D0561344

TRANSGRESSIONS *of* POWER

DAW Books is proud to present the novels of Juliette Wade

The Broken Trust

MAZES OF POWER (Book One)
TRANSGRESSIONS OF POWER (Book Two)

TRANSGRESSIONS *of* POWER

Book Two of The Broken Trust

JULIETTE WADE

DAW BOOKS, INC.
DONALD A. WOLLHEIM, FOUNDER

1745 Broadway, New York, NY 10019
ELIZABETH R. WOLLHEIM
SHEILA E. GILBERT
PUBLISHERS
www.dawbooks.com

Jacket design by Adam Auerbach.

Varin font and numerals by David J. Peterson. Varin alphabet by Juliette Wade.

Interior design by Alissa Rose Theodor.

Edited by Sheila E. Gilbert.

DAW Book Collectors No. 1874.

Published by DAW Books, Inc.
1745 Broadway, New York, NY 10019.

First Printing, February 2021
1 2 3 4 5 6 7 8 9

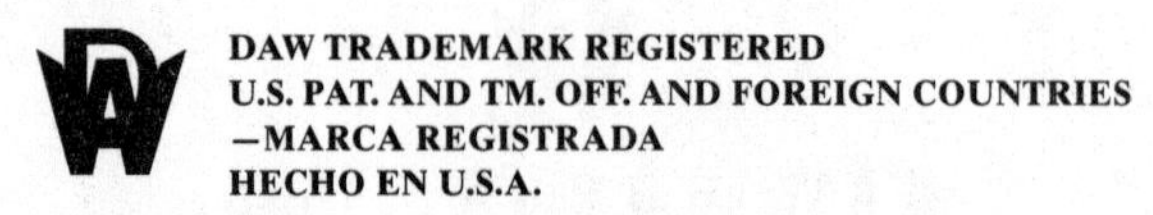

PRINTED IN CANADA

To Alixi Unger, Captain Keyt,
and Fifth Sahris

VARIN IS A PLACE WHERE HUMANS HAVE ALWAYS LIVED ON AN ALIEN WORLD.

IT IS ALSO YOUR HOME.

The Castes of Varin

Grobal–the Noble Race

Arissen–the Officer Caste

Imbati–the Servant Caste

Kartunnen–the Artisan Caste

Venorai–the Laborer Caste

Melumalai–the Merchant Caste

Akrabitti–the Undercaste

The Eight Cavern Cities of Varin

Pelismara

Selimna

Safe Harbor

Erin

Herketh

Peak

Daronvel

Vitett

CHAPTER ONE

Singled Out

Birthdays just weren't the same when everyone expected you to live. Adon loved the excitement of the preparations, but today, on the eve of turning thirteen, he knew tomorrow was going to be anticlimactic. He'd been singled out as a lucky exception to the decline of the Grobal Race since the day he was born. This morning, Mother had caught him moping, and asked if he'd prefer the kind of pawing congratulations other noble boys received for managing not to die of hemophilia, heart defects, or inherited cancers. He shuddered at the thought, yet the fact remained: he just wasn't like most people.

Soft-footed, he moved among the boisterous boys who ran between classes in the vaulted stone hallway of the Grobal School. Usually he would linger to avoid the rush, but for role-play class, it was important to arrive early. And to stay unnoticed, if possible. So, not a day for fashion innovations. The sapphire velvet suit and white gloves he wore had already been adopted by several classmates, and wouldn't draw any attention.

Not far from the bronze doors of the play hall was a column, half-embedded in the wall; Adon tucked himself behind it and pressed his nose to the cool stone. He evaluated the others with his right eye. Boys in gangs, scheming for the hour to come. If not for them, role-play would have been his favorite class. He could have talked to Imbati-caste servants his own age, gotten to know them with an eye to hiring a bodyguard when he turned seventeen—which was supposed to be the whole point. Not, *who can be rude to the most Imbati in an hour?*

Adon scanned and found a gang of his cousins from the First Family. Xeref and Cahemsin were in that group, but they never seemed to agree on which servant to approach first. Running it was, then, as usual. He tugged his gloves tight, and shifted his weight to his toes.

With a click, and a shift in the cool air, the heavy doors swung open.

Adon dashed forward, dodging between gangs into the hall where Imbati awaited their testing. After he'd bumped a couple of older boys and gotten elbowed for it, he slowed a bit. *Don't try to get out ahead, just find Imbati Talabel.*

Talabel: she stood calmly in her maroon uniform. Though she stood within arm's reach of a brass chair at one of the tables, she didn't touch it. Tall, graceful, eighteen—she wore her hair in twists, and her eyes seemed to speak. Adon wished he could erase the small Imbati castemark of black paint between her eyebrows, so he could see her whole face, just once. Sometimes, in secret, he tried to stand like her. He never could find that Imbati poise.

Just as he drew close, Venmer of the Eighth Family veered off another nearby servant and tried to beat him to Talabel; Adon leapt past and blurted, "Imbati-Talabel-I-require-your-service!"

The Imbati girl bowed. "Yes, Grobal Adon, sir."

"Adon, you took my servant," Venmer drawled behind him.

He didn't want to answer. He wanted to talk to Talabel. He glanced up at her; she seemed to approve of him staying put.

"Adon," Venmer said, louder this time. "Give her to me."

He shook his head, *no.*

"Your mother's a muckwalker. She brings fever-carrying Lowers to contaminate our air."

Lies. Adon's cheeks burned, but he said nothing.

"Tunnel-hound." Venmer shoved his shoulder, hard enough that Adon stumbled forward by a step. "Your mother wants doctors to inject us with Lowers' blood."

That's not true. That's not how inoculants work. But he'd heard all of this before, and arguing never helped. "Come on, Talabel," he said, "let's go somewhere el—"

Venmer grabbed him roughly by the back of his coat.

Adon squeaked, "Talabel, defend me!"

The servant took a step forward. "Please release him, Venmer, sir."

"Ha!" Venmer scoffed. He shook him so his teeth rattled. "That's not going to work this time. You can't fool me."

Adon winced, and caught Talabel's gaze pleadingly.

"Sir," the Imbati girl said. "Please release him. This will be my final request."

Venmer laughed. "What are you gonna do, Imbati? I've called your bluff; admit it. You can't do a thing to me."

"Grobal Venmer, sir. I shall simply role-play as manservant and bodyguard to Adon of the First Family, as requested, according to the play hall rules."

The gloved hands on Adon's jacket slipped slightly. "You wouldn't dare."

"Pardon me, sir."

She flashed past. Adon spun around as Venmer's hands dragged down his body. He jumped and pulled his leg away, and found Venmer lying face-down on the floor. For an instant, Talabel's eyes came up to his and she smiled. Actually smiled! Then the moment was gone, and her face returned to its Imbati calm.

The Eighth Family boy surged up with a roar. Adon took three steps backward, every nerve afire, intensely aware that Talabel was taking a place beside his left shoulder.

"You can't do that!" Venmer shouted. Rage pulsed in his face. "Whose side are you on?"

My own? Adon took a breath, but Talabel murmured down to his ear, "Don't answer."

He pressed his lips shut. He could feel all eyes in the room on them. But role-play was how you tested a servant's qualifications, and wasn't that exactly what he was doing? What those other boys did—sneering at the Imbati, or humiliating them—made no sense.

Venmer raised gloved fists as if to strike, but then shook them instead. "I'm reporting you, Imbati! That was a *fault*, you hear me? You're not allowed to touch your betters!"

Adon relaxed slightly. Venmer had it backward: nobles of the Race were the ones expected to keep their hands to themselves. Imbati were allowed to touch those they served—Mother's Aloran styled her hair, and dressed her, and helped her in the bath.

Venmer stormed off toward the Schoolmaster Supervisor. Imbati faded out of his path, but when younger schoolmates were too slow, he shoved them out of his way.

Adon's breath came faster than he liked. Would the Schoolmaster Supervisor intervene? Surely he wouldn't be told his actions reflected badly on the First Family, or Mother . . .

He whispered, "You were perfect, Talabel. Like a certified manservant." Which, in a few months, she would be. If only he were older . . .

"Thank you, sir."

"If he asks, I take full responsibility for my orders. I won't let the Eighth Family get you in trouble."

An unexpected shift in the air brought his head up; he stood on his toes to look toward the entrance. The massive bronze doors were opening again, and a hushed stillness spread outward. All eyes swung to the man who entered: tall, thin, commanding, with a streak of gray in his sandstone hair, a noble nose, and a gaze that seemed to stab right through you.

His least favorite birthday inevitability was here a day early. Every time he saw his older brother Nekantor, Adon felt a sudden urge to hide.

Murmurs chased through the room. "By Varin!" "It's the Heir." "Nekantor." "The Heir!" "Nekantor of the First Family, impress him and he could make your career!"

Those words started a sinister change. Boys shifted—Imbati tensed—and suddenly two Twelfth Family boys started throwing punches at the servant they'd been working with. Next thing Adon knew, all the boys were doing it, the air filling with jeers and cheering while the Imbati tried to dodge. Nekantor didn't seem to notice, or care, but the young manservant behind the Heir's shoulder did. Professional as he looked in a black silk suit with his hair in long braids, he would know firsthand how the students felt, because he didn't look that much older than Talabel. His tattooed forehead pinched—a look that made Adon's stomach hurt.

There was a quiet grunt, and Adon jumped. A punch had landed on an Imbati boy right behind him. *Merciful Heile, please make them stop!* But there was no reprimand after the contact, which only made things worse. Adon could feel terror and desperation all around him, while his classmates renewed their attack.

"T-Talabel," Adon stammered, clutching at the nearest brass chair.

"Sir." Even in that single word, her voice shuddered.

Adon's mind whirled. Play hall rules said not to damage the Imbati—that's what they *said!* Under the eyes of the Heir himself, how could these boys justify what they did? Why didn't they cringe at their own behavior? And why did the Supervisor not enforce the rules?

Then the hard brass of the chair in his hand gave him an idea.

"The chairs, Talabel. Stack them."

She nodded. "Yes, sir."

"Wait. Not just the chairs. Stack everything. Chairs, tables. You'll—you'll need help. Take as much as you need. Take all you need."

Her eyes widened. "Yes, sir."

Talabel ran to a small Imbati boy who had managed to hide near a curtain, and spoke into his ear; in seconds the two of them were running through the room. They never raised their voices, but each time they drew near, the next servant would turn away from their attackers and seize the nearest chair. Something in how effortlessly they wielded the heavy brass gave the noble boys pause. It also clearly disturbed his brother. Nekantor's fingers flickered over his vest buttons, once, twice. Then he looked down at his watch.

Adon felt the Imbati's pleading gaze come to him. His breath hitched in fear, but he ran to the center of the room.

"Here!" he shouted. "Imbati, bring them here, tables on this side, chairs on this side." He added recklessly, "In the name of the First Family!"

Cries of outrage echoed through the hall, but it worked: the Imbati broke free of their tormentors and came to him. They began to create a pile of chairs, higher and higher.

Adon couldn't help a fearful glance toward his brother. Nekantor was looking directly at him, this time; it made him uncomfortable. Adon turned away instead to the servants. Every Imbati who came near had eyes full of gratitude, and his heart swelled, big enough to burst.

The next time he looked, the Heir had turned away. His servant opened one of the bronze doors for him, and the two of them vanished into the hall outside.

The Schoolmaster Supervisor moved into the room, waving baffled schoolboys out of the way. "Halt, halt!" he shouted. "This session is adjourned. Boys, early dismissal."

Those were powerful words. The rest of the boys broke into cheers and mobbed the doors. The Supervisor shouted instructions as he followed them out into the corridor.

Adon's throat felt tight. Most people had no idea how to relate properly to servants—Mother often said so—but that was worse than anything he'd ever seen. Worst of all, his brother had caused it somehow. With a deep breath, Adon took a first step toward the exit.

And found Talabel standing in front of him.

He lifted his eyes to her golden face, and his breath caught. Her graceful brows were serious, just that small circle of black paint between them. A drifting wysp cast light that gleamed on the black buttons of her uniform. Her lips curved into a faint smile.

"Adon, young sir," she said. "Thank you."

His cheeks burned. "No, thank *you*. It was a stupid idea, but it was all I could think of. You made it work—you were wonderful." More reckless words tumbled out. "Come to my birthday party tomorrow?"

"Sir." She looked away.

Adon blushed harder. "I mean it! We're not like those boys; we're nicer. You'd be welcome, and the Household would take good care of you."

"It's—kind of you, sir."

Behind her, the heavy door swung open again, and moving air caused the wysp to drift upward toward the chandelier. Most likely, the Supervisor was here to get him in trouble. Adon hung his head. But instead, a strange woman entered, causing Talabel to glance over her shoulder.

Adon frowned, searching for the woman's castemark.

Talabel slammed her hands into Adon's chest. He flailed his arms and toppled backward.

Zzap!

His head struck the carpet; the play hall spun. When he could see Talabel again, she and the strange woman were fighting hand to hand—and the stranger was winning. The stranger knocked Talabel down across Adon's legs, then jumped over them both and crouched as if to pick something off the floor.

An Imbati in black sprinted through the open door and aimed a high kick that struck the stranger in the back, pitching her forward. She rolled to her feet and ran for the door—

Zzap!

The stranger's head exploded. Blood and worse spattered in all directions, dripping down the bronze door. The headless body stiffened strangely, then crumpled. Standing beyond the open doorway, an Arissen guard in the orange uniform of the Eminence's Cohort lowered her weapon and shouted for reinforcements.

Oh—oh, mercy—

The Imbati in black came to Adon, bending down. A brown braid swung forward; Adon followed it up to a face he recognized: Nekan-

across Varin, and he'd risen to the rank of apprentice. He deserved better, honestly, because he was a brilliant musician and composer. Tamelera often had him play at her salon gatherings, because his music relaxed people while they discussed uncomfortable issues like the Grobal decline, and the role of inoculants in preventing deadly outbreaks of Kinders fever.

"Good afternoon, Lady Della," Vant said, bowing. Still so formal and polite, after all these years.

"Come in, come in, I'm so happy you could make it. No big audiences today; it's mostly just practice for Adon's birthday. We'll be playing farther in." She led him across the sitting room and through the bronze double doors into the private drawing room. She watched him look around the space, taking in the hangings of embroidery and tufted cloth. "How have you been?"

"I'm well, Lady. I had a concert with my master last week, and I think it went well. It was my first time playing the triscili for a concert audience."

So that was a triscili case. "I'd love to hear you play it," Della said. "But before you practice, I'm going to introduce you to a couple of people."

Vant's face changed, suddenly guarded with a hint of . . . alarm? How could he play in public concerts and still be so shy?

"Don't worry," she said. "They're Kartunnen, not Grobal. I took the liberty, recently, of sending one of your compositions to the director of the Selimnar symphony . . ."

"Lady," Vant said, very quietly. "Did you really?"

"Of course I did. It was marvelous, and I can't imagine you'd want to spend your entire life living in your master's shadow."

"I . . . well, I don't suppose . . ."

She took his elbow. He smelled of hand oil, and something else, a gentle waxy scent. "I had the opportunity to meet a sweet couple from the symphony who've been visiting Pelismara this month. They asked if they could meet you, so I've invited them here."

"Oh," he breathed, and laid one long-fingered hand on his chest. "Oh, Lady. You're too kind."

Imbati Serjer looked in from the sitting room carrying a pair of cases, which he set to one side of the doors. "Lady, your other guests have arrived."

"Yes, thank you, Serjer." She turned back to Vant. It was hard seeing

tor's young manservant. Concern showed in the lily crest tattoo on his forehead.

"Young Master Adon, are you hurt?"

Adon panted through clenched teeth, unable to speak, unwilling to throw up. He shook his head.

"You remember me, young Master. I'm Nekantor's Dexelin. Come with me, please, sir. I'll take you to where you'll be safe."

Talabel had already hopped off him to one side; Adon managed to stand. His legs shook. Dexelin's arm came around his back, guiding him firmly to the edge of the room.

No way was he going to look at the body. Or at the floor, at what might get on his shoes. Dexelin wouldn't let him trip. He glanced over his shoulder instead, back into the room.

Just below the edge of a wall hanging, a black burn mark smoked on the stone. That sound he'd heard . . . His head spun again, and he clenched his teeth harder.

Someone expected me to die.

him so nervous. "Vant, promise of Bes, it'll be all right. We've known each other long enough for you to trust me, haven't we? I'm only trying to give you the success you deserve."

"Thank you, Lady."

Though it made her awkwardly self-aware, she sheltered him with her body as the other two guests came in. Kartunnen Simi was tall and angular, with golden skin and short black hair that stood up like a kanguan's crest; her pale-skinned partner, Benyin, had a beautiful soft body and wore a thick braid forward of her shoulder. Like Vant, they wore the gray coats and green lip-paint unique to the Kartunnen caste; unlike him, they also wore black lines across their eyelids. When she introduced them, Vant gave a formal bow. Simi returned the bow, and Benyin curtsied.

"So grateful ever, noble Lady," said Benyin. She and her partner both had strong Selimnar accents, speaking slowly with stretched vowels, and lots of 'so.'

"We're deeply pleased to meet you, Vant," said Simi.

"Deeply pleased," Benyin agreed. "Your style—"

"Oh, yes, my true, the style."

"It shines, and your energy, too. Both distinct in your composition, so."

"Thank you," Vant replied, and glanced at Della. "What did you send them?"

She couldn't help smiling. "Just the piece you wrote for me."

Vant's cheeks turned red. "But—but that was nothing. You can't have loved it that much; I wrote it in an afternoon."

"You don't understand." Della shook his arm. "You're *brilliant*. I've seen it all along, and you deserve to be known as a composer in your own right, not just as Ryanin's assistant, or his apprentice. Simi and Benyin agree with me."

"So does Selimna," said Simi. "We played it in concert at the Lady's Walk, so."

"You—!" Vant covered his mouth with both hands.

"What's the Lady's Walk?" Della asked. "Is it a concert venue?" She had to be careful—discussing Selimna would mean skirting some dangerous secrets—but this question was surely innocuous. She and Tagaret had been studying Selimna for years, poring over maps, and listening to Tamelera's stories about living there. It was hard to believe there could be a venue there she'd never heard of . . .

"It's not really a venue," said Simi. "It's an open zone near the Alixi's Residence, so."

"It is a venue, though, my true," said Benyin.

Simi nodded. "It is, because the walls of the whorl are so tall, and the acoustics they provide are so fabulous." She waved one hand in a circle above her head. "Once, though, markets used to set out there. At that time, it was named just The Circle, so."

"The Circle!" Della exclaimed. "I've heard of that. I've always wanted to go. They changed the name to the Lady's Walk?"

"Road signs still read The Circle, noble Lady," Benyin chuckled. "I suppose, the name changed within the last twenty years or so, Simi, yeah?"

"Yes, after the Lady Alixi chose it for her everyday healthful."

"Lady Tamelera. She wanted music, so."

"Music, art, fashion, too—she made careers."

"Did she really?" Della asked, delighted. "That's wonderful." And Tamelera would be delighted to learn she'd had a lasting influence, but for the moment, Vant was still looking a bit too shocked. "Vant, are you all right?"

"L—Lady Della, I—" He took a deep breath. "I guess I just have a hard time believing it's true."

"It is true, so." Benyin went and opened one of the cases that the First Houseman had left beside the door. There was a pair of foot-drums inside it, but she pulled out a piece of paper. "Do see here, Vant. It's the program from our performance, so. Perhaps one day you'll travel to Selimna and play beside us."

"Oh, I love that idea," Della said.

Vant took the program, and she looked over his shoulder. Simi and Benyin's names were printed in machine script on the soft paper, and beneath that, *The Lady's Walk* and a list of pieces. One was entitled, 'For Della,' with Vant's name beside it. At the bottom of the page, smaller script read, *Paper provided by special arrangement with Dorlis and Nenda, Melumalai.*

Della blinked. The secrets kept insisting. Just two days ago, Tagaret had asked her to be on the lookout for any information about paper merchants in Selimna.

"May I have this, if you don't mind?" she asked. "I'd like to show it to Tagaret."

"Of course, noble Lady."

A strange sound came, muffled, through the double doors. Della turned toward it just as the First Houseman looked in, eyes wide. "Lady Della, please come into the sitting room."

Her stomach twisted, but she made herself turn to her guests and smile. "I'm sorry. You'll have to excuse me for a moment. Feel free to get to know each other." She tried to slip through the door, but her hip caught painfully on its edge, making her hiss. She stumbled into the sitting room, where Adon was standing beside a very young manservant with long braids. She frowned.

"Lady," said Serjer. "This is Nekantor's Dexelin."

"Oh, gods!" she exclaimed. *Nekantor's eyes are in our house. Our preparations won't stop Dexelin if his Master isn't here.*

Then Adon barreled into her, flinging his arms around her chest. She would have toppled if her Yoral hadn't been standing by; Yoral caught her, and she fought back to her feet.

This was all wrong. Adon never hugged her unless she asked him to, and never like this.

"Adon, what's going on?"

He looked up. "Someone tried to shoot me and now she's dead!"

"Shoot you?!"

Those words plunged her fourteen years into the past. Instinctively, she grasped at implications, at action plans, as if the Eminence Indal had just caught his fatal fever, the epidemic had started, and this was the Heir Selection all over again. *Who else is in danger?*

No, wait. Now was now; they'd come a long way toward repairing the rift between the Grobal and their doctors that had followed the epidemic; the Eminence was Herin of the Third Family, who was quite alive; and no one should be attacking Adon. There was no reason to, was there?

"Lady," Serjer said. "Nekantor's Dexelin brought young Master Adon home."

Music started playing in the drawing room. Della held Adon tighter, keeping her eye on Dexelin, memorizing him in case she saw him again. Nekantor's servants were not glass icons, but he broke them, systematically, which meant she constantly had to learn new Imbati who were far too young. It wasn't exactly Dexelin's fault that he worked for someone awful, but his vow of service required him to report to his Master. Fortunately, he didn't seem overly curious. He'd glanced only once at the double doors, when the music began.

"Please excuse my confusion, Dexelin," Della said. "We have musicians by. They're practicing for Adon's birthday party tomorrow."

"Lady," said Serjer, "I'll get the Mistress." He hurried through the double doors into the back.

"And thank you for bringing Adon home, too," Della said. "Can you tell me exactly what happened?"

"I'll tell you what I know, Lady." Dexelin bowed. "My Master and I were leaving the Grobal School when I saw an unmarked Arissen intruder, and begged permission to follow her. When I found her, she had already taken a shot at young Master Adon and was fighting an Academy student. I fought her off, but before we could capture her, a guard of the Eminence's Cohort arrived on the scene and shot her in the head."

"Heile's mercy!" Della cried. "That's awful." Adon's arms tightened until she could hardly breathe.

Dexelin inclined his head. "Indeed, Lady. So I brought young Master Adon straight home, for safety. But now, if you will excuse me, I should return to the scene to answer the Cohort's questions."

Oh, thank heavens. But she mustn't sound too eager for him to leave. "Of course, by all means," she said. "Thank you again."

The servant bowed and departed.

Della squeezed Adon's head against her chest. "Sweet little brother. He's gone. You're safe, now."

"I think my suit is ruined," Adon mumbled. "I need to change my clothes."

"Do you think so?" Hard to tell from this angle whether he had blood on him. That thought was just—ugh! And an attempt on Adon's life couldn't be random. Some unseen motive lurked behind the act, deadly and terrifying, urging her, *do something.*

Do what?

"Oh, Adon! Oh, my love!" Tamelera swooped in with a rustle of silk skirts, her manservant, Aloran, close behind her. Half her hair was in a braid; the other half fell in a red-gold cloud down past her elbow. Aloran must have been in the midst of styling it.

Adon instantly unwound himself and ran to her. She held him, kissing the top of his head. Even Aloran placed a hand on Adon's shoulder.

"Della, did he tell you what happened?"

"Nekantor's Dexelin said an Arissen entered the Grobal School and tried to shoot him."

Tamelera's eyebrows shot up. "Nekantor's servant came *here?*"

"He's gone now, don't worry."

"M-mother," Adon said, voice shaking. "Imbati Talabel s-saved me. Like a real bodyguard. I have to, I have to thank her. And Nekantor's Dexelin, too, for saving us both, and bringing me home. And—oh Heile—" He broke off, and gulped hard.

"Come, love," Tamelera said. "Let's get you cleaned up." She shifted him slightly to one side and walked, with him still molded against her, into the back.

Tamelera's Aloran turned his dark eyes on Della. "Mistress Della, if you please."

Oh, right. The musicians were still here, still playing. "Yes, of course, I'm coming." She took the heavy door from him and went into the back. Vant, Simi, and Benyin were sitting on a single couch together, playing. A wysp had drifted into the room, and now sparkled above their heads. That joy, in the face of what had happened to Adon, brought tears to her eyes. "I'm so sorry," she said. "We've had some bad news. I'm afraid I'm going to have to ask you to go."

Vant stood up, the slim triscili still held in his fingers. "Are you all right?"

Why should she be reacting like this? She brushed the tears off her cheeks. "I'm fine."

Simi and Benyin stood and bowed. "Vant told us about playing for your brother's birthday party, noble Lady," Benyin said. "We've offered to join him, so. If there's been bad news, will you still celebrate?"

That was surprisingly easy to answer. Anyone who attacked the First Family would be looking for signs of the impact of their scheme—for fear or weakness—so they must show none. "We'll hold the party as planned," she said. "We'd be honored to hear you play."

"So grateful ever, noble Lady." They carried their instruments to the wall and began packing them into the cases. Vant took apart his triscili and laid the pieces into the small case he'd brought.

Della shook her head. Poor Adon. A *child* should have no enemies! But Nekantor and his Dexelin had been at the Grobal School this afternoon, and Nekantor had plenty of enemies.

As did the whole First Family.

Oh, dear gods, *Tagaret!*

She clenched both fists instinctively, caught by an impulse to run in several directions at once. Nausea shuddered through her. "Yoral?"

Thank the Twins, he was still at her shoulder. "Yes, Mistress?"

"We have to go—you'll have to excuse me, Vant. Simi and Benyin, my apologies. Our First Houseman will show you out."

Della hurried across the Eminence's Residence to the offices wing. In thirteen years living here, she'd learned to agree out loud that this was the most prestigious and perfect place to live, far better than the large Grobal neighborhood to the north, where she'd grown up. However, this emergency reminded her again of all its problems. Too many people in too small a space. Too many outward-facing windows. Too many doors, both in the main halls and in the halls of the servants' Maze, all of which had to be guarded by Arissen or Imbati. Tagaret had lived here his entire life, and thought nothing of it—but an Arissen assassin had just walked into the Grobal School and straight to her intended victim, unchecked until the last possible moment. If any of the people assigned to those doors failed, or betrayed them . . .

Let it be all right. Let the attack be over. Della knocked on the bronze door of the First Family's cabinet offices.

The door did not immediately open.

Panic seized her throat. What if Tagaret had been attacked too, or killed, when she had nothing to keep of him? No. No. She pressed her hand to her stomach and took a deep breath, another. Tagaret must be in a meeting; surely that was it. She knocked again, harder.

The door swung inward on Tagaret's bodyguard, Imbati Kuarmei.

"Oh, Kuarmei, thank Heile," Della exclaimed. "The First Family is under attack!"

"Come in quickly, Lady," said Kuarmei.

She hopped over the threshold, and then she was in, and here was Tagaret, opening his arms to her. Dizzy with relief, Della pressed her face into his chest, gave herself to his embrace, breathed him in, squeezed him tighter and tighter. *Oh, to have him alone, right now*—the shockingly inappropriate thought sent a hot blush from her cheeks down to her knees.

Not in the cabinet assistants' office! Where had *that* idea come from?

"Della, are you safe?" Tagaret asked. He stroked her cheek with one gloved hand; she wished for his fingers. "No one is after you?"

How handsome his sweet, serious face was. His brown eyes, full of fear, were also full of love. Had she failed to look at them this morning, or just failed to see?

"No, I'm safe," she said. "Adon is, too—but an assassin found him in the Grobal School! If it weren't for one of the Imbati students, and Nekantor's Dexelin, he wouldn't be. You haven't seen anything here, have you?"

Tagaret frowned and took half a step back, looking over his shoulder. Della suddenly became aware of the room around them. It was broad enough to hold four steel desks, one for each of the cabinet assistants: Tagaret, his younger cousin Pyaras, and two other cousins, one of whom was a known informant to the Eminence Herin. However, of the four, Tagaret was the only one here. He served as both Nekantor's informant in this office, and as a secret informant on Nekantor's activities to the First Family's cabinet member, herself.

Who was standing just behind him.

"Lady Selemei!" Della exclaimed. "Oh, heavens, I'm sorry."

Lady Selemei was the first lady ever to hire a gentleman's servant and claim a seat on the Eminence's cabinet. She was small, with golden skin and tightly curled gray hair, and her gloved hands rested atop a silver cane. If not for the gently softened shape of her body, you would never imagine she had borne five children—*five,* imagine it! She herself was miserable in comparison. *I'm too tall, my hips are too narrow, my stomach feels all wrong, my breasts poke out . . .*

"Please don't worry, Della," Lady Selemei said. She smiled up reassuringly. Behind her, her broad-shouldered Imbati woman remained expressionless. "You have an excellent reason to interrupt, but honestly, I don't consider it an interruption. We'd finished up for today."

Tagaret smiled. "I was actually about to come home and ask for your help with the inoculant program."

"Really?"

Tagaret nodded. "We need to reach the people who live in the northern neighborhoods. That's over half of the Pelismara Society. If you could ask your parents to talk to my mother . . ."

"I'm not sure how they'll feel about that, but I can ask this week."

"There's more, though." Tagaret got a mysterious look on his face. "Even bigger news."

"Wait—bigger news? Besides the attack?"

Tagaret squeezed her arm. "It's about Selimna. Della, the old Alixi *died.* The city has no leader."

"What?" She stepped backward, looking from Tagaret, to Selemei's hinting smile, and back. "He—he *died?*" Too many plans, fears, and hopes whirled in her head at once. But if holy Mother Elinda had taken the Alixi to join the stars . . .

"Yes," said Tagaret. "This is what we've been waiting for."

Their chance. To escape Nekantor's unrelenting gaze, to escape the Residence, the stifling Pelismara Society, and the capital itself. Imagine! Selimna could be their own city, a place where they could begin to break down the oppressive rules of caste, just as they'd dreamed and planned for so long. And as it happened, she was holding a small piece of it in her hand—a little sweatier for having been clenched in her fist on the run over.

"Tagaret," she said. "I found paper merchants for you. Is that part of our plan?"

Tagaret considered the paper. "*Paper provided by special arrangement with Dorlis and Nenda, Melumalai.* That's intriguing." He glanced at Selemei. "Is this still useful to you?"

"What's it for, Lady?" Della asked.

"It's for my piece of the Selimna plan," said Lady Selemei. "I've learned that the city government is choosing a paper supplier for the next four years. It's a huge contract. I thought if I could get involved, even indirectly, I could potentially help you both—maybe arrange some favors and set you up with reputation in the Selimna Society."

"I think this looks perfect, don't you?" Tagaret asked, gesturing with the program. "I like the idea of Melumalai who've negotiated directly with Kartunnen. Since we want to break down caste rules, that kind of open-mindedness could help us a lot."

"Mistress," said Selemei's Ustin, "any unfinished negotiations will have been suspended when the Alixi died. They may resume with the appointment of the new Alixi, or they may even start over."

"Thanks, Ustin," said Selemei. "That's helpful information."

"Even better, I would guess," said Tagaret.

Della nodded. "So now, Nekantor just has to appoint you."

Behind her, another knock sounded, and she pressed her lips shut. No more secrets. Who was this at the door?

Tagaret's Kuarmei went and opened it. The moving air wafted in the odor of mustache wax, which intensified with the arrival of Arbiter Lorman of the First Family Council. His job was to protect the continuance and reputation of the First Family, so understandably, he was agitated. Instead of preening his whiskers as usual, he was wringing his hands, to the significant detriment of a pair of brown gloves. If they were lucky, he'd be unsettled enough to spare them his usual lectures about duty, tradition, and Tagaret's late father Garr.

Lady Selemei went to Lorman and took his hand. "Arbiter, are you well?"

"No," Lorman said bluntly. "We're under attack."

"I heard," Selemei replied. "But we're safe, and so is Adon. My other assistants went home half an hour ago. I haven't yet had time to contact my sons at work, but we've had no emergency messengers."

Arbiter Lorman pursed his lips, bunching his mustache. "I'll go check on your sons next, then, Lady. Thank Heile all of you are well. And you've seen nothing out of the ordinary?"

"No, sir," said Tagaret.

"This attack is an outrage; we have to respond. Have any of the attackers been identified?"

Della took a step forward. "The attacker was an Arissen woman," she said. "That's all we know right now. She was killed by a Cohort guard."

Lorman turned to her, blinking. He frowned and started twisting his whiskers.

Of *course* he hadn't noticed her at all until this moment. Della forced a smile and tried not to breathe through her nose. When he next spoke, Lorman no longer used the tense clarity he'd entered with, but his favorite poorly affected Selimnar accent.

"So, so. We'll see who was responsible." He cast a keen eye at Tagaret. "So, is that *paper* you're holding?"

Della froze. Had he overheard their earlier conversation? How could he? She could see Tagaret's shoulders tense, but he answered calmly enough.

"Of course it's paper. It's a program Della was showing me, for some musicians who are visiting Pelismara."

Hand of Sirin, she shouldn't have brought that program here—now Lorman would get suspicious, and Nekantor would have an excuse to move against Selemei, and their thirteen years of planning would be for nothing, even if their subversion weren't fully discovered . . .

"So, paper is so ridiculously expensive," Lorman said meaningfully.

"Indeed it is."

Della braced herself for some dreadful accusation, but Lorman only reached into his pocket and pushed something into Tagaret's hand. "So, so. I'm glad you're safe. So I'll go check on the others, now. I wish your father Garr were here; he'd know just how to respond to this atrocity." He strode out the door that his manservant held open for him.

Della took the first deep breath she'd dared since he came in. "Mercy of Heile, that was close." Even what remained of his smell was awful; she tried to wave it away from her nose. "Ooh, that mustache wax—why can't he depilate like everyone else?"

"I'm sorry, darling." Tagaret gave her a squeeze. "It does have an odd perfume. Selemei, do you think he suspects anything?"

The Lady shook her head. "For a moment I worried, but surely if he did, he would have pursued it. What did he give you?"

"A blank card." Tagaret turned it over, looking puzzled. "Maybe it's a paper sample? I don't see how it can have anything to do with Selimna's paper contract negotiations." He held it up: it was heavy tillik-silk paper, edged with gold on one side, corners dipped in gold on the other. Precious; and beautiful enough to display on a bedside table.

"May I have it?" Della asked.

"Yes, absolutely."

Tagaret's gloved fingertips brushed hers as he passed it to her. She removed a glove to feel it with one finger. Its surface was soft, its gold-dipped corners cold.

"Unfortunately, we now have a different problem," said Lady Selemei. "I implied to Lorman that Pyaras had gone home."

Della's stomach flipped. She glanced to Tagaret, who had dropped his face into his hands. "Tagaret, did Pyaras tell you where he was going, when he left?"

Tagaret looked up from the cover of his gloves, wincing.

"Of course not." Della felt sick all over again. "This is all wrong. Why a *child*, the very future of the Grobal Race? Why Adon? It's disgusting."

"I agree." Lady Selemei's deep brown eyes glittered with outrage. "The only time assassination attempts even begin to make sense is during an Heir Selection, but I've heard nothing to suggest that Eminence Herin is unwell. I don't see this as a plausible response to the inoculant program—most objectors I know are demanding more guards to protect them from exposure to Lowers."

"There are already more guards," said Della.

Lady Selemei nodded. "I mean, even more than we have now."

"My first thought is Heir Selection," Tagaret said. "Adon's excellent health makes him obviously suitable as an Heir candidate. But it would have made more sense to attack him when he first turned twelve and became eligible."

Selemei pressed her lips together. "I agree. It's worth looking into, though. The Fifth and Third Families are the most likely suspects for an attack like this. Let me see what I can learn about their recent activities."

Della pulled her glove back on, shaking her head. "I can't believe this—I just can't. How can this kind of thing keep happening? Who just *decides* to hire an Arissen to kill someone, as if murder were an item in a shop? Is there a *murder shop?*"

"Yeah." Tagaret grimaced. "I've even been targeted, and I've never heard the question asked in quite that way."

"The Pelismara Society accepts a lot of dangerous traditions," Selemei said. "I suspect the three of us work well together because it's in our nature to question such things. For now, you should both go home where you'll be safe."

"Lady, you should, too," said Della. "Shall we walk you to your suite, or will your Ustin be sufficient protection?"

"I'm quite confident in my Ustin." Selemei smiled. The blonde Imbati woman bowed.

"We'll wish you a safe evening, then."

Tagaret came to Della and kissed her. The tips of his brown hair brushed against her forehead. Desire rose in her again—a familiar feeling, but so long gone its return was a shock. She twined her fingers in his, and they hurried back through the stone halls, while their bodyguards stalked on either side, wary of every window, every door.

The thought of their younger cousin nagged at her. Pyaras had unusual habits that he didn't even share with Lady Selemei, much less Arbiter Lorman.

Where was he? How could they warn him?

CHAPTER THREE

Transformation

Pyaras leapt out of his dressing room with a flourish and cried, "Transformation!"

Nobody was here. The aisle between the rows of blue curtains was empty.

"Oh, come on," Pyaras said. "Veriga, aren't you out yet?"

There was a mirror at the turn of the row; glimpsing his reflection, Pyaras grinned. He looked nothing like a dutiful cabinet assistant in the costume the club had provided: scandalous short trousers, and a vest of brass-studded leather. His bare knees tingled. Oh, and if he pulled the tie out of his hair—yes, that was it. Shaking his dark locks out past his shoulders he looked like the domo card from dareli. Sort of. Really, he was nothing the Pelismara Society had ever seen—something from another place, another planet! He was ready.

"Veriga, where are you?"

"Over here." His friend's gruff voice echoed from beyond a curtain. "I'm not in such a hurry to take my clothes off."

"That's not fair." But Veriga wasn't wrong. He did love to strip out of the sense of obligation that the Pelismara Society placed on him; and there was no denying he felt thirsty, from his throat all the way down to where it counted. Kethani, the woman he'd met here last time, had worn a similar scandalous costume: tight pants and a top that left her arms and navel bare. Taking that off her had been an interesting challenge. Maybe she'd be here tonight.

He licked his lips and realigned the sexual-health bracelet on his left wrist. The bracelet stored medical information, and he'd promoted it heavily to other young men of the nobility, until it became the most popular medical invention of the last eight years. It felt great to know he'd boosted the health of the Race—and it sure spared him a lot of awkward conversations on his evenings out. "You ready yet?"

The older man grunted. "Do we have to do this?"

"Are you serious? We've paid, and we've got food to eat, drinks to drink, and people to meet." Pyaras walked down the aisle toward the door, hung with a blue-tinted mirror above which the name 'Lake Club' was traced in blue neon. He checked back over his shoulder for Veriga, and gaped.

He was pretty used to Veriga looking like a stone giant, but in costume, *whoa.* Veriga's muscles bulged from beneath a drape of silver net, and his short skirt looked like . . . knives? "You're in the mood for attention."

"This is nothing."

"I get it, you're playing with me." But no point in arguing. Veriga would do well to pull attention down off his face, which was prematurely aged with the scars of a poisoning soon after they first met.

No, don't think like that. No outside thoughts in Lake Club.

Pyaras pushed through the mirrored door. The space beyond was large and dim. Strings of false jewels dangled like illuminated blue stalactites from the ceiling, raising a weird city of jeweled towers in the mirror that covered the floor. In between were tables, chairs, and a stage where a beautiful man in ribbons sang a throbbing song. Mysterious masked and costumed people moved, rightside-up and upside-down, between the jeweled realms, and *he couldn't tell what caste they were.* In this one place, people could just be human. Delicious!

He found his way to the drinks table first. Mystery was the flavor of the night—he chose a glass at random. It turned out to be only smoked chatinet. Drinkable. He swigged it with a shrug. Veriga was offered a drink by a graceful person who seemed to know him. She led him off to a table by the stage.

Eh, let him go. Maybe company would improve his mood.

Pyaras inhaled the fantastical world of costume and desire. Was that Kethani over by the waterfall? He pushed closer between the spectators . . . No. It was only some stranger. He would have to start all over. Disappointed, he drifted to a nearby table.

A couple was here, already halfway through their drinks: a woman with long, straight hair and a ruffled costume, and a pale, muscular young man with a shaved head that gleamed in the blue light. Impossible to join their conversation, when they were already enthralled with one another.

Pyaras leaned his elbows on the table, pressed the glass circle of his

rounded the corner; a broad dark figure brought him upright with a gasp. "Varin's teeth!"

"Please excuse me, sir."

Pyaras recognized her then—powerful body, golden skin, black suit and tattooed forehead—*thank heavens.* "I'm sorry, Jarel. I didn't see you." But something was wrong; his manservant was not supposed to come into the club.

Imbati Jarel bowed. "Sir, we should go. I've identified a spy lurking out front."

"That's bad."

"It's worse, sir. He shows signs of having recognized me."

Plis' bones. Pyaras ran for his dressing room, fumbled open the locker, and almost tore his velvet suit getting it back on. Something was coming. Something bad. He burst back out.

Veriga was here, startling in white shirt and Arissen-red trousers. Beside him, powerful Jarel was minimized by her Imbati black.

"I'm on this," Veriga said.

Good enough for an apology. Veriga could handle himself; he'd been a bodyguard in the Eminence's Cohort even before he joined the police. Veriga headed around the turn and out the way they'd first come in; with Jarel now at her station, Pyaras followed into the dim, blue-lit entry hall. Clients entering through the windowless front door of the club strategically refused to look at them.

Veriga pushed out with police boldness, and the door swung shut. *Thud.*

Oh, holy Twins, had he just sent Veriga to be shot?

Panic tried to split him from the top down. Pyaras squeezed his head between his hands. He shut his eyes—he shouldn't have. The old images flooded in: Veriga in that hospital bed, twitching head to foot, a needle in his arm, a tube down his throat, all because he'd been assigned to protect Nekantor.

Why had he let Veriga try to protect him?

"I have to go out there," he choked out. "I can't let Veriga face a death meant for me!"

"I understand, sir," Jarel said quietly. "But this is Arissen Veriga's choice."

Heart flailing, Pyaras fought the panic. *Gnash it, gnash it . . .*

Veriga's gray head popped back in. "You're clear. Come on out."

Pyaras gasped. "Really?"

Veriga shrugged. "Whoever he was, he's gone. Maybe he realized the Imbati saw him."

I'm stupid and childish. One thing to say so; another to make his heart stop pounding. Walking into the street, Pyaras searched for signs of danger. The atmospheric lamps on the cavern roof had gone dark for nighttime not long ago. The mercantile district's shops and restaurants were busy with Lowers—the gray coats of Kartunnen artisans were weirdly luminous under streetlights, while darker clumps of people occasionally flashed with bright reflections of silver from Melumalai castemark necklaces. No obvious threats, but it would be easy for a spy or assassin to hide on a shop roof, or vanish in shadows among the moving bodies.

They returned to their parked skimmer without a word spoken. Pyaras took his seat beside Veriga, Jarel engaged the vehicle's repulsion, and after maneuvering around a few stray pedestrians, they accelerated into the circumference.

Around the corner from the next radius, two skimmers came heading in their direction. Something was odd—neither seemed to be passing the other. Pyaras tensed.

As the vehicles drew closer, they caught the aura of a streetlight, revealing three Eminence's Cohort guards, and Cousin Nekantor.

Oh, sweet Heile, not Nekantor! Had that spy been one of *his?*

Imbati Jarel braked to a stop. Pyaras gripped the cushioned edge of his seat to stand up, and glared into his cousin's face. Nekantor had cheekbones as sharp as his wits, and that touch of gray hair that everyone said made him look even more handsome—but Pyaras had never been fooled. Nek was ugly underneath. You had to look right at him, or risk drawing his attention to something he might destroy.

Varin's teeth.

If that spy *had* been Nekantor's, then he would take Lake Club apart until nothing was left but bare limestone.

Sure enough, Nekantor narrowed his eyes and sent a scathing gaze over the surrounding buildings. His mouth pulled into a grimace of disgust. "Pyaras, come back to the Residence at once."

Pyaras gritted his teeth. "Why?"

"You're in danger."

Tell me something I don't know. "Not that you care."

"I do care. The Fifth Family is after you."

If that information was some kind of bait, he wasn't going to take it. "Look how you give yourself away, Nek. You only care because I'm a First Family asset."

Nekantor twitched. "Come home. Leave your pet Arissen here; he can find his own way. You would be a lot easier to protect if you weren't constantly muckwalking."

"Easier to control, you mean." This place was less safe by the second, but gnash it, he wasn't just going to *do as Nek said.*

Nekantor shifted, now a gaunt shadow outlined with orange on one side; he flicked one hand along his sleeve. "Pyaras, if you come back now, I'll name you Executor to the Pelismara Division."

What he'd wanted for years. A bribe? More likely a lie. Pyaras snorted and bent forward to Jarel's ear. "Do you believe thi—"

Zzap!

Pyaras screamed. *It burns, it burns!* He clutched the top of his head—mercy, his hands were burning! The skimmer jerked forward, knocking him into his seat. Heavy fabric smothered him. Blows pounded his head—*gods!*—the skimmer swerved sickeningly—*I can't see*—

The heavy drape dragged away. It was Veriga's coat; Veriga shook it, and laid it across his lap. "Fire's out," he said. "Name of Plis, I'm sorry."

"Aaaaargh," Pyaras moaned.

"That assassin was a Paper Shadow, or I wouldn't have missed him. You're lucky to have a face, young nobleman."

"Thank Sirin—aaaargh." His head still felt on fire. His hands stung. Somehow, they'd come to the top of a level rampway near the edge of the city-caverns. A fall of limestone created a wall behind it. Their skimmer dropped into the bore, and Jarel braked down the steep slope beside the pedestrian steps until they arrived in the well-lit neighborhoods of the fifth level. Tentatively, Pyaras felt for his burning head with his stinging fingers.

A huge clump of hair and ash fell off in his hands.

If he hadn't bent to talk to his Jarel, he'd be dead.

Sirin's blessed luck. At least it was me, and not Veriga.

Jarel was driving at legal speeds now. Pain stretched the seconds. Home, home, come on, come on—at last, the iron fence of the Residence grounds loomed out of the dark.

And Veriga was still here.

"Gnash it, Veriga, I forgot to take you home. I was hurting instead of thinking."

"Eh," Veriga grunted. "Doesn't matter. Police will be called. I should be there."

"So you can make a statement? All right." Pyaras winced. "But I'm not letting my Family question you. You shouldn't have to deal with those people again."

"I'll talk to the police. Officer to officer. I saw more of it than you." He shook his head, and his voice fell to a growl. "And I *should* have seen him before."

"It's all right. I'm all right."

"Yeah."

Jarel turned into the Conveyor's Hall, pulling the skimmer in beneath the wide stone arch. She braked to a halt and turned off repulsion. Pyaras got up slowly. So much pain—was his hair still smoldering? Jarel was talking to the team of Imbati, all attentive in their black suits with their crescent-cross Household tattoos.

He hadn't thought this far ahead. The Household team wouldn't just return the skimmer to their collection of vehicles; they'd also inform every other Imbati in the Residence about the attack. So now, everyone would know what had happened. And where. And who he'd been with. He'd lost so many friends over Veriga . . .

Varin's teeth, I'll never hear the end of it.

No, go home. Just get home, where medicine cabinets built by Lowers for weak-blooded nobles would be helpful for once. He gritted his teeth walking across the gravel pathways, entered the suites wing, and climbed the spiral stairway.

Jarel pressed her palm to the front door lock, got the door open, and immediately vanished through the curtained door into the servants' Maze.

The First Housewoman asked, "Would you care to sit, sir?"

"Not yet," said Pyaras. "I have to tell Father what's happened."

She got the inner doors and Father's bedroom door for him, because he couldn't have done it with his hands in this state. Pyaras walked in with his bracelet hand behind his back, guilty as if he were sixteen and not twenty-five—that feeling, at least, wasn't unusual.

It smelled of soap in here, and medicine. Father's servants had carefully arranged painted screens to hide the medical equipment from view, but they couldn't hide that smell. Father had been reclining against his pillows, playing with a handheld ordinator. As Pyaras walked in, though, he looked up and his eyes widened.

"Oh, my Pira—!"

"Father, I'm all right. Someone sent an assassin after me."

"Holy Mother Elinda, thank you for staying your hand," Father murmured.

"Yeah." Pyaras held out his right hand: the palm was bright red, shiny, speckled with fragments of hair and ash. "I should get cleaned up. And I guess the police will be coming by in a little while."

"I should be there to receive them." Father tried to sit up straighter, and grimaced. He couldn't always hide his frustration at the chronic inflammation and pain that had forced him to retire as a bureaucratic Administrator. His servants hovered near, attentively, but he waved them down.

"Please, Father," Pyaras said, "it's all right. I can talk to them, and if you have questions, we can have them come back to speak with you. Don't ruin your whole week trying to do this."

Father subsided, looking annoyed, but also relieved. "Please do have them come back, then."

Pyaras nodded. He leaned over and patted the air just above Father's arm so neither of them would be hurt. "I'll just go get cleaned up."

If it had just been him, he would have gone to his rooms. With Veriga here, though, and the prospect of an impending police visit, he went back out to the sitting room. Without thinking, he sat down on Mother's brightly striped pouf, then realized he had no idea where to put his hands. Not *down*, obviously.

No dirty hands on your Mother's pouf, Pira. Don't stain her memory.

Pyaras sighed, and made a wry grimace at Veriga, who was sitting on the couch with forearms draped across his knees.

"Sir." Imbati Jarel had set up a steel folding table with a towel, a basin of water, and a pair of scissors. The First Housewoman spread a cloth, and placed one of the brass dining chairs in its center.

"If you would have a seat, sir," she said.

Pyaras moved to the new chair, but glanced sidewise at the folding table. "Jarel . . . what are the scissors for?"

Jarel leaned her head to one side. "Sir, your hair is—uneven."

"Oh, gods, no." This hair had taken years, and saved him endless harassment.

"Very good, sir."

He nodded, and allowed them to wash and dry his hands. He would have preferred just to keep them in the cooling water. Jarel applied a medicinal salve, which made him hiss in pain but felt cool on his palms and the top of his head.

"We'll have a pain pill for you in a moment, sir."

He held on until it arrived, and gulped it gratefully while the First Housewoman held the glass. Then, in the corner of his eye, he saw Veriga making a face.

"What?"

Veriga rubbed a hand across his mouth. "Imbati," he said, "you owe him a mirror, at least."

"The heart that is valiant triumphs over all, sir," Jarel replied stonily.

"What?" Pyaras demanded. "She owes me a mirror?" He looked between them.

Veriga shrugged. "Just saying."

"Jarel, please get me a mirror."

He didn't miss the glare Jarel cast at Veriga as she brought it to him. He looked.

It wasn't just that a chunk of his hair was missing. Half of the top of his head was essentially bare. Long strands at his left temple straggled pathetically, and even if the remaining hair on the right side hadn't been damaged to a frizzle, it would have looked ridiculous.

"All right," he sighed. "Do it, then."

"I'm sorry, sir."

The First Housewoman wrapped a cape around his neck, and Jarel came at him with the scissors. Snip, snip: the hard-won locks fell on the light cloth beneath the chair.

"Cousin Della will be so disappointed. She'll think I changed my mind about her advice."

"I'm sorry, sir," Jarel said again.

"I didn't, though. She was the one who finally figured out what would stop people calling me Arissen. It even looked good." It had been a few years, now. Mai willing, they'd gotten over it.

Fool thought. How could anyone just 'get over' his size and health, almost unheard of amidst the decline of the Grobal Race, when their own continued to fail?

Whatever. He wasn't a child any more. Anyone that petty could just go and die in a hole.

Call me Arissen. I dare you.

CHAPTER FOUR

A Pinpoint Shot

Score one for the Arissen!

Melín grinned as the all-clear whistle died away across the sunblast air. There was nothing more satisfying than walking away from a field with a cold weapon—the grain loaded, the firefighters and harvesters safe, and not a single shot fired.

The shadeline drew cool over her skin. She waved away a cloud of tiny insects, wiped sweat from her lip, and entered the overforested zone.

This place never got less incredible. The ancient bark-trees had trunks broader than a city street, roots that wrestled through the dirt, and massive arms that sheltered her from the gulf of sky. The shinca trees had silvery-bright cylindrical trunks as smooth as glass, rootless feet, and slender branches. The birds fluttered and bickered in tangles of bushes. The flowers burst with sudden scents. It had, maybe, rightness?

Peace. That was the word—but not a peace that belonged to people.

A wysp winked past at knee level, splashing shadows among the bushes and vines it passed through. Aimless, and harmless: agitation-level zero. For now.

That was why she carried a weapon of war.

The rust-red tent of headquarters was a beacon in the green: small, but strategically placed. Behind the door-flap, the radio officers sat to one side with their steel desk of maps and equipment, coordinating the field teams.

"Specialist First Melín reporting to Captain for reassignment," she said, to the officer who had his headphones pushed back off one ear.

"Confirmed, Specialist. You're scheduled for a break."

Already? "Understood, sir."

"Captain wants to talk to you. Report to her first."

"Yes, sir."

From the coordinators' desk, a bundle of electrical cords ran across and down a tumble of stones into a cave opening. Melín boot-stepped down stone to stone beside it, then ducked into the tunnel and jogged deeper until it opened up.

The Division had used this cave pocket for upwards of eighty years, because everybody preferred underground, and because it saved on equipment-hauling. The large inside space was warm and bright at all hours and in all seasons, because the trunk of a shinca tree passed straight through its center. This did have drawbacks: shinca trees attracted and absorbed energy, so you couldn't store weapons in here for any length of time or their batteries would drain. And it was too bright to take a nap.

Captain Keyt was at her desk, earphone in one ear. She had evenly sunmarked skin and a scar where her right eye used to be. Her left eye was busy over maps and schedules.

Melín saluted, a chop of her right hand to her left shoulder. "Specialist First Melín, reporting as requested, sir."

"Thank you, Specialist." Captain didn't stand. She kept a folding chair on the side of her desk that she could keep her eye on; she glanced over at the man sitting in it. "Someone's here to speak to you. Won't tell me what it's about." She glanced up meaningfully. "He's been waiting a couple of hours."

Oh boy. This man had never seen surface duty in his life: overly stiff with knees and heels together, external sun lenses held awkwardly in his fingers, not a single sunmark on his skin. He stood up like police—and with just a bit of edge to him, something to prove. Definitely not a Cohort First.

"Yes, sir," Melín said.

"Third Solnis," said Captain Keyt, "you have four minutes. Then I need Specialist Melín to report back to me."

"Yes, sir," the man said.

"First, I gotta set this thing down," said Melín. She headed past the shinca and through the tunnel to the weapons room. Here, the weapons racks were shielded from the shinca by a thick wall of rock; Specialist weapons were first inside the door. She slung the bolt rifle off her shoulder—finally!—and slotted it into the charger.

The weapons officer posted at the rack called, "Nush, check!" His tunnel-hound lolloped over, running its broad, electrosensitive snout over the weapons on the shelf before giving a musical yelp. The officer rewarded it with a treat.

"Quite a weapon," Third Solnis said.

Melín glanced at him. *Gods. Save me from police attitude.* If Solnis ever made Division, he'd probably be one of those guys that tried to mark particular weapons as their own. She shrugged. "It is what it is." She whistled to Nush, and crouched down to scrub the hound's velvety, eyeless head between her hands.

"I'd think you might have more respect for it, seeing as you're the pinpoint shot of the Division."

Melín laughed out loud. "Is that why you wanted to talk to me?" The hound wriggled with excitement and draped its forepaws over her knee, so she crooned to it. "He thinks I'm the pinpoint shot of the Division, yes he does."

"I'm not known for getting bad information."

"He's not known for getting bad information, Nush, no he's not." She shot a look at Solnis. "You talk like an Imbati." She winked at the weapons officers. "Doesn't he, seni?" Both of them laughed, and Solnis reddened.

"There's no need to insult me."

There was no need for him to stand around and be insulted, either. Just like there was no need for him to wait around under Captain's eye for a couple of hours. He wanted something. Melín stood up.

"If you want the pinpoint shot of the Division, go talk to Sixth Elovin. You should know, though, he got demoted off the Specialist team because he took a perfectly accurate shot at the perfectly wrong time, and got five people killed. Those things—" She waved at the bolt rifles. "A bolt rifle's a tool for one job. In the wrong hands, it's worth less than my ass." She enjoyed the look on the weapons officers' faces; they weren't the only ones who appreciated her ass. "Come to me when you want the top Wysp Specialist of the Division."

"I want the top Wysp Specialist of the Division."

He sure was persistent. "What for?"

"This team I'm a part of, we recently . . . lost a member. We appreciate people with your skills."

"You might have noticed I already have a job."

"Oh, I'm not trying to poach you."

She raised her eyebrows. "Mai's eye sees you, seni."

"No, no. This is more of a . . . a contracting position. You might appreciate the extra pay."

"I got two words for you," Melín said. In one motion, she reached over her shoulder, drew her Division blade from its sheath across her back, and touched its narrow, curved tip to the end of his nose. "My. Ass."

To the laughter of the weapons officers, she smirked and returned the blade to its sheath. Third Solnis reddened and left in a hurry. Melín sauntered until she reached the room where Captain was sitting, then resumed her professional gait. She waited until Captain's eye came to her.

"Captain, Third Solnis was trying to offer me a second job."

"Was he, now?"

"Yes, sir. Somehow, he'd heard I was a good shot. I refused, though, sir. I'm ready for my next assignment."

Captain Keyt regarded her levelly. "What is the most important skill of a Specialist?"

That was Specialist training question number one. "Good judgment, sir."

"Exactly. I appreciate that you never forget that. You've been a positive influence on the other Specialists in your cohort. If you began giving some hours to training new candidates for Specialist, you'd provide great benefit to my cohorts, and to the whole Division."

"Sir?"

"Specialist Melín, I'm offering to promote you to Captain's Hand. I want an instructor who can give our Specialists the perspective they need."

"Captain, thank you, sir. But no, thank you."

Captain Keyt studied her face. "Are you sure I can't convince you, Specialist?"

"Sir." Her throat felt dry. "I'm honored that you feel I'd be a good instructor. I'd be happy to volunteer hours when I'm not on duty."

"But you don't want to be taken off the fields."

Melín stood to attention. "Thank you for understanding, sir."

Captain sighed. "I hope you'll—" She straightened suddenly, one hand to her earphone and fire in her eye. "Specialist, wysp emergency, field three."

"Thank you, sir. Up and out!" Melín ducked through into the weapons room, snatched a fully charged bolt rifle from the upper shelf, and slung it over her shoulder. She ran through the tunnels and up the tumble of stones. Once she was clear, she drew her blade. She had the field map in her gut at this point; field three wasn't far.

Then the Imbati walked to the main door and opened it. "Lady," he said, "we're ready for you."

Mother stood outside. Imbati Aloran offered her his hand, and she took it, allowing him to escort her into the room. The two of them were so pure. He was to her exactly what the ideal manservant should be: a bodyguard and nurse, a faithful companion, a confidant, a comfort. She was so lucky to have hired him after Father died. Today, she was wearing a hand-painted silk gown with a tree design. Its leaves were precisely the same shade of green as his new coat. That couldn't be coincidence.

"Mother, you've been planning this." Adon started to grin again.

"Of course!" she said. "When it comes to clothing, I always plan. Congratulations on your thirteenth birthday, darling boy." She reached for him with her free hand, and leaned down close; her lips brushed his cheekbone.

Adon blushed. "I guess I made it." *Zzap!* "Barely."

She'd started to pull away, but now she leaned forward again, her warm cheek pressing firmly against his. In his ear, her voice trembled. "I'm grateful for you every day, Adon. But now, more than ever."

Any other day, he might have argued. "I love you, Mother." He looked up. "You, too, Aloran."

Aloran's reply was clear in his eyes.

"Oh!" Adon remembered. "Tagaret and Della will just love this suit—I have to show them."

At this hour, chances were they would be having breakfast. Adon ran out across the private drawing room, pushed through the double doors to the sitting room, and nearly ran smack into Tagaret's back. He threw up his hands and managed to stop just as they hit.

Tagaret's body swayed, but he didn't react to the collision, except to feel behind him. That wasn't normal. Alarmed, Adon let his brother take his shoulder and guide him to his side—into a confrontation.

Nekantor was here.

Heile help him.

Nekantor and Tagaret were staring at each other. Silence vibrated in the air between them as if echoing with years of terrible words. Had they been fighting? Adon looked to Imbati Dexelin, but the servant with the braided hair didn't meet his eyes. For someone who'd just saved a life, he looked awfully unhappy.

"Why?" Tagaret said. "Here's Adon, but why do you need to talk to him?"

Nekantor snorted. "Don't pretend you don't understand what's going on here, Tagaret. Adon and Pyaras were targeted. You know what will happen if we let such an attack go unanswered. Everyone will think the First Family is weak, and you know what that means . . ."

"Yes, yes, I know what it means."

Adon pressed his lips together. They were talking *about* him, not *to* him, which he hated. Usually.

Tagaret gave an exasperated sigh. "Nek, one of those Arissen is dead, and we're never going to find the other one."

"I don't need to find Arissen," said Nekantor. "I know who's really responsible. Innis of the Fifth Family."

Gods, he *knew?* Adon glanced up at the side of Tagaret's face; Tagaret's eyebrows had pinched skeptically.

"*How* do you know? How do you know it wasn't, say, the Eminence Herin?"

"Oh, don't be stupid," Nekantor snapped. He glanced up at the wall behind them, and started opening and closing his hands. "Herin already has all the power he could want. Innis, though—Innis would have been Heir if *I* hadn't beaten him. He hasn't forgotten his humiliating defeat. It shows in his choice of targets."

Adon swallowed.

Zzap!

Tagaret opened his hands. "There is a police investigation going on, and they'll—"

"Fah. The police won't pin it to him. When have you ever heard of an assassin being arrested? Arissen will protect their own."

Or shoot their own. Adon didn't dare say it.

Zzap!

All Tagaret said was, "I'm not sure that's how it works, Nek."

"Even so, Tagaret. Even so." Nekantor started wringing his hands. "Innis has plans. Secrets. He's going to do something worse, and I'm going to find out what it is, and teach him a lesson before he can catch us unprepared again. So I've challenged him to Imbati Privilege."

Adon blinked. Wait . . . *Imbati Privilege*, did he mean like—?

Tagaret's mouth fell open. Maybe he was too shocked to speak.

Adon wasn't. "Imbati Privilege, are you even *serious?*" he demanded.

"Nobody's done that in a hundred years! This isn't *The Great Grobal Fyn and the Duel of Secrets*."

Nekantor's gaze snapped to him, latching on like a grip. It squeezed his breath. Adon tugged his new jacket straight and tried to stand taller.

Nekantor said through clenched teeth, "If it's good enough for the founder of Varin, little brother, it's good enough for me."

"Well," said Tagaret reasonably, "so long as Innis doesn't laugh at the suggestion."

"Shows what *you* know, Tagaret. He's already agreed to meet at the Imbati Service Academy this morning. And you're coming. One hour from now, with Adon and Pyaras." He waved a hand. "Don't even start telling me you have important work. Lady's politics can wait." He smiled at Adon. "Take a day off school for your birthday; you're welcome."

Adon managed not to grimace.

"Nek," Tagaret protested. "Aren't you worried about exposing First Family information in this competition?"

"That's for my Dexelin to handle."

Just look at poor Dexelin flinch! Holy Mai, no wonder he was so miserable. Shoved into a public conflict of questions with absolutely no training? Adon tried to catch the Imbati's eyes sympathetically, and Dexelin stared at him in shock.

"See you both there," Nekantor snapped. "With Pyaras. One hour." He turned on his heel and walked out.

Adon blinked after him for a minute before he could even shake his head. "Tagaret?"

"Yeah?"

"That—doesn't make any sense."

Tagaret squeezed his shoulder comfortingly and called, "Serjer?"

The First Houseman stepped out of the vestibule with a bow. "Your brother has left, sir."

Tagaret's tall frame sagged. "I'm sorry, Adon. I'm so sorry. Nekantor . . . he's very fearful, sometimes. There's nothing we can do about it."

"His Dexelin is really upset."

Tagaret raised his eyebrows. "Is he? Well, Mai's truth. Of course he would be." He rubbed his hand across his mouth. "One hour? I have no idea how to prepare for this."

Adon almost laughed at that. "Who would? They'd have to be a hundred years old!"

Tagaret nodded. "I just wish we had more basis to accuse Innis of the Fifth Family than our brother's insistence. He's putting our information at risk, and for what?"

Adon shrugged. "Innis' plan?"

"If he has one." Tagaret sighed. "But I suppose, if Nek *is* right that Innis is behind this, he must have *some* plan. One that starts with assassinations."

Zzap!

Adon's stomach flipped as the truth hit: in one hour, he'd be standing in the same room as a man who might have tried to kill him. *Twins stand by me.* He gulped hard. "Tagaret?" his voice quavered on the word.

His brother turned, face falling. "Oh, Adon, I'm sorry, I should have thought . . ."

"Can I just—? I need a minute. I'll be in my rooms."

"Of course. Are you all right?"

Adon closed his hands on the edges of his new jacket to stop them shaking, and forced a smile. "I'm fine."

I'm not fine.

Hot water felt good when it pounded on the top of his head. Getting in the shower had been the right idea; he wasn't about to wear his celebratory suit to some bizarre Imbati competition, anyway. Everyone knew Nekantor couldn't keep servants, but it had never felt this personal before. If only the whole situation could swirl and drain away between his toes . . . Adon angled his head so the shower hit the nape of his neck, watching the water run down over his body into the marble tub.

It would be all right, though. Tagaret would be there. Pyaras would be there. And Tagaret's Kuarmei, and Pyaras' Jarel.

Poor Dexelin.

A knock and click came from beyond the shower curtain.

"Adon, darling, are you all right?"

Bless her for wondering—but not for coming into his bathroom! "*Mother*, what are you doing? I'll be ready to go, I promise. I just wanted to change my clothes."

"Oh, of course. Did you want me to bring them in, then?"

He sighed. "Can you get me my old Kartunnen Ober suit, with the lace?"

"Be right back."

Might as well get out, then. He shut off the water and toweled dry, then quickly clamped one corner of the towel under his arm and wrapped it around himself. Mother came back in with the requested amethyst-colored suit over her arm, her face carefully angled away. She set it down.

"I need to talk to you, Adon," she said.

"Now? When I'm not dressed?"

"I can step out into your bedroom if you prefer, love. But I need to talk to you about your brother before you leave."

"Oh. Well, you can stay, then." A tremor ran down his legs to his toes. He grabbed his underwear, just barely getting it up far enough before the towel slipped out from under his arm and landed on the tiled floor. Clothes first. This wasn't a conversation he wanted to be naked for. "So, Nekantor?" He stepped into his pants and pulled them up.

"Nekantor's . . . not safe," said Mother. "It's important that you know that."

He couldn't remember ever feeling safe when Nekantor came around. Besides, he'd just seen what happened when Nekantor walked into his role-play class; it made him sick. Good thing putting on his silk shirt and arranging the lace gave him something to do with his hands. "I get that."

"I'm not sure you know how much effort Tagaret and Della and I, and the Household, have put into keeping him away from you. Especially over the last year. You've surely noticed that we started holding salon gatherings here at the house, in spite of the pressure that puts on our Household."

Adon's fingers paused on a button. "Why the last year?"

"Are you dressed?"

"Dressed enough."

Mother turned around and looked him in the eye. "Because ever since you turned twelve, you've become potentially useful to him, as a possible Heir candidate for the First Family."

"Useful?" Adon echoed. "Who thinks that way?"

"Nekantor does," said Mother. "If you ever see him in person, you can be sure he's assessing you. Your intelligence. Your skills. Your potential contribution to the First Family's interests."

That sounded like some conversations he'd had with Schoolmasters. "A lot of people do that, though."

"It's different with Nekantor," Mother insisted. "To him, the entire world is a game of kuarjos. Every person is a gamepiece. A warrior for our side—the First Family's side—or the other side. To be used or sacrificed as necessary. He's tried to use me before."

"You?" Adon shuddered. "He didn't, though, did he?"

Her face was deadly serious. "No. That time, he found a way to use Tagaret instead."

That explained the echoing silence in the sitting room. "All right, Mother, I understand. I'll be careful."

"Stay near Tagaret and Pyaras when you go to this meeting, but especially Tagaret. If Nekantor talks to you, it's safer to have someone nearby listening."

"I will." He turned to hook his crystalline-patterned coat with one finger.

"One more thing, love."

He looked up into her face; seeing her fear so plainly made the world shiver. "Yes, Mother?"

"Never fight Nekantor when his eyes are on you. He's too dangerous. Too cruel." She reached out her hand. "Promise me."

Adon took it. "I promise."

I can do this." Adon took a deep breath, tugged at his gloves, huffed the breath out again, and repeated to the door handle, "I can do this."

Bang-bang-bang-bang!

He leapt backward. "What in the name of Mai!"

The door cracked open, and his older cousin came in. "Are you in there, Adon?"

"Varin's teeth, Pyaras! Were you trying to break down my door?" Pyaras was the only grownup he knew who overdid absolutely *everything.* He was probably strong enough to break a door. The finely tailored sleeves of his ruby-red suit stretched over his arm muscles. He wasn't even wearing gloves today, as if he didn't care if people questioned his commitment to the health of the Race.

Of course, then he realized why Pyaras looked so different, and gulped.

Pyaras' mouth quirked sideways. "Sorry."

"Uh, I'm sorry, too." It was one thing to know his cousin had been shot; totally another to see the injury. At the top of his forehead began an area of blistery red, nearly hairless skin, glistening with some kind of salve. The rest of his hair was so short it stuck straight up. "Shouldn't you have a bandage on your head?"

"Probably, but I'd rather not treat this like some big drama. I won't be made into some kind of show object for Nekantor."

"Ugh," Adon grunted. "Nekantor."

"I couldn't have said it better."

"Mother said we were only kuarjos pieces to him."

Pyaras nodded. "You should listen to your mother. You feeling all right?"

"Um." Adon glanced away toward the window, where the rest of his gloves were arrayed in a star pattern on the stone sill. He grimaced.

"Yeah, me neither," said Pyaras, with none of his usual bombast. "That was terrifying."

"Whoa, really?" Of course it had been terrifying—but it was weird to hear *Pyaras* say it.

His big cousin's mouth quirked. "Who needs sleep, right? I almost passed out while jogging this morning."

"Ha!" said Adon. But that idea brought back the sound: *zzap!* He fought down the horrible images that lingered in his mind with the smell of smoke. He shook his hands at his cousin. "Crown of Mai, why do Arissen weapons have to exist in the first place?"

"Now, there's an interesting question." Pyaras made a grab for the brass desk chair, but hissed and snatched his hand away, hooking the chair with a foot instead.

Right, Heile's mercy, his hands were injured, too—Adon could have kicked himself for forgetting it. Of *course* Pyaras wouldn't wear gloves today.

Pyaras sat on the chair backward, forearms across the top. "Well, first off, energy weapons weren't designed for police work. They're ideal for the cities because they don't create physical waste or release toxic gases—but they were designed to be used against wysps on the surface. We couldn't put food on our tables without the Division to protect the harvests."

"Arissen Veriga told you that, right?" Adon asked. "They said he was with you when you got shot."

Pyaras jutted out his chin. "If my *friend* Veriga hadn't been there, he couldn't have put out the *fire* on my *head*."

That was news! Adon blinked. "You're pretty lucky, then."

"Yes. I might have no hair at all."

Zzap! "Or no head."

"Mai's truth."

"Actually, my friend Talabel saved me," Adon found himself saying. *Oh, gods, did I just call Talabel a friend?* But Pyaras had just called Veriga the same . . . He flushed. "Well, I mean, not—she's, I saw her in play session and she's my bodyguard sometimes. Mostly for roleplay. Yesterday, for real. She'll be certified soon." He grimaced, bracing for a lecture—Arbiter Lorman would chastise him for being soft on Imbati; Mother would explain what was Not Spoken Of with people from outside the house. But Pyaras raised his eyebrows and smiled.

"Some people are just good people," he said. "It's the gift of the Twins that we have them in our lives."

"Wow." Adon stared at him for a second. "You're right."

"I'm sorry you're getting yanked out of school for Nekantor's dug-up farce."

Adon shrugged. "Better than walking into a place where the next person in the door might try to shoot me."

"They won't try again," said Pyaras.

Adon shook his head. "How can you be sure?"

"Here's the thing." His cousin counted awkwardly on reddened fingers. "One, the Eminence Herin is alive and well. Big factor there. Two, assassination attempts are dangerous to the assassin, as you saw. Three, the whole Family is on alert now. Also the whole Household. The whole Society."

"The whole Society," Adon murmured. A weird euphoria tickled up his spine, as if the two of them had been thrust into a spotlight on an invisible stage. Still, it couldn't banish that sound.

Zzap!

Now Pyaras chuckled. "And even if these guys today *were* the ones who tried to get you killed, they wouldn't do it with the Heir and cabinet members around."

"Ugh." Adon checked his watch. "I guess we'd better go."

"Don't worry; I got you." Pyaras stood up, and they walked out together.

Thank all the gods, Nekantor hadn't shown up at the house. Instead, Lady Selemei and her Ustin had come, and also Fedron, the Speaker of the Cabinet, with his Chenna. Nothing like having gray and dignified cabinet members walk you out the front entrance of the Residence to make something feel consequential.

There were more Arissen guards in the hallways than usual. Adon hung back between Tagaret and Pyaras, watching cautiously past Lady Selemei's head toward the Plaza of Varin.

This gravel path was in plain view of all the Lower tourists circulating in the Plaza. At first, they seemed to be looking at all sorts of things—the columns of the Courts building, the housing of the old Alixi's Elevator, the Old Forum where the Administrators worked, or the single silver-glowing shinca tree that pierced upward through the Plaza's center. But soon they all started turning toward the Residence grounds. None of them were brave enough to goggle between the iron bars of the fence, given the presence of four Eminence's Cohort guards beside the main gate, but at least one Kartunnen pointed in this direction.

Yes, Lowers, enjoy, because we're all fancy and on display.

Not that the members of this group were dressed for show. Lady Selemei's gray silk gown had panels that gleamed like steel armor, so she was taking this seriously; Speaker Fedron wore an amber suit so basic it was clear he couldn't be bothered to dignify the proceedings. Tagaret looked defensively formal in Grobal green, while Pyaras in ruby red wore the brightest color of the group. His own Kartunnen Ober suit was of higher quality than any of them except maybe Lady Selemei's custom piece.

As the Arissen opened the gates, Selemei's Ustin and Fedron's Chenna moved to the front. Tagaret's Kuarmei and Pyaras' Jarel moved out to the sides, causing any nearby Lowers to pull back. The four Imbati created a square of safety, allowing the group to cross the near corner of the Plaza toward the Imbati Service Academy.

Nekantor was standing by the Academy gate. So was Arbiter Lorman of the First Family Council. Something was obviously wrong, because Arbiter Lorman had his hands on his hips, and Nekantor was practically quivering. In addition to their bodyguards, Nekantor had brought an Arissen with him: a woman with an orange Eminence's Cohort uniform and brown sunmarked skin. The closer you got, the better you could hear him above the hum of the Plaza's activity, spitting fury at the Academy gate wardens.

"How dare you speak to your superiors that way! Let us in."

Both of the wardens bowed deeply, but they didn't open the gate.

"Heir Nekantor, sir," said one of them, "I deeply apologize for the inconvenience. The invitation that was extended to you naturally applies to your Dexelin, but we are not permitted to allow Arissen to enter the Academy."

"Not permitted? Of course you're permitted!"

"Regretfully, sir, I must inform you that we are not."

"You'll do as you're told. Open this gate!"

"I will be happy to do so, sir, when your Arissen agrees to stay behind."

The Arissen woman didn't move or speak.

"Unacceptable," Nekantor snapped. "Get me someone in charge."

"Of course, Heir Nekantor, sir," replied the warden. He ran away across the courtyard. Another warden, who had been standing beside the columns of the main Academy building, ran forward to take his place.

"So, so, Nekantor," said Arbiter Lorman. "So, I mean, you could agree just to let your Arissen stand by the gate."

"It's principle, Lorman," said Nekantor.

"So, your fa—" Lorman began, but Nekantor wheeled on him, and he didn't finish his sentence.

That was when 'someone in charge' walked out into the courtyard of the Academy. You might not have realized he was important at first glance. He wore the manservant's tattoo, but nothing distinguished the black silk suit he wore from that of the wardens; he was quite small, of a height with Lady Selemei, and a good deal older, with white hair falling to his shoulders. However, he moved smoothly and with dignity, and every warden's posture shifted around him, realigning to orbit his gravity.

"Heir Nekantor, sir, greetings," he said calmly. Adon found himself on his toes, wanting to hear him speak again.

"Headmaster Moruvia," said Nekantor, sourly, but without the venom he'd used for the wardens. "I must be allowed in with both my attendants, Imbati Dexelin and Arissen Karyas. Your people have terrible manners."

Headmaster Moruvia bowed. "Have pity on them, sir, trapped as they are between the wills of two powerful men." His voice was more than calm; it was as still as a hidden cavern pool.

"What? You haven't been speaking with Eminence Herin, have you? Or Innis?"

"Our contract is with the Great Grobal Fyn, Heir Nekantor, sir," the Headmaster replied, bowing again. "I request your understanding in his name, just as you have requested ours."

Nekantor seemed baffled by this turn of the conversation. "What are you talking about?"

"My apologies, sir. Every manservant's contract rests upon a charter from the hand of Grobal Fyn, a document four hundred years old, preserved in the Academy archives. The Academy and its environs, sir, are preserved from uninvited entrance by Highers—in return for our oaths of silence. Our wardens only strive to protect the Great Families and their information, sir."

"Fah," said Nekantor. He lashed a look at Arissen Karyas, who snapped to attention with a loud click of boot-heels and stepped away to one side. The gates opened, and the Headmaster turned and walked calmly across the worn limestone courtyard, with the muttering Heir and everyone in their party following behind him.

Walking through the broad doorway, Adon ran his eyes up the nearest stone column; its capital was carved into golden flames. In the vaulted foyer, more wardens approached, subtly inviting them in different directions. Adon found himself directed into a group with Tagaret, Pyaras, and Arbiter Lorman. Their manservants stayed behind as a stocky warden directed them through a pair of doors on the left, into a spacious office. You could tell it was an office because the silk carpet had dents in it where a large desk and chairs had been removed.

It didn't stay spacious long. The stocky warden took them straight ahead to the far wall, and seated them on metal stools against the stone, snug beside each other so he could feel Tagaret's soft arm on one side, and Pyaras' hard arm on the other. Nekantor and his Dexelin were seated at the wall to his left, as were Lady Selemei and Speaker Fedron, all of them carefully spaced so they wouldn't touch. On the wall to his right, the Fifth Family's party had been seated already: Grobal Innis was there, and his manservant, and two more men who had to be the Fifth Family's cabinet members. The wardens who had seated them pushed the bronze doors shut so quietly they barely clicked, and then took places at the corners of the room, vigilant and silent.

The Headmaster walked to stand before the doors, bowed gracefully until his tattooed forehead touched the floor, then stood again.

"I am honored to convene this gathering in the tradition of the Great Grobal Fyn," he intoned. "The challenge having been issued by the Heir Grobal Nekantor of the First Family, and having been accepted by the Arbiter Grobal Innis of the Fifth Family, Privilege will be contested by their manservants, Nekantor's Dexelin and Innis' Brithe. If the two of you will step forward and face each other before me."

Adon swallowed hard. Dexelin's braid today was tight and precise, beginning at the crest of his head; the line where his lips met was less certain. He looked incredibly young compared to Innis' Brithe, whose hair was entirely gray.

The Headmaster spoke again. "Privilege is a competition of eight questions. Each competitor asks four questions in a row. The order of competitors is determined by a coin toss."

Solemnity broke into amusement on faces around the room. Adon bit his lip to keep from smiling. It was one thing to read the words in a children's book, another to imagine dignified Moruvia taking a coin that belonged in the hand of a Melumalai, and throwing it in the air. What was it supposed to do?

"Arissen do this all the time, you know," Pyaras whispered. "Before targetball games."

"They throw money?"

"Who's that talking?" Nekantor snapped. "Pyaras, do you have something you'd like to explain to everyone about Arissen?"

"This is Headmaster Moruvia's event," said Pyaras through his teeth. His eyes flashed fury. "I don't presume to know what Grobal Fyn intended."

"Thank you, Grobal Pyaras, sir," said Headmaster Moruvia. He held up a silver coin. "Innis' Brithe, as the target of the challenge, you will choose either Varin or eight, and we shall see which design faces up when the coin lands. If you guess correctly, you may choose to question first or last."

Brithe nodded. "Varin, please, sir."

Moruvia threw the coin, which flipped and glittered in the air until it landed on the carpet at his feet. He looked down. "It's Father Varin," he said. "Brithe?"

"I wish to question last, sir."

"Very good. For each question Brithe answers, Dexelin must also answer one. To decline a question, use the polite denial. Any imbalances in the number of questions answered by the end of questioning shall be resolved by returning to previously asked questions. Are the rules understood and accepted?"

"Yes, Headmaster," replied Brithe and Dexelin, bowing in unison.

"Are they also understood and accepted by the Masters of the competitors?" the Headmaster asked.

"Yes," said Innis. "Frivolous little event you've set up here, Nekantor. But anything that lets me access more First Family information, I already consider a win."

"It's a win for both of us, then." Nekantor crossed his arms tightly. "Yes, Headmaster, I accept the terms. Let's go."

"Nekantor's Dexelin, you may begin," said Headmaster Moruvia.

There was a silence. The two manservants stared at each other, as if each wished the other would speak first, even though Nekantor's Dexelin was designated to start. Someone's stool squeaked.

At last, Dexelin cleared his throat. "Question one," he said. "Who has Arbiter Innis most recently identified as the top possible Heir candidates for the First Family?"

Brithe's lips tightened. "Tagaret, Pyaras, and Adon of the First Family."

Adon tensed. It was awful, hearing his own name. He shouldn't assume it meant anything, because everyone knew who the three of them were. It didn't mean Innis had tried to kill them, necessarily. No one had tried to kill Tagaret, so far as they knew.

It just didn't sound like coincidence, either.

"Question two," said Dexelin. "Has Arbiter Innis ever contacted the Paper Shadows?"

Against his arm, Pyaras twitched. Adon nudged him; his cousin leaned to his ear and whispered, "Assassins."

Adon gulped. How would Brithe answer that?

"I don't know," Brithe said.

That was the polite denial. The room tightened, as if everyone had leaned forward.

"The question has been refused," said Headmaster Moruvia.

Innis' Brithe shifted feet. Nekantor's Dexelin winced slightly, and continued. "Question three: has Arbiter Innis conferred with his cousin Unger within the last week?"

Brithe's lips tightened again. "Yes."

"Question four: has Arbiter Innis conferred with any representatives of the Seventh Family within the last week?"

"Yes."

"Thank you, Dexelin. Thank you, Brithe," said the Headmaster. "Please, everyone, remain seated. The competitors may now have two minutes to confer with their Masters." The room filled with quiet murmurs.

"That was odd," Tagaret said. "Why would Dexelin ask about *the last week*?"

Adon frowned at him. Was *that* what he picked up on? *Last week*, but not the way both of the manservants hated every second of this? Imbati considered questions offensive when asked without consent—and this was basically an interrogation conducted at one-sixteenth speed. Brithe hadn't even been able to answer without tensing his mouth, and now, Nekantor was giving Dexelin some kind of talking-to.

Tagaret took Adon's shoulder. "You all right?"

"I guess." He didn't like the way Dexelin was standing as Nekantor spoke to him.

"If Heile's merciful, this'll be over soon," said Pyaras. "I'll get stiff." He stretched his legs far out in front of him.

The wardens announced in unison that the competition would resume, and the Headmaster returned to his presiding place. Adon rubbed the amethyst silk on his knees, uncomfortably. Thinking of Dexelin having to take questions put a sour taste in his throat.

"Innis' Brithe, you may begin," said Headmaster Moruvia.

"Question one," said Brithe. "Has the Heir Nekantor ever contacted the Paper Shadows?"

Dexelin swayed, as though he'd received a blow to the chest. "No."

The answer seemed to dismay Brithe—or at least, he hesitated before proceeding. Maybe it was because he had refused to answer the same question. Had he expected Dexelin to refuse it also?

"Question two. Whom has the Heir Nekantor appointed to what positions in the last week?"

Dexelin swayed again. "My Master has made three appointments. Wenmor of the Ninth Family to Director of the Pelismara Secure Facility. Pyaras of the First Family to Executor of the Pelismara Division. Unger of the Fifth Family to Alixi of Selimna."

"What?" Pyaras half-hopped out of his seat. "I thought that was a joke!"

"Pyaras!" Adon hissed. He grabbed his arm and pulled him down again. "Shhh, you'll get in trouble . . ." He turned to look pleadingly at the Headmaster.

"Please continue, Brithe," the Headmaster said—thank Heile, before Nekantor could make any sort of comment.

"Question three." Brithe took a breath, but appeared to stop himself, and cleared his throat. "How long have you worked for the Heir Nekantor?"

Dexelin swayed, and glanced aside.

He's looking at me. Adon felt a tingle behind his ears. He leaned forward slightly, trying to help Dexelin be strong.

"Three weeks," Dexelin said.

Brithe definitely didn't like that, probably because Dexelin had him cornered. There was only one question left, and Dexelin hadn't refused a single one. If Dexelin answered the last one, Brithe was going to have to answer the question about the Paper Shadows.

"Question four," said Brithe. "Is Nekantor planning to assassinate the Eminence Herin?"

Quiet gasps came from people around the room, but Dexelin didn't even sway this time, even though he had every right to be shocked.

"No."

Brithe swallowed.

"Respectfully, Brithe," said Headmaster Moruvia. "I request you give an answer to the refused question. Has Arbiter Innis ever contacted the Paper Shadows?"

The older servant's lips parted and he didn't answer for several seconds. Finally, he said, "Yes."

Yes? Adon stiffened and bumped his head against the stone wall. Mai help him, Nekantor was *right?*

"This competition is concluded," announced the Headmaster with a bow. "The Academy has been honored by your visit. You are free to return to your other obligations."

Nekantor got up first, with a smile. His Dexelin came to his side, and they left together through the bronze doors, which the attending wardens pulled open for them. Lorman and Pyaras stood up and started stretching their legs, so Adon joined them.

Innis didn't seem to be in a particular hurry to leave, despite what had come out of the questioning. In fact—

Adon tugged at Tagaret's shoulder. "Innis is coming!"

Tagaret stood up slowly. Adon's heart pounded. He tried to position himself between Tagaret and Pyaras.

"Tagaret, Pyaras," said Innis casually. "I thought I'd be remiss not to say hello while we were all here." He was shorter than either of them, and balding, with a long forehead that fell into a nose so noble it dominated his face. His fashion sense was careful and refined. His suit was a deep sapphire blue with occasional fine stripes of red through it, and his gray gloves had pearls at the wrists. "I'm sorry about the circumstances."

"That's a thing to say," said Pyaras. "Given what we've just learned."

"Oh?" Innis raised his eyebrows. "I don't think we've learned very much. The Courts won't consider any of this legally binding. Who knows how many times I've contacted the Paper Shadows, or when, or how successfully?"

Adon gulped. Innis was right; no matter what Nekantor thought, the Courts had nothing.

Innis smiled politely; Adon could see straight up his nostrils. "Tagaret, I hope you and Lady Della are well."

He knew Della by name? Adon glanced between them. Tagaret's expression looked strange, though he answered politely enough.

"Yes, of course. As I hope for you and your young partner."

"I can't complain about how that part worked out," Innis chuckled. "We'll be announcing her pregnancy soon."

Tagaret's answer was strained. "May Heile and Elinda bless you."

"Won't you introduce me to your brother?" Innis asked.

"Of course. This is Adon. Adon, this is Arbiter Innis of the Fifth Family Council."

A bolt of fear zapped from Adon's neck down into his shoes, but he extended his hand. Glove fabric made the Arbiter's grip shift and slip. "It's a pleasure to meet you, Arbiter," he said.

"As it is for me, young man."

Selfish cat. You should never have put your Brithe through that. He didn't say it out loud. "I think we need to go home," he said instead.

"Of course," said Innis. "Excuse me." He rejoined his party and they left together, looking sour.

Adon exhaled. "Let's go." Pyaras came with him immediately, but they hadn't gone two steps before Lady Selemei called after them.

"Adon, Pyaras, please wait."

Adon turned around. Tagaret hadn't moved at all. Lady Selemei was standing beside him, gently rubbing his upper arm.

"Tagaret," said Adon, "are you all right?"

"I'm so sorry," said Lady Selemei.

"Don't tell her," Tagaret whispered. His voice made Adon feel cold. "Selemei, Pyaras—you can't tell her."

"She's your partner," Lady Selemei said gently. "It should be between the two of you."

Adon looked between them, stomach twisting. "Please, tell me what's wrong."

"Adon, just promise me something," Tagaret said. "Say you won't talk about this with Della. I have to be the one to tell her."

"All right," he said. "I promise. I'm sorry . . . ?"

"Thank you for hosting us, Headmaster," said Pyaras. Adon made sure to look gratefully at both the Headmaster and the wardens as they passed by. Their servants rejoined them in the foyer, taking bodyguard positions as they exited the front doors.

"Tagaret?" Adon whispered. "Why can't we talk to Della?"

"She—" Tagaret grimaced, and his voice was hoarse and strange. "She still has to host your birthday party."

CHAPTER SIX

How to Respond to Disappointment

This birthday party was doomed. Knowing that Tagaret and Adon were out facing threats from Innis of the Fifth Family made Della's spine feel cold, and dread permeated every detail of the preparations. Even the smell of food drifting in from the kitchen seemed somehow wrong. Tamelera had designed an excellent plan to protect Vant and their other Kartunnen visitors from harm whenever Nekantor showed up, but all of the house's usual defenses felt fragile. This was a terrible time to be inviting outsiders in.

She'd also trapped herself when she'd offered to help the Household with preparations. Serjer the First Houseman and Premel the Household Keeper were moving furniture, but Tamelera had asked her to put away the collection of ceramic statuettes that sat on a shelf in the dining room—and today was one of her clumsy days. Every move she made seemed to bump her into a doorjamb, a table corner, a chair. Though she wasn't wearing gloves, she fumbled a delicate figurine of a dancer, and nearly dropped it.

"Mistress," her Yoral said. "May I get you anything?"

She set the figurine into its box, and took a deep breath. No; this was worse than a clumsy day. The odd aches she often suffered were worse than ever. Today her body almost didn't belong to her. "No, thank you."

"May I check your blood pressure?"

"Not now, all right? I just need to take a break for a minute."

Unreliable product of the decline of the Race, down to her very core. But you had to keep moving forward; it was that, or give up completely.

She walked out into the sitting room. Her Yoral, bless him, stayed close. He'd been marked to her since she was born, and his steady presence fended off panic.

The front door clicked. Through a gap in the front vestibule curtain, she glimpsed movement. Then Tagaret's Kuarmei pushed the curtain aside.

"Kuarmei, is it over?"

"Yes, Mistress," said Kuarmei, bowing. "If you'll excuse me, I'm just stopping by to pick up something in Lady Tamelera's room." She crossed the sitting room quickly.

Della tried to catch up with her, and just managed to stop the bronze doors before they could quite swing shut. She shoved them open again and followed into the private drawing room. "Can you please tell me how it went?"

The compact Imbati woman paused beside one of the couches. "It was a strange proceeding, Lady," she said. "I believe the Heir Nekantor would claim victory, but likely so would Arbiter Innis of the Fifth Family. Information was exchanged."

"Oh." Della frowned. "That's odd. I can't believe nothing would happen, with all those enemies in the same room. Innis works hard to get what he wants." He'd worked hard to get *her*, all those years ago. Thank heavens, she and Tagaret had stopped him.

"I do believe certain things were learned, Lady," Kuarmei said. "Excuse me."

"Of course."

Kuarmei knocked on Tamelera's door. The door swung slightly open, and she slipped through.

"Where's Tagaret?" Della asked, too late. "Did he go straight to work?"

The door had already closed. Kuarmei didn't come out again. After a minute or so, Della frowned and turned to her Yoral.

"Yoral?"

"Yes, Mistress?"

"Was that—odd?"

His dark brows pinched together, creasing his tattoo. "I believe so, Mistress."

Della planted her hands on her hips and chewed her lip. "Something's going on. Why would Kuarmei need anything in Tamelera's room?"

"I can't imagine, Mistress."

"Hm." What if Kuarmei had done that on purpose? But why—to

draw her out of the sitting room? When she turned around, her thigh bumped the corner of the couch. She snorted disgust at herself, and rubbed it, walking out to the sitting room again. The Household was still working on party preparations: Serjer and Premel were adjusting the placement of food tables along the wall of the dining room. No Tagaret.

Della pursed her lips. There was one place he might be. "Yoral, stay here for a minute, please." She crossed to Tagaret's office door, and opened it.

Tagaret lay motionless in his formal green suit in the middle of his office floor, between the desk and the couch. His long arms and legs were splayed out, and he stared into the ceiling arches without blinking. For an instant, her blood turned to ice—but then Tagaret startled and tried to scramble to his feet.

"Heile have mercy, Tagaret!" she cried. "Are you going to scare me like that? I thought we'd be rushing you to the Medical Center!"

Tagaret lost whatever momentum he'd had, and sank back to a sitting position, hiding behind folded knees and elbows. "I'm sorry."

Della clasped her shaking fingers together. "What in Varin's name is going on? Did Lady Selemei cancel your work for today? Why didn't you want me to know you were at home?"

"I didn't know how—Love, I didn't want to worry you."

"So instead you scared me to death?"

Tagaret sighed. "Oh, Della. I'm sorry." But he didn't say he was all right.

"What's going on?"

Tagaret took a breath as if to speak, then shook his head helplessly.

Della gathered up her skirts and sat down awkwardly across from him. "Is it me? It is, isn't it. Did Innis bring his partner with him? How old is she, eighteen? Is she pregnant already?"

Tagaret winced, but then he looked her in the face. "Della, I love you. Nothing that happened is about you, darling, not at all. I love you so much. It's just—I don't want to hurt you."

"I don't want to hurt you, either." But she had, gods knew she had. Failed him, and hurt him, and herself, so many times. She hardly knew how speak about it anymore, but she had to try. "I know I haven't managed to be—" *A mother* . . . the word so dripped with shame that she couldn't even say it. The last time they'd been intimate had been more than two months ago, and she'd wanted it, and hated it—herself—both, really—and ended up in tears. She took a deep breath, and a second, before she managed, "—what you expect me to be."

"I don't expect you to be anything," Tagaret insisted, shaking his head. "Didn't we decide long ago we weren't going to play their games?"

"We aren't, but the decline isn't a game."

"It *is.* Just a much larger and more implacable one." Tagaret shifted to sit beside her, and removed his gloves. When he touched her hand, the form of her objections dissolved on her tongue. His touch made her skin tingle again, just when she'd almost convinced herself that yesterday's feeling had been her imagination. He twined his long fingers in hers.

Her whole body came alive at his touch. Della caught a breath, and held his hand tighter. "What's wrong, then?"

He sighed, as if out of a well as deep as the city. "Well—everything."

There was a lot. "The attacks? The Privilege competition? Adon's birthday? Or do you mean the inoculant objectors?" She gulped. "Do you think all this is going to threaten our Selimna project?"

Tagaret looked at her, stricken, for several seconds. Then he dropped his head. "I'm just so *tired,*" he whispered toward the floor. "So tired, Della. All the measures we've taken to keep Nek out of this house. All the efforts to keep him away from Adon. And, meanwhile, I have to work between him and Selemei every day—it's exhausting. Playing his ally while constantly running to keep us ahead of him. Trying to keep him calm so he won't lash out. Creating distractions so I can have decent conversations with allies from the Second and Ninth Families. The secrecy. The vigilance. The plans that never come to anything. They wear me down. All these years, and we've never even set foot in Selimna."

These were echoes of the fears that played in her head at night. She stroked the back of his hand; it felt as musical as shiazin strings. "Sweet love of my heart. If you think back to how bad the decline was right after Herin took the throne, you can see how far we've come. And with Selimna, well, we're almost there."

"You don't understand. Everything depends on Nekantor, and we can't—we *can't* depend on him. We can't trust him."

He was right, of course.

"I—I don't know what to say," she said. "Except that nothing's changed. We've never been able to trust him."

"Nothing's changed, that's exactly it," said Tagaret. "This is his world, Della. The more I understand it, the more I see it's just like him. Everything in the 'right' box gets left alone, and everything outside it gets destroyed. No one is safe from exploitation. I talk to Selemei about our inoculation numbers, and I feel like we're making progress. But immunity to Kinders fever doesn't magically confer comfort interacting with Lowers. The Pelismara Society is still afraid to look outside itself. Our goal was to help *everyone*. How many people are we really helping?"

"I don't know," Della said. "But even if you only helped one person, wouldn't that make a difference?"

"There are only two ways to keep Nek's trust. First, I have to make sure he sees me 'report' to him. Second, I have to be careful what gets discussed in the assistants' office so nothing can reach him independently through the Eminence. Every time I lie to him, it feels like he's changing *me*. I used to think he was like my father, and he is, but it's worse than that. He's like gravity. And he's not even Eminence yet." He pulled away from her and dropped his face into his hands.

Della took his shoulder. "You're still yourself, Tagaret. You still believe that the Grobal Trust meant for us to care for everyone. We're still planning. He still doesn't know."

"But what if I'm torturing myself for no reason? What if I'm waiting for something that will never happen? What's our grand plan, anyway? Lady Selemei's paper contract?"

"We have to start somewhere."

"Who says Selimnar Melumalai will have any interest in talking to us?"

"We'll find an excuse. You can bring the card Lorman gave us and ask them to duplicate it, or something."

"In the end, we're nothing but weak-blooded, meddling nobles who think they run the place."

Weak-blooded. To her very core.

No. Their success depended on not giving in to despair. Defiantly, Della lifted Tagaret's hand and pressed it to her lips. She inhaled in shock at the incredible scent of it, which sent a hot blush racing all the way to her toes.

"Mm—blessing of Eyn, Tagaret, kiss me quick, before this feeling goes away."

"All right, but—"

She covered his mouth with hers. Gods, why did he taste so sweet? By some miracle it was exactly as it had been when their love was still forbidden, unsoured by duty, pain, blood. *Great heavens!* She couldn't let him go long enough to cry for joy, just kissed him, again, again, deeper, buried her fingers in his hair, filled herself with the scent and taste of love for which she had been starving.

The ancient stories said that Eyn the Wanderer journeyed through the dark, praying that her lover Sirin would not forget her. Della's own dark journeys, all these fruitless years, had felt as long. But Tagaret had never forgotten her—he hadn't. He hadn't! He met her with desire both solemn and fierce. His embrace, his lips, his tongue, his hands on her body, they were nothing short of holy. Their touch changed her into something beautiful.

She couldn't have explained how she got her clothes off, or he his, but they managed it. He guided her down to the carpet and kissed down her neck and chest. When she tried to pull him over her, though, she couldn't breathe. She flipped onto her side, pushed him onto his back, and tried again. Yes, like this! Now he was the foundation of her world, and they were one. She gasped in joy, gasped again at each rising wave until bliss lit her like a star.

She fell forward into his arms.

"Oh, Della." Tagaret took a deep breath, and her head rose and fell. In this moment, her body felt perfect in the way it shaped over his. She could still feel where her nipples pressed against his skin, and where they were joined. She nuzzled the fine hairs on his chest, mixed with the copper strands of her hair. He stroked her head and sighed. "Mmmm, Della."

"I love you."

"Sirin and Eyn, yes," he agreed. "I love you so much." He rummaged one-handed in the pile of his clothes, and came up with a handkerchief.

Della took it, shaking her head incredulously as they separated. "Oh, dear gods, what are we doing in your office?" The desk and couch loomed.

She gathered up her clothes, some of which had landed draped over the arm of the couch, and put them on as best she could. Tagaret finished dressing before she did, moved behind her and worked on the back fastenings of her gown. She couldn't help leaning into him, rubbing against his legs. It wasn't gone. *The feeling wasn't gone.*

"Della . . . uh, mm . . . darling . . . ?"

She wanted him all over again. It wasn't remotely sensible. They had guests coming. She laughed out loud at herself. "I know. We should probably get changed for the party."

Tagaret nodded, and offered her his hand. Together, they processed with great ceremony out of the office, across the sitting room, and through the double doors into the back.

At that moment, Tamelera emerged from her own room, strikingly dressed for the party in a silk dress hand-painted with a tree on it: converging lines of brown that twined downward from clouds of green. Her braids were wound upward, decorated with bright green enamel pins like closed eyes. She looked ten years younger in that style—even more so because her hand rested over her Aloran's, as if she were a young lady, and he her nurse-escort. Imbati Aloran was also wearing something new—a suit that was very dark green instead of black.

Della blushed. She and Tagaret were scandalously rumpled in comparison.

Tamelera smiled knowingly. "Take your time," she said. "I'll greet Vant and the musicians and the tailor's family when they arrive, and make sure they're comfortable. Adon should be home from school shortly."

"Of course, Mother," Tagaret said.

Della nodded. "We wouldn't miss it."

Even after she'd helped Tagaret get properly dressed, he looked wounded. Something bad had happened at the Academy this morning, and telling him it was all over didn't seem to help. Della squeezed his hand as they left their rooms, but their gloves came between them.

They couldn't go straight through to the party, either, because Pyaras was blocking the way, holding the double doors shut. He was dressed in red and wearing perfume, but even so, she could smell medicine on his head.

"Pyaras? What are you doing?"

Pyaras flushed. "Lady Tamelera is impervious to Arbiter Lorman's complaints, so he decided to pick on me."

"And so you *hid?*" Della demanded. "Mercy, are you four?"

He winced. "I don't need you attacking me, too. I even scented up, and he still says I look like an Arissen."

Tagaret snorted. "Oh, crown of Mai, *that* again? I'm sorry. You know we support you in your friendship with Veriga, don't you?"

Pyaras flashed a split-second smile that quickly fell away. "Yeah."

Della managed not to roll her eyes. "Of course we do. Keep in mind, Pyaras, you can survive *assassins*; you should be able to survive the Arbiter. If he does it again, tell him there's nothing quite as noble as nearly getting killed for mysterious political reasons. Are you going to let us go to the party?"

Now Pyaras' face brightened. "You're never going to believe what Lady Tamelera did. This is so much better than all the stupid politicians last year. You should have seen Adon's face when he realized." He pushed open the doors.

She knew what Tamelera had done. She smiled as they followed Pyaras into the sitting room, which was hardly recognizable. Vant and the Selimnar musicians were playing in the front corner near Tagaret's office door. Delicious-smelling food was arrayed on the tables on the wall near the dining room. Serjer and Premel had also pushed the chairs and sofas back against the walls. A folding screen of geometric brocade hid the corner directly to her right, while along the wall of Tagaret's office stood an array of open garment cases bursting with colors. A gray-coated Kartunnen tailor and her two children were picking things out of the garment cases and handing them to the guests.

As they walked out, Tamelera's voice said, "Oh, come now, Arbiter. This is a curated fashion show. This young employee is only doing her job."

Della looked over. Arbiter Lorman was standing across from Tamelera in the front corner near Lady Selemei and her grown daughters, twisting his mustache. He'd obviously tried and failed to suppress the general mood of excitement. The open space at the center of the room was full of children in fabulous outfits, dancing to the music. Adon flourished a gold-edged cape of black velvet, to the obvious delight of Lady Selemei's four-year-old granddaughter, who was twirling and clapping at once. Adon's friend, Nayal of the Second Family, was marching alongside Adon's older cousins Xeref and Cahemsin, all three of them wearing bright bicolor jackets. Another of Adon's friends, Igan of the Ninth Family, called out,

"Adon—hey, Adon. Let me try the cape next."

"Get your own."

The tailor's son raced to provide Igan with his desired cape, while the tailor's daughter carried an armful of silk scarves around the edge of the room to tempt the adults sitting on the couches.

Lorman left Tamelera and walked toward them. Della quickly bent, took a scarf from the tailor's daughter, and wrapped it dramatically around her face. It didn't entirely block the smell, but it helped.

"Hello, Arbiter," said Tagaret.

"So, so, Tagaret," said Arbiter Lorman loudly, obviously meaning everyone in the room to hear. "I'm so glad you're hosting us here on this wonderful occasion."

"You're so kind."

"Well, so, yes, I'm honored to find myself in your home alongside members of the Second Family, and the Ninth Family, great allies in our political projects." He gestured toward Tagaret's friends, Menni of the Second Family and Gowan of the Ninth Family; they nodded back politely, though they kept their true smiles for the children. "So, so, may I say I only wish that the great Garr could be here at this moment, to see his third son reaching the age of thirteen. And, so, as someone who worked with Garr for years in Selimna, I believe I understand his spirit of Grobal tradition; and, because the last Family Arbiter, Erex, shamefully abandoned the Race and Fell to become a Kartunnen, he chose me to guide the First Family—"

Della could have screamed. What was Lorman thinking? Erex's son was right here among the children . . . She managed to push through the guests to poor Cahemsin without letting Lorman see her smile drop. She bent to the frozen boy's ear.

"I'm so sorry," she whispered. "Please, ignore his terrible manners. We're so happy you're here . . ."

Cahemsin didn't move, so she couldn't tell whether he was at all consoled. Gnash Lorman—they'd cut down the guest list this year, because a thirteenth birthday wasn't the kind of political occasion that a twelfth birthday was. Why couldn't they have left him out?

"I feel it's my solemn duty to carry on the spirit of the great Garr in saying that I'm as proud of your family as if it were my own. So, Adon, you are our bright light and our future. Congratulations. How do you feel?"

Adon was glaring at Lorman. Della wouldn't have blamed him if he'd responded rudely, but Tamelera had raised him too well. "Thank you, Arbiter Lorman. I definitely feel glad to be alive today. I also feel . . . that I'd like to introduce everyone to Kartunnen Jaia." Adon looked over at the folding screen, beckoning. The tailor didn't appear for several seconds, but then finally she came out, arranging her billowy gray coat. "Jaia's my favorite artist working in fashion right now, and she's provided all of the clothing today. Thank you so much for coming, Jaia."

"Sorry that took me so long," Jaia said, curtsying to the guests. "I was just finishing up something. Thank you, Grobal Adon, sir, and Lady Tamelera, for inviting me."

At that moment, they discovered what she'd been finishing: out from behind the screen stepped Lady Selemei's nineteen-year-old daughter, Lady Pelli. Pelli wore a long-sleeved gown of sapphire blue with a gorgeous embroidered neckline that traced curves against her albino-white skin. Her curly orange hair looked like a crown. Menni and Gowan and their partners burst into spontaneous applause.

How could that gown possibly fit Pelli so well? That should have been impossible for something pulled out of a case. Blessing of Heile, was Jaia modifying garments on the spot?

Della glanced up at Tagaret. "Your mother is cleverer than I gave her credit for. I have to see if Jaia brought anything for me."

Tagaret smiled. "You should, absolutely."

Fortunately, Adon's attention to Jaia had effectively ended Lorman's speech, and Cahemsin had resumed exchanging garments with the other children. Della waded through them to the edge of the privacy screen, and discovered that Lady Selemei had come to study the open cases, too.

"You can go first, Lady," Della said, pulling the scarf down from her face now that Lorman was no longer near.

"Don't be silly," said Selemei. "We're not in the cabinet office; of course you should go first. Jaia, do you have any gowns to fit my cousin Della, here?"

Della blushed, instantly conscious of their attention on her body, its vague discomforts, its bony points and soft curves in all the wrong places.

The tailor looked her up and down. "I believe so, Lady. Come in."

It didn't sound like any of the gowns had been *intended* for her. Nervously, Della entered and considered the beautiful pale blue and gold gown the Kartunnen presented to her. She took a deep breath. *This is a party. Don't expect it to fit; it doesn't matter if it fits. Just try it.*

Her throat felt tight.

It wasn't long before she discovered the secret, though. The gown had hidden laces underneath the arms on both sides of the bodice. When Jaia's deft fingers finished the adjustments, she would have sworn it had been sewn just for her. The implications were stunning—if she had a weird day, or a puffy day, Yoral could still make it fit, easily. Comfortably.

"May I buy this from you?" Della whispered.

"The Lady Tamelera has purchased everything here," Jaia replied. "You are welcome to keep it."

"And if I want another one?"

"I do have one more here, but you may also contact me any time, Lady." She handed her a card, which Della immediately passed to her Yoral.

Then she steeled herself and stepped out, to a flurry of applause. While she'd been changing, Pyaras had put on an adult-sized bicolor jacket, and Tagaret a cape of emerald velvet. Della walked over to Pelli and embraced her; she smelled wonderful, her crown of hair scented with kalla oil.

"Thank you for coming, Pelli. You look so lovely."

"Thank you for inviting me," said Pelli. "I wouldn't have missed it. Mother is very fond of your family."

Abruptly, the music stopped. The triscili played a high warning note that pierced the laughter and conversations.

Della backed up quickly, reached out and stopped the motion of the nearest children. Jaia's son frowned in confusion.

"Kartunnen, get behind your changing screen, quick," Della said. She shooed him as fast as she could; Lady Selemei had Jaia and was hurrying her to cover. The musicians took an instrument in each hand and joined them, though the space behind the screen became crowded. Serjer and Premel swept through the room gathering stray garments with astonishing speed. The garment cases were closed and locked in less than a minute.

"What's happening?" Jaia's son whispered.

"Hush, doll," said Jaia. "The Eminence is here. You don't want him to see you."

Not exactly, but close enough. Della tugged her gloves tight, and adjusted her position to block the gap at the edge of the screen just as Jaia's daughter escaped behind it.

Serjer scanned the room, then returned to the vestibule.

A second later, the Eminence Herin walked in. His golden looks seized every eye. He held his head high; the white and gold drape of office shone around his shoulders. His velvet suit was a conservative amber color, and matched his perfectly curled, golden-brown hair. He even *smelled* good. If anything, he'd only become more handsome over the years. She'd always found him a decent man; he prioritized his own Family, the Third, but worked hard to keep the rest of the Families' demands in balance.

The Heir, the greater danger, joined him quietly. It was some time since Nekantor had looked his age, two years younger than Tagaret. The gray hair at his temples, and the tension lines around his eyes, could easily have convinced a stranger that he was forty instead of twenty-nine. He was clothed impeccably in pale brown silk, down to the tiniest detail. Never fancy, always careful never to usurp Herin's place at the center of attention. But while the others watched the Eminence, his hungry brown eyes consumed them.

Della refused to fall into the Eminence's thrall, and watched Nekantor's eyes. With absolutely everything in the room either put away or moved, there was a real chance he'd become angry. What would he notice first? What might he attack?

The Kartunnen were safe out of sight behind her, so long as no one disturbed the screen; all the servants had vanished into the Maze. Menni and Gowan had both stood up; they knew Nekantor well enough to try to draw his attention off people who could less easily handle it. Della stood taller. *See me, partner-brother, if you'd like. I know all your insults.*

Lady Tamelera approached the Eminence Herin with a graceful curtsy that swayed through the painting on her dress. "Welcome to our home, your Eminence."

"Lady Tamelera." The Eminence Herin nodded magnanimously. "Thank you for receiving me among your guests. I see the Second and Ninth Families represented. Hello, Menni. How are you enjoying your work on the Second Family Council?"

"Very well, your Eminence," Menni replied in his resonant voice.

"And Gowan, already working so closely with your father Amyel on cabinet business." Herin smiled, and Gowan bowed; his long hair swayed. "Did I hear correctly that he received an inoculant this year? Is that a requirement these days in alliances with the First Family?"

Della met Tagaret's glance. Was Herin trying to provoke Gowan? He was unlikely to succeed; Gowan was far too smooth.

"You heard correctly, your Eminence," said Gowan, smiling. "I received one as well—but there are no requirements. My father tested negative for allergies and wished to feel confident in his interactions with Lowers; that's all. I do believe I heard a rumor that your beautiful partner, Lady Falya, had expressed interest in getting tested."

Herin's answering smile was even more brilliant. "You're absolutely right. I'll be getting tested, too, inoculated if possible—we must make sure to avoid Heir Selections, after all."

"Your Eminence," said Lady Tamelera, curtsying. "You do us a great honor with your consideration."

For an instant, Herin preened at the compliment, and Della had to hold back a chuckle. Then the Eminence held up one finger. "I don't wish to disappoint my objector supporters too much, however. That is why I've made a personal gesture to them as well." Herin made a flourishing gesture with his hand, and smiled as the crowd's eyes followed the motion. "Drenas, ho!"

The vestibule curtain shrieked open. Inside stood a huge man in a bright orange Eminence's Cohort uniform. Della, startled, felt an instant's sympathy for Serjer, who must have had to cope with this man invading his entry hall. A stifled sound of shock came from the Kartunnen children hidden behind her.

"Imbati make fine bodyguards," Herin said. "However, there can be no finer specimen than Drenas, here. We must keep safe every way we can." He looked around. "Where's young Adon of the First Family?"

Adon had been behind his mother; he stepped forward with admirable poise, still wearing his gold-edged cape. "I'm here, sir."

The Eminence gave a beaming smile. "Congratulations on your birthday, young man." He pulled a folded paper from an inside pocket of his coat—that special perquisite of boys, the birthday letter from the Eminence—and placed it in Adon's hands.

"Thank you, your Eminence."

"You're looking quite well. Bit of a luckier thing than you expected, getting to thirteen, wasn't it?"

Della almost snorted. What a thing to say! There was a second's affronted silence, followed by a spattering of polite laughter.

Adon answered seriously. "Yes, sir, it was."

Pyaras pushed forward out of the crowd. "Surely that's not disappointment I hear in your tone, your Eminence?" he asked, with an assumed lightness that wasn't very convincing. "We've just been through a bit of drama with the Fifth Family today. Surely *you* wouldn't have anything at stake in the safety of the First Family?"

Wow, he dared! Of course he did; he was Pyaras. Della held her breath, but fortunately, the Eminence only laughed out loud.

"Getting your hair burned off would make anyone testy, Pyaras of the First Family. You should know that I'm taking these attacks very seriously. Arissen Drenas isn't the only bodyguard who has recently come on duty. No; I've decided to make full use of our expanded Eminence's Cohort, in order to protect all of the Race, here, and in the northern neighborhoods."

Della raised her eyebrows. Wouldn't that put the Cohort in conflict with the police?

Herin began to walk in a circle, meeting the eyes of the guests. "Some of you may have noticed the increased number of guards in the Residence, on the grounds and at the Grobal School. It's my goal to make sure every person of quality within these grounds will be able to feel safe, including—" He gestured as he arrived back at his initial position. "—young Adon, here."

Nekantor clapped, so Della quickly joined in, as did everyone else standing. It was important to cover any uncertainty among other party guests.

The Eminence flourished his hand, and nodded his head. "Thank you for your hospitality, Lady Tamelera. I am due shortly at an important meeting."

Mother curtsied. "We are grateful for the honor Your Eminence has bestowed upon us."

The Eminence Herin gave one last brilliant smile, and left. Fortunately, his huge Arissen bodyguard went with him.

Less fortunately, the Heir stayed behind.

"Ahh, Adon," Nekantor said. "I'm so sorry about Herin's inappropriate comment." His gaze flickered around the room, and he gave a cough. "I see you've changed the arrangement of the sitting room."

"It's what I wanted for my birthday party," Adon answered.

"I see." Nekantor touched the three buttons on his vest with his fingers, one after the other. "I hope you're enjoying it."

"Yes, I am, thank you."

"Sorry, of course you are. I should have said this to you when I saw you earlier, but we were busy: congratulations on your birthday."

Della shifted uncomfortably. Hearing apologies out of Nekantor's mouth made her stomach squirm; this had to be some kind of performance.

"Thank you," said Adon, and bowed. "I'd like to thank your Dexelin for rescuing me yesterday."

"Oh, really? Considerate boy." Nekantor gave a strained smile. "We'll be protecting you better, after this. Why choose between Arissen and Imbati when you could have both?" He gritted his teeth and lashed a look at Tamelera. "You shouldn't have moved the furniture. And you didn't invite Caredes of the Eighth Family; he was expecting it."

"It's my home, and I'll do as I like," Lady Tamelera said. "This isn't a political birthday. It's only for an afternoon."

"Well, enjoy your party, then."

Would he leave? Without ruining anything? Della held her breath.

Nekantor began to turn away, but then turned back again, opening and closing his fists. "Actually, before I go . . ." He smirked at Pyaras, who stiffened. "Cousin, I'm glad you cut your hair for your new job as Executor of the Pelismara Division. The Arissen there will like your new style. I imagine that will keep you busy more appropriately now that Lake Club has been shut down and all its employees arrested."

"What?" Pyaras cried. "Arrested!"

"Aww." Nekantor's smirk grew wider. "Are you sure you shouldn't thank me, Cousin? I gave you a job perfectly suited to your temperament."

"Gnash you!"

Della winced. Pyaras was so easily baited.

Nekantor waved a hand. "Poor manners won't matter in your new job—one of its many advantages. Oh, and Tagaret, I have to apologize for this morning."

Tagaret jerked as if he'd been struck.

Oh, no.

This was why she'd found him on the floor. When he spoke of despair, *he'd been trying to tell her something.* Whatever Nekantor had done, it was so terrible that Tagaret hadn't even been able to put it into words.

But of course, Nekantor could.

"I should have told you that I'd appointed Unger of the Fifth Family as Alixi of Selimna."

For a second, all she could do was blink.

No, no, no, no, *no, no, no, no, no*—!

The horror tried to accelerate into a scream, but she would not permit it. She would *not* let thirteen years of work be destroyed. She would *not* let Tagaret lie devastated where she'd found him. She held her breath, and compressed the scream into a single burning demand:

Do something.

"I don't accept that," she snapped.

Nekantor's gaze whipped to hers. He showed his teeth. "Oh, don't you, my darling sister? And why not?"

She would not flinch, and risk revealing those who hid behind her. She had his attention; now she had to remember what Tagaret had taught her.

Never try to stop Nekantor. Try to turn him. Change the game.

"I know you, Brother," she said, glancing down at her gloves and assuming as calm and reasonable a tone as she could manage. "I don't accept that you'd cave in to Innis' threats, or concede Selimna to the Fifth Family without a larger plan to reclaim it. I mean, you're the Heir. Nekantor of the First Family! Cowardice is below you."

Nekantor's gaze sharpened. "Ha! It is, indeed."

"You're playing games again. You've planned to come here, to test how we respond to disappointment, and then tell us you're sending Tagaret as your agent to keep the Fifth Family from consolidating its hold over the city." She forced a smile.

Nekantor stared at her silently. Della breathed fast between smiling lips, struggling against the scream, until she felt dizzy and her ears started to tingle. At last, a slow answering smile slid across Nekantor's lips.

"How clever you are to find me out, Della. I knew there must have been *some* reason my brother brought you into the family."

I know your insults. She gave a curtsy. "Thank you."

"Unger left for Selimna this afternoon. I need you ready to leave tomorrow morning."

A hot flush rushed to her cheeks. "We can do that, can't we, Tagaret."

"This really isn't the appropriate time to discuss plans," said Nekantor. "Tagaret, when this party is over, you'll report to me immediately."

Della dared a glance over at Tagaret. He was standing straight again. It made her heart leap.

"Of course, Brother," Tagaret said.

"And—" Nekantor wagged one finger. "Make Mother put the furniture back where it belongs. Enjoy your birthday, Adon." He turned on one heel and stalked out.

Della swayed on her feet, but Tagaret rushed up behind her, his warm arms holding her, supporting her.

Lady Tamelera smoothed her skirts and walked to the center of the room. "Oh, my dear friends, I'm terribly sorry about that. The good news is, now that the unfortunate but necessary portion of the party is over, we have more refreshments for you. Desserts are in the dining room!"

Lady Selemei responded with a light laugh—the reassuring sound that was her signature, even in the face of danger. "We would be delighted to try them."

The party broke into small groups, parents telling their children that everything was all right, and that this Household was known for unsurpassed food and drink, so why shouldn't we all have some?

Della turned into Tagaret's arms. He bent down to her ear; buoyed by his nearness, she kissed his jawline.

"Della, my beautiful, amazing Della, Mai was standing by you just now," he whispered. "That was brilliant! He came here to hurt us, and *you made him change his plan.*"

Della leaned her head against Tagaret's collarbone. What *was* Nekantor's plan? Had she really changed it? Or had she only managed to change their role in it?

Right now, it didn't matter. She closed her hands on Tagaret's lapels, and stood on her toes.

"Oh, my love, we're finally going!"

CHAPTER SEVEN

A Round of Drinks

Tomorrow, she'd lose the sun.

Melín liked duty rotation about as much as a kick in the head. A hot shower could rinse off the sweat of her on-duty hours, but not the feeling of being torn away. It was starting early this time—the headache, the twitchy feeing in her thigh muscles. *Gnash it.* She turned the water up hotter, though it made the tips of her ears burn.

You're a professional. You know the rotations extend a soldier's career. You know they lower the injury rate, and the error rate. The Division can keep the fields safe without you for thirteen weeks.

She pummeled her thighs with her fists under the water.

Listen, gnash you. Descent's not till tomorrow night. Can't have you twitchy now or I won't sleep.

"Plis' bones," she swore, and slammed her hand against the handle. The water stopped.

She wrapped herself in her robe and shoved one hand into her pocket. Found her bracelets first, so she pushed her hand through, distributed them to both wrists, then scooped up her ear rings. She put them in while walking back to her cot: one steel ring in each lobe, and the three memorial rings along the top edge of her right ear. Those had to go in delicately—stupid disruption burns. The pain made her wince, but she wasn't in the mood for Lowers right now; she could see a Kartunnen medic tomorrow.

After nightfall, the glass roof of the barracks dimly reflected her face, and also the heads of a mob in off-duty casual that had gathered between the cots. She was forced to sidestep along the lockers to her own. Somewhere in the crowd, someone was telling a story. She caught the gist while she pulled on a rust-red skirt and white shirt.

Wysps! Flames! Action!

She snorted. Someone was either lying or it wasn't their story. Nothing so exciting had happened in the last rotation. Bracelets jingling, she pulled her blade from its sheath to double-check that it was clean, returned it to the scabbard, and buckled it across her back. Then she studied the crowd again.

Oo, look—Drefne was here.

She pushed through the mob to his elbow, and saw the storyteller.

A veteran? This woman had brown wrinkled-leather skin and gray hair in a braid long enough to drape across her lap. She wore a uniform style sixteen years old, complete with the blade that meant Division.

Huh. Maybe it *was* her story.

"Isseni," Melín whispered. "Dref."

Drefne glanced down, grinned, and wrapped his lean arm around her. She ran her fingers lightly over the muscles of his stomach.

"So we had three soldiers down at that point," the veteran said. "And then—have you ever seen agitation level six?"

"No," voices answered.

"There is no agitation level six," said Drefne.

Ah, trick question. Melín called out, "There *was* an agitation level six but we're ordered to shoot no later than level five, because by then the wysps are already attacking." She touched the platinum ring nearest her head.

"Specialist reporting to storytime, I see," the veteran said. "Well, she's right. You don't want to see level six. Because at level six they get *smart.*" She gave an ugly smile. "They identify you and *hunt you down.*"

A couple of people called out, "Oooo." Drefne gave that little adorable chuckle of his.

Melín couldn't laugh. Her fingers found the ring again. Was the veteran exaggerating? If she was right, it would explain some of the casualties she'd seen—but why would anyone remove that kind of lifesaving information from Specialist training?

"Specialist," said the veteran, with understanding in her keen eyes. "Maybe we should talk?"

"I'd rather drink, actually," Melín said. "Anybody want to join us?" She tugged on Drefne's forearm. "Dref, you free tonight? Drinks, bed after?"

"Ah, Melín." Drefne looked rueful. "Already scheduled for tonight, sorry. Tomorrow?"

She raised her eyebrows at him. "Descent night? Are you sunblasted?"

He laughed and planted a kiss on her forehead. "Point. Talk to you after we get settled downlevel."

The mob broke up. Melín led the veteran and a few others out the door into the alleyway; at the corner of the barracks they turned to the right. Tomorrow they'd turn left to go to the Descent, but the food block was down this way. It was better than the Division's mess, if you didn't mind paying.

"I'm Treminindi," the veteran said, hurrying ahead of the others. "Call me Tremi. Can we hit Blades?"

Melín looked at her. "Why, you looking for a bed partner?"

Tremi frowned. "At Blades?"

"Best place for it."

"Ugh," the older woman said. "It wasn't like that the last time I went."

"Maybe it's been a while?" Melín smiled. "But you know what? I don't mind the attention. You'll be fine. And Blades does have the best drinks."

The food block was in a massive stone curtain that intruded far into the first level. Three restaurant-sized spaces had been scooped out of its base. The eateries farther back changed every so often, but Blades occupied the triangular point, and had been here so long the columns that formed its sides had been carved into eight-foot versions of the Division's ceremonial and practical symbol. Black leather couches filled with mates blocked the space between them, and at least two people sat on top with legs draping out, their backs against the stone blades. Talk, and recorded drumming, poured out into the air.

Melín took point, to draw attention off Tremi. It worked: she'd barely made it four steps inside before the first come-on, from a stocky sunmarked woman with pale patterns like a map across her shoulders.

"Long day, seni?" the woman asked. "Care to make it longer? Bet you'd be good at bedtime."

Melín chuckled. Not the best line ever, but the patterns on her skin were sexy, and the energy in the woman's pose said she could be fun. "Busy right now, but if you can find me at the Descent . . ."

"Pff. Chances of that?"

"I don't know. It's the best I can do."

The woman pressed her lips and nodded. She lifted her health bracelet between them. "Tap if you're serious, and I'll look out for you."

"Sure." Melín pushed most of her bracelets up out of the way and touched her health bracelet to the other, and two lights flashed: a match. She smiled. You'd never catch *her* saying medics were a waste. A pain, maybe, but never a waste. "See you then, I hope."

She pushed into the crowd. Gnash it, what if they bounced all the way out again without a single place to sit? By the back wall, that might be a gap . . . It turned out to be Chezzy, clearing dishes off a steel table onto the tray of her skimchair.

Melín moved around to her side. "Chezzy, hey, this table taken yet?"

"Plis in a mist—Melín!"

"That's me."

"Where've you been, anyway, seni? Go ahead, sit down. Why haven't we seen you?"

"I don't know, got enough attention most nights, I guess."

Chezzy pulled a sly smile. "Yep, the place is full of hungry cats these days. How you been?"

She shrugged. "Headed downlevel tomorrow and not happy about it."

"Oo, that's me every day after the accident. Give me sunblast every time."

"Well, Mai's truth. I'd carry you with me if I could."

"Don't leave without seeing Durkinar, all right? He'll be thrilled."

"Gotta see him anyway or I won't be drinking." But she felt her cheeks flush.

Chezzy skimmed off toward the kitchen doors, hollering so drinkers had a chance to hop before her foot-wedge cleared them. When Tremi finally arrived, she came alone. Surprising that none of the others had stuck with them, but it was simple, then, to settle the veteran on the bench against the stone wall, get her order, and head for the bar.

The bar was a multilevel brass circle under a rack of glassware that hung from the ceiling. This section was at her elbow level; when Melín leaned on its edge, the twitches in her thighs were joined by a more pleasant flutter in her stomach. She called out, "Durkinar, hey, Melín here, can I get some drinks?"

"Melín!" Durkinar turned toward her voice instantly, though he never stopped working. She could have watched him all day. He'd run thumb and finger along the curve of a glass stopper, pluck it up and unstopper it with his three-fingered hand, run it under his nose, then find the glass and pour, replace it and grab the next one. Disruption burns had ruined his eyes, but he knew just where the bar stepped down, and the position of every bottle and glass down to the length of a fingernail. He'd told her once the feel-check and the sniff-check were just like when he was a weapons officer triple-checking a rack full of bolt rifles. He placed two drinks on the lower section of the bar for Chezzy to deliver, pulled two new glasses, and started again. "So, seni, tell me why you haven't come to see me."

"You know me," she said. "Busting sparks as usual."

"Don't be sending us any new workers, now."

Guilt punched her in the stomach. *Blast that paper field.* She picked at the engraved menu on the bar surface with her fingernail. "No way, seni, just trying to keep your fridges full. Can I get one Grobal's Tears and one Bush Duel, please?" She kept her tone light, but he apparently heard the difference despite the bar noise. He slid his undamaged hand across the bar until he found her arm, and patted it. She put her hand on top of his without thinking.

"You've stayed away too long, Specialist. I've been pining away." He grinned, pulled his hand back, and plucked up a tall slender bottle of clear liquid. "Watch yourself with this one or it'll knock you on your ass. Grobal's Tears aren't made of water."

"Noted." Durkinar wore a bracelet, too, but for some reason she was too nervous to ask him to tap, though she could have eaten that grin whole and kissed his scars from his face down to his missing fingers. He flirted with everybody, and what if he said no? The mystery was fun in its own way.

A wiry-looking man pushed in on her right. Instead of announcing himself to Durkinar, he looked her up and down with unsteady eyes. Eyes that paused in predictable places.

Yeah, yeah, I know.

"Durkinar, someone's just arrived beside me," she called. "He's already started his night." She dropped a comment over her shoulder. "Where're your manners, seni?"

The man leaned forward on the brass. "Getting friendly with the bartender, isseni? Wouldn't you prefer someone who can actually read the menu?" He wore his health bracelet with the sensor on the inside of his wrist. Great—to tap, you'd have to open yourself to him grabbing you.

Melín snorted. "Near anyone can do that. Durkinar's got the menu in his fingers."

"Oh, you like fingers?"

"You gonna ask me a question, seni? 'Cause right now you're wasting my time."

The man licked his lips. "Want a hop?"

"No, thanks. I got a table to get to."

"Sure you do. I know your name, and I heard you're always looking for a good hop. I got the best weapon there is."

"I said no. Everybody's got weapons, yours aren't—" In the corner of her eye, his hand moved low toward her ass. Melín swiveled on her right foot, stomped his near toe with her left heel, and struck, elbow into his chest. The man toppled into the crowd behind him, though a few mates grasped at his arms to stop him hitting the floor. "I SAID NO," Melín bellowed.

The helpful hands changed instantly. A pair of mates with Cohort Second pins on their jackets hauled the man to his feet as Chezzy came skimming up.

"You're going to leave now," Chezzy said. "But first let's get your identification. Bracelet."

The man struggled. "No."

"What does that word mean again?" Chezzy snapped. "Bracelet!"

More bar patrons were turning toward them. Someone behind one of the Cohort Seconds sneaked a punch and hit the man behind the ear. The other Second forced the man's bracelet hand out.

"Durkinar, there's a snake here name of Ostem, note him down. Don't come drinking at Blades any more, Ostem, you'll leave dry and be lucky not to find your ass in your hand."

The man spat and struggled. "A tribunal—"

"A tribunal's a waste of time," said Durkinar. "Everyone saw you, and I heard every word you said. Now, out." The Seconds and Chezzy between them hauled the man off toward the door. Durkinar set two drinks on the bar. "Sorry about that, Melín. Don't stop coming around just because of that piece of carrion."

"No way." She set her coins down. "Or hey, seni, you're always welcome to come find me."

Had she really said that? Would he take her seriously? She walked determinedly back to Tremi's table, and no one bothered her on the way. She set the glasses down on the shiny metal: Grobal's Tears was Tremi's choice, stiff enough to make her eyes water just carrying it; Bush Duel was a taller glass with a meadow in it, murky red velut under green sprouts growing from a layer of gelatin.

"Sorry, Tremi, that took a while."

"Oh, not a problem." The older woman downed half her drink in one gulp. "I already knew you were as good at driving off amateurs as you are at gauging wysp shots."

Halfway through a mouthful of bittersweet sprouts mixed with heady, fruity alcohol, Melín figured it out. "Plis' bones, you're not saying you sent *that* guy? What was his name?"

"Third Solnis, yeah, sorry about that. I should have known to send Division to the Division."

"Treminindi, you were Division," Melín guessed. "A Specialist."

The veteran smiled, and wrinkles flexed in her cheeks. "Right you are. Now I'm retired, and I'm master assassin of the Paper Shadows."

Melín blinked. "What?"

"I won't say it again. I saw you at storytime earlier—lose a mate to the sparks at level six, did you?"

Melín grunted.

"So did I, more than once. Look, you know you've got a reputation as a pinpoint shot. I sent Solnis to talk to you because I figured you'd be good at my job. Not that there's a lot of this kind of work, but we keep a few contractors for the busy times."

She sounded so blasted *casual* about it. The fingers of the veteran's hand still rested around the half-empty glass of tears, and she draped the other along the back of her seat.

"You don't forget the ones you lose," Melín said, weaving her fingers around her drink so she wouldn't touch the rings in her ear.

"No, you don't," Tremi agreed.

"They stay with you. And when you're not on surface rotation, you know they're losing people out there without you."

Tremi nodded. "Yes. If anything, retiring is worse."

"So how do you figure the leap from saving people to shooting people?"

Tremi thought about that, and tipped back the rest of her glass. "Haven't you ever shot anyone? Even on adjunct rotation?"

"I'm not police, thank Mai the Right."

"Hm. Well, our targets aren't mates, and my thinking is, if I didn't do it, somebody else would."

"Somebody else in the team *you* run."

"Not my point. The thing is, nobles are bloodthirsty." Tremi dipped a finger into her glass, brought it up glistening, and licked it—*Grobal's*

Tears aren't made of water. "They're willing to pay ridiculous sums to have their political rivals killed, but they want to keep their own hands clean. They could get a Venorai or a Melumalai to do the job, but imagine the mess! We, on the other hand, have finesse. If someone's going to live well off their cruelty, no reason it shouldn't be us."

"You're totally fine with being a nobleman's tool."

Tremi gestured around at the bar patrons. "We're all noblemen's tools. I'm a person with unique skills I'd rather not leave behind. I'm not in charge of the demand."

I'm not a nobleman's tool.

"Look," Melín said. "I'm not sure I'm comfortable with this. I—"

"I don't need an answer now," Tremi said. "Think about it, and get back to me. Here's my card, so you know where to find me. Enjoy your Descent."

Melín watched the veteran's back as she disappeared into the crowd, and shoved the card into the pocket of her skirt. Taking a Grobal Executor's orders in the name of feeding the city was not the same as shooting a nobleman's enemies, gnash it! She took another mouthful of her drink, crushing sprouts between her teeth.

"Varin's teeth," she muttered.

I am not *a nobleman's tool.*

CHAPTER EIGHT

How to Disappear

How was it possible for your whole life to fall apart so quickly? Adon stood with his hands clenched, watching catastrophe pile up in the sitting room. Serjer and Premel and Tagaret's Kuarmei moved in and out, bringing bags and boxes, and more bags and more boxes. Nekantor's orders about the furniture had been totally disregarded, because they needed room for all of it. So many boxes, some larger than he'd ever seen. They contained Tagaret and Della's things, and it meant—

It meant they were going to—

He couldn't stand it!

Adon forced his hands open and shook them out, but of course it didn't help.

How could they leave? Selimna was thousands of miles away! Across the *surface!* What if wysps got them? What if cave-cats got them? What if they fell off a cliff?

Mother had said to stay out of the way, but he couldn't do this; he might have only minutes more before they disappeared. He shoved through the double doors into the private drawing room, and walked in through Tagaret's door without knocking.

The room was unrecognizable. The art from the walls was all gone; the bed was stripped, and the wardrobe doors hung open; even the door to the servants' Maze had been propped wide. Tagaret was leaning over an open case on the bed, talking with his Kuarmei about its contents, and Della sat on a brass chair in the corner while her Yoral moved folded gowns from the top of the mattress into a large canvas bag. Two stranger Imbati from the Residence Household were also here, running in and out from the Maze with smaller cases and trays of miscellaneous items.

Holy Sirin help me.

Tagaret looked up. Adon opened his mouth to speak to him, but nothing came out. His brother turned and murmured a few more words to his Kuarmei, then walked over.

"Adon, are you all right?"

"Uh. No."

His brother's hand squeezed his shoulder. "I know this is sudden. I'm sorry."

Adon's head, when he shook it, felt heavy with horrible feelings. "Tagaret, you *have* to stay safe on the surface. You *have* to come back."

"Well, we've hired an excellent driving team," Tagaret said. "It's a non-stop voyage company, and they're prepared for all eventualities. As for coming back—I wish I could tell you when that will happen. But I promise to write to you."

"*Write* to me? Oh, come on!" He jerked away, and stomped out the door into the private drawing room. Couldn't bring himself to go out into the sitting room, though, where all the boxes were . . .

"Hey," Tagaret called after him. "Hey—please, can we talk?"

Adon clenched his fists. Anger made his eyes burn.

"Look, I'm sorry," said Tagaret, behind him.

He clenched his teeth.

"I hate leaving you," Tagaret admitted softly. "It's not fair, even though we've wanted to go to Selimna since before you were born. I get what you're feeling, honestly, I do. The same thing happened to me."

Adon grunted. "It wasn't the same, though."

"No, it wasn't. Mother and Father both moved to Selimna, and I was left alone with Nekantor and the servants for five years."

Wait—alone with Nekantor for *five years?* Disbelief turned him around. He stared at Tagaret. "That sounds like Varin's teeth!"

Tagaret's mouth pulled to one side. He went to the nearest couch and patted the spot beside him. "It wasn't easy. I got through it with music, and by writing letters. I wrote to Mother almost every day."

"What about Father?"

"I wrote to him when I had to."

Adon sank down next to him, trying surreptitiously to memorize what Tagaret's arm felt like, wrapping around his shoulders. "All right, I will. I'll write to you."

"And I promise I'll write back. You might not realize this, but I write letters all the time. I wrote one to my best friend Reyn last night."

"Weren't you busy packing?"

Adon felt him shrug. "It wasn't a long letter. But I couldn't exactly not tell him he'd have to write to me in Selimna after this." Tagaret was quiet a moment. "I'm sorry; I should have told my Kuarmei to leave some writing paper for you."

"I can get some. Mother probably has some."

"I'm sure she does." Tagaret's arm lifted slightly as though he'd considered getting up, but then it squeezed around him again. "Hey, so, I need to get back to the packing. Will you be all right with that?"

"Sure."

"I'm sending Della out to talk to you. Don't go anywhere."

"Wait—"

Tagaret didn't wait.

Adon scowled, but stayed put. Holy Mai, how had Tagaret done that? Trapped him into a conversation that made him clench his teeth just thinking about it? Della was the one who'd brought on this disaster. Tagaret adored her—and of course he would, not just because she was his partner but because she was the most beautiful Lady in all Varin besides Mother, and she was sweet and loving and had impeccable fashion sense.

But, of them all, she was the one who knew best how to disappear. Between one day and the next, sometimes, she'd vanish. Mother said it wasn't his business why, that they were lady's concerns. Aloran said she was in the Medical Center because she was fragile—and also that it wasn't his business. Sometimes she'd be gone for a day. Sometimes she'd be gone for two months.

This time, who knew how long she'd be gone? And she was taking Tagaret with her.

He dropped his eyes to his hands when Della came out. She was wearing traveling clothes: wide-legged flowing trousers, a high-necked white shirt, and a velvet jacket, all of which would have been near-impossible to acquire overnight. She must have been saving them for this moment. The trousers brushed the couch as she sat down, with a velvet-on-velvet sound.

"Sweet Adon," she sighed. "I'm going to miss you so much."

"Why?" he blurted. "Why did you do it?"

She was quiet, maybe surprised. He didn't want to look up at her, only looked high enough to see her emerald velvet knee, her pale hand on top of it, and the tips of her striking copper-red hair.

"You mean, why did I confront Nekantor? To protect Tagaret."

Adon scowled. "How does going off to Selimna protect Tagaret?"

"You know that he's been trying to go to Selimna since before you were born."

Of course I know that. I'm not stupid. "He's been *trying* to get promoted to Alixi."

"No, actually." Della sighed. "It would be easier if he were Alixi, but really he just wanted to go to Selimna. He had his heart set on this being his chance. And then Nekantor denied him, so I had to change Nekantor's mind. Or, at least, turn him aside."

Adon snorted. "I don't see how you can say this is all Tagaret's fault."

"Where did you get that idea? The plan has always belonged to both of us."

He crossed his arms.

"Adon." Della's hand reached out, and her fingertips touched the back of his wrist, just where his hand tucked into his elbow. "Do you really want to know why we want to go?"

Her voice was different, more cautious. He almost looked up.

"Can you keep a secret?" Della whispered. "I mean, truly keep it, as Aloran would?"

Startled, Adon looked up into her green eyes. Twins help him, she really meant it. In anger, he'd walked out onto a cracked cave floor. Could he safely walk off it again?

"Of course I can." It came out a little surly. He took a deep breath, uncrossed his arms, and tried again. "Yes. I'll keep it in my heart."

Della leaned forward until her copper hair brushed his shoulder. "We don't want what Grobal always want," she said quietly. "We've been trying to go to Selimna so we can do something important."

He shook his head. "But this is Pelismara. Everything important happens here. You can do anything you want."

"You know we can't do everything we want, Adon. Everything in Pelismara is under Nekantor's eyes. Why else would we have worked so hard to keep them off you?"

He knew what Nekantor's eyes felt like. "What do you want to do?"

"We want to teach people to treat each other properly, with love, *no matter who they are.*"

"What, like Lowers?"

"Listen. Imagine if we didn't have to hide musicians in corners. Imagine . . . a place where Aloran could be loved the way he deserves."

"Oh . . ." A warm flush spread from Adon's cheeks down his neck. Mercy, could she really see his heart so easily? "Oh."

"Tagaret and I both wish it could be here, with you—but it just can't."

"I understand." The most shocking thing was, he actually did. "I'm going to write to you."

"I love you, Adon." She put her arms around him briefly, then stood and walked away.

Heart of Bes. Imagine—a place where he could make friends with Talabel if he wanted to. A place where no one scoffed if he sat for hours watching Kartunnen Jaia, or Ober, working with silk, needles, sewing machines. A place where he wouldn't be chastised if he ever dared to mention Aloran outside the house.

The only problem was, they needed Mai the Right's own miracle, because then Tagaret and Della wouldn't have to disappear.

A surface-worthy floater looked like a big glass-and-steel bubble with a flat bottom. It hovered mysteriously above the stone surface of the road. It couldn't fit inside the Conveyor's Hall, which meant more work for the Household who were loading Tagaret and Della's luggage into it.

Adon stood by Mother and her Aloran watching the process, trying to ignore how many wysps were drifting about. The tiny sparks cast their light unevenly across the floater, the luggage, the Arissen guards, and the people who moved back and forth from the open compartments to the stone arch of the Hall.

Ordinarily, wysps were easy to ignore. Now, all he could think of was danger. Tagaret and Della weren't just going to another city; they would be traveling through wild wysps' territory. Having wysps drift near was supposed to be good luck, but he definitely didn't appreciate the reminder.

"Adon," Della called. She walked nearer, a gorgeously bright figure in her noble colors leading a paler Kartunnen who wore canvas overalls and a gray coat with elbow-length sleeves. "This is our engineer, Adi."

He drew himself up. "Hello, Adi." What did she expect him to say? He glanced at Mother.

"We're grateful for your skill in caring for our family, Kartunnen," said Mother.

"We're honored, Lady, and we'll do our utmost," the Kartunnen answered with a fancy bow.

"Don't you have questions, Adon?" Della asked. "You were worried about our trip, right? Adi's the one who will be on hand in case we have any difficulties with the floater. Her sisters Arri and Odri will take turns driving so we don't have to stop."

Adon tried to think of a question that wouldn't be rude. "You've done this a lot, have you, Kartunnen?"

"Yes, sir," the engineer answered. "We've recorded sixty-three surface voyages."

"Just—be safe, all right?"

"Of course, sir. If you have any factual questions about our route, please direct them to Odri, sir. She's wearing blue stripes."

"I will."

Adon glanced at Mother again, but she seemed lost in thought. Most of the questions he wanted to ask, he'd already asked Della. Part of it was that this didn't seem real. It was like some kind of street theater performance with the floater as a stage, where eventually the Kartunnen actors would close all its various panels and doors and carry it away, leaving their lives unchanged.

But of course the moment came. Mother started crying, and Tagaret embraced her, and then came and folded Adon into a dark space of safety that felt tight and real. Adon clung to Tagaret's jacket for longer than was proper. And then Della hugged him, too, and Tagaret and Della vanished into a compartment. The compartment doors closed and the floater drove away.

Gone.

It was just him, and Mother, and Aloran. His lungs felt raw, as if something had been pulled out of them.

Tagaret . . .

"Adon," Mother said.

Adon held her hand, wishing he could take his glove off. They walked back along the familiar gravel paths toward home. Passing by the Grobal School, he couldn't help noticing each entrance had three guards, not two. He tried to ignore it.

He couldn't ignore Nekantor, though. His brother stood waiting for them, blocking the path to the Residence.

Adon tensed and almost bolted.

"Adon," Nekantor said. "I thought you might be returning to school today." His Dexelin stood behind his left shoulder, and the Arissen, Karyas, behind his right.

"No, Nekantor," Adon growled. Anger joined the churn of loss in his stomach. *We were saying goodbye.* He didn't say that; it shouldn't have been any of Nekantor's business.

"Nekantor," said Mother, "he'll go back when he's ready."

"Yes, of course." Nekantor smiled at him.

He hated it.

"Well, Adon," Nekantor said, reasonably. "I know it must be hard with Tagaret leaving. I'd like to offer you an opportunity."

"No," Adon said. And when Mother squeezed his hand, added, "Thank you."

"It's not a good time, Nekantor," said Mother.

"But it's nothing really. I'd just like to take you on a tour. I discovered when I became Heir that there are a great many beautiful spaces in the Residence that the public doesn't have access to. I could take you around and show you some art that you've never seen."

From anyone else, even the Eminence Herin himself, he would have loved the offer. But from Nekantor? How had Nekantor learned what he liked? Spies?

He glanced instinctively to Dexelin. The young servant's eyes widened a little in surprise. It was clear, though, that Dexelin could offer no reassurance regarding his Master's motives.

"No, thank you," Adon said again.

"I guess you'll have to wait, then. Maybe if you become Heir one day, you'll see them."

"I need to go home now."

"Of course. Take care of yourself, Mother."

A hand—Mother's hand—squeezed his elbow so hard Adon startled and began walking forward.

"Thank you, Nekantor," Mother said. "You take care of yourself, too."

Adon walked fast, but even after they'd entered past a trio of guards into the Residence proper, he still felt shudders down his back.

"Mother," he whispered. "He's watching me."

"He's always watched you," Mother replied. "How else do you think his Dexelin was able to save your life?"

"But he *shouldn't.*" He couldn't shake the feeling of Nekantor's eyes on him, every time they passed one of the new Arissen guards. "I should have gone to Selimna with Tagaret and Della."

"Not at all. It's not safe for children to leave Pelismara."

He snorted. "I bet Lowers take their children out of Pelismara."

Mother paused in front of their suite door and looked at him. "It's not the same, Adon. Lowers have lots of children, because they don't have the decline."

He was an exception to the decline. He would be safe to go. But, at the same time, that only made him more valuable to the Race. They would never want him killed by a wild wysp.

He wasn't exactly safe, here, either. Nekantor expected him to go back to school. How could he go back to school?

Imbati Aloran touched his palm to the lock pad, and the front door cracked open.

Adon blurted, "Mother, may I take your Aloran as my bodyguard?"

Mother froze.

Oh, no. Why had he said that? But he couldn't help it—the words had welled up from a deep place, like a shudder in the earth that had waited too long and could no longer be kept down.

Mother clenched both gloved fists, as if fighting her own earthquake. Her ice-blue eyes, when they locked on his, blazed with terrifying fury.

"Under *no* circumstances. Will you *ever.* Take my Aloran."

Adon stepped backward. His face felt hot. "I'm sorry, Mother. I'm so sorry. I shouldn't have said it."

"I'll go in, now, Aloran."

The servant pushed the door fully open, and she swooped inside. Aloran followed, as close as her shadow.

Adon crept in alone, slowly. His throat and chest hurt. His heart beat too hard.

"Welcome home, young Master," said the First Houseman.

Adon couldn't speak, just looked at him.

"I'm very sorry, young Master," Serjer said, closing the front door. "Would you like me to speak to her on your behalf?"

No, thank you. He couldn't get the words out.

Serjer nodded. "Let me know if you change your mind."

Adon wandered in through the double doors to the private drawing room, but couldn't sit down with Mother's bedroom door right there looking at him. Instead, he found himself drifting into Tagaret and Della's rooms.

Empty.

Empty walls, empty floor; stripped bed and vacant wardrobe left behind because they were too large to fit in a floater compartment and weren't easy to break down. The wardrobe's glass and metal doors hung open. This space was no longer theirs.

Adon sank down on the foot of the bed. He stuffed his gloves in his pocket, rubbed his face, and waited for his heart to calm. It was too early to write a letter when they had barely left. Maybe he'd feel better if he changed his clothes—but that would mean erasing the feel of Tagaret's arms around him.

A sound crept under the door: murmurs in a high voice.

Mother was coming.

Oh, Twins help me . . . Adon sprang up and hopped into the wardrobe, pulling its doors shut behind him. He slid to the floor and wrapped his arms around his knees.

What in Varin's name was he doing? He could already hear Mother asking it: *What do you think you're doing, Adon? Hiding? At your age?*

He listened hard to the silence outside. Maybe he'd been wrong; maybe he'd just have to grimace at his own immaturity and climb back out.

But then he heard Mother sigh. "He's not here either. That was my fault. Mercy of Heile, he didn't need me snapping at him. I suppose it was inevitable he would ask."

"I'm so sorry," Aloran's voice replied.

"I should have seen this coming. I tried to protect our guests from Nekantor; I didn't think he'd hurt *us* instead. Now, Lady Selemei is having to cope with the loss of the two assistants she trusted, and I don't know how to keep him away from Adon. I won't be able to create political distractions the way Tagaret did. And I can't convene the salon every day."

"Please, my Lady, don't blame yourself. It's impossible to prepare for every form of harm."

"That's exactly what I mean."

"Come."

There was a rustling sound. Mother's silk gowns always rustled; maybe she was sitting down on the bed. Would the bed still be warm where he'd sat? Would she figure out he was in here? Adon held his breath, but exhaled when after a few moments she spoke again.

"Are Serjer and Premel all right? With Tagaret's Kuarmei and Della's Yoral gone so suddenly?"

"It is a loss. I'll pass on your sympathies; they'll appreciate them."

"Crown of Mai, I wish we still had Kuarmei here! She could bodyguard him."

Aloran answered after a long pause. "Lady, we may need to prepare for the worst."

"Oh, gods, do you mean . . . ?"

"Everything about our life was designed to protect Adon. Nekantor just split that shield, and we have to assume he did it deliberately, out of self-interest. It's clear he doesn't intend to bring Adon harm, but there's no way to anticipate what will happen next. Adon may need to disappear."

"Mercy of Heile," Mother moaned.

"I will always protect you, Lady," Aloran said. "I have vowed my honor, my duty, my love—" He fell silent abruptly. There was more rustling, and then footsteps, and then nothing.

After waiting so long he couldn't stand it any more, Adon cracked open the cold metal door. The room was empty. He stepped out of the wardrobe slowly, terrified by new questions he should never have had to ask.

What did they mean, he might need to disappear?

CHAPTER NINE

The Road

As hard as it was to say goodbye, not saying it would be worse.

They left through the back gate of the Residence grounds. This was driving, but it didn't feel like it, because the vehicle felt like an entire room. It *was* luxurious—it had silk carpeting, a padded couch that faced forward, another padded couch that faced sideways, a narrow desk, a small door into a bathroom, and curtains along the upper sections of the side walls. If Della hadn't been this way so many hundreds of times, she wouldn't have recognized the road to her own house.

Then the floater stopped, and the door opened.

The familiar arched entry, with its iron gate, was directly in front of her. Her house wasn't unusual for this neighborhood—it was large, multi-story, with all its windows facing inward on a central courtyard. When she and Tagaret got out, members of the Household greeted them and ushered them into the entry hall, which was as large as the dining room at home.

Her family was waiting. Liadis rarely ever left the path between her bedroom and her music room, but today she stood with Mother and Father, holding Father's hand. She had two caretakers with her; the younger one supported her elbow to help her walk. Liadis had always been more comfortable sitting on a bench, fingers and feet flying over the stone keys of her yojosmei, bathing in music.

Mother ran forward and embraced Della so tightly their hairpins got caught, and Yoral had to help extricate them. By the time they had gotten separated, Father and Liadis had caught up, and they all held one another.

"I can't believe Nekantor," Mother exclaimed. "We were just planning to spend time with you, and then he sends you off with no warning at all?"

"I'm really sorry, Mother," said Della.

"I'm sorry, too," said Tagaret, who had taken a step backward when they all converged.

"Your brother is not your fault, Tagaret," said Mother, firmly. "Eyn bless you."

"Thanks."

"Please be safe," added Father. "Send us a radiogram when you arrive, all right? When will you be back?"

Della glanced at Tagaret. "I'm not sure."

"Where are you going?" Liadis asked, with a broad smile that showed her small teeth. "Why are you wearing trousers?"

They'd probably told her—but if she'd been concentrating on her music at the time, she wouldn't have heard. Della stroked her sister's short coppery hair back from her face. "We're going to Selimna, Lili," she said. "These are my traveling trousers. I'm going to see the surface, and Father Varin, and when we get there there will be lots of music. I wish you could come."

Liadis made a face. "I want to come play music but I don't want to see Father Varin. Not at all."

"Well, you don't have to. I'll write you letters, and Mother can read them to you while you play. And I'll send you some new music, all right?"

Liadis grinned. "Yes! Send me music. Promise."

"I promise."

"Della," said Mother, "I don't imagine Nekantor had the decency to arrange a doctor for you in Selimna, did he?"

She gulped. "Honestly, Mother, I wouldn't want him to. I have my Yoral."

Mother could have started scolding, but thank Heile, she only pressed her lips together and shook her head. "Please, love, let one of our caretakers check you before you go. Just to ease my mind."

Della didn't roll her eyes. The suggestion was infuriating, but it *was* sensible. She didn't have a doctor she really trusted in Pelismara; who knew how long it would take to find a decent one in Selimna? She sighed.

"All right. Mother, come sit with me, at least." Together, they went to one of the brass benches by the wall, padded in malachite-striped velvet. The older caretaker, Imbati Bestao, followed them. Mother sat beside her, stroking the side of her arm; Bestao produced a device from one pocket that he attached to her finger, and pressed another briefly to her forehead.

"Looking good, Mistress Pazeu," he said as he removed them. "I'll just check her blood pressure."

He wrapped a cuff around Della's arm. It tightened; her breath tightened with it. Della tried not to think about it. "Mother, I have a favor to ask you."

"What's that?"

"Please reach out to Lady Tamelera while we're gone. She would really like your help with the inoculant program." Her fingers tingled, and then the cuff began its slow release.

Mother had never really connected with Tamelera, mostly because of the gap in reputation between the Sixth Family and the First. She blushed, and glanced at Tagaret. "She does? Are you sure?"

"Absolutely," said Tagaret.

Della nodded. "I've told her about Liadis, and she knows plenty of ladies with unconfirmed children, so that's not an issue. The two of you could reach out to people in the neighborhood. Think if everyone could be as safe as you and Father, and keep their children as safe as Liadis."

"Well . . ."

"Please, Mother, do it as a favor to me." Finally, the cuff released completely.

Mother gave a small smile. "All right."

"Everything checks as normal, Lady," said Bestao. "That's as much as I can do here."

"Thank you, but I don't have time to stay for more," Della replied firmly. "I'm afraid our drivers are on a schedule." It was an exaggeration, but not a lie.

"Oh," said Mother. "Oh, mercy, Della, love, be safe!"

Della kissed her mother's soft cheek. "Of course, I will. I love you." She stood and hugged Father, then Liadis. Then she took Tagaret's hand.

Tears welled in her eyes as they returned to the floater.

Don't think about it. Think about the future. Think about what you're going to do.

I'm going to leave everything behind.

Della pressed her tears away, and tried not to breathe too fast. She stepped up into the compartment and went to her seat.

Tagaret focused immediately on the curtains. "I don't like this. We have this opportunity to go up to see the surface, and they're trying to hide it?"

She smiled at him, though something fluttered disconcertingly, low in her stomach. "Some people are frightened, love."

His face shifted from disapproval to concern. "Darling, are you frightened?"

"Yes." She managed to shrug. "I think you should still open the curtains, though."

Tagaret leaned one eye to the crack between curtains for a second, then pushed them wide open. The arch of her own front entry was visible through her reflection on the glass.

Yoral came and bent over Della to fasten her seatbelt. When it was done she felt quite normal except for the reminder of the strap constricting her across the thighs. Tagaret joined her a moment later. The two Imbati took seats on the side couch. The floater started to move, left her house behind, and soon left the neighborhood entirely, entering a major circumference. A minute later, the floor tilted.

"Oh!"

Tagaret took her hand.

"Let's take our gloves off." She felt so much better with his hand touching hers. She inhaled deeply, and breathed out slowly. Long minutes passed while the floater tilted and leveled, tilted again and leveled again up the city rampways.

Then, they left the world.

The reflection of her face on the window peeled back, replaced by luminous green. Della held tighter to Tagaret's hand while her eyes tried to make sense of it. Some of it moved so fast it was incomprehensible, but if she looked farther out, there were rooms—halls—caverns of green!

A space opened. Far off in the center of it was a glowing white column her mind recognized instantly as a shinca tree. This one was an absolute giant, wider than their whole vehicle. It split as it rose higher, then split again, and—it vanished behind them, swallowed by green that whipped past them in a chaos of speed.

The green was a whole universe. It shivered with gold light that sometimes landed in speckles and sometimes pierced like needles. It was full of weird movements, shudderings, a sudden diagonal burst upward and outward that her eyes could scarcely grasp before it had passed by. She sat, with no awareness of time, trying to make sense of it, but there was always more, another shade, another color, another whir of close movement, another flash of light. There would be no grasping this, or comprehending it.

"Wow," she breathed at last.

"It's beautiful, isn't it?" said Tagaret.

She nodded, though she would have chosen a different word. Overwhelming.

"Was this what it was like for you?" she asked. "When you went up?"

Tagaret chuckled. "Not at all. I was on a skimmer, in a Venorai field. I think it's easier when you're not moving quite so fast. Scarier, being outside in it, but easier."

She looked out again just as a new green room opened up, and at the far edge of it, she saw something that looked exactly like Mother's tree dress. Her heart leapt with the unexpected spark of recognition.

"Oh!" The entire room fled past in less than a second, but some mystery had come unlocked, because suddenly she saw them everywhere. "Tagaret," she said. "Look, trees!"

"I love you." Tagaret patted her hand, and she realized she'd been gripping his other hand so tightly his fingertips were turning purple. She let go and shook her fingers out.

"Sorry," she said. The green outside the windows sucked her attention back.

"I know exactly how you feel." His warm arm curved around her shoulders, and he sighed. "Look at us, Della."

"We're on the Road."

"More than that. You got us here. We're together, we're free."

"We can do what we've always dreamed," she sighed. "With no one watching."

"I'm sorry we're having to leave Mother and Pyaras and Adon, and your family, but—" Tagaret flicked his fingers. "Gnash the whole rest of the Pelismara Society. And the Selimna Society, for that matter. Maybe it's even Sirin's blessing that I don't have to be Alixi. There won't be a cramped space full of people I have to fear or please. No rules I'll have to follow. No eyes. No expectations."

"That's wonderful," she sighed.

"No expectations for you, either, darling heart." Something in his voice had changed.

Della pulled back and looked up at him. "What are you saying?"

Tagaret glanced down, nervously, but then looked into her eyes again. "No one has children in the provinces."

Everything inside her clenched. She breathed shallowly, staring at the seatbelt that held her down.

"Della, please, listen. Since no one has children, no one will be looking for them. The two of us will be enough. We can think about our project. What we create together—will be our vision."

"But you said—" She shook her head. "What if no one cares about our vision? What if they hate us?"

"They won't. We'll find a way; that's what you said."

Abruptly, the floater slid downward.

Della turned to the window. Outside, now, was distance: a gray-brown dimpled surface that moved constantly, extending on and on until it ended in an eerily straight line. Above that was pale blue, and gray, and white, that looked flat as a painting.

"What is it?" Della asked.

"Are we on water? Kuarmei?"

"We're crossing a river, sir," said Kuarmei. "The Ordala, which constitutes the official border of Yrindonna forest. One of its sources is in the mountains ahead."

"If I may remark, sir," said Yoral, "it's much broader than I thought it would be, based on maps and books."

"It's huge," Della agreed. It was its own whole world, and thinking about a river so large was airily delightful. Much better than what they'd just been talking about.

"Master Tagaret," said Kuarmei, "we should probably offer you a drink before we leave the flats and serving becomes more difficult."

"I would appreciate that," said Tagaret. "Della?"

"If you feel comfortable enough to move around." She most certainly would not have, though she'd have to use the bathroom soon. It was right next to her, fortunately, behind a small door where the bench ended.

Something big and reddish flashed by the window. The surface outside had changed again. It was still quite flat, but closer to window level than it had been before. It moved differently, in speckled billows. Also, it was punctuated with house-sized stones. Those, aside from being in a place without a roof, were quite easy to comprehend.

Out in the middle of that space was another shinca. This one wasn't like the giant from the forest, but slender, comprehensible. And so much like a tree! When she could see the whole of it, the splitting pattern looked like branches, as if one of the forest trees had had its flesh stripped off and its hidden soul revealed. Instead of leaves, it carried a thousand thousand globes of light at the tips of its branches.

Yoral recalled her to the inside of the floater by appearing in front of her, holding a glass of ilma juice. It was amazing that he could stand so steady while they moved so fast. She took the glass anxiously. "I shouldn't have asked you to get up, but thank you."

"It's not that difficult, Mistress," Yoral replied. "Are you hungry?"

"Not—" A weird flutter like fear hit her in the stomach, and she gasped and nearly dropped her glass. Juice sloshed and dripped over her fingers; she grasped the glass with both hands, panting and dizzy, her heart pounding. "Tagaret," she gasped. *Bestao was wrong; something bad is happening. The decline has caught up with me. Oh, holy Elinda, I'll never reach Selimna; I'm going to die . . .* "Tagaret . . ."

Tagaret took her shoulders and squeezed tightly; her Yoral swooped the juice glass out of her hand. She didn't see what happened to it after that. Her lips tingled. The edges of her vision paled.

Yoral came, holding a damp cloth, wrapping it around her hands. "Hold this over your nose and mouth, Mistress," he said.

He was her nurse; she did as she was told. The damp cloth was cold and had an odd smell, maybe from the ilma juice on her fingers.

Oh, so gradually, something changed. Not that she could explain it, but the tingling in her lips stopped, and she could see again. Her heart still raced. She lowered the towel.

"I don't know what happened . . ."

"The towel, Mistress," said Yoral. "Just a little longer, please."

She raised it again, and mumbled into it. "All right."

The servant's warm fingers touched her wrist. "You had a minor panic. Remember when I explained that to you? If you breathe slowly, it should subside."

She lowered the cloth again. This time, though, she focused on not breathing too fast. Her heart gradually slowed. "But I don't understand; why should I panic?"

"Is it the surface?" Tagaret asked. "Should we close the curtains?"

"No, please don't. I love this." Her body was being fickle, just when she didn't need it to be.

"Is it . . ." He put his hand on her knee. "What I said?"

She didn't want to answer that. "Let's do something different. Let's talk about Selimna. Tell me something you're looking forward to."

Tagaret rubbed his nose thoughtfully. "I'm looking forward to . . . being so cold in the city that I have to wear hats like a Selimnai. I would say I'm looking forward to talking with Alixi Unger of the Fifth Family, but I'm really not. I'd prefer to talk to Melumalai."

Surely he was saying such things just to make her laugh. "Darling, seriously?"

"Absolutely," said Tagaret. "Kuarmei, are you looking forward to anything?"

"Sir," his Imbati replied, "I'm looking forward to Selimnar bread."

Della couldn't help but smile. "Bread, really? Are you looking forward to anything, Yoral?"

Yoral unwound the towel gently from her hands. "I'm looking forward to you being safe underground, where I can care for you properly," he said. "But, I suppose, also bread. They say it has a tangy flavor."

"I brought a few things with us," Della said. "I mean, I know we brought all sorts of things with us, but I brought things to help us talk to people."

"Oh?" Tagaret's brow wrinkled. "You did? I mean, we can always just talk to people . . ."

"Things to talk *about*," she explained. "Sort of like tangy bread, only things from Pelismara. A stone from the Residence gardens. A miniature pen-and-ink portrait of the Eminence Herin. That silk-paper card Arbiter Lorman gave you. It helps if people have questions."

"What? Who gave you a portrait of the Eminence Herin?"

"He did. Over a year ago."

Tagaret made a face. "Why does that not surprise me?"

Della sighed. "This is going to be hard," she said. "Maybe Lowers won't care about any of those things. Maybe we'll talk about tangy bread. I'll think of something."

Tagaret squeezed her, and leaned his head against hers. "I know you will, darling. You always do."

She hadn't expected to see the gate of Daronvel Crossroads. After their departure from Pelismara, she'd imagined it would just be wild semi-comprehensible surface and then suddenly darkness, her own face reappearing on the window glass as they returned to safety underground.

But, in the mountains, the Road wasn't straight. It weaved back and forth as if it had drunk too much chatinet. Sometimes she felt vaguely ill, like *she'd* drunk too much. She'd seen faces of rock, dark green forests, shinca trees on otherwise barren slopes, fields covered with white as if hidden under bedsheets. More and more as they went on, there were mysterious fields of broad black metallic stripes that reflected orange sunlight. Some of these last had helmeted Kartunnen standing far off in the middle of them. But whatever she saw in one window, the other window always held a shivering sight: a beautiful light-filled painting of a mountain on the far side of the most terrifying crevasse imaginable. She couldn't bear to look at it, but couldn't stop stealing glances. And on one look, suddenly, she saw it.

Far below where they drove, closer to the bottom of the crevasse, was a shiny black structure: a dome with arched openings on four sides, like a protective hand. It sat atop a sort of hill, and four pale lines of Road draped from between its fingers, wriggling in among the green and brown humps of the surrounding valley.

Safety. Once she'd seen it, she couldn't stop looking, though many minutes passed in the descent, and it would disappear for long periods and then reappear again on a curve, only to vanish again seconds later.

At last they came down far enough that the mountains were too tall to see. She counted five shinca as they wriggled among the humps, and then the floater hit the final rise, and the blessed black hand of the Daronvel Gate reached protectively over them.

The floaters drew to a stop.

Sounds came from beyond the floater walls, and then the outer door opened. Freezing air invaded their compartment. Della got out of her seatbelt and stepped out first, with her Yoral behind her.

Under her feet was a wide, curving walkway of concrete. In spite of the Gate's protection, there was wind here. Gusts of ice! Sunlight in shades of orange and blue poured through the openings on the Gate's far side. She hugged herself.

One of their drivers approached, her pale curly hair ecstatically gyrating in the wind. The weird sunlight cast the shadows of her legs in stripes that matched the fabric of her blue-and-white trousers.

"I'm Odri, Lady," she said. "Welcome to Daronvel, or as the Daronveli say, 'A-greeting the time.'" Della had to pluck her words out of the rush of the wind. "Daronvel is famous for its hospitality, but also for its power generation facilities and its battery industry. We've arrived four minutes ahead of schedule."

"Thank you for delivering us safely, Kartunnen." The cold air tasted strange when she spoke. A strand of her hair, caught in the wind, tickled across her face.

"We'll resume our journey tomorrow morning at eight forenoon."

"Yes, thank you."

She only noticed Tagaret arriving behind her when the chill against her back turned to warmth. She reached back for his arms and wrapped them around her. "Oof, it's cold."

"I'm sorry," Tagaret said, above her ear. "It will be warmer in the Crossroads Suites. I wonder where our transport is."

Della rubbed one hand back and forth along his forearm. "We're a little early, I think. In spite of our delayed departure."

"Sir? Excuse me, sir." The Kartunnen was back; or, since she wore no stripes or overalls, this had to be the third sister. "Sorry for the trouble, but the dockmaster is refusing us a spot to park the floater overnight."

"Refusing?" Tagaret asked. "Why?"

"Sir." The Kartunnen rubbed her nose on her sleeve. "I've been *told* the space is being taken up with a cargo delivery, but we'll be fined if we remain on the dock overnight."

Della frowned. "That's not nice. If they require you off the dock, they should have a spot prepared."

Tagaret squeezed her. "Let me take care of it. I'll be right back."

The wind was even colder with him gone. She started to shiver. Yoral opened one of their overnight cases and wrapped a shawl around her shoulders.

"We need to get you indoors, Mistress."

"We do," Della agreed. "The Daronvel Alixi is sending a skimmer." The inner side of the walkway's curve was a city road circle that sloped downward into a smooth bore where shinca light shone. Down there was warmth, and dinner, and a place to sleep—but even though they were here, somehow, they hadn't entirely arrived. "They're supposed to. But Tagaret's busy anyway, for the moment."

"Mistress," Yoral said, "the Daronvel Alixi is Seventh Family." When she blinked at him he added, "And we're First Family, and our parking spot is mysteriously unavailable, and our skimmer is late."

"You're saying it's Family pettiness?" She sighed. "But this is *travel*."

"I don't know, Mistress. Travel is more normal at the Crossroads than it is for us." Dryly, he added, "And antagonizing Master Tagaret might be more fun than the Alixi usually gets in this remote location."

Sirin's luck appeared to solve the problem for them. Only moments after Tagaret returned from arranging the parking, their skimmer arrived.

"A-greeting the time, Sir, Lady," said the Imbati woman at the controls, in a cute Crossroads accent. "I'll be a-driving you in."

Della felt so much more comfortable bundled into a seat beside Tagaret, with Yoral and Kuarmei behind them. Their driver wore the mark of the Household, and drove at a sedate pace compared to Pelismar drivers. Shinca light increased as they entered the tunnel, but instead of the freestanding trunk Della might have expected, silvery light poured from what looked like a window. The tunnel leveled in front of it and made a sharp turn to the right, into an even steeper bore.

No more wind, or strange light, or noise. Thank Eyn. Della exhaled more completely than she had in hours.

A faint sound grew on the air, like a raucous crowd, far off but getting closer. Ahead was another shinca window, another sharp turn. They'd reach the source of the noise, soon.

Suddenly, the walls and ceiling flared open into a cave pocket that glittered white with miniature tiles on every surface. The magnificent face of Eyn the Wanderer, patron of travelers, gazed down at them. Her wild hair covered the walls and ceiling, and the tunnel passed between her welcoming arms.

"Blessed Eyn," Della whispered. "This is gorgeous! How have I never heard of it?"

Tagaret only shook his head. "Mother never mentioned it. Maybe we've been so busy asking about Selimna, we forgot Daronvel. But I'm glad I've seen it."

Through the arms of Eyn they entered a tunnel-crossing. Here was the source of the noise: talking, yelling, something that sounded like singing, and a cacophony of competing musics, all of it echoing off a roof so low she could have sworn they were indoors. The space straight ahead was either a broad hall or a two-lane street, lit by a line of slender shinca trunks down its center, where Lowers of many castes walked among tables full of merchandise. There was a mouth-watering smell of food. Even if there had been enough room in the crowd to drive forward, however, a row of waist-high poles prevented the skimmer from entering. Their driver turned right instead, then followed a sharp curve to the left into a long narrow tunnel with numbered steel doors on both sides. The skimmer stopped.

"Through door five here are your pockets where you'll be a-staying, Sir, Lady," the Imbati said. "I'll help with a-bringing in your bags."

Behind the numbered door was a long, straight hall, its stone walls corrugated with excavation marks. A steel door at the far end of it was painted with the word 'Marketplace.' Their rooms—the local word *pockets* made her smile—were accessed through three carved openings in the right-hand wall. The one nearest the entrance was for Yoral and Kuarmei, the one in the middle was a small common room with a bathroom beyond, and the one on the Marketplace side was for her and Tagaret. They were snug, cozy, lit by golden lamplight that reflected on bright flecks in the stone. They were also a disgraceful mess. The beds were unmade; garbage sat in cans in the corners, on the small common room table, and even here and there on the fringed rug in her bedroom. It smelled appalling.

Sickened and dismayed, Della picked up a glove from the floor at the foot of her rumpled bed and brought it out just as their driver and Tagaret's Kuarmei came in carrying bags.

"Imbati," she said to the driver, holding up the glove apologetically, "I think there may have been some mistake. I hope we're not invading a room that's already occupied."

The Imbati's eyes widened, and she bowed. "Lady, I'm a-grieving. I believe the glove must belong to Alixi Satenya of the Seventh Family; I drove him and his party up to the Gate early this morning."

"I'm afraid we can't return it to him," Della admitted. "We won't be returning to Pelismara any time soon."

"I'll take care of it, Lady," the Imbati replied, blushing. "If you don't mind a-stepping out for a few minutes, I'll get the situation remedied here, and then be a-bringing you your dinner. I believe I can mail the glove on to Alixi Satenya at his new assignment in Peak."

Tagaret ducked in through the low doorway, shaking his head. "I'm starting to think the Alixi of Daronvel dislikes us."

"Let's go out for now, Tagaret," Della said. "Our kind Household has offered to fix it."

"I'd love to. Imbati, I'm so sorry that you'll be put to extra trouble."

"No tears a-falling, sir."

Tagaret pressed Della's hand warmly between his palms, concern on his face. "Are you sure you're feeling well enough?"

"I'm fine. And I'm tired of sitting, after being strapped down all day." She pulled him by the hand out into the corrugated hallway.

"Master," said Kuarmei, "take us with you, please, in case of pick-pockets."

"Really? All right, then," said Tagaret.

"Besides," Della added, "I can't wait until dinner. Aren't you all hungry?"

Her Yoral took the key from the door and slid it aside for them, and they walked out into the Marketplace. The noise, echoing inside this contained space, was overwhelming.

"Pauura!" "Roast kelo, roast kelo!" "Come see our jewels!"

Everyone around them seemed to be talking at once, either buying or selling something. Some kind of unfamiliar spice drifted on the air. Della's mouth instantly started watering. Melumalai tables on either side of their pocket door sheltered them from the movement of the crowd, which had a sort of current from left to right.

"Can you smell that?" Della asked.

"I smell lots of things," said Tagaret.

"I want to find where that smell is coming from." She took him by the elbow, and with Kuarmei and Yoral following, they joined the flow. Tables were either near the wall, or at the center near the row of shinca.

A golden-skinned boy of about eight, with a glittering Melumalai necklace, waved to her. "A-greeting the time, Lady, come try our hot soup!"

She nodded, and walked nearer to the table he indicated, but a deep sniff told her this wasn't what she'd smelled before, so she moved on. A table by the corner sold strong liquor in tiny metal cups, which smelled so bad she literally had to run away. There were cheeses, dried fruit, and candies. It wasn't just food, though. There was also jewelry, and tableware, and cloth, and clothing. One table had nothing but tiny city scenes carved out of dark wood.

As the flow started to double back, an even smaller hawker crossed their path, crying, "Pies an' pepper! Pies an' pepper!" over and over. She might have been two or three. She had a tiny chrysolite that gleamed against her pale, chubby neck.

"What's pepper?" Della asked. "Is that what I smell?"

The Melumalai girl fearlessly took her hand. "Pepper!" she said. "Secrets a-keeping. Pies an' pepper!"

"Show me?"

The girl led her by the hand to a table near the center of the hall, where a woman who had to be her mother had two basket-trays laid out. One had fruit and cheese; the other had rows of pastries, and in one corner, a row of small stoppered containers full of grayish powder. The look of the powder was worrisome, but this was definitely the source of the smell.

"Good girl," said the Melumalai mother. "A-greeting the time, Sir, Lady, may I tempt you with dinner? Tastiest pies and pockets in the Marketplace."

"What's pepper?" Della asked. "Is that what I'm smelling?"

"Cling-pepper, Lady," the Melumalai answered. "You'll only find it a-growing in secret locations in the Daronvel tunnels. Gives dimension to any dish. Nothing better." Her daughter, who had been poking around between the tables, found a coin and gave a cry of delight. "Ameyan, no, that belongs to our neighbor, give it back." At her reluctant cry, the mother insisted, "Generous means a-giving." She shoved the girl toward the Melumalai at the neighboring table, then looked up and smiled. "Lady?"

"I'll try one of the pockets," Della said. She waited, stomach growling, while the Melumalai heated the pastry inside a machine. Finally, she had it in hand and took a bite. Underneath the pastry was a warm, meaty filling with a flavor that flared and expanded up into her nose. "Mm!" The second bite was even more intense than the first, almost painful on the tongue, but absolutely incredible. "Tagaret, this is—you have to try it."

In the end, they bought out all the woman's pastry pockets, and purchased two bottles of cling-pepper powder.

"Generous Lady," said the Melumalai mother. "I'm a-wishing you good evening."

It really was a good evening, at last. Della took Tagaret's arm again, and grinned. "Now that we're not starving, let's go see what we can see before dinner."

CHAPTER TEN

Descent

A gift from Nekantor wasn't a gift; it was usually a trap.

I'm the Executor of the Pelismara Division. The most joyful declaration he could think of, and now all he could do was prod at the idea like a rotten cave floor, trying to find what cracks Nekantor wanted him to fall into.

Cracks would be there somewhere, no question. Nek had wrecked Lake Club, totally true to form. This wasn't the first time Nekantor had tried to use him for his knowledge of Arissen, but acting as Executor was a lot more complicated than choosing a bodyguard. It must have something to do with controlling the Division's functions, which were . . . protecting harvests, and patrolling the adjunct caverns outside the city. Why would you want to mess with either of those? Was there something else? He should have asked Veriga more questions about the Division, and not just the police.

Two things were certain. First, he would have to be ready for the Division to distrust him because of his association with Nekantor. And second, he couldn't let his own distrust of Nekantor affect his treatment of the Arissen.

Pyaras crossed the gardens toward the Arissen Section, passing the Medical Center on his right. His footsteps crunched in the gravel. His Jarel followed far more quietly, attentive to threats as always. She was on guard, and that meant he could let himself smile at the idea of being with Arissen every day.

Maybe that was Nekantor's motive—to hide a cousin's inappropriate interest in Arissen by making it official so the Family couldn't look bad. And maybe that was why, when it came to telling Father he'd been promoted, he'd hesitated.

If that was it? Well, fine.

At eleven, hearing stories from a real Arissen had been the most exciting thing ever, but now he could walk right up to the Arissen Section itself: a large square stone building of two stories which housed offices for the Division, the Police, the Firefighters, and the Eminence's Cohort. It had been built at least a hundred years after the much fancier Residence. An engraved plaque announced 'Division' above the south-facing bronze door.

Pyaras pushed the plate-sized handle in the center of the door, and entered. Inside was a large hall with a woven-fiber mat on the floor, metal benches along the stone walls, and a steel cross-beam ceiling. The panels between the ceiling beams were painted, which seemed incongruously artistic.

An older man with sunmarks on his face emerged from a door straight ahead: Arissen-red uniform, diagonal strap of white leather leading to—yes, there was the handle of the Division soldier's blade peeping from behind his shoulder. And where the front of the strap crossed his line of buttons, a narrow rectangular plaque held rank pins . . . one, a silver circle with a band of gold across the center, that was the Division pin, and then the other, a silver circle with crossed gold bands, for the rank of . . . Pyaras almost grinned, but managed to keep his face sober so he wouldn't look like a fool.

"Commander?" he asked.

"Yes, sir. My name is Tret," the Commander replied, with a forced smile. Smiles probably didn't visit his face very often.

"I'm Pyaras of the First Family, and this is my manservant, Imbati Jarel. I'm very pleased to meet you."

"And I you, sir. Let me show you to your office."

The office was very easy to find: the door in the center of the left-hand wall had a plaque above it engraved with the title *Executor* in fancy serif script. Tret led him into a space that was ridiculously plush compared to the sturdier decor of the entry hall. There was a green silk carpet, a large steel desk and padded chair. There were also three uncushioned metal chairs: one for Jarel, and two facing the desk for Arissen to sit in. There were tables in the corners: one of glass and brass, and one with a floor-length cloth draped over it. The walls were hung with large paintings of surface scenes which he could have studied for hours—forests and fields, all in fine detail, all featuring Arissen busy working.

"Please make yourself comfortable, sir," said Commander Tret. "You may further decorate the space as you wish. Come find me if you have any questions."

"Thank you."

Commander Tret saluted, a chop of his right hand to his left shoulder, and left them.

"Jarel, feel free to have a seat if you like, while I figure this place out."

"Yes, sir." She sat down in her metal chair.

Pyaras almost clapped his hands, decided not to challenge his painkillers, and took a deep breath. This place was a lot fancier than the Cabinet Assistants' office. Exploring, he found a door that led to a private bathroom. He peeked under the table with the cloth and discovered a tiny refrigerator containing juice, cheese, bread, and mushroom cakes. Finally, he sat down in the chair at the big desk, and opened the top drawer.

It contained nothing but a stack of white paper and a pen.

"What?"

He checked each of the three drawers on the left side, but they were totally empty. The drawer on the right, which should have contained files, had a single folder in it.

"Jarel, do you see this?" The folder contained what looked like one-page report summaries. "Is this how Arissen keep records?"

"Sir," said Jarel dryly, "I would call that the absolute minimum of information necessary to give a report before the Eminence's cabinet."

Pyaras snorted. "Makes Imbati look like archive masters."

She hummed, almost a chuckle. "Yes, sir."

But then, in the topmost drawer, he found a handheld ordinator. It was exactly like the one Father used, to keep from getting bored during long helpless hours. Ugh! He slammed the drawer shut.

Varin's teeth.

He looked around the room again. This was a fancy, cozy, totally self-contained play space. It had essentially nothing to do with the work of the Division—there wasn't even a door into the spaces where Division business was conducted. He even found himself distrusting the paintings. What did *artists* know about Arissen, anyway?

The Division didn't distrust him because Nekantor had appointed him; they distrusted him on principle. They didn't welcome an Executor. They didn't want him here at all.

Was this what Nekantor had intended?

No, couldn't be. Nek was all about big secret plans, not about office decor. Plus, he usually tried to avoid thinking about Lowers unless he needed to control them.

How could anyone do this job, when the Division didn't want him to do it?

Pyaras sighed through his nose. If he could talk to Tagaret, Tagaret would advise him—but Tagaret had run off to Selimna. Father would surely have advice—but because he'd been keeping secrets, Father didn't even know he was here.

On the other hand, he knew exactly what Lady Selemei would say. *Stick with it. Figure it out.* Selemei had been unwelcome in the cabinet—in every place men were expected to wield power—but she kept going. It was why she'd kept her influence as long as she had. It was impressive.

"All right, Pyaras," he muttered. "Figure it out."

He took the pen from the top drawer, along with a piece of white paper, and sketched out everything Veriga had ever told him about the Division. Commander was at the top. Then Captains came next. Below that was Captain's Hand, and then came the cohorts, which were also called eights, each soldier ranked First through Eighth. They would be on the surface, in the adjunct caverns, in offices, and possibly in other places as well.

It was time to start asking questions.

"Jarel, I'm going out."

She stood up from the chair. "Yes, sir."

"Actually, I'm guessing you might prefer to stay here while I go talk to the Commander?"

Jarel didn't immediately answer. At last she said, "If you insist, sir."

"I mean, Highers are a big hassle, right?"

Jarel's mouth twitched into a subtle smile. "Yes, sir."

Pyaras smiled back. "I shouldn't be long."

He took the pen and paper with him. The entry foyer was empty, but he pushed through the door out of which Commander Tret had initially appeared.

Whoa.

This room was many times larger than the foyer, and full of uniformed Arissen. Some worked at desks arrayed in lines like a maze, while green interlinked text climbed their ordinator screens; some strode about as if on urgent errands. Farther in, the space was closed off and divided into smaller sections with panels of metal and glass. Pyaras stopped a pale young woman whose cheeks were sprinkled with sunmarks. He *could* get away with calling her just *Arissen*, but with everyone else around he'd rather do better, so he looked at her rank pins. At the center of her jacket, there was the plaque with the Division circle, and then another circle with a hand in it. *Captain's Hand.*

"Hand," he said. "I'm Executor Pyaras of the First Family. Please take me to Commander Tret's office."

The young woman saluted. "Yes, sir. Follow me, sir."

Heads turned. Arissen eyes tracked him as he followed the Captain's Hand down between the desks toward one of the glass-framed enclosures, which had a metal bench sitting outside it. Nobody was waiting there to see the Commander, fortunately. When the Captain's Hand stepped aside, Pyaras knocked on the Commander's door, and leaned it open.

Commander Tret looked up from his work in surprise. "Executor Pyaras?"

"Please, don't get up, Commander," he said. "I'm sure I'm interrupting, but you did say I should ask questions."

"Ah. Yes. I did say that."

"I hope you can fill in some of the blanks in my understanding." Pyaras set his sketch in front of the Commander. "And could you please introduce me to some of the workers here?"

"Truth be told, sir," said the Commander, "it's not worth your time. None of these people will be here tomorrow."

It felt like a slap. Pyaras swallowed. Was Tret lying to put him off? No; *stick with it.* If Tret was telling the truth, why would none of these people be here tomorrow?

"It's their rotation day," he guessed. "So they're about to head up onto surface duty?"

Tret raised his eyebrows. "Yes, sir, they are. The ones currently on adjunct duty will be coming here tomorrow, and the ones on the surface are on Descent tonight."

"Well, I'll wait to be introduced to people tomorrow, then," Pyaras said. "But I'd appreciate it if you could help me fill in my understanding of the rotation schedule, and the duties your cohorts are assigned to."

"Yes, sir." Commander Tret gestured past him. "Hand, bring that chair over here for the Executor, and then you may be dismissed."

"Sir."

Pyaras sat down beside the Commander, but Tret didn't refer to his rough sketch. Instead he opened a file drawer of his desk, sorted through it, and extracted a paper, which he unfolded across the other things he'd been working on. It held a far larger, impressively precise diagram of Division organization.

Pyaras grinned. "Excellent. I can see I've got some studying to catch up on."

Pyaras banged on Veriga's steel front door—*ow*—shook his hand out, and banged again with the other one. "Come on, Veriga, be home. Don't be off Arissen-ing around town right now . . ."

Behind his shoulder, Imbati Jarel murmured, "You could have sent me ahead to check, sir."

He turned to look at her, then huffed out a sigh. "I know."

The Imbati woman hinted a smile at one corner of her mouth. "You just didn't want him to refuse you."

"No." He frowned. "That's not it at all, I just wanted to get away from—argh, never mind."

He turned back to bang again, and the door opened. Veriga's iron hand stopped his fist in mid-air.

"Hello, Grobal Pyaras of the First Family," the Arissen said, without smiling. "You here to apologize for skipping our jog?"

Oh, mercy. He'd been so busy this morning, getting himself to the Executor's office . . . "I forgot, I'm sorry, it's entirely my fault."

Veriga grunted. "Yes, it is. I'm surprised; you usually send Imbati Jarel rather than trying to break down my door yourself. Ah, but I see she's here, too. Good evening, Imbati."

Jarel inclined her head politely. "The heart that is valiant triumphs over all, Arissen, sir."

"Veriga," said Pyaras. "I know I missed this morning, but I'm free tonight, so let's go out."

"Sorry, no."

"What? No?" Veriga couldn't be going to work; he was out of uniform, wearing fitted knee-length pants of Arissen red and a sleeveless white shirt that showed his gnarled shoulders.

"No, sir. I'm already going out, and you can't come."

Stung, Pyaras shook his head and hid his health bracelet with one hand, though Veriga had surely already seen it. "Wait a minute, why can't I come? Where are you going?"

Veriga leaned against the doorjamb, scowling, arms folded. "Descent. Arissen only."

"Descent," Pyaras echoed. Then he placed it. "Wait, Descent, that's what Commander Tret said."

Veriga lost his scowl. "Commander Tret? You mean the *Division's* Commander Tret?"

At that moment, Veriga's tunnel-hound burst past him onto the sidewalk. She rubbed her head on Pyaras' knees, wriggling gleefully. "Aw," Pyaras said. "Hi, Evvi. Hi, pup!"

"To me, Evvi," said Veriga. Then he sighed. "Come in, Pyaras, don't stand around outside."

Pyaras did. Veriga's house was more welcoming than he had been. It smelled like childhood escapes—chalk, rope, shoe polish, and tunnel-hound. The hound in question ran circles around the rug-and-pillow floor until Pyaras had finished putting his shoes on the shelf by the door. When he sat down, she flung herself on him, climbing up to rub her broad, sensitive snout against his ears. She made the most adorable crooning sounds in her throat. The smell of hound was musky but wonderful—almost sweet—and her fur was softer than velvet. Her head was totally smooth where another animal's eyes would have been. The hard nubs of her foreclaws pressed through his shirt and jacket.

Tunnel-hounds are not pets, young nobleman, Veriga had told him a thousand times. He was right, too—she was more. Kartunnen doctors had allowed Veriga to survive, but Evvi had brought him back to life.

She'd also taken over the house. Three walls of this room were her playgrounds, criss-crossed with interconnected ramps of steel shelving to climb, and decorated with toys including three pumice wheels to keep her foreclaws from growing as long as his fingers. The fourth wall was Veriga's. Besides the doors into kitchen and bathroom, it was fastened all over with colorful polymer handholds. Veriga used them to climb to the loft where he slept.

It was a wonderful place.

Pyaras held Evvi's head against his shoulder, and stroked her—the first sensation his fingers had really loved since he was shot. "Yeah, so I should explain Commander Tret," he said. "It's been the weirdest day. Thank the Twins for you, Veriga, honestly. Nekantor appointed me as Executor to the Pelismara Division—that's where I was instead of meeting you—and I'm actually thrilled, but nobody wants me there. If it hadn't been for the things you taught me, I wouldn't have known where to start. And then tonight, after everything my father's said about you, he starts telling me how I need to be the best Executor in history? I mostly just don't want to be useless. I'm glad you taught me enough that I can ask decent questions."

Veriga folded down nearby and leaned on one elbow. "Questions are good. Listening to the answers is even better."

"Well, I've been listening. When I was talking with Commander Tret, I remembered duty rotations just in time."

"I'm sure the Commander appreciated that."

Pyaras ran his thumbs along Evvi's head from snout to ears. "Blessing of Sirin, I hope so. I wish I could get a tunnel-hound. I know, I know, tunnel-hounds aren't pets, they're responsibilities."

Veriga didn't say it with him. Pyaras looked over and found the Arissen shaking his head. "I don't get you," Veriga said. "Sometimes you behave like an utter nobleman, and other times I could swear you care."

"What?"

"Want to know what happened at the Lake Club?" Veriga didn't wait for him to answer. "You *should*. It happened because of you. That's the thing, Pyaras; you walk into things and never think about what you're doing, or what consequences you might bring to others."

Mercy, this wasn't about jogging at all. Pyaras let his hands fall, though Evvi continued to nuzzle them. He whispered, "Nekantor had the employees arrested . . ."

"Your stinking cousin only waved his hand. Who do you think actually had to arrest them?"

Police. *Oh, Mai strike me.* A wave of cold sank into his stomach, and his mouth felt dry. "You?"

"Oh, I insisted." Veriga stabbed one finger into the rug between them. "A lot of my friends get way too happy when they have a chance to break up an unlicensed brothel. I *had* to take charge, to make sure no one got seriously hurt. Bad enough they'll be accosted and fined—I can't have anyone shot just because my idiot friend can't tell what kind of club he's walking into."

"Wait," Pyaras protested. "It was a *brothel?*"

Veriga waved a hand at him in exasperation. "I thought you knew!

That place had a good look, but everything it was made of was cheap. Not near fancy enough to warrant the entry price. How else do you hide your sex fee? We went there twice, and you were about to be two for two, still thinking it was Sirin's luck? Gnash it, you're good-looking for a Grobal, Pyaras, but you're not *that* handsome. Just for a second, just *think*."

If it had been anyone but Veriga, he might have stormed out. Being dumped unceremoniously into reality made him feel dirty all over. "You had to arrest Rivai because of me."

A muscle flexed in Veriga's jaw. "I did. Evvi, up up." The tunnel-hound went to him immediately, snuggling in, allowing him to lay hands on her while she laid her head against his chest. She made a gentle warbling sound. "Good girl." He took a deep breath. "Pyaras, back at Lake Club, you knew the caste of everyone I showed you the minute you stopped pretending. I could tell. And that means you know why Rivai deserved better."

Oh, he knew. Why one could dance, why one seemed to understand him . . . "One was born to the Grobal Race," he said brokenly. "A member of the Great Families, until one was chosen by Mai the Right. And then one Fell."

"You're blasted right. Same person, born to the Arissen, wouldn't have had to Fall. One might have worked as police or Division, or trained as an arbitrator. Born to the Imbati, same—one could have trained as a servant of the Courts. Now? Who knows where one landed, or how one will earn the money to pay the fine? The Grobal see justice's favor and throw it away—I've never understood it."

"I'm sorry." The words were for Rivai, but he had no idea where one even was. And even if he had, words wouldn't have helped. Pyaras shook his head.

"I'm sorry, too. Those arrests are Nekantor's doing, not yours, but I couldn't let you think you had no part in it."

Pyaras sighed. "You probably want me to leave now."

"Nah, you should stay."

After all that? Pyaras looked at Veriga sidelong. "Maybe I'll use your bathroom," he said, and excused himself. He sat on the closed toilet, studying his partially healed hands. After the shame eased a little, he used the toilet and washed his hands, watching the water chase soap bubbles off the pink skin.

Did he want to go home?

Did he want to go out?

Actually, he wanted to hold Evvi.

When he came back out, Veriga was gone. Probably up in the loft, because Evvi was running up her shelves, claw-nubs clattering on the metal. The only one still down here with him was his Jarel, standing by the front door.

Who had just watched all that. Pyaras grimaced.

"My heart is as deep as the heavens," Jarel said quietly. "No word uttered in confidence will escape it."

"Thanks. Maybe we should go."

Veriga's voice called from above. "Hey, young nobleman. How strong are you?"

Pyaras shook his head in confusion. "Uh . . ."

"Maybe I should have you climb my wall a few more times; what do you say?"

"Sure, but—what are you up to?"

Veriga's hands appeared at the edge of the loft, and then his head. Though his tone just now had been playful, his scarred face was deadly serious. "If I teach you a lesson, young nobleman, will you listen?"

His stomach squirmed a little. "Um, not like the last one . . ."

"Oh, not at all." Veriga's gaze intensified, and he shook his head. "This one will be much worse. I protected you during the last one."

Pyaras opened his mouth to stammer some kind of refusal, but before he could get out anything coherent, Veriga said,

"You said you wanted to come with me to the Descent, didn't you?"

Holy Twins.

"Sir," said Jarel behind him. "I would strongly advise against that."

He glanced at her, than back up to Veriga. "What's a Descent? Didn't you say Arissen only?"

"It's a Division thing, but any Arissen can go. You could call it a party, to let off steam when you come down off surface duty alive. Frankly, I'm not sure you can handle it."

"That sounds like a dare." Veriga knew him too well; already he wanted to prove him wrong. But *Arissen only* meant no Jarel. It also meant something else. Pyaras glanced over his shoulder again. Behind Jarel's head, a line of handkerchiefs hung from clips beside the front door. Because they were vivid rust-red, the regulated color of the Arissen, any one of them could serve as a castemark. Veriga kept them there so he'd always be legal to go out, even if he were summoned at midnight on an emergency. "I would have to—" He licked his lips before saying the distasteful word. "Crossmark."

"And if you get caught, I won't protect you."

"Sir." Jarel leaned her head to one side. "Please, sir."

Pyaras looked at her. "Your oath of silence on this, Jarel."

The Imbati didn't immediately respond. At last she said in an expressionless voice, "My heart is as deep as the heavens. No word uttered in confidence will escape it."

"Get up here, then, you fool," said Veriga.

Pyaras climbed onto the wall, and made it up in seconds, though his hands hated him for it. Fortunately, Evvi had been trained not to greet climbers too enthusiastically. She butted him only after he'd achieved hands and knees at the top. He leaned his cheek against her shoulder, then got up and walked to where Veriga stood by his steel wardrobe. The Arissen glanced at him, tossed a pile of white clothes into his face, and chuckled as he scrambled to catch it.

"So," Veriga said. "Rules."

"I get it." Excitement grew in his stomach. He started changing out of his beryl-green silk suit. "This is a lesson. Lessons always come with rules."

"One. Don't drink anything but yezel, and even that only if you get it directly from me, or from uniformed monitors—rank pins the Monitors' gold diamond, and a number of whistles."

That was easy. "All right."

"Two: no pills or powders."

Pyaras paused, stepping into the short white pants Veriga had given him. "Easy enough, since I don't know what you're talking about."

"Three. And this is the hard one, young nobleman."

"All right . . ."

"If anyone tells you no, to *anything*, you have no right to insist. Forget this one, and you better be ready to get your face broken by several people. In fact, if you don't want to be questioned you should consider yourself ranked at Cohort Eighth, and that means doing exactly as the monitors tell you."

"I will do as I'm told, I promise." He pulled the shirt on, carefully avoiding the sore areas of his head. When he emerged he found Veriga frowning at him skeptically. He flushed. "Crown of Mai, Veriga, I *promise*."

"Give me that shirt back," Veriga said, tossing a different one at him. "We'd better cover your shoulders."

The new shirt had elbow-length sleeves. Pyaras caught a glimpse of himself in the mirror, and shivered. His nose, though not as obviously noble as Tagaret's, was still a bit too Grobal, and he just wasn't muscular enough; the clothes, while not baggy, didn't fit him like they fit Veriga.

But his hair was perfect.

"This works," he said.

Veriga looked him up and down. "Close enough. Though . . . someone might ask why you're wearing your dress shoes."

When they climbed back down, Imbati Jarel stood blocking the front door. She bowed herself in half.

"The heart that is valiant triumphs over all, Veriga, sir. In the name of Eyn the Wanderer, please bring him back safe. Or I'll never work again."

"Like he was my own little brother, Imbati," Veriga said solemnly. "You're welcome to stay here with Evvi and wait for us." He plucked a handkerchief from one of the clips and tied it around Pyaras' neck.

Pyaras tried not to look at Jarel as he walked out. In the light of street lamps, the cavern roof was a dim looming presence overhead. Excitement had expanded into his limbs, a little too close to fear; he took deep breaths. But it would be fine. Veriga would bring him back safe. Like a little brother.

"Pyaras, one last thing."

"Yeah?"

"If you get found out for any reason, remember I'm *not* going to be the one arresting you."

They walked all the way up to the first level. Pyaras was grateful for his many hours spent jogging, but well out of patience with machine-hewn limestone steps, by the time they passed through the last upward tunnel. The scale here was awesome: a vast, mostly dark space crossed by columns of reinforced rock, and pierced by bright silver shinca trunks. Away to the left floated an island of orange lights and buildings, strangely framed by solid black. The air smelled musty, of water and plants, yet very unlike the gardens of the Residence. Pyaras turned his head and sniffed.

"That's field smell," Veriga said. "Venorai territory, for farming—the safe kind. The kind you don't need firefighters or Descents for."

They started along the road toward the lights. A faint, regular thudding sound grew in the air, too prolonged for rockfall. Skimmer headlights flashed long shadows along the smooth stone ahead of his feet as vehicles full of Arissen hummed along the road past his ear, one after another. The left side of the black framing pulled slowly back from the illuminated area as they drew closer; it proved to be an enormous intruding curtain of cavern wall. The lighted district featured many long, single-story buildings with dimly lit translucent roofs. The view of the right side had been cut off by the side of a building, a giant black cube so tall that only a narrow band of shinca-light showed there was still space between it and the cavern roof. The thumping sound emanated from there. At this angle, he could see neon red words splashed across the front of it: PLIS' PLAYGROUND.

The closer it loomed over him, the more the thumping tugged at his heartbeat. Pyaras licked his lips. *Holy Plis, do teach me a lesson, but please spare some favor from your warrior Arissen to give this nobleman a bit of extra courage.*

The entry to the giant building was through a smaller cube with a front wall made entirely of woven rope, each strand as thick as his arm. Uniformed Arissen—monitors, because they wore the uniforms and rank pins Veriga had described—hailed them out front, raising voices above the thumping.

"Veriga!" one called. "Checking weapons tonight, seni?"

Pyaras didn't hear Veriga's response, because a monitor built like a stone column was approaching him.

"Checking weapons?"

"No—" he snapped his mouth shut before he could call her 'Arissen' and give himself away. Raised his voice a bit more forcefully. "No, sir."

"Remember the rules. No needles, no fighting."

"Yes, sir."

She waved him forward. Pyaras hurried to Veriga's side as the thumping grew even louder. "Veriga, I didn't ask you about—"

The thumping stopped abruptly, and he found himself half-shouting into the low crowd murmur, "—money!" He flushed, and held out both hands. His expense card was back at Veriga's, in the pocket of his silk trousers, and chances were Arissen would want real orsheth anyway.

Veriga laughed. "I got it, don't worry." Then the thumping started again, a different rhythm this time, and Veriga raised his voice again. "Do you have a watch?"

Pyaras held out his wrist.

"Take that off. Put it in your pocket." As he obeyed, Veriga handed him a plastic ticket. "Meet back here in an hour."

That would be half past nine. "Got it."

"Now—drinks!"

Veriga pushed ahead. Pyaras moved forward into the converging mass of Arissen bodies. Bare sweaty shoulders pressed against him, hips bumped, and hands pressed on his back. A monitor loomed up and took his ticket.

They passed under the rope wall.

Inside, under red lights, there was barely room to move. The Arissen were a famously large caste—the Division alone numbered four thousand—but this felt like it was every last one of them. Pyaras sidestepped around two shirtless women, one pale, flushed by the lights to tourmaline pink, the other darkly sunmarked, with muscles that looked carved in garnet. He caught up with Veriga just as the police officer reached the long drinks table. Veriga leaned across it, raised two fingers, and yelled, "Yezel!" at a helmeted monitor.

Veriga received two plastic cups from the monitor, handed him one, and then knocked his own cup against it.

"To life, Pyaras!"

"To life, Veriga!" He took a swig. Cold, cold yezel, a brew sharper and more sour than he was used to, but marvelous in the heat of the pressing bodies.

Veriga grabbed his arm and pulled him forward. Here were swinging doors, flanked by monitors. A flashing white light strobed over their heads as the doors opened, and Pyaras stumbled forward—into the incomprehensible.

He was inside the beating drums. Wild whistle notes pierced the throbbing air. The space pulsed and flashed, pulled at his nerves, his heart, his breath. He almost froze, but Veriga dragged him forward. The floor was soft; he stumbled and fell to one knee before scrambling up again into a swinging wall of pale hair that stung his face. A woman's body collided with his, and her hands grabbed him; he shoved her away and spilled yezel over his own arm. Bodies, hard as stone, converged from either side to crush him, then spun away.

Pyaras panted. *Keep moving, keep moving, we'll get through this—*

But what did 'through' even mean?

He didn't realize Veriga had stopped until he ran right into the police officer's back. Veriga turned and yelled into his face. "You all right?"

"Yeah?" He struggled to think through the noise. It felt like he'd been tumbled through rockfall. His clothes were wet in places, and his cup of yezel was gone. This wasn't 'through,' but there was enough of a gap among the moving Arissen to get his bearings. He scanned around for landmarks. He hadn't seen any walls since they entered, but above the crowd he could see a pole just beyond Veriga. He followed it downward, and his mouth fell open. A bald, naked man was tied to it with ropes. His face was ecstatic; a woman in sleeveless shirt and short pants had mounted his bent knee, her hands tangled in the ropes above his head. She thrust him against the pole in time with the drums.

"Oh," he breathed. "Oh gods."

Veriga glanced over his shoulder and broke into a lascivious grin. "Want to leave?"

Pyaras gulped sweaty air. The drums stopped again, for an instant—this time he could hear screams, shouts, moaning. He was hot and cold, and hard, and terrified. He clenched his fists. "No."

The drums resumed. Veriga started moving forward.

Now he didn't have to be pulled. Getting free of this wasn't the point; being *in* it was the point. Push, breathe. Now he recognized the rhythm of the movement—the crowd was a lover's body. Push, breathe; push, breathe; push, deeper in. He stumbled, and fell into a pit of multicolored foam cubes, crawled across it and out. Here was a writhing pile of human bodies. There, three men of markedly different ages were wrestling each other, or having sex, or both. Over there, the air flashed strangely with light and shadow; a group of at least fifty people stood, body to body, faces turned up toward a luminous cloud of real wysps.

A hand tugged at him, and when he turned, offered what looked a tiny plastic bag full of powder.

No powders.

He shook his head and pushed the hand away.

Not far ahead, a shinca-trunk glowed, and the space seemed less full; he slid diagonally toward it. As he arrived, a rolling body smacked him in the ankles. He looked down. An Arissen, gender and age uncertain, gazed up at him with mouth open like a laughing child, and started petting his calves with both hands. He allowed it by pretending the contact was Evvi, at the same time looking to find where anybody could have rolled from.

The ceiling over his head ended within two body-lengths, and in the flashes of light he could see a sloping expanse: a rope net, wider than a room. People were climbing up and down it. It was much less crowded than the floor—he should tell Veriga they should go up.

Where was Veriga?

Fear flashed inside him, then vanished into the pounding of the drums. Veriga wasn't Jarel, bound to his left shoulder. He'd been warned this was a lesson about being unprotected. He should be able to handle himself.

Pyaras pulled his legs free of the petting person's hands and stepped onto the net. Gods above! The farther he went, the more its slope increased, and beyond the edge of the partial ceiling, the white light of three shinca revealed nets webbing everywhere—some slanted, some flat, layering upward through beams of colored light to a gulf of dark ceiling. Way up there, a man was flying—how could he be flying? Pyaras climbed, leapt the gap to another net, rolled and climbed again, trying to reach the top. A shinca trunk beckoned ahead, silhouettes moving around it; he passed through the edge of the group, and on the other side, found himself in a forest of ropes strung from somewhere on the ceiling above. Panting, mouth open, he wove between them with his arms outstretched. They twanged against him. His mind beat with the heated sound. A woman with one lower leg missing zoomed out of the air and flew down on him. She was going to knock him down—he opened his arms and braced to catch her, but when she landed her face pressed to his; her mouth sucked him into a kiss. Liquid heat melted down him from lips to hips.

"Life!" she shouted, and shoved off him, crouching and then sitting down, removing something from her foot. When she stood up again she pushed a handful of straps into his hand and dived into a roll down the expanse of net.

Wow.

He panted, still tasting the flying woman, scarcely able to comprehend this thing that now pulled at his grip. Looping straps, metal rings, and a cord tugging up into the darkness. No way to ask. He searched among the people in the rope forest and realized someone was detaching a similar set of loops from a hook on the net, stepping into them, like trousers. How could straps be like trousers? The tugging cord attached at the waist, and the loops went around his legs? Suddenly someone was helping him—Veriga? No, not Veriga, but a grinning young man scarcely old enough to drink, who directed his feet into the right loops, then tightened the straps around his waist and thighs.

The young man pressed a rough cheek to his and shouted in his ear. "First Descent, seni? You're enjoying it, I see." He pointed to Pyaras' erection, made all the more obvious by the tight harness, and then ran a hand appreciatively over his own parts. "Want company?"

"Uh—no . . ."

The young man nodded. "Can I launch you?"

"Like, fly? Yes?"

"Life!" the young man cried, seized the harness at his waist and dragged him into a crouch, then flung him into the air.

Pyaras screamed. He clutched at the rope that pulled him up into the darkness, then screamed even louder when gravity captured him again. He hit the net, knees buckling as it rebounded; he clung to it, heart and lungs like to explode. The ropes were hard and slippery in his hands—or was that the sweat? At least it didn't hurt at all. He scrambled to his feet and leapt again, this time under his own power. By the time he lost count of his leaps, he could no longer tell if he was screaming or laughing. Lights and bodies wheeled around him. This was the ecstasy of the gods in their orbits!

But now, coming down, he found too many people below. He tried to aim for a gap, spun out of control, caught his feet on someone's shoulder and sank into the crowd like a knife into meat. The drums stopped.

"Sorry!" he shouted, into an awful silence.

The drumming started again. Rough hands grabbed him, unceremoniously stripped the harness off, and flung him. Pyaras curled to protect his head, rolled, and found the net so steep he couldn't stop. Several spinning seconds later, he lost his tuck and slammed out flat on his back. A shinca wavered and whirled in his eyes, directly in front of him; beating drums and vibrations in the net slid him toward it. He tried to get up. Hands pulled at his arms and got him standing, but standing was worse. His stomach lurched and his knees wobbled. Arissen running from behind him bumped him farther down the slope. The shinca was almost close enough to touch, radiating heat, its silver glow pricking light from beads of sweat that ran down the converging Arissen bodies.

Someone in the crowd in front of him jumped, then dropped out of sight.

What?

He got closer, and a woman came running in from the right side, leapt onto the shinca, and shot downward like a stone. They were all doing it, from all sides, sliding down the shinca trunk like grains of sand through a funnel.

"No!" he shouted. "No!"

But no one heard. His toes hit the edge of the net, and the crowd momentum shoved him forward. He grasped desperately for the shinca, and just barely got his arms around it. Its surface was hot to the touch, slicked with sweat, and offered no friction at all. He hurtled down in one long throat-breaking scream. An eternity later his feet punched into foam, and his grip broke. For a second he blinked, too stunned to move.

Oh, Heile help me, someone's going to land on my head!

He struggled down the enormous pile of foam cubes until he found real floor. He crawled out onto it. Solid, thank heavens—yet it was a long minute before he stopped feeling it moving.

He had to get out.

Panting, he dragged himself to his feet, searching for an exit. No sign of one—only the wanton chaos. He picked a direction and fought his way into surging crowds, while panic tightened his throat. A uniformed monitor loomed up. He pushed until he reached him.

"Where is the exit?"

The monitor scowled.

Oh, holy Twins. What was he doing wrong? Descent, Arissen only . . . "Where is the exit, sir?"

The monitor pointed.

Pyaras moved in that direction as fast as he could manage, but it took two more pointing monitors before he got back to the strobe light over the swinging doors. He pushed through into the room with the drinks, but it was even more tightly packed than before. He kept going, across a floor slippery with spills, out past the rope wall and into the night.

Cool air, and quiet.

He stood for a moment, breathing. Slowly, his ears began to recover from the noise, and the quiet resolved into the low throb of drums, overlaid with the talk of Arissen who were still arriving in droves, checking their weapons with the monitors. He looked down at his hands, sure that they must be bleeding, but the stickiness appeared to be only sweat.

Carefully, he put his hand in his pants pocket. His watch was still in it. He fished it out—Veriga wouldn't meet him for another twenty minutes. In other words, forever.

No way was he going back in. Veriga's lesson—learned.

A monitor approached him. "Picking up a weapon?"

"No, sir."

The monitor nodded and turned away toward one of the new arrivals. "Checking a weapon this evening?"

Pyaras stepped away to one side. There was still ringing in his ears, and his body felt battered, but there seemed to be nowhere to sit. A pair of Arissen women had chosen to sit on the ground with their backs against the rope wall of the Playground. They were kissing playfully; one of them had her leg crossed over the near leg of the other, who kept sagging forward as if she wasn't quite sober, and wanted to dive into the first one's bosom. Then, in a breath, they both looked up and saw him.

Plis help me, I hope I look Arissen enough. His throat felt dry, but the last thing he wanted was yezel.

"Police Eighth, are you, Handsome?" one of the women shouted. "This your first Descent?"

He didn't answer, but edged away from them, farther toward the darkness. *I'm not here. Don't notice me.* The woman didn't shout again.

His heel tipped on a curb. He nearly fell backward into the street, where a straggling crowd waited to be approached by the monitors. He caught himself before the nearest Arissen could try to help him, decided this was the best seat to be had, and sat on the curb with his feet in the gutter. That put his face right at the level of at least three weapon holsters.

He glanced away toward a wysp drifting along the sidewalk, and shivered. *I wish Jarel were here.* Who knew what Veriga was doing right now? He didn't want to know.

"Eminence's Cohort is the best!" A shout arose out of the murmurs of the waiting crowd. The speaker was a big man who meandered closer in a group of friends—easy to pick out because his shirt was orange instead of red or white.

Pyaras' stomach turned to stone. That guy had better not be a Residence guard . . . what if he recognized him? He angled his head away.

"You would say that, you hound's anus," one of the friends remarked.

"We *are,*" the Cohort man insisted. He sounded drunk. "We have the good faith of the Eminence! Herin! Himself!"

"For what a Grobal's faith is worth," scoffed a woman. "Till he falls apart and *dies.*"

The group burst into laughter.

"Gnash you! The Heir got that Melumalai collector off my ass; you can't say as much."

"Wow, what for?"

"Being brave, slime-ass. We're the *bravest.*"

"Tell that to the cohort on Descent," another voice snapped. "Tell that to someone who's faced wysp fire and survived."

Pyaras sighed, and glanced at the drifting wysp again. It looked so pretty and harmless here, but the surface was different. Tagaret told stories—Lady Tamelera and her Aloran had taken him up there once, and he'd seen the danger with his own eyes. Who would travel, after that?

"I laugh at wysps," the Cohort man declared, weaving closer. "The Cohort laughs. Kill one and everyone bows down."

"Plis' balls! *Kill* one, are you crazy?"

Movement by the rope wall caught his eye. The less sober woman had slumped over sideways, but the other had gathered herself into a crouch, watching with an intensity that sent alarm racing down his backbone.

"You're jus' not a good enough shot, Figo. Plenty in the Cohort've done it. Hit one juuuust right . . ."

Pyaras glanced back toward the rope wall; the woman was on her feet now, eyes ablaze, tensed like a cave-cat ready to spring.

"Get it wrong and die, seni," one of the others said sourly. "Along with everyone within twenty feet."

It was like being doused in ice. *Twenty feet?* Good gods, and him here within arm's length? Adrenaline buzzed behind his ears. Was the man just bragging? Would a drunk Arissen actually try to shoot a wysp?

Plis knew, the pride in that man's voice was too familiar—too much like his own words to Veriga: *That sounds like a dare.* And the holstered weapon was now inches from his face . . .

The Cohort man shook one finger in his friend's face. "I told you, you're jus'—not—a good 'nough—shot."

Gnash this! Pyaras snatched fast, freed the holster strap and yanked the weapon out, just as the man's hand swung down.

The Cohort officer pulled at nothing and aimed at the wysp; when he found his hand empty, he roared, "Figo!!!" Then he saw Pyaras, and his eyes turned murderous.

Pyaras dropped the weapon and scrambled backward.

A figure flashed between them—the woman from the wall. Her elbow smacked the Cohort man straight across the face, snapping his head sideways, and he staggered. His friends erupted in outrage as they leapt to break his fall. He landed heavily in the road.

"I am Specialist First Melín; Division cohort on Descent under Captain Keyt!" the woman shouted, cutting them off. "It's a *thirty*-foot fireball, and unless you're suicidal, you'd better be grateful he's knocked out. Monitors!!" She waved over the officials.

Pyaras sat mute and frozen.

The woman plucked the weapon from the ground near his feet and handed it over to the monitors as they arrived. They called her Specialist. She explained things to the nearest one, who scowled and nodded.

His breath came quick and shallow. *Oh holy Mai cast down your eyes—don't let them arrest me!*

But the monitors joined the Arissen group in carrying the Cohort man away. The Specialist walked up—buckled black boots—and reached down to him. Her arm was strikingly sunmarked, jingling with copper bracelets. What could he do but take it? She pulled with such force he was on his feet in an instant. As strong as she was, he'd have sworn she should have been taller.

She looked up, evaluating him, keen brown eyes in a brown face sprinkled with darker sunmarks. Sirin and Eyn, she had holes in her ears, with rings in them!

Her full lips curved into a smile. "You're a sharp one, Police Eighth.

That was well done. I like a man who thinks ahead about as much as I like lives saved."

Pyaras tried to turn air into something like speech. It took a couple of tries. "Varin's teeth! Who wants a thirty-foot fireball? Have you seen one, Specialist?"

"Felt one. Lost my eyebrows and most of my hair. Seni, did you get shot recently?"

"Uh," he said. "Yes."

"Bad luck." She grinned. "But hair grows back, right? That's not news." She pursed her lips thoughtfully. "I'd sure like to kiss you. How would you feel about it?"

He stared at her. "What?"

"Kiss you. You look like you'd be good. I'm up for bed, too, if you'll tap. It's Descent night, and a rock roof's safer than a blanket."

He flushed hot from head to foot. Just look at her—could it be that simple? He swallowed hard and offered his bracelet. "Yes."

She pushed up her copper rings, tapped, and when the lights flashed, broke into a wide smile. "To life! Come here, you."

Pyaras bent down. Next thing he knew her hands had seized him shoulder and backside—she closed on him, mouth, breasts, hips, grinding her muscular body against his. Pleasure exploded through him, burning away all pain, all sense of the eyes around. He fought to match her, and for several seconds, entirely forgot to breathe.

She pulled back with a throaty chuckle. "Oh, this is going to be fun."

He couldn't even form words. Mouth open and incredulous, he gulped a breath and dived back in. The sheer power of her—she erased the entire world. He found handholds, at her waist, her bottom, and took a step forward, but it was she who climbed him. He staggered.

She spoke in his ear. "I have a place close by, where we can go."

"Go?" he panted, still grasping her, convulsively. This wasn't right. Veriga—oh gods, what if Veriga saw them? "Where?"

"Come on."

He followed her away from the Playground, in among the low buildings, around a corner or two, and in through steel double doors. Whatever this place was, it had no internal walls, only lines of lockers, and steel-framed beds all along its length; but whoever should have slept here must still be at the Descent.

Walking ahead of him, she stripped off her shirt, jingling. The sunmark spots on her dark arms and neck faded into her golden, densely muscled back—magnificent, even in the low light. He ran to touch her; she stretched back, looped a lazy hand around the back of his neck, and slowly turned against him. His heart raced. He found himself fascinated by the gradient sunmarks at her collarbone.

"Distracted tonight?" she asked, pulling off her jingling bracelets.

He said, hoarsely, the only words he could think of. "Sirin and Eyn, you're beautiful."

Her mouth pulled to one side, then opened into that irresistible grin. "Get your clothes off."

Pyaras woke to a hand on his neck, caressing slowly downward. Neck, shoulder, chest, stomach . . . leg. His body roused faster than his mind; just as he recalled who the hand belonged to, it moved upward again, grasped and pulled.

He moaned; his hips thrust upward involuntarily.

"Oo, hoo," she chuckled. "You *are* fun."

He turned his head. She was watching him in near-darkness.

Courage surged in him along with desire. "Kiss me again, then."

Her breath escaped, almost like a laugh.

"If you want," he added, or tried to—she pulled again, and the words gasped apart. He reached for her with arms and mouth, found her, thrust his tongue in deep. Her tongue pushed past his, curled behind his teeth, and sneaked under his upper lip.

He tried to pull her closer.

"Hang on," she said.

"W—hang on?"

She pulled herself higher against him, so her lips were just above his ear. "Melín."

He stroked down the arch of her back. "Mmm, Melín," he murmured.

"You?"

"Pyaras." Only when the word was out did panic hit. Oh gods, he'd told her his name! But how could he not? She'd have known he wasn't being honest. She might already know something was wrong; he'd soon see.

He squeezed his eyes shut and prayed for Sirin's luck.

"Pyaras," she echoed, thoughtful. "Pyaras—isseni, I want to have you again."

He should say no. He should leave, now, before she had time to connect that name with the latest news of leadership changes in the Division. She edged downward, into another kiss that left him gasping. Her hand rubbed up his side, and her leg swung over him. Soft damp hairs tickled his stomach.

He grabbed her hips, and lost the world again.

CHAPTER ELEVEN

Passenger

The second half of their journey felt more difficult than the first. It was hard to say exactly why. Why would the way down from the mountains bother her so much more than the way up? Was the Road so different? Why would it take so long for the haze of nausea to recede when at last they reached the flats? Thank the Twins for Yoral, who provided her with juice and foods to nibble on.

At the moment, they were in another forest, spikier and sparser than the Yrindonna forest which covered Pelismara. Yoral had most recently given her a sour candy to suck on. Della rolled the last sliver of it around her mouth, and opened the padded case that held her final purchase from the Marketplace: an oval tray with an array of miniature sculptures forming a spiral from the center to the edge.

"That's beautiful work," Tagaret said, as she set it on her lap.

She smiled. "I finally found a worthy successor to our old set." The tray was simultaneously a map of the solar system and a complete set of icons of the Celestial Family. Its dark wood had been engraved with concentric elliptical grooves, and in carefully placed cradles along their paths rested the deities, exquisite sculptures each the size of an eight-orsheth coin. Father Varin was at the center, wrought in gold, his gnashing teeth hidden in favor of his gentle life-giving smile. Mai the Right, in bronze, began the outward spiral, followed by Plis the Warrior in iron—if she rotated them just right, their armored forms faced one another sternly.

The Kartunnen she'd bought the set from had told her that each city was represented in the materials; he'd found them in raw form at the Marketplace, worked them, and then returned with the final piece to sell. Beside Plis the Warrior rested the Silent Sister, rendered in fossil-rich stone from Herketh, with Mother Elinda in Daronvel silver as her own smaller elliptical companion. Next were the holy Twins,

Bes the Ally and Trigis the Resolute, rendered in lapis and malachite from Peak. Heile the Merciful had been carved into a green beryl from Pelismara, and Sirin the Luck-Bringer into Vitett red marble. His incomparable love, the comet Eyn, traveled the only ellipse that didn't quite align with the others, and was carved in white marble from Erin. The dark wood of the tray itself came from a tree species of the Safe Harbor region.

"It's too extravagant for a conversation piece, unfortunately."

"That's all right," Tagaret said. "It's the perfect way to remember our voyage together."

"Maybe I could take one or two of the icons to talk about with the Lowers."

She replaced the tray in its box but, unwilling to hide it entirely, picked up the graceful depiction of Mother Elinda and tested the weight of the silver in her hand.

She shouldn't have. Maybe because she held the Mother of Souls, this time when the flutter hit her in the stomach, she recognized it for what it was, and dropped the icon of Elinda onto the floor with a gasp.

"Oh, merciful Heile, no!"

She had to get out.

If I screamed, maybe they would stop. Maybe I could run out the door . . .

Into what?

Struggling not to hyperventilate or throw up, she fumbled her seatbelt off and leapt for the bathroom. Oh, gods, mistake—the tiny space inside was a thousand times worse, a trap she recognized from all the times she'd filled it with vomit or blood. But how could she go back out with Tagaret there? She found a strange latch on the side wall that looked like it might be for Imbati, and pulled it.

The wall gave way, dumping her through into the baggage compartment. It was dark in here, full of cases and boxes, all strapped down so they wouldn't shift with the floater's movements. The hum of the vehicle was louder than in the main compartment. She was alone.

But not truly alone. The flutter was still there. If she could, she'd have torn it out of her with her bare hands. Instead, she sank to her knees, curled over the defective inner moon that made her a failure to herself, to her partner, to the future of the Grobal Race. She clenched her fists, shaking.

Don't pretend you're a child. I know what you are, traitor: nothing but blood and death. Like last time. Like every time, year after year after year.

Light sliced across the darkened space. A soft voice spoke.

"Mistress, I'm here."

She tried to speak, and almost choked. "Y-Yoral . . ." She tried again. "Yoral, I'm—" The words dissolved on her tongue and turned into a moan.

"I know, Mistress." He went to one of the stacked cases, opened it, and pulled out a small device the size of his hand.

"You know?" She should have realized; he always knew.

"Months already. Are you in distress?"

Distress, yes, but what he meant was—horrors flashed through her mind, and she clenched her teeth against nausea—not this. "No. I felt movement, that's all."

"May I perform one brief check?" Yoral asked. "I'll omit the ones Bestao took care of."

She gulped a deep breath. "Yes."

Della braced one hand on a luggage rack, and lowered her trousers enough for him to press the device against her stomach. It emitted a soft pulsing sound that cut into the floater's hum.

"Thank you, Mistress," he said.

"Yoral, you can't let them order me into a bed," she said. "You can't let them drug me."

"I can see no reason for us to consider this an emergency," Yoral said. "Besides, at the moment, that would be difficult."

She almost laughed—almost. "Well, but we won't be in a floater forever." A new dimension of the nightmare hit. "Heile have mercy, we'll be in Selimna!"

A vision of Tagaret flashed into her mind, shy-eyed, saying, *No one has children in the provinces. The two of us will be enough.*

"Sirin and Eyn help me."

Yoral was silent for some time. Finally he said, "Mistress, you are not known to the Selimna Society. They won't expect anyone to have traveled in your condition."

"But what if—" She shook her head. "No; they have hospitals in Selimna. Of course they do. When we need them."

"Excellent ones, Mistress. There is no law against having a child in the provinces."

She shook her head. *It's not a child.* "So we won't tell anyone, not a soul, unless we have to." He knew better than anyone what would happen if people found out.

Yoral bowed. "My heart is as deep as the heavens. No word uttered in confidence will escape it."

She didn't want to return to the main floater compartment. She'd rather climb out of her own skin. Nevertheless, she allowed her Yoral to help her onto her feet. To lead her back through the bathroom. To lead her back to her seat.

She couldn't bear to look at Tagaret. She would have to tell him. How could she possibly tell him?

"You're safe, Lady," Yoral said quietly. "I'm sorry this voyage has made you so anxious."

"Th—thank you, Yoral." By the time she'd said his name, her voice worked almost normally.

Yoral seated her again, and she pulled the seatbelt across herself, swallowing hard at the way her belly curved over the strap. Why hadn't she noticed before?

No, don't panic again . . .

She focused on breathing evenly. One breath. Two.

"I love you," Tagaret whispered. His arm found its way around her shoulders. Bless him, he didn't ask any questions.

Every time, it was worse. One more restriction, one more humiliation, the price she paid rising higher and higher so maybe this time she'd keep the pregnancy. And while she lay supine under doctor's orders, she could only watch Tagaret's agony for her at war with his hopes—hopes that inevitably ended up torn in bloody fragments.

The one time she'd got close, there had been nothing human to keep.

Here she was, soon to arrive in their new city, and desperate to run away. She laid her hand gently against her stomach.

Movement does not mean soul, small thing. Mother Elinda has turned her back on me. Nothing you can do will make me hope.

CHAPTER TWELVE

A Lesson

W*here am I?*

Noises had awakened him, and even with eyes closed, he remembered that the answer was a very, very bad one. Clomping footsteps; people moving. Whatever he did, he'd have to do it carefully. He cracked his eyes open just enough to see an Arissen walk past his feet. Another lay sleeping in the neighboring bed.

Melín was gone.

Pyaras tried to breathe. *Don't panic. Pretend everything is normal.* He sneaked a hand off the side of the bed, and felt awkwardly for his clothes on the floor.

Slowly, he sat up, keeping the sheet draped over his lap. He pulled Veriga's shirt on over his head, found his underwear and Veriga's pants, Veriga's handkerchief, his watch. Nothing was missing. The watch read seven o'clock forenoon, and he felt like he'd been pummeled with a club. He tried to rub his face with his hands, but it hurt too much.

A nearby Arissen laughed aloud.

Oh, gods, he had to get out of here—his face was probably as red as Veriga's handkerchief. He slipped his feet into his shoes, and stood up. There were still plenty of empty beds in the hall, as well as a large number of sleepers. He tried to walk as they did, casually, but his breath felt too shallow.

"Well, Melín's Descent lottery has a winner," a man commented, smirking. "I see you wore your dress shoes for the occasion."

A woman nearby added, "Seni, consider yourself lucky you can still walk."

Oh Mother Elinda, take me now.

At last, he reached the exit door. The only problem was, he was right in the middle of the buildings, still surrounded by Arissen, with only the vaguest memory of how he'd gotten here. He didn't dare ask the way, but when he reached an intersection, he glimpsed the giant stone curtain. That meant he should turn over this way . . .

He wandered until he reached the edge of the Arissen neighborhood. The sight of the fields was a relief, and the road to the rampway clearly marked. If only he could have run. His throat ached with thirst. Down the rampways he kept hold of the railings, because they were cool on his hands, and because his feet kept stumbling.

He was about ready to collapse by the time he turned into Veriga's street on the third level. But he had to hold it together—what if Veriga's Arissen neighbors glanced up when he passed their windows? Before he could reach the house, Veriga burst out the front door and ran up the sidewalk. The police officer grabbed his head and looked him in one eye, then the other.

"Varin gnash you, Pyaras!" he hissed. "Get inside."

Pyaras hustled the last distance in Veriga's hard arm, and turned into the house. Toeing off his shoes automatically, he mumbled, "I want to lie down." The rugs on the floor looked awfully comfortable.

"No, you don't," Veriga growled, and dragged him into the kitchen, where he sat him down on an aluminum chair. There was large glass of water on the table. "You're going to drink that water. The entire glass, this instant."

"All right." Pyaras reached for the glass, but Veriga grabbed the handkerchief, and it cut into his neck. "Ow!"

Veriga tugged again, and this time the handkerchief came off. "Drink!"

He drank. It tasted funny, like medicine, but it soothed his rough throat, and cooled his stomach. "Thank you."

Veriga scowled. "If you're planning to throw up, the bathroom is over there." He pointed.

Pyaras shook his head. "I don't think so." He'd hardly drunk a thing; this bruised exhaustion was something else entirely.

"Fine." Veriga slammed a plate of bread and fruit down in front of him, so hard that one of the rolls bounced off onto the aluminum surface of the table.

"Veriga," Pyaras mumbled, through a mouthful. "I'm really sorry. I learned my lesson. It's all right, though—nobody found out."

"I certainly hope you're right," Veriga growled. "The lesson *I* learned was that if I stop trying to protect you from your own stupidity for a single second, whatever consequences come to you will be nothing compared to those for me and everyone else. Do you realize neither of us has slept all night?"

Oh, Heile have mercy—what was he thinking? Veriga was the last person who should have been serving him breakfast! "Where's Jarel?"

"Varin's flaming asshole!" Veriga flung up his hands.

"Veriga, I'm sorry, I'll never do it again."

"Not if I have anything to say about it! How Imbati put up with your behavior I'll never know. She's in the loft."

Pyaras pushed back from the table, aching. The food and water helped. He walked out of the kitchen and considered the wall. This was part of his punishment, no question. He climbed up, slowly. His hands throbbed, and his limbs shook, but he made the top.

Jarel was sitting on top of Veriga's weapons locker, back flat against the wall, her eyes cast aside. Evvi sat at her feet, head resting on her knee. Jarel's face looked strange, as if she'd been crying. But Imbati never cried. No wonder Veriga was so angry.

"Jarel," Pyaras said. "I was remiss."

"Yes, sir," she whispered. "You were."

"I swear, as Mai the Right is my witness, I'll never treat you with such disrespect again."

She only looked at him, silent. After a long moment she took a deep breath. "Let's get you clean and back into your proper clothes, sir. I'm pleased to see you escaped unscathed."

For a guilty instant he heard Melín's voice again, murmuring into his ear. "Pyaras . . ."

He hadn't escaped at all. What a mess—it would be a miracle if Veriga ever spoke to him again.

CHAPTER THIRTEEN
A Nobleman's Tool

Adjunct duty was all about the weight. Weight of the lamp helmet on her aching head. Weight of dark, that only ever made her wish harder for sunblast. Weight of dragging a duty-partner around in case one of them fell in a crack. With the way memories kept flashing in her eyes—bright fire, cold velut, delicious night—it was a possibility. Melín kept a hand outstretched. This tunnel section dripped on them constantly, and Fourth Luun could only talk about targetball. *Gnash it, I'm trapped in a stinking penalty box.* Her head hurt, and her thighs twitched.

"Melín, sir. You hear me, seni?"

"What?" The front edge of her lamp gave off a cluster of drips.

"Seni." With obvious exasperation. "*Who's* your *team?*"

Just watch if she tried to avoid an answer. She sighed. "Pelismar Cave-Cats."

"Gnash the Cats!" He went serious. "Sir."

She snorted. "Are you from the provinces, then? You don't sound it." The tunnel narrowed, and she had to climb over a clammy knob of rock to get through. She managed not to catch her blade handle on the ceiling. "Watch your head."

"My father's from Herketh, sir. On the other hand, seni, if the Cats hadn't tied last week against the Thunderers, I would have missed the start of the playoffs on barracks, and, seni! Imagine Cats hosting Herkethi for the championship? Match of the decade! Everybody will be there!"

She shrugged. "Plis knows I'll probably be there, too. I mean, I can't follow targetball from surface rotation, but I do like it. Makes underground rotations less boring." At last they left the drippy section. The light of her headlamp showed a stone cascade where the loop portion of the route started; shinca light showed in the right-hand passage. The minute she ducked into it, though, she caught the smell.

This was not shaping up to be a good day.

"What about wrestling, sir?" Luun halted at her shoulder. "Ugh, *seni!*"

Melín activated her radio. "Team Four to Station."

"Sir, wait. We don't even know what it is."

"It's carrion, Luun. Akrabitti burnouts." Smell that mix of decay and smoke once, and you'd never forget it.

Luun made a face. "Here I thought trashers smelled bad *before* . . ."

The radio beeped. "This is Station."

"Asher cleanup team needed on the Three-Shinca route. First shinca beyond the split."

"Understood, Team Four."

When she'd signed off, she went to resume walking, but Luun grabbed her arm. "Seni, is that like drugs or something? Hand and Captain won't be happy if you're wrong."

"Go look if you like. You won't find drugs, though. Burnouts are more like suicides than overdoses—have you ever seen a wysp lurer die, up top?"

He shuddered. "Yes."

"Well, it's like that. Except undercaste." Off he went, nose in his elbow. She wasn't about to tell him how much it scared her to see wysp deaths underground, where wysps were supposed to be safe. At least it was only ever the burnouts, and only ever trashers. Let the ashers deal with their own.

Luun was back quickly. In the light of her headlamp, he looked ill. "Heile's mercy, there were two, in the cave pocket right beside the shinca. A tunnel-hound already found them. You're right, I never want to see that again."

A sound of scraping, and boots, came from behind them in the tunnel. Melín turned. "Arissen! Identify yourself."

"Second Berios, sir." Following the voice up the tunnel was a tall man who would get headaches from adjuncts quite directly if he wasn't careful. "First Melín, you're relieved. Report to Captain Keyt." His nose wrinkled in disgust. "Burnout?"

"Already reported; we were about to move on," she said. "Fourth Luun can give you the details. And I hope you like targetball."

As she turned back toward Station, she could hear Fourth Luun ask, "Second Berios, sir, seni, who's your team?"

Not that she minded backing out of four damp hours with Fourth Luun, but a summons from Captain didn't sound good. It was twenty minutes' climb and squeeze to get back to the ring road at the edge of the city-caverns. She crossed and entered the concrete cube that was the local access point station.

The officer at the door said, "Specialist Melín, Captain's waiting for you."

"Thank you."

No, not good at all. She marched down between the coordinators' desks and knocked on the captain's glass door. Captain Keyt waved her in.

Melín stepped in and saluted. "Specialist First Melín, sir, reporting as requested."

"Good morning, Specialist." Captain's voice was stern. "Please, take a seat."

"Yes, sir." Melín sat at the front edge of the nearest chair. Headache buzzed behind her eyes; the twitches in her thighs made her itch to move. She kept her back as straight as her blade.

"I've been informed that you've received a summons to tribunal. A complaint has been lodged against you by Eighth Helis of the Eminence's Cohort after an incident at last night's Descent. At nine sixteen afternoon, do you recall?"

Oh, gods, the wysp fool? She clenched her teeth, but answered, "Understood, sir."

Captain's dark eye glanced down at the paper in front of her, then up again. "The complaint states that you assaulted a soldier of the Cohort and stole his weapon."

That lying piece of carrion!

"Specialist Melín, you know I value your work in my cohorts," said Captain. "If you want to explain this incident, I'm listening."

She wrestled the fury down. "Yes, sir. Thank you, sir. I had stepped out of the Descent. I heard Eighth Helis talking in line for weapons check. He was bragging to his friends that soldiers of the Eminence's Cohort didn't fear wysps and knew how to kill them in one shot."

Captain Keyt raised her eyebrows, stretching the scar tissue where her right eyelid used to be.

Huh. This place was fancy. Talk about Grobal whims.

White marble arches imitated the shinca branch-pattern across the ceiling over her head, and three brass tables had been placed below: two facing each other across the room, and the third in the safest position, directly by the shinca trunk at the far end. Did they think someone might take a shot at the arbitrator? No; Grobal had arranged this, and that was Specialist thinking. Near the deep-silled windows on her right sat Eighth Helis, bruised and obviously hung over—from the drink, or the blow to the jaw, or both—with the commander of the Eminence's Cohort.

"Commander Abru doesn't look pleased," Captain Keyt murmured. She took the chair facing the commander, leaving Melín to sit opposite Helis. The monitor sat on her right, and gave a resigned smile that twisted across a scar on his lip.

This whole accusation was a sham. And because of Helis, Captain now had doubts about her honesty. *Gnash it.*

Melín sat for long minutes, resisting the urge to rub her thighs under the table. Eighth Helis tried several times to whisper to Commander Abru, but he obviously wasn't having it.

Finally, the hearing arbitrator came in. A bronze medallion hung at the neck of one's red robes, and one was carried by a black-suited Imbati under each arm. If not for the Imbati, the arbitrator would most likely have been in a skimchair.

Honestly, if this hearing had been at all sensible, it would have been held in a station outside the grounds, and one wouldn't have had to be carried at all. Stupid Grobal and their whims—and their stairs. The Imbati knew they weren't wanted, though, and left through a side door once the arbitrator was seated.

One scanned the papers on one's table, then lifted a transparent block of polymer from a silver tray and set it down again with a bang.

"I call this hearing to order. Arbitrator Demni presiding. In the matter of Eighth Helis of the Eminence's Cohort, claimant against defendant Specialist First Melín of the Pelismara Division, is the claimant present?"

Eighth Helis and Commander Abru both stood. "Yes, Arbitrator," said Helis. "I am Helis."

"Claimant's representative?"

"Abru, sir, Commander of the Eminence's Cohort."

"Is the defendant present?"

Melín stood up. "Yes, Arbitrator. I am Melín."

There was a soft click, off to her right. When she glanced over, the main hall doors were opening again. She focused on the arbitrator.

"Defendant's representative?" the arbitrator asked.

Captain Keyt stood. "Keyt, sir, Captain under Commander Tret of the Pelismara Division."

Footsteps. She couldn't help another glance: a Grobal was walking straight up between the tables. He was tall and spindly, backed on one side by an Imbati man and on the other by a sunmarked woman in the orange uniform of the Eminence's Cohort.

Ah, now, *this* was the guy with the whims. The way he looked around, it was clear he had no patience for anyone in the room.

"Heir Nekantor," said the arbitrator. "We are in session."

"I know that."

Commander Abru saluted him. "We're honored by your presence, sir." He kicked Eighth Helis, who attempted to match his commander's salute but started trembling.

Plis' bones, she wouldn't have expected that. To turn away from the arbitrator was bad manners; to speak out of turn was against protocol. But it was also bad manners for this arrogant ass to have walked in here at all. The things Grobal managed to get away with!

Melín shared a glance with Captain Keyt; maybe out of caution, Captain saluted, so Melín joined her. The monitor did the same.

The Heir made a slicing gesture with one hand. "Word has reached the Eminence that a member of our Cohort had his weapon stolen last night," he said. "Unacceptable. He has sent me to set it right."

"Heir Nekantor, sir," said Arbitrator Demni. "The purpose of this hearing is to determine the events that occurred last night, and whether action needs to be taken."

"Of course action must be taken!"

"Please, sir. We haven't yet had time to establish the facts of the situation, if you'd just—"

"Did you, or did you not, have your weapon stolen?" The Heir stalked to Eighth Helis, and pointed in his face. "The Eminence wants to know."

Melín managed not to snort, *Oh, does he really?* Too dangerous to speak, but Helis was an Eighth. Why would the Eminence care what happened to him at all, much less while he was off-duty? And hey, maybe the Eminence didn't—but the Heir quite obviously did. Walking in here in complete disregard of the arbitrator's authority, cutting through protocol as if Mai's justice were nothing but underbrush before a blade . . .

"Sir," said Eighth Helis, still trembling, "I was just standing in line for the, for a party. She came out of nowhere, punched me in the face and took my weapon."

It wasn't a punch, you toad, it was an elbow. My fingers are too valuable.

"Is that the full extent of your claim, Eighth?" the arbitrator asked.

"Never mind," said the Heir. "It doesn't matter. He lost the weapon, or he wouldn't have reported it stolen in the first place. The Eminence's Cohort can't tolerate such irresponsible behavior. Arissen Helis, you are hereby expelled. Go find another job."

Eighth Helis broke salute, and took a step backward. "Sir?"

"Please, sir, wait," the arbitrator protested.

The Heir turned away as if he hadn't heard. He looked at Melín.

Plis' balls, this guy was something else—that was a look no one should ever be fool enough turn their back on.

"What's your name, Arissen?" the Heir asked.

"Specialist First Melín of the Pelismara Division, sir."

"Arissen Melín, come with me."

She stared at him. "Sir?"

The Heir smiled, an alarming expression. "You've exposed a weakness in our Cohort. I'm grateful to you, and you'll be rewarded. Come."

Melín glanced desperately at Captain Keyt, whose eye had widened. Captain gave a tiny shake of the head, but nudged her and whispered, "Go. I'll speak to Arbitrator Demni."

Plis help me. "Yes, sir," Melín said.

The Heir turned on his heel and left the hall. The Imbati man and the Cohort woman fell in behind him as if it were natural; Melín ran to keep up.

Holy Mai, don't let them punish her for abandoning a tribunal under a Grobal's orders . . .

"Arissen Melín," the Heir said. "You're to take orders from Karyas until I say otherwise."

No, no . . . "Yes, sir."

"Karyas, take her to the Ring. We'll meet you there."

"Yes, sir."

Gods, the Ring? That was where she'd fought her certification bouts to finish up at Norendy Arissen Academy—they meant her to *fight?*

It wasn't the first time she'd been grateful for her combat instructor at Norendy, who'd punished her pinpoint-shot flippancy with hours of extra training. It had helped her against bullies before. But it had never before seemed likely to save her life.

Down the twisting stairs Karyas marched, and out onto the grounds; Melín could only follow, dragged by an order as if on a string.

The Ring was close to the Residence Stations, but not close enough that anyone there might conveniently intervene. If she was really lucky, there might be students there practicing for their bouts . . .

Nope, not lucky. Today the Ring was silent. Inside the curved metal wall, not a single student sat on the spectator benches, or practiced on the sandy circle; and not a soul sat along the low wall around it, nor in the roofed section with the fancy Grobal chairs.

She knew what a trap smelled like.

Melín watched Karyas. The older woman was taller, with smooth sunmarks of faded brown. Beatable, if they fought by the rules, but that wasn't guaranteed. Maybe the Heir wasn't planning to show up at all, just to let Karyas play until she was satisfied. Some reward. Better hope someone was coming, that time would make a difference.

"So, seni," Melín said. "Were you Division?"

The woman bared her teeth. "Call me First Karyas."

"Understood, First Karyas."

"You Specialists have a lot of pride."

Ah, that explained some things. Melín had heard that line before, plenty of times. When she heard it from mates in the Division, she knew not to answer. Bet you anything Karyas had gone out for Specialist training, and failed. *Got some resentment to work out, do you?*

"Well, pride won't help you here. In the Cohort, favor is our coin, which you're going to have to earn."

"Understood, First Karyas." But she wasn't going to fight until she had to.

"Don't play dumb. The earning starts now. Take off your blade and coat and give them to me."

My ass. If Captain were here, or if she weren't here on a Grobal's order, she would have refused. "Yes, sir."

Slow it, slow it. She removed her rank pin with care, tucking it into her pocket. She unbuckled the strap of her blade, breath measured, skin tense. She caught Karyas shifting stance, and quickly interrupted.

"If favor is coin, First Karyas, then how do you spend it?"

"Hurry up, gnash you. It doesn't matter. Right now, you don't have dirt."

Hurry? So maybe the Heir *was* coming—someone must be. Melín took a strategic step back as she held the blade out, hanging from its strap. Karyas swiped it from her hand. Melín ran her tongue along the edge of her teeth. When she took off her jacket she moved fast, because she was *not* having her hands behind her back while the person in front of her held a blade. *Not just any blade,* my *blade . . . gnash you, Karyas, I'm getting that back.*

Raucous laughter exploded somewhere just outside the Ring wall. Footsteps came closer. Saved?

Maybe not. A group of mates sauntered in, but they weren't students. They were adults in orange uniforms, who looked at her like they'd found her on the bottom of a boot. Too many of them for this not to be a setup; there were seven. One more, and they'd make a cohort.

Oh, Plis help her, these were Eighth Helis' mates. *They've been told I got him fired. They're going to kill me.*

"She's all ready for you, Crenn," Karyas sneered, tucking the jacket and blade underneath her arm. "She's a fancy Specialist."

"Shouldn't be too hard to break in," the broadest of the men chuckled.

Break in? Gnash it, no way—did they think she'd just been reassigned in Helis' spot?

Varin's teeth and wysp-fire, *had* she just been reassigned? As an Eighth in the Eminence's blasted hound's-ass Cohort? From Crenn's smirk, she would guess that was a yes. The constant glance-checks he got from the others indicated he was Cohort First.

She'd show them she didn't live for her bolt rifle. "Well, Crenn?" she asked. "Have you decided? Are you breaking me in, or not?"

The big man's nostrils flared, and he smirked at her. "You don't deserve it. This is an honor cohort; we worked to get where we are."

"Did you, now?" What was an honor cohort? The Eminence's Cohort had been expanding for years, but had they also established new rank distinctions?

"Fifth, you go first."

A woman stepped forward. Every last one of this eight was taller than her—all with shaped citydwellers' haircuts—but this woman was closest to her size, pale, dark-haired, and built like a whip. "Hey, seni," she said under her breath. "I'm Sahris."

"All right." Melín backed onto the sand, shifting weight left to right. The sound of her feet on the sandy ring brought back hours of one-on-one instruction in humility. Don't underestimate the opponent. Fight hard; fight clean.

Sahris tried a punch. Didn't pull it back fast enough; Melín closed and grappled her. She tried to pull Sahris backward and down, but with her other hand, the woman grabbed Melín's arm across her chest, and pinched a nerve.

Gnash it!

Pain forced her into a partial release, but Sahris' punching hand was still extended. Melín grabbed her wrist and bent it back over her shoulder. Rather than let her break it, Sahris fell. She landed on her side and sensibly slapped sand.

They separated. Melín stood up, brushing sand from her hands.

Someone started clapping, slowly.

She looked around. The Heir had arrived. He sat, tense as a spider, in the centermost of the fancy chairs, shaded by the roof that prevented drips from above. His servant stood at his left shoulder. Karyas had taken her place at his right.

"Well done," the Heir said. "You'll be quite an asset. Tell me, do you have any betting debts?"

She stared at him. "No, sir." She didn't tell him to go and die in a hole, which was a victory in itself. But now she knew precisely the hole *she* was in: its name was Pelismara. Reassigned by the Heir, stuck underground in a pointless guard cohort that was bound to hate her. One fight down, six to go, and if she didn't make a good impression, they'd never stop harassing her.

"Why don't you fight me, Crenn?" she asked. "Afraid you might lose? Got to let six mates tire me out before you dare?"

The Heir chuckled.

Crenn crossed his meaty arms. "Second Fetti," he growled. "You're up."

This guy was bigger, heavier. He had reach on her, and she didn't like the glance he shot at Crenn, like they'd reached some kind of agreement.

"This is for Helis," he said.

Speed would have to be her strategy here. She let him circle for a few seconds. He tried for a punch, missed. No overcommitment, though. He lunged. Melín aimed a sweep at his knee, but he was faster than he looked. In a blink he trapped her leg, one hand above her knee and one below.

Gods, no, that wasn't a legal hold—*Mai help me!*

Melín flung herself backward. Sand or sweat slipped his hands down her leg, but just as she was about to slip free he wrenched. Pain exploded in her ankle. She hit the ground, rolled, came up, tried to stand on the foot—gods!

Bam!

A shocking blow sent her flying sideways. By the time she'd figured out it was a kick, she'd already slammed out on her back on the sand, gasping for air.

Now he could pin her instantly—but for some reason, he didn't. He grinned down at her while she struggled to breathe.

Remember, Melín, if you're down, you can still fight.

"You deserve this," Fetti said. She caught her first real breath, but stayed limp and watched him take one more step closer. As his leg swung forward she kicked upward, driving her good foot into the soft spot between his legs, a classic club-the-fish. Fetti howled and collapsed in a ball on the sand.

Get up now, while he's down.

She couldn't actually get up, only managed to scramble at him hands-foot-knees. She grabbed the arm she could reach and yanked it straight backward, shoved her knee in between his shoulder blades, and pushed him face-down into the sand. With his arm locked in this position, it would be easy to wreck his shoulder, just like he'd intended to wreck her knee.

"Tap out, you cheating piece of carrion," she said.

"Eat dirt, snake."

She leaned forward until the joint gave. Now suddenly he was interested in slapping sand.

Slowly, Melín got to her feet. Every other step was a knife up her leg, the ankle able to take her weight, but only just. And she was still in trouble—the Heir had a disturbing expression on his face, somewhere between fascination and delight. Crenn gave a furious snarl.

"Get her."

The rest of the cohort jumped for her all at once. No question now of resting her injury, or of what was legal. A big woman came at her—she ducked a heavy swipe, leapt up and open-handed her in the ear. Another one, from the side this time. Melín pivoted sideways—pain stabbed up her leg—braced lower, and grabbed the woman's hips, swinging her around and straight into a man coming the other way. The helmet-on-helmet crash echoed off the cavern roof; they fell under the feet of the last man, who tripped and toppled forward. Melín slid forward on her good foot, bent her elbow and slammed it up underneath his chin. She re-balanced as he fell, checking for more adversaries. Ear-slap woman had started to turn as if to charge again, but Sahris put one hand on her arm, and she stopped, shaking her head.

No one was coming at her anymore. Three of them were on the ground, and at least one of those would have a hard time getting back up. She, meanwhile, was hurt. As bad as the pain was now, it would get a thousand times worse the minute she stopped fighting. Melín hopped awkwardly to face the First.

"Not happy till you've seen me taken apart, Crenn?"

"Stop," the Heir said, before Crenn could answer. "I've seen enough. Go home, all of you."

"Yes, sir," Melín spat, between panting breaths.

Luckily, the others were saying it, too.

The Heir gave her another one of his alarming smiles. "I'll be keeping my eye on you, Melín. Impress me, and there will be benefits, not only for you, but for your family as well."

Go die in a hole. Panting heavily, she forced herself to reply, "Thank you, sir." Maybe his attention would keep them from trying to dismember her every chance they got. Maybe it wouldn't.

"So? What are you all waiting for?" The Heir flung himself up from his chair, and stalked away. Karyas followed him, keeping pace, but his Imbati man hung back. The message was clear: don't disobey me while I still have eyes on you. When she and the expressionless Imbati were alone in the Ring, Melín finally dared to turn and hop to the edge of the sand. She always carried injury tape in her jacket pocket, but First Karyas had stolen it, so she tried the door of every locker along the inner wall. By Sirin's hand, she eventually got lucky.

She sat down on the low wall, removed her boot, and taped her throbbing ankle as tightly as she could. Then she shoved her boot back on and limp-hopped to the exit.

Plis knew how she managed to get home. Hopping, limping, hurting, *get home just get home just get home.* She dragged her body up two level rampways with both hands on the brass rails, never pausing more than a few seconds because if she stopped, she'd probably spend the entire night right here on the pedestrian stairs.

She couldn't say when exactly nightfall had come.

She was almost to her own dark neighborhood when a familiar figure came running toward her through pools of streetlight. She should call to him, but all she managed was a moan.

"Drefne . . ."

Drefne put his hand on her shoulder, and she nearly fell over. He scooped her up in his arms. She yelped in pain.

"Varin's teeth, Melín, what happened to you? We expected you an hour ago. Where's your coat? Where's your blade? Aripo's frantic—I was too worried to go home. I've been searching the whole neighborhood."

"Gods—isseni—" At least she didn't have to keep going any more. She leaned her head into his shoulder. "Home."

She couldn't relax completely. Pain spiked with every step he took. He maneuvered her carefully in the apartment door, calling, "Aripo, quick. Melín's hurt."

Thumping came from the main room, and swearing.

"Get her some ice." Drefne's low voice vibrated through his shoulder into her ear. "Her ankle's bad."

Aripo's voice floated higher, harder to catch words.

"What do you mean you don't know where it is?" Drefne demanded. "*I* know where it is. Get her some water, then, I'm putting her on the bed."

The bed was softer than Drefne, but didn't hold her nearly as well. Aripo came in—Twins, it was good to see her—lifted her with one big arm behind her neck, and gave her water.

"Isseni," Melín sighed. "I had the worst day."

"Varin's teeth," Aripo spat. "I'm going to break somebody."

"I already broke him."

"Good girl."

Drefne came in with three bags of ice, lifted her leg up on pillows, and packed her ankle in them. Pain throbbed with her heartbeat.

"Medicine?" Aripo asked.

"She's got some," answered Drefne. "Locker in the bathroom, top shelf."

"You stay where you are," Aripo told her, totally unnecessarily. "Gnash it, I need to pay better attention to where things are in this place."

". . . since you live here as much as I do," Drefne put in.

"Ha!" Aripo replied. Even just walking out the door, she strode with magnificence and power. If only she'd been at the Ring this afternoon—she outweighed Drefne, and would have outmuscled Fetti easily, and Crenn too.

Aripo came back with the medicine, which Melín gratefully swallowed. While they fussed over her, her muscles slowly unknotted. She'd always worried how they would get along—this would have been marvelous if not for the pain.

"How bad is it?" Melín asked. "Can you tell?"

Aripo bent down and kissed her. "Hmmm, wish I could say."

"Don't think we'll really know until tomorrow," Drefne said. "Should I stay over?"

Trigis and Bes, she wanted him to. To sleep between them would be the safest place she could imagine. But this was already more than she'd ever asked of them.

"I'm all right now, isseni," she said. "I can tell Aripo where everything is."

Drefne chuckled a little. "Sense of humor's coming back, I see." He found her hand and squeezed it. "But I'm going to make sure you see a medic tomorrow."

"Yes, sir."

When he was gone, Aripo carefully climbed into bed alongside her. "Holding you now," she announced.

"Give it a try." The warmth and weight of Aripo's arm over her stomach was the best thing to happen to her all day.

"You want me to break somebody, you just tell me, isseni, all right?"

"You couldn't break the guy who really deserves it," Melín sighed.

"Why not?"

"Grobal."

"Spineless fishes."

"Worry about it tomorrow," Melín said. "That's what I'm going to do."

Plis only knew, tomorrow there would be plenty to worry about.

CHAPTER FOURTEEN

Welcome to Selimna

Oh, blessed Eyn, deliver us from the sky. Take us down.

Down, to safety.

Down, to new hazards.

Della looked out the window. Beside the Road ran the river Arzenmiri, a small but fierce waterway nothing like the enormous river Ordala, or Pelismara's well-controlled river Trao. She studied the draping plants at its edge, the flash of light from its waters, the stones and the places where the water turned white. The road inclined alongside the river, and walls rose up on either side of them. Now it was a ravine. There was a waterfall. Then another, and now it was a canyon. Before long, the bright sky persisted only in a narrow gap above, while the canyon cupped them like a pair of hands.

On the other side of the river, rock formations bulged out of forest and reeds, dripping down into the fast-moving waters.

Della forced herself to think about the task ahead. Without the executive power they had counted on, it wasn't going to be easy. Nekantor should have appointed Tagaret as Alixi, not Unger. Tagaret had discussed it with him many times. Had the assassination attempts forced Nekantor to change his mind? Surely not. Nekantor never gave in to pressure; he didn't even give in to good advice.

Mai's truth, he'd accepted her suggestion far too easily.

There had to be hope here, too, however—for others, if not for herself. In the unbalanced time before the Fifth Family solidified its hold, there should be room for action.

"I can do this," she said. She looked at her Yoral. The shape of his tattoo hinted at sadness, but he didn't put his thoughts into words.

"Of course you can do this," said Tagaret. "We can do this together."

I have to tell him. How can I tell him?

The urge to *do something* filled her all over again. Whatever they did here, she would have to act while her health was still stable. *Soon,* she promised. *The moment we arrive.*

At last, blessed Eyn answered her prayers: the high walls of the canyon folded overhead into the arch of the Selimna Gate. Road and river entered the tunnel side by side. Too-harsh sunlight vanished, replaced by very yellow-looking daylights. As yet, no buildings were visible. The reflection of her face returned to the right side window, while on the left the Arzenmiri stepped down alongside them in a series of small waterfalls. She couldn't see through the wall of the drivers' compartment, but watched out her window for the tunnel to open on the city.

It did—and didn't.

The wall of the tunnel curved away from them suddenly. The river tumbled over another fall and vanished. They descended into a broad space that looked like some kind of transport hub, then leveled out into a curve to the right. It didn't reveal the city, though; the tunnel walls closed down again seconds later. Skimmers began to pass by in opposite directions, on both sides.

Strange. This roadway had the feel of a major circumference. She could have sworn it was the main city road; these were the curves on the maps in her mind. But why would there be no rampways down, only this intermittent steady descent? And why was the road entirely enclosed? She must be missing something behind her reflection in the window.

A curve pressed her against her seatbelt so strongly that she reached a hand to the wall beside her. It was a long one, too, which could only mean one thing: they'd hit the Bend. But that was the center of town. Why had they had no glimpse of the city? The road doubled fully back on itself, then meandered into another series of descending curves. A gap of light flashed by, and then another. She pressed her hand to the window and tried to see what they were. Another one—this one, at least, an opening into a well-lit area full of parked skimmers—and then another.

Finally, the tunnel walls vanished, and she gasped.

"Tagaret, look!"

The real Selimna faced them at last. Far across a gulf of yellow-bright air rose a cliff that seemed too high to fit into a city—maybe even as tall as three Pelismar city levels. It was densely packed with rectangular buildings, layered all on top of one another. The road they now traveled had a counterpart halfway up the other side of the city, which seemed to run across the roofs of the lower buildings.

She should have oriented her maps vertically.

A great many slender bridges stretched across the gulf, and transports ran up and down the city-cliff at intervals—not skimmers, but funiculars of some kind. If the floater hadn't still been moving, she'd have run to the window opposite to see how far down it went.

Then the floater followed a curve leftward, bringing the two converging cliff-sides of the city into view, and slowed to a stop.

"Sirin and Eyn," Tagaret said. "We're here."

"Thank the Wanderer for her grace." Della pulled her gloves on, released her seatbelt, and stood up. Her legs wobbled, but Yoral came and offered his arm. She took it, thanked the Kartunnen driver who opened the door, and stepped out.

The rock under her feet now was tame, not wild: a roadway of heavy stone that crossed the chasm. Beside the floater, the Residence of the Selimna Society of the Grobal rose up. Its wings stretched outward to the cliffs on either side, their carven balconies and bright windows forming a rock face almost like its own small city. That wasn't the city she cared about, though. She turned her back on it and crossed to the rail to look out.

The two sloping cliffsides of Selimna converged far below on the banks of the Arzenmiri, which looked narrow enough for her Yoral to jump across. She could see shockingly far up the river, miles maybe, before the view was lost to the Bend; and in all that space she could identify maybe twelve shinca trees. No wonder the air was so chill, and the daylight so yellow. A buzz of faraway voices and traffic floated on the air.

There had to be close to a hundred thousand people living in just the areas she could see—people she needed to talk to.

Tagaret joined her at the stone rail. He sighed, laying his gloved hand over hers. "Dear gods, we're really here."

She nodded. "It's real. Do you feel it?"

"I'm trying."

She was, too. She'd rather dive into those voices, but the movement in her stomach kicked her back into herself. *I have to tell him.* She took a breath, but the words wouldn't come.

"Noble sir, noble Lady, greetings of the day," a Selimnar voice said.

They turned around. A delegation of servants had emerged from the near doors of the Residence. It appeared they had already spoken to the floater drivers and begun the process of unloading. The Imbati who'd just hailed them was an older woman in a black silk dress and velvet cap who wore the crescent cross tattoo of the Household.

"Thank you, Imbati," Tagaret said.

"So, your pardon, noble Sir," the Imbati said, subtly smiling. "Forgive while I presume, but I believe I have made the acquaintance of your noble mother, the Lady Alixi Tamelera?"

Tagaret's face lit with a grin more delighted than Della had seen in years. "Yes!"

Della prompted, "We're pleased to meet you . . ."

"My name is Aimali, noble Lady." She bowed. "I'm the Household Director, so. If you'll allow me, I'll escort you to your suite."

"Yes, please." Della took Tagaret's hand, and they followed Aimali into the Residence. Its internal architecture demonstrated a clear nostalgia for the Eminence's Residence in Pelismara, and several prominent paintings of the capital hung on the walls. A stone alcove outside the main central hall held a fancy portrait of the Eminence Herin. Tagaret didn't slow down, but Della paused in front of it, shaking her head at Herin's grandly tilted head and brilliant smile.

"I guess I didn't need to bring a portrait, after all."

Household Director Aimali led them into a long residential corridor. The view out the windows here was not into gardens, but into a strikingly lit vista of wild river-cavern: the path of the Arzenmiri continuing beyond the city's limits. Aimali walked some distance down the hall, and then turned into the entrance of a spiral stairway. Tagaret and his Kuarmei headed right in after her.

Della had begun to follow when movement back along the hall caught her eye. An Imbati manservant was walking nearer, purposefully enough that her Yoral interposed himself between them. Beyond the unfamiliar manservant, though, a balding man with a sharp noble nose entered the hallway and vanished into one of the suite doors.

No.

That man was not supposed to be here.

She'd done no more than shiver before the unfamiliar manservant reached her. He bowed formally.

"Excuse me, Lady." His accent was fully Pelismara, striking after the speech of the Household Director. "My name is Unger's Fyani, of the Household of the Fifth Family. I'm here to inform you that my Master, the Alixi Unger, expects your attendance, and your partner's, at an official tour of the city beginning in one hour."

Della made sure to look at him, rather than staring down the hall over his shoulder. She also made sure to smile. Their travel would not have been secret, and naturally, the new Alixi would want to keep eyes on them—as they did on him. "Thank you very much, Fyani."

"Please meet us at the Residence funicular at six afternoon," the servant said. "I hope you will understand that your attendance at the tour is not optional."

Della forced her grin wider. "Oh, don't worry! We'd be delighted to attend. Now, if you'll excuse me, we've just arrived, and we have to clean up. So kind of you to include us." Sick to her stomach, she walked away quickly and entered the spiral stairway, calling, "Tagaret? Tagaret!"

"Della? What is it, love? What's wrong?"

She found him, paused on the stairs; the back of Director Aimali's dress was just visible by the central column beyond him. She would have preferred to cling to him, but she pulled him down by the shoulder and whispered in his ear.

"I think we're in danger. I just saw Innis of the Fifth Family."

Punctuality seemed the best approach to—if not engender good will, then at least deny Alixi Unger additional excuses to surveil them. Also, conveniently, a tour of the city would provide a perfect way to look for places where the caste system might not quite be working as intended. For gaps of opportunity.

Neither she nor Tagaret had caught any further glimpses of Innis, but most of their scant hour had been spent in their new suite, showering and changing clothes. His presence here could not be a good sign. If Sirin was smiling, he might only be here trying to escape from whatever retaliation Nekantor intended to bring upon him. If not, Innis might be operating on some kind of new plan. She hated thinking of him moving in places where she couldn't see.

She also hated to imagine the awful conversation with Tagaret that, somehow, she would have to initiate.

It was a blessing that they would have the distraction of going out.

Their new friend, Household Director Aimali, assigned a messenger child to show them the way to the funicular—a word, the girl archly informed them, that true Selimnai never used. "We name it the Ride, so." Her name was Xira, and she wore the same style of black velvet cap that Director Aimali had. It left her forehead uncovered, showing the Imbati child's circle of black paint between her eyebrows. She was quite willing to volunteer information, which instantly made her more talkative than any Imbati Della had ever met.

"So here, on your right, noble Lady, noble sir, is the Lady's Walk," Xira said. "Many ages ago, the Arzenmiri whorled and shaped this magnificent formation, so. Now it's a cultural center for Selimna's Kartunnen community."

Della squeezed Tagaret's arm in excitement. It was astonishing to think of the river creating this vast smooth cylinder; its walls rose at least a hundred feet high. Only a single row of stone buildings had been built along the curve at its bottom, but heavy steel scaffolding rose above it in layers, supporting less permanent shops. Here, where they were walking, they just passed through the edge of a colorful crowd. Deeper in, she could see Kartunnen painters and dancers. A painted street sign read, *The Circle.*

"Tagaret, the Circle!" she said. "Simi and Benyin were right."

"Noble Lady," said Xira, indignantly. "Nobody names it that anymore. It's the Lady's Walk, so."

"Exactly, thank you, Xira. We should definitely ask to have the sign changed. I wish we weren't keeping Alixi Unger's time tonight, or I'd stop."

Tagaret chuckled. "Darling, we live here now. We can stop by tomorrow, or the next day, or the day after that."

She couldn't help a grin. "Mai's truth, we can."

Xira left them not far from a graceful arch of braided metal that indicated the Ride stop. It was a shorter walk than she'd imagined; they were eight minutes early, and Alixi Unger's party had not yet arrived.

The Kartunnen had done beautiful work here. Pedestrians were prevented from falling into the deep, angled track by a surprisingly delicate barrier in the same style as the arch. Where the street met the barrier, a huge metal plate was embedded in the ground; the sound of their footsteps changed as they stepped onto it.

Beyond the barrier, and well below their feet, the track began to hum.

"I have so many questions," Tagaret sighed. "I wish Xira had stayed.

Ooh, what's that?" He walked to a console near the barrier, beside what looked like a maintenance stairway. "Della, it has buttons like an elevator."

"Tagaret, don't press—"

Too late. Beneath her feet, the metal plate lurched. She reached out in a panic, but Yoral was quick, and steadied her. They were going down—in seconds, the gap between her and ground level was too far to jump.

"Tagaret, what did you *do?*" It was an elevator, all right.

"Sorry . . ."

As her downward movement stopped, the funicular car rose up from the lower part of the city. It was quite big. Its decorative roof passed her position; then the empty passenger compartment, large enough for at least twenty to stand; then its floor. A second, lower compartment stopped right before her feet.

Clearly, *someone* was supposed to board here. "Tagaret," she called, stepping into the spacious bottom of the car. "Come look at this."

Tagaret hopped down the maintenance stairway and joined her. He wrapped his arms around her, warm in the cool air. Her body tingled, and she breathed in his scent. Seconds later, a hiss drew her eyes back to the elevator plate; it was returning automatically to its previous position.

Tagaret laughed ruefully. "Sorry about that, love."

She shrugged. "I survived. But look: what do you think this space is for?" She gestured around. The opening into this section of the car was nearly as wide as the car itself, and the walls were dinged and dented. "Luggage?"

"Freight, Lady," her Yoral murmured.

"Freight." She weighed the word. "Of course. If there's only one road, you have to have a way to get everything up and down the citysides."

"I suspect it's also for Akrabitti," said Tagaret.

She sighed. "That makes sense." Akrabitti were going to be so hard to reach—she hardly knew how to start looking. It was almost sad no one was here.

Footsteps resounded on the elevator plate, moving into the upper part of the funicular car. Della blushed and pressed her hands to her cheeks. That had to be Alixi Unger's party. *They're counting on us to be punctual, and here we are, exploring the freight area?*

"Arbiter Innis, get off my back," came a voice from above. "Of course I'll be signing the papers. I'm not going back to Pelismara. I deserve this."

Della looked at Tagaret, and found him staring, eyes wide. He laid a finger across his lips, and waved to his Kuarmei. The small Imbati woman moved instantly to assess the situation, creeping to one side of the freight space and peering up the side of the car.

"Gnash it, you're missing my point," Innis replied, in the nasal voice that made her shudder. They had never spoken much, even when Innis had bargained with her birth Family Council against her parents' wishes, trying to take her as his life's partner. "This isn't about whether you *deserve* an Alixi position. It's not about you or your skills. They're just fine."

"Maybe it's about you, then," Alixi Unger retorted. "You wish *you'd* accomplished so much by twenty-seven. Well, sorry. I won't give up this opportunity just to soothe the pride of my Family's Arbiter."

Innis gave an exasperated sigh. "Unger. Stop thinking so small. The Heir Nekantor sent you out here. He's also sent people to keep an eye on you. Don't you think there's a reason for that?"

Yoral touched her sleeve, and Della remembered herself with a start. He was right—they had to get out of here before Unger, Innis, or their manservants realized they'd been overheard. Kuarmei was already shooing Tagaret into the maintenance stairway on the opposite side of the car. Della scooped up her skirts and followed, with Yoral steadying her from behind.

"You forced Nekantor's hand," Unger said, while Della tried to keep her footsteps from making noise on the tight metal stairs. When she reached the top, she found Tagaret's Kuarmei indicating they should cross the narrow alley and enter the side door of a building nearby.

"I did no such thing," said Innis. "And this isn't your particular accomplishment, or Satenya's."

What does that mean? But Yoral touched her sleeve again, so she tiptoed across the alley and into a door that Tagaret's Kuarmei held open. The air inside smelled delicious and indescribable.

Their arrival caused some fluster. A round-armed Melumalai woman wearing a snug white hat and a chrysolite pendant on a silver chain gaped at Tagaret across a scratched steel counter, stammering.

"Oh! Oh, noble sir, noble Lady, the wrong—not this door—oh,

your honorable graces—Heile aid me! Please, I implore you, come this way, so." She pulled aside a plastic curtain, and ushered them into a tidy, well-appointed shop that appeared to specialize in breads. Here, the indescribable scent was so overwhelming that tears sprang into Della's eyes. A Melumalai man who looked like he must be the woman's brother bowed and apologized to them, and pressed warm, leaf-wrapped buns into their hands.

Della blinked away her irrational tears. "Thank you, we should pay you for these . . ."

"Oh, noble Lady," said the man, "No need, no need, so."

"Thank you," added Tagaret. "We'll bring you our custom another time." He opened the shop's front door decisively, and walked out into the street. Della flashed a smile at the Melumalai, and followed.

At least now they had an excellent excuse for a few seconds' delay. She was hungrier than she'd thought. But it wasn't as if she could eat this, after her reaction to the smell alone. She was *not* going to cry with food in her mouth in front of Innis.

"Tagaret of the First Family," exclaimed Alixi Unger. He'd taken a seat on one of the benches along the wall of the Ride car, his arms extended across the back and his legs crossed. He looked even younger than twenty-seven, long and lean with pale cheeks and flowing blond hair down past his shoulders. "So good of you to join us."

"Why, it's our pleasure, Alixi," Tagaret replied, bowing. He had always known how to maintain a polite façade as a form of self-defense. "Della wouldn't have missed it."

"I most certainly would not," she agreed. "Selimna is such a beautiful city." She took Tagaret's free hand in hers, hiding the bun behind her back. Her Yoral immediately plucked it away. She brushed the crumbs from her fingertips, and placed herself so Tagaret's body was between her and Innis' calculating smile.

"It's a pleasure to see you both," said Innis, though surely it was not.

"Is that *all* that brings you here, Lady?" Alixi Unger asked.

"Oh, I'm sure!" she gushed. "Alixi, I've dreamed of this place. Have you seen the Lady's Walk?"

Alixi Unger smiled—polite bafflement. "I'm not sure what you're referring to, Lady."

Uncertainty struck her. Of course, it made sense that he wouldn't know the local names for funiculars, or for The Circle. He'd just arrived, and Aimali had apparently not provided him a guide. But, if she explained, he'd surely disdain her interest in the arts of Lowers. She'd seen Tagaret receive more than enough pitying looks because of his choice of her. Not today.

"It's a fascinating district I've heard of, sir," she replied. "There are so many."

Alixi Unger nodded. "Indeed, there are. We'll be surveying them today."

And I'm going to know them better than you ever will.

A new voice said, "So, so, Lady, you're correct! So it's a perfect opportunity for a tour."

Lorman? It couldn't be! She jerked her head around. But, no—the voice was wrong, and there had been no stench of mustache wax. The man who'd just arrived was older than Innis, with a streak of white in his long black hair. He wore a blue velvet cap with a long white feather that trailed over his shoulder, and moved in a cloud of some kind of sweet leaf perfume. Hearing that same accent out of his mouth, though, was weird. There were three other men with him, all of whom wore similar feathered hats. Unger stood to greet them.

Innis excused himself.

One of the four newly arrived manservants pressed a button near the door, and the Ride started to glide upward.

The men introduced themselves as the leaders of the sub-districts of Selimna, who directed the city in the absence of an Alixi. The perfumed man was Chaile, in charge of the Up-Bend district nearest the Selimna Gate. The Bend district was run by a handsome, heavy man named Kudzina. Down-Bend, which included the Alixi's Residence, was in the care of Orindi, a golden-skinned man with frown lines who nevertheless gave Della a warm smile as he kissed her hand. The last man was Vix, who ran a district referred to as the Venorai tributary. He was pale, but had actual sunmarks across his cheeks.

By the time she'd heard the same accent out of every one of their mouths, she figured it out: Arbiter Lorman hadn't invented this. It was obviously the speech adopted by Grobal transplants to Selimna. She didn't need Imbati Xira to explain how 'real Selimnai' would feel about that. But she couldn't ever be a real Selimnai, even if she tried to learn a real Selimnar accent. What should she do to escape the Selimnai's scorn, and earn their trust?

Mai grant her good judgment to find the right way.

The Ride car passed upward for several minutes, stopping at stations where Lowers ceded them right of way and didn't bother to board. Finally, the buildings on either side of the track disappeared, and the car passed through a woven deck of metal, followed by another. The doors opened.

They walked out onto the deck. This place was up high, right against the cavern roof. She could actually see the bulky shape of the atmospheric lamps, and their light struck at an odd angle. Stalactites had been lopped into stubs above her head, so close she could reach up and feel the texture of the saw-cuts with her fingers. Tagaret was stooping cautiously.

Her stomach growled. Della crossed her arms tightly, but then her Yoral slipped something into her hand. Through her gloves, she couldn't feel what it was, but when she looked, it was a small pinch of bun. She feigned rubbing her mouth, and popped it in.

Oh, dear gods, bread was not supposed to taste so good. She blinked fast against the tears, and glanced over her shoulder, nodding. Yoral gave her another piece, and she chewed it gratefully.

"So, so. These roof transports were first built a hundred and fifty years ago," explained Orindi, rubbing his frown lines with one gloved hand, and extending the other toward the edge of the deck, where a new type of car awaited them. It had broad windows, and its body was painted all over with clouds. "So they were restored fifteen years ago, now. The paint is new last year. So they give the best view of the city."

It was weird to climb into the car, knowing that it dangled over nothing. The view from the inside was magnificent, though, and its action was perfectly smooth as it carried them gradually upslope along the cityside. The buildings below were so tightly packed that only occasional alleys could be glimpsed between them. Della spotted at least two places that looked like restaurants with seating areas on their roofs. Orindi, whose district this was, narrated the entire way, ignoring the stations they passed. Alixi Unger was either not curious enough to ask questions, or unwilling to show any weakness by suggesting lack of knowledge. "And so, you see those? The green buildings across there," Orindi said with a proud smile. "So that is the University of the Selimnar Kartunnen."

Alixi Unger didn't react.

Della swallowed a bite of bread. "What a wonderful resource."

Orindi chuckled. "So, so. They have good ideas, but they're always asking for more money." Kudzina laughed with him, but Chaile and Vix put on smiles that didn't touch their eyes. The car angled slightly left and passed through another station. Orindi sat down, and Kudzina took his place to talk about the Bend.

Kudzina was a storyteller. Not only did his delivery make the odd accent tolerable, but he made his district seem both lively and interesting. Not necessarily full of the potential she and Tagaret were looking for, though. The car's path curved dramatically here; below, the cityside curved as well, into a shape that was almost like its own small mountain, with a peak directly below them. The Alixi's Residence was no longer visible. Silver light entered the car, and they passed a large shinca trunk on the left side.

"So, now, you might think a district's night attractions might be its most famous feature," Kudzina said, and raised a finger. "We have plenty of those, rest assured. So, see the lighted tower there? You wouldn't want to miss the restaurants and dance clubs surrounding it. So we have the arena of the Selimna Thunderers. We also have the banking district, and ah, the things I could tell you about our business dealings, so, so. What's more, we have the largest, busiest, most successful medical center in the entire city."

"Really?" asked Tagaret. "Fascinating."

Chaile spoke up coldly. "Except. The Iyemmelim Medical Center is not actually in Bend. Strictly speaking, it's in Up-Bend. So, look, there, where you see the green globes."

Kudzina looked annoyed, but there was a blush on his cheeks suggesting Chaile was correct. "So it's in Bend, too."

"Two of the Center's twelve buildings are in Bend," said Chaile.

Della tried to distract the men from their disagreement. "Are you saying then, sirs, that it's a draw for people from the entire city?"

"So, so. Well, not the *entire* city," Orindi of Down-Bend put in. "So the Residence has its own medical facility, naturally."

"Of course," said Alixi Unger. "I would expect no less."

"So, Doctor Iyemmelim has treated people from every district," Chaile said.

"Including mine," said Vix.

Tagaret raised his eyebrows. "That seems quite a workload for one doctor. I imagine he has a team. He can't be in twelve buildings at once."

"Yes, well, of course," said Chaile.

The car passed into another station, and stopped. The doors opened.

Chaile indicated the open doorway. "So, so. Come out onto the deck for the best view. Vix and I will be presenting from here."

Della squeezed Tagaret's hand, and glanced up at him. He met her eyes and nodded. Stopping here meant they wouldn't get a full tour of the remaining two districts. There had to be reasons for that—best guess, those reasons would be poverty and disrepair.

The view from here was marvelous, though: it was a river confluence, lit in a familiar silvery light by several shinca trees. Traveling by the entry road, she could easily have imagined the Arzenmiri as the sole waterway of Selimna, though the maps she'd studied said otherwise. Before her now, the Arzenmiri's path curved off to the left between the citysides, and on the right side, there was a gorgeous waterfall. Water from the path of a second river at least a hundred feet above the Arzenmiri fell in a cascade that glittered in the silvery shincalight, landing in a wide zone of glowing white mists, and then continuing down via a stone chute to join the larger river below. In the shadow of an opening above the waterfall, she could just glimpse the first buildings of another section of the city.

"So, Kudzina is more interesting than I could ever be," said Chaile, "though I will draw your attention to our medical center. It has *expanded into* two buildings in Bend in recent years. So we produce labor, and we have the Mist Market, located just below us, where everything is kept naturally cool. So, so. It's a commodities market, where Venorai produce is distributed to the rest of the city, and sold for export."

"So, well, it's the natural place for a market," agreed Vix. "Just at the entrance to the Venorai tributary."

Della nodded. "Why is your district called that?"

Vix gave a blushing smile that made his sunmarks stand out even more sharply. "It's actually the Arzenmiri tributary, Lady," he said. "But, so, with all its access points to the fields, it's where all the Venorai live."

"What, *all* of them?" That wasn't good. Could a caste entirely isolate itself? That would make accessing them far, far harder. Her tone brought everyone in the car around to look at her, and all the strangenesses of her body sprang into sharp focus.

Dear sweet Heile, don't let any of them realize she was in a condition . . .

"So a small number do live in Up-Bend near the Mist Market, Lady," Vix replied.

"Oh, naturally."

Tagaret squeezed her shoulders and kindly relieved her of the group's attention. "And where do the Melumalai live?" he asked. "Do they have an extreme concentration, too?"

"Less so," Chaile answered easily. "So a great many are naturally concentrated in Up-Bend, but they are also in the Bend, and a few in Down-Bend."

"So, so. Our banking centers would not function near as well, otherwise," agreed Kudzina.

"Nor our business districts," added Orindi.

Della felt Tagaret's arm tense around her—he was about to take a risk. "And where do the Akrabitti live, then, sirs?"

She held her breath.

Alixi Unger's mouth dropped open; he was clearly too appalled to protest aloud.

Chaile, though, only seemed resigned. "So, I'll be honest. You can't keep a city *clean* without them. They are a challenge, because Akrabitti who are asked to work in the Venorai tributary often become . . . so . . ."

"So insubordinate," said Vix.

Chaile nodded. "So they're generally housed near their workplaces."

Now Alixi Unger found his voice. "They're not near the *medical* clinic, are they?"

Chaile grew cautious, and didn't meet the Alixi's eyes. He answered, "So, well, I'm not sure where all the garbage centers are located, Alixi. So, so. The crematory is in its own cave pocket not far from the Selimna Gate."

"Well, we need to find out where they are," Alixi Unger declared. "I need to understand exactly how to contain the Akrabitti and keep them away from places like the medical center."

Della's heart went cold. She held Tagaret's arm tightly. "Akrabitti get injured, too, Alixi, sir. They get sick, and need care."

Alixi Unger made a face, and cast a look at Tagaret that she'd seen all too many times: a mix of pity and disgust.

Della clenched her fists on the fabric of Tagaret's sleeve. Varin gnash Nekantor. They had always known this was going to be hard; with a new Alixi on a rampage against the Akrabitti, now it would be near impossible.

Della couldn't sleep, though fatigue penetrated to her bones. *You have to tell him.*

They had a window in their bedroom, and she was unreasonably pleased about that. Their suite was at the far end of the Residence closest to the Lady's Walk, and from here, with her elbows leaning on the stone sill, it seemed no distance at all to the upper scaffolds. No one was there to see her in her nightgown.

"Della, love?" Tagaret's voice spoke behind her, and she startled. His warm arms enfolded her. She hadn't felt the flutter in a few minutes, but she couldn't forget it—looking out the window was easier than looking at him.

"Imagine," she said. "Imagine if we could get someone to sit right there and play for us. A piper, maybe, with her legs hanging down off the end of the scaffold and her elbows on the rail."

He chuckled. "There's an idea. But I'd rather go out, I think."

She nodded. She'd rather be out there, lost in that view that went on for miles, than here inside herself. She had to tell him. What would happen when she told him?

Tagaret held her closer and kissed her hair. "The sooner we go to bed, the sooner we'll be out there in the morning."

"Tagaret?" Her voice shook on the word.

He squeezed her tighter. "Are you all right?"

Tell him. "I can't."

"You can't? Can't what?" She could hear a frown in his voice.

Fear and necessity wrestled for her tongue. She blurted, "I won't go back to Pelismara!" and started to cry. Her face twisted up and her body shook—feelings that seemed outside her, almost as if they were happening to someone else.

"No, no, sweet Della, love," Tagaret said gently. "Of course not. Of course we won't . . ."

His voice cut off. For a long moment, he didn't say anything at all. In the gap that should have been silence, her uneven sobs were unseemly, ugly. Why was she still crying?

She pressed both hands to her face, trying to press the tears away.

"Oh, gods," Tagaret breathed suddenly. "Heile and Elinda help us, are you—"

NO! she wanted to shout, but only a moan came out. She turned in his arms and buried her face in his chest. He was breathing fast, chest heaving, but he gently stroked her hair.

"We shouldn't have come," she whispered.

"Of course we should have. I want to be here with you, right now."

"It's going to be the same."

Tagaret nudged her back from him. His hand lifted and touched her hair, pushing it away from her face. "We don't know how it will be, love. But don't forget why we're here. We're here to break traditions, and if the first one we break is 'no children outside of Pelismara,' then so be it."

He sounded braver than he looked. But maybe here, in a new place, it could be different.

"I was checked at my house before we left," she said. "And my Yoral checked me, too, on the way here."

"Bless Yoral," said Tagaret. "We're so fortunate to have him."

"We can't tell anyone."

"Not a soul, I promise."

She looked up at his face, which trembled on the edge of hope and fear. "That means no visits to the Grobal medical center. But I have Yoral, and I have time to look for a doctor here. In case."

Tagaret pressed his lips together.

"I can ask Director Aimali for help finding someone."

He nodded. "Good idea."

She pressed her face into his chest again, and wrapped her arms around him. "I'm so tired."

Without letting go of her, Tagaret started backing away from the window toward the bed, which had already been turned down for nighttime. When he reached it, he climbed backward into it, keeping hold of her hand. "Of course you're tired. You've been traveling all day, and I sent you down an elevator, and we walked through an Akrabitti door into a bakery . . ."

She gave him the smile he was trying for, and climbed into bed beside him. It was different from their bed at home, but soft, with smooth sheets that caressed her skin. When she lay down, exhaling, she could feel herself sink in. There came the flutter again—she curled around it, toward him.

Don't panic. In Selimna, everything could be different.

"Can I hold you?" Tagaret murmured.

"Mm." She pulled herself so her head lay on his shoulder, and her arm across his chest. Tagaret stroked her hair, her shoulder, her side, down to her hip. It felt amazing, but the fatigue was too powerful to resist. "Sleepy."

He kissed her forehead. "All right, sleep, then."

She could do it, now that she and her secret were no longer alone.

CHAPTER FIFTEEN
Unexpected Guardians

You weren't supposed to feel alone in a classroom full of cousins. Adon struggled to keep his mind on the Schoolmaster's math lesson, while his cousin Xeref kept reaching back and writing notes on his paper, and Cahemsin kept poking his back and whispering. Safety was worth it, though. It was.

Really, it was.

He sighed, and forced his hand to copy down another triangle, another rectangle. Calculate the areas. Calculate the circumferences. Calculate the shooting angle from the classroom door to his head. Maybe he could duck under the metal desk, if it came to it? At least Xeref was in between.

"I don't know why we're learning this," his cousin Ganni drawled at Schoolmaster Churon's back—Churon was chalking up a new series of shapes that would have looked better embroidered on a velvet coat. "Math is for merchants. Are you a Melumalai?"

"*You're* a Melumalai," one of the girls snapped. "Do your work."

Cahemsin whispered, "Actually, math is for Kartunnen."

Schoolmaster Churon turned and scowled straight at Adon, hands on his hips. "That's enough. If you fail to study, Lowers who *do* know math will cheat you and make you look ignorant. Ten extra problems for everyone. Better copy them down fast before the bell rings." He started chalking a series of rectangles, triangles, and trapezoids.

"See what you've done now," Adon murmured under his breath as his pen flew. Too many cross-outs; he was going to have to write this over again on new paper, and also get ink smears washed off his gloves. Cahemsin kicked at his heels. This sort of thing was why he didn't join their gang. If Tagaret and Della hadn't left, he wouldn't have had to.

Maybe something terrible would happen, and bring them back, so that everything could start to be all right.

He checked the angle to the door again, and the bell rang. The sound zinged down his nerves. He leapt up.

No, slow down. You're going to role-play with Xeref and Cahemsin.

He forced himself to tag along as his cousins sauntered out of class and into the hall. The hall was busy with colors: lots of students bright as jewels, a few more soberly toned Schoolmasters. Orange was the unwelcome presence of extra guards beside the columns, beside the foot of the grand marble staircase that led to the second floor, and beside the classroom doors.

He should have been able to borrow a bodyguard. It made no sense for Mother to be so upset about the suggestion. If only he were older, he could hire Talabel, who was about to be certified.

They arrived just as the bronze doors of the play hall swung open. Cahemsin pushed past him, knocking his shoulder hard enough that it was easier to spin than stop himself.

"Come on," said Xeref, and ran after.

Twins help him. Adon ran to keep up, and found they'd both converged on an Imbati in a spot beneath the embroidered hanging of the Great Grobal Fyn, between two brass tables.

It was Talabel. Her golden face was carefully blank, not a single wrinkle in the cosmetic dot between her brows.

Adon tensed. "What are you doing?"

"Why shouldn't we test a top servant?" asked Xeref. "You've done it plenty of times."

"Top servant," Adon said, skeptically.

"Sure. Saved your life, didn't she?"

He flushed, and looked at Talabel again. Her normally expressive face said nothing. "She did save my life," he agreed. "Nekantor's Dexelin helped her."

Cahemsin smiled. "So that makes her special, right?"

"She's your *favorite*," said Xeref.

Adon swallowed.

"In fact," said Cahemsin, "Cousin Jorem will be turning seventeen soon. Maybe he should hire her."

"*No*." The word escaped before he could stop it.

"What? Adon, are you saying he can't hire her? All he'd have to do is write a letter."

"And turn seventeen," Adon said. "That won't be for—" He couldn't remember; too many cousins. "Well, it isn't going to happen tomorrow. *I* could hire her first."

Xeref laughed out loud. "Not likely. Your Age of Choice is four years off."

"Not if I become Heir."

"Get a bit of attention from your own brother and you start thinking you're better than us, eh?" sneered Xeref.

Cahemsin got an infuriating smirk on his face. "Hm, so you're going to arrange Herin's death, and survive everyone trying to murder you for three weeks, just for this one servant. Yeah, sure. I see what's really going on." He spat. "Imbati-lover."

"Son of a Lower!" Adon retorted.

Cahemsin slapped him across the face.

Adon kicked him in the shins. For an instant as his cousin fell, his heart filled with triumph, but then he realized Talabel had vanished. Not only that, but now everyone in the entire hall was looking at them, and here he was standing over his cousin, and Cahemsin was . . . crying?

"Adon of the First Family," said the Schoolmaster Supervisor, grasping him by the collar of his jacket, "you're coming with me."

Within moments he'd been dragged off through the vaulted stone hallway to the office. The Schoolmaster Supervisor sat him in a brass chair against the wall, and told him to stay. Then he stomped off, probably to hear from Cahemsin what had happened.

Adon stayed.

He felt sick to his stomach; his face felt hot. You weren't supposed to say such a terrible thing. Not to a cousin. Especially not when it was true.

Mother was going to be so angry.

There was a click. Adon straightened up fast, tightening gloved fists on his thighs. The main hallway door didn't open, though. A curtain on the wall beside him moved.

Nekantor's Dexelin stepped out from behind it. "Young Master Adon, please forgive me."

Adon frowned. "You've been watching me. For the last three weeks, anyway. Don't try to deny it; I can tell."

"I won't deny it, young Master."

"And now you're here because I got myself in trouble, so you can report on me to Nekantor?"

"I don't know, sir."

He knew the polite denial when he heard it. He crossed his arms. "Well, you probably are."

The servant said, "I'm sure you didn't mean to draw your cousins' attention to Talabel, sir."

Rage flashed in him again. "I certainly did not! I don't want my brother's attention on her, either. Or on me. Or on *you*, Varin gnash it! Nekantor is cruel and horrible. I see how he talks to you."

A flush reddened Dexelin's face.

Adon quickly looked away. "I'm sorry; I know it's none of my business, but I can't stand it. You deserve better than that. The Headmaster of the Academy should be giving you a medal, and instead Nekantor makes him force you into a Privilege contest."

"Young Master, where . . . ?" Dexelin whispered. "I came to ask . . ."

"Where what?"

"Sir . . . where did you learn . . . what you know?"

Adon shook his head, baffled. "What I know? I know something?"

"Never mind."

"Do you mean Nekantor is looking for some kind of information from me?"

"No, sir," the Imbati replied. "He is not."

That was a shockingly direct answer. Adon raised his eyebrows. "Well, that's good, at least. You're generous with me." He glanced at Dexelin cautiously, wondering what he could get away with.

"You . . . wish to make a request, young Master?"

Adon took a deep breath. "Dexelin, obviously you've been asked to watch me. I won't stop you. Just . . . can you let me know when you're nearby? It would be nice to know you were there protecting me." He hugged himself. "That is, if you *are* there to protect me, and not just steal my secrets."

Dexelin looked at him as if to answer, but the arrival of a hand rattled the handle of the main door. Dexelin leapt up and vanished behind the curtain.

Adon braced himself, looking down at his knees contritely. The Schoolmaster Supervisor would punish him, and he deserved it; he had to endure it.

Mother's voice drifted in as the door opened.

"I'm very sorry, Supervisor." First in the door was the leading edge of a pale blue gown, and then Mother swooped in, followed by the Schoolmaster Supervisor. She reached out her hand to him, but Adon didn't take it. He stood up and went to her left side, as close to Aloran as he could reasonably manage. "Adon's been upset ever since his brother Tagaret left, haven't you, Adon."

Adon gulped. "Yes."

"Look at the Supervisor and tell him it won't happen again."

Adon glanced up at Mother's face. She was tense around the eyes; her eyebrows were raised expectantly, her lips a firm line. Heile's mercy, going home to *her* punishment would be worse. But he deserved it; he had to endure it.

"Well?" the Schoolmaster Supervisor demanded.

Adon looked up just enough to see the Supervisor's angry, bloodshot eyes. "I'm sorry, sir," he mumbled. "It will never happen again."

Mother didn't take him home. Instead, she grabbed his forearm and dragged him out into the grounds.

Where was she taking him?

Adon tried to meet Aloran's gaze as he stumbled along, but Aloran kept his eyes studiously on Mother's shoulder.

"Mother," Adon said.

She didn't answer. Maybe she wasn't speaking to him, now. They crossed the gardens to the sound of swishing silk and crunching gravel, until they reached a small side gate.

The Arissen guards saw Mother and immediately let them out.

Once off the Residence grounds, Mother seemed to relax slightly. Her pace slowed. This was the corner of the plaza closest to the Imbati Academy, less crowded than the others, because the radius in this corner only led out toward the northern Grobal neighborhoods. The tourist crowds were thinner today. One group was looking up at the cylindrical housing of the Alixi's Elevator. Another was near the shinca, and another near the Academy gate.

Mother took a deep breath, then released his arm.

"Mother," Adon pleaded. "I'm so sorry."

"Of course you are. You weren't thinking at all."

That hurt. "I'm really sorry, I promise. Can we go home, please?"

"This is more important, love," she said. "I've been putting it off, but now I see that was a mistake. We're going to visit the Academy for a few minutes, and I need you to be on your absolute best behavior. Use your manners; you know how."

"I'm *sorry.*" Then he saw the gate wardens. "Are we invited?"

"Not yet, but we will be." Mother looked down at him and, unexpectedly, flashed him a smile. "Just think, this is where Aloran went to school."

It was, too. The thought hadn't even occurred to him when he'd been here last. The Imbati Service Academy wasn't supposed to be a building for hosting Privilege competitions; it was a school. Aloran had told him about the classes there, which had funny names like 'Hands,' or 'Types,' or 'Waiting.'

A Kartunnen toddler in a baby-sized gray coat was squatting down beside the Academy gate. Under the tolerant attention of the gate wardens, she was patting her hand on the red stone threshold below it. When her parents spotted them coming, they scooped her away.

Mother's Aloran stepped to the front, and bowed to the wardens with their diamond-within-diamond tattoos. They exchanged quiet words, and a warden ran off toward the main building.

Adon looked down at the red stone the child had been patting. There was an inscription carved into it—one barely legible at the center where feet had trodden it smooth. 'Cross this threshold with'—one or two unreadable words, and then, maybe, 'heart'?—'and the Mysteries shall be revealed.'

Mysteries? He looked up at the Academy building. Its stone columns burned at their tops with golden fire, and its two wings folded around its front courtyard, hiding what lay behind. Secrets and safety for Imbati. Maybe the missing word was 'selfless,' since Imbati vowed themselves to others. He could easily believe that the Headmaster knew mysteries—he had a document signed by the Great Grobal Fyn himself!

At last the warden returned. She opened the gate, escorted them across the courtyard, and ushered them through the main entrance. Now that they weren't being herded with a crowd, Adon could see the full layout of the foyer, which had several heavy bronze doors, as well as corridors leading out of it on both sides. The doors to the Headmaster's office were closed.

"Mother," he whispered. "What do we do now?"

"Not to worry, young Master," said Aloran. He turned to Mother and gave an unusually deep bow. "With your permission, Lady, I'll go in ahead."

She gave the tiniest nod.

Aloran slipped through the doors into the Headmaster's office.

He was gone a long time. At least, it felt long. That might have been because the two of them were standing alone in a formal, empty hall. Adon glanced up at Mother; she looked more tense now than angry, alternately wringing her hands and smoothing her skirts. What were they doing here? Surely it couldn't have anything to do with Cahemsin—oh, Heile's mercy, was it about making him disappear?

He'd lose his mind if he just stood here wondering.

"Look, Mother," he said. "There are flame emblems in the vaults where the arches meet, too."

Mother didn't immediately respond. Just when he thought she wouldn't reply at all, she looked at him. "What?"

"*Art*," he said. "There are flame emblems on the ceiling, and these floor tiles are amazing." They were white, with a branching pattern in gold that looked almost like the tree on Mother's dress.

Mother sighed. "I love you, Adon."

At last, the office doors cracked open. The first person he saw was Aloran, whose face clearly said, *be on your best behavior.* Adon glanced at Mother; she gave a tense smile.

"You go on in, love. I'll wait here."

Adon swallowed, and walked in. The inner office furniture was in its proper place this time, and his mouth dropped open. The chairs were normal enough, but the large desk was topped with a thick panel of wood. Wood! It even looked like a single piece . . . Gods, where would you acquire such a thing? Cut it whole from a tree? How could you, without being attacked by wysps?

"Welcome, young Adon of the First Family," said the Headmaster, from behind the incredible desk. "I'm pleased to see you."

His calm voice was so soothing, washing Adon's worries down around his feet. Adon bowed impulsively. "Headmaster, thank you for seeing me."

"Young Adon, I've just spoken with Tamelera's Aloran. He has explained to me the fear you and your family feel after the attempt on your life."

"Yes, Headmaster." He swallowed. "Maybe he also told you about how Nekantor is sending his Dexelin to follow me. Again—or, still."

"He did," the Headmaster agreed. "I'm sure it's particularly difficult now that your Household has been diminished."

Adon nodded.

"Aloran has asked me to protect you in the event that your life is . . . at risk of catastrophe."

Adon blinked, and looked for Aloran. The faithful servant was standing by, watching the Headmaster with an expression of deep respect. "Did he? Thank you, Aloran."

"Please tell me, then, young Adon: do you also wish for my protection?"

Adon gulped. The Headmaster's solemnity filled every tiniest corner of the room; the next words spoken would have import. At that moment a wysp drifted up out of the floor, as if summoned by the strength of his wish. Maybe this one could bring him good luck. He took a deep breath.

"Headmaster," he confessed, "I've never been so scared. If you can offer protection, then yes, I would wish it. Please."

The Headmaster paid no attention to the wysp, but inclined his white head. "You understand, I suspect, young Adon, that the grounds of the Academy are intended for the protection of Imbati—that, as it stands, we could not entirely ensure your safety."

He frowned, and shook his head. Did that mean no? "Yes, I do understand, I'm sorry . . ."

"I will therefore ask you first: do you wish to join us?"

"Wh—" Adon blinked. "Do I—*what?*"

"Young Adon. Should you wish to Fall, to become Imbati, you would need a sponsor among us. I am willing to serve as that sponsor. Is this your wish?"

His breath vanished; his tongue refused to form speech. Had he thought his life could fall apart quickly? Had he imagined his words might have import?

Disappear . . .

Now, knowing what it meant, he saw that the ground under him had dropped by a thousand feet. He dangled, breathless.

"A—uh," he stammered. "Headmaster, it's kind of you, but no. Thank you."

Wait—dear gods, had he just refused all help? That wasn't a fair choice! His heart started pounding.

The Headmaster's face changed, in no way he could understand. "Here is our offer, then, young Adon. Please be aware that, given your refusal, it comes with strict conditions."

"All right."

"Should you feel your life is in imminent danger, you may enter any door into the servants' Maze."

"Wow." *Any* door? He was only rarely permitted to enter Aloran's room. And to think of it—*any door*—that was a kind of safety he could believe in. Something that had seemed impossible since the shooting.

"Here are the conditions," the Headmaster said. "First, no one must see you entering a Maze door."

"All right."

"Second, once you enter, you must immediately announce yourself to the first Imbati you see. If you see no one, you must wait to be found, without returning to the main hallways."

It only made sense, since he had no idea how to tell if he would walk into a room full of observers. "I understand."

"Third, you must never speak to anyone but me or Tamelera's Aloran about having this permission. If any of these conditions are broken, our offer will be instantly rescinded, and anything you have told anyone about it will be a lie. Will you accept?"

More powerful Grobal than he had accepted terms from the Headmaster. He stood straighter. "I accept, Headmaster."

"Then I wish you safety."

"May I say something?" Adon asked.

"You may."

"I wouldn't be alive without Imbati Talabel and Nekantor's Dexelin. I'm sure you know that, but I'd like to do something to thank them."

The Headmaster nodded. "Rest assured, sir, that young Talabel and Nekantor's Dexelin have been commended for their actions in saving you."

"Can you help Dexelin?" The question popped out all on its own. "Nekantor is being awful to him. Is there anything you can do?"

"I don't know."

"Oh."

"Thank you for seeing us, Headmaster," said Aloran, with a solemn bow.

Adon bowed, too. It seemed too little respect in the face of the offer he'd just accepted. Had the Headmaster agreed to it for Aloran's sake, or was there something unusual about *him?* The thought was both heady and frightening. As he straightened, the Headmaster said,

"Not even your mother, young Adon."

"No one," Adon said. "I'll respect your conditions—I swear by the crown of Mai."

He walked out, shaking. Mother turned to him with a wan smile, and his throat constricted. He'd kept secrets before, but this one felt different.

"Are you coming home?" Mother asked.

His stomach dropped into his feet. Mercy—she'd thought he might actually Fall? "Yes, of course I'm coming home," he said. "Sorry if I scared you."

Mother looked to Aloran, and then back to him. Her eyes filled with tears.

Adon took her hand. "Are you all right?"

She squeezed his fingers so tightly he had to squeeze back so she wouldn't hurt him. "Yes, love. Let's go home, and I'll ask Keeper Premel to get us some tea."

You could change clothes as many times as you wanted, but you couldn't really change your heart. Deep breaths only barely touched these shakes. In front of the mirror, Adon checked his new green jacket, and straightened the emerald at his throat. Why had they done it?

Of course it was for his safety. He *had* nearly been killed. But Falling was such a . . . *complete* solution, it was frightening. And why Imbati?

But of course, that question also answered itself. He knew more about Imbati than he did about other Lowers. Maybe Cahemsin's father had known a lot about Kartunnen.

Guilt washed over him. He'd done a terrible thing today.

Four more minutes, or eight, or even twenty, wouldn't make this any better, and Mother would be waiting for him at dinner.

He went out.

Pushing through the doors into the sitting room, he discovered Pyaras, who had apparently just finished greeting Serjer. Pyaras wore a loose garnet-red house coat as if he were in his own home. His Jarel stood behind him. Pyaras looked over at Adon and grinned.

"Adon! You're looking fabulous tonight. How are things?"

His new secret caught in his throat. "All right, I guess."

"Come here and give me a hug."

"Uh . . ."

"And before you start wondering, yes, your mother asked me to come, but it's not her fault. I should have realized I ought to come around more, with Tagaret not here to look after you."

Adon hesitated. "All right, that's fair."

Pyaras came close, but thank all the gods, he didn't grab. His muscular arm was gentle, wrapping around Adon's shoulders. "Do you know what's for dinner?"

Adon laughed; it came out sounding nervous. "No."

"It'll be good, whatever it is; your Keeper's great. Good evening, Tamelera."

Mother had appeared in the door of the dining room. "Thank you so much for coming, Pyaras," she said. "Come in; we should sit."

As he sat down, Adon glanced at Mother. She'd arranged this. She would expect him to talk to Pyaras about something. Today was the last thing he wanted to talk about.

Pyaras wasn't short or wide, but he looked both when he sat in Tagaret's chair. Keeper Premel and the manservants brought appetizers of poached fruit to their places.

Adon took a bite. His new secret made it hard to swallow.

"How are you enjoying your new job, Pyaras?" Mother asked.

"I love it when I'm with the Arissen," Pyaras said. He flashed a smile that quickly subsided. "But of course, I had to give a report to Eminence Herin today and he didn't care one bit about anything I said. And then there's Nekantor, who's surely using me for something, coming around with all his demands."

Nekantor. Adon's stomach turned over, and he set down his spoon. "He came around? Is he watching you, too?"

"He's always done that," said Pyaras. "What's new is, now he's pressuring me. He keeps stopping by at weird times, full of things he wants me to order the Division to do, and none of them make any sense. Here's one: he asked me to raise paper yields and then refused to acknowledge any costs. Not that I expect his requests to make sense; I mean, this is Nekantor we're talking about. He's always messing with me." He sounded so casual about it, as though he had no idea how dangerous his cousin could be.

Mother had quietly finished her fruit; she passed her empty plate to her Aloran. "It sounds like he's testing you."

"I'm sure he is."

Awful thought—Adon shuddered. "So . . . did you do what he said?"

Pyaras barked a laugh. "Of course not. I have no desire to make the whole Division hate me."

"Mercy of Heile, you said *no?*"

His cousin raised one dark eyebrow. "Saying no, now that's a different question, isn't it? I just let Nek say his piece, nodded my head, and then ignored it. I haven't even told Commander Tret."

Mother raised her eyebrows high. "I hate to say this, Pyaras, but I'm afraid you're just postponing your problem."

"Fair enough. I am." He scooped up the last piece of fruit from his plate. "But enough about me. Adon, I notice you haven't told me anything about how you tried to beat up your cousin."

Adon froze, ice in his spine, fire in his face. He gulped hard. "I didn't like the way he was treating my *friend*."

"Oh, I see." Pyaras rubbed his napkin across his mouth. "Is it the friend you told me about? They gave you trouble about her, didn't they."

He couldn't answer. *Mother, why did you have to invite him over tonight?* It still hurt, thinking about how Talabel had vanished. And then there had been Dexelin sneaking in to find him, and then Mother grabbing his arm, dragging him off to—

The secret rose in his throat again, hard as a stone. He fought it until his throat started to hurt. He couldn't talk to anyone about the Academy . . .

No, wait. He'd sworn not to tell anyone about the Maze. But Mother already knew what had happened at the Academy, and so did Aloran, and Pyaras understood about Talabel, so . . .

"Something scary happened today," Adon said. "I got asked if I wanted to Fall."

CHAPTER SIXTEEN

On Thin Rock

Pyaras gaped at his small cousin. Had Adon really just said . . . what he'd just said? Caste insults were one thing, but this was something else entirely.

"Varin's teeth!" he swore. "No wonder you tried to beat him up." He caught Tamelera aiming a steely-eyed reproach at him, and quickly added, "Not that it was the right thing to do. Just—I understand it."

Adon glowered up through the dark fringe of his hair, and dropped both palms to the surface of the table. "You don't understand anything! My cousins never told me to Fall. Someone asked me *if I wanted to.* Did you realize you can Fall without taking a partner? All you need is a sponsor. It shouldn't be allowed to be that easy. What about the future of the Race?"

Every bit of his own indignation vanished instantly, and Pyaras swallowed. That wasn't insulting, it was frightening. *Someone tried to take my cousin from me.* "But why did they ask you, Adon? Who would ever do such a thing?"

Adon huffed and glared. "I don't know."

What an Imbati thing to say. Twins knew he wasn't going to call Adon on it, though, when he was already so upset. Pyaras grunted, and looked down at his Jarel's hand as she took the empty plate from his place.

"I suppose your friend Veriga has never asked you?" Adon said.

Pyaras looked up at his cousin. "Heavens, no. People don't ask questions like that—and besides, you don't know Veriga. He constantly reminds me I'm a nobleman."

Though he might never do it again.

A plate of roast galiya and greens appeared by his shoulder; Imbati Jarel lowered it to the table in front of him. It smelled delicious, but he couldn't stop thinking of Veriga slamming that plate down on the aluminum table.

"Actually, I think he might hate me now."

"This has been a difficult time for all of us," said Lady Tamelera. "With Tagaret and Della moving away, and your new job, Pyaras, on top of everything else. I just hope some good things can come of it."

Melín leapt into his mind, grappled him, her mouth on his, her voice ordering, *Get your clothes off.*

Worst, absolute *worst* thing to think of at your cousin's mother's dinner table.

Pyaras grabbed his glass and took a gulp of cold water. He speared a mouthful of galiya and greens with his fork, and crossed his legs.

"Good things," he said. "Yeah, that would be great."

"Mother, do you have writing paper I could use?" Adon asked. "I'd like to write to Tagaret."

Tamelera looked over at Pyaras, meaningfully.

Pyaras tried to smile. Hopefully, he wasn't blushing too hard.

She said, "Maybe you could write one together, Pyaras."

"Oh." He cleared his throat. "Sure, of course."

After lunch, Tamelera sat them down together and they composed something friendly and meaningless. It wasn't as if he didn't want to help Adon. He just wasn't good at this. He couldn't be the father Adon had never had, and it made him ache. Adon didn't much seem to want his help, anyway. He might have given up if the horror of what had happened to Adon hadn't remained, clinging in corners of his heart. *Someone asked my cousin to Fall.*

Tamelera seemed remarkably composed, considering.

When the letter was finished, Adon returned to his rooms, and Lady Tamelera walked with him politely to the entry vestibule. She put a firm hand on his arm before he could walk out.

"Pyaras. You're on thin rock." Her eyes were sharp, her tone icy. "Watch Nekantor. You're the only one who can at this point."

He swallowed, but couldn't argue. "I know. Lady, you've known him longest. What do you think I should do?"

"Get help," Tamelera said. "If no one knows he's pressuring you, no one can help you. Learn as much as you can about *why* he requests what he requests. There are ways to influence him, but not many, and most aren't safe. Ignorance won't help you. No one can tell him what to do."

"Wait." Pyaras frowned. "What about Herin? The Eminence can tell him what to do."

"That's not a bad thought." She nodded. "But Herin tends to err on the side of caution, and I can't really blame him. He's got all twelve Great Families to balance."

"Maybe Herin's Argun could convince him this was important."

"Or his partner, Lady Falya. I've spoken with her, and she has a good head. Find as many allies as you can, Pyaras. Don't stand alone."

Don't stand alone.

But he did stand alone—just as he sat alone now, at a table with a pristine white tablecloth in the middle of Society Club Four. He had cousins here; he could see a couple of them over at the bar. But they didn't treat him like family. Tagaret had been the only one who understood Veriga; and now Veriga was gone, and so was Tagaret.

Tagaret had left, and taken Della, his perfect partner, with him. Nekantor was threatening, and Tamelera warning; and Adon wanted nothing to do with him. He and Adon had never much connected. Why should it be bothering him so much now?

But someone had tried to take Adon.

The healthy child.

Pyaras shuddered, and took a last large swig to empty his glass of yezel.

Society Club Four was precisely the sort of place where he was *supposed* to do his drinking. Silk curtains, brass tables, carved wood centerpieces. Recorded music. Ordinary lights. He wasn't going to argue that the Trao Falls mixer he'd drunk first hadn't been exceptional. But.

The Lake Club had been a brothel, and he hadn't even noticed.

You weren't looking, Pyaras.

Veriga was right.

And now, here he was, alone.

And his drink was gone.

Pyaras got up and wandered past tables of late-night diners over to the bar. It was crowded, all the chairs full, lots of men standing around talking while Household Imbati served them. He angled between a pair of backs in velvet jackets, and sidestepped around the side of a chair.

"Is that Pyaras? Cousin!" A curly-haired man on elbows at the shiny brass bar, who'd been talking to someone, turned and grinned at him. He knew him: Lady Selemei's son.

Pyaras managed a smile. "Corrim, nice to see you."

"Have you been here long?"

"Not that long," Pyaras said, although he had. Three drinks long, now.

"I heard about your new job," Corrim said. "Mother's disappointed to lose you, but I can't complain, because she hired me instead."

"Congratulations."

"Hey, do you know Odil of the Eleventh Family? Odil, this is my cousin Pyaras."

"A pleasure." Odil had the kind of face you'd never mistake for anything but Grobal, with a prominent nose and sharp cheekbones; he wore his black hair partially pulled back. Pyaras took the hand that Odil offered him, and shook it.

"I'm buying this round," Odil announced. "Join us?"

After two more drinks, he could feel the loneliness subside just a little. Talk at the bar had gotten louder, and pushing against it was harder. He wandered back to the bathroom, the door to which was in a back hall where the walls were all green leather stamped with Grobal insignias. He used the toilet, washed his face with a bit less coordination than would have been ideal, splashing water in some places he shouldn't have, but managed not to hurt his injured head. As he walked out, he discovered Odil about to walk in.

"Hey, Pyaras, funny meeting you here."

"Really?" He shrugged. "Hazard of the evening's activity."

"It's an activity I like, though." Odil pressed his lips together. "Corrim told me about your head. Sorry."

"Eh, could've been worse."

Odil leaned closer to him. "Are you in the cold and dark?"

Oh, gods. He'd heard that verse fragment a hundred times, but somehow, he was never ready. Loneliness rose again like dead air, suffocating. Life would be so much easier if only he could teach himself to like men! What reputation of duty to the Race did he really have to protect? But the Song of the Twins wasn't his verse; he replied with Sirin's Lament. "I'm waiting to glimpse my lover's hair."

Odil turned and walked away.

Gnash this.

He didn't go back to where Corrim was sitting. At a different section of the long bar, he set down his expense card, ordered a straight double chatinet from a stone-faced Imbati bartender, and downed it in one gulp. Then he wandered to the exit. His Jarel had been waiting in the manservants' anteroom; she joined him with the faintest look of disapproval.

He stubbed his toe on the threshold on the way out, and stumbled a few steps before righting himself again. On the front walk, a thin woman with a blue dress and gray coat waved to him.

Kartunnen, offering company. They were common enough outside the Society clubs. Why shouldn't he talk to her?

"Good evening," he said.

"Good evening to you, sir."

"Care to tap?"

"Certainly, sir."

Lights flashed. Not surprising, since a prostitute with bad health would quickly be run out of this neighborhood. She was fine-looking. But she wasn't Melín.

"Can you be . . . active?" he asked.

"Yes, sir."

"No, no. I mean . . . assertive?"

"Yes, sir."

"Can you tell me what to do?"

"Yes, sir."

"Yes, sir, yes, sir?!" *Varin's teeth!* He managed not to swear in her face. "No thank you, never mind."

"Sorry, sir."

"Jarel," he said. "Please—please get me out of here."

Imbati Jarel was better than he deserved. She wordlessly escorted him to their skimmer, nudging him straight when his feet lost their direction. The skimmer hummed and lifted.

"Jarel, can we go somewhere?"

"Where do you have in mind, sir?"

Melín. He flushed with desire, and shivered. *Plis' Playground. The crowd—the drums—the barracks—oh, Sirin and Eyn . . .*

No. No one would be there, tonight. Melín wouldn't be there.

He could still hear her voice, exactly the tone she'd used. *I'd sure like to kiss you. How would you feel about it?* Direct. Unashamed. The way she'd told him to take his clothes off. And softly, her delicious lips right in his ear: *Melín.*

He closed his hands on the edge of his seat so he wouldn't do something indecent with them. Arousal wrestled with guilt. "If she saw me right now she'd hate me."

"Sir?"

"Don't. Don't think about her." Jarel had asked him where they should go. "Lake Club, Jarel. No, it's not there. Gnash Nekantor! No, let's go anyway. It's a fun neighborhood. Veriga can't blame me if I'm not going to a brothel."

"I understand, sir."

The wind of the skimmer's passage felt good. Jarel skimmed them up the rampway. Of course, when they got to the Lake Club neighborhood, there was no Lake Club. The streets were just as busy, but people crossed the sidewalk before the old building without even looking up. Jarel pulled up to it. If there had been windows to look inside, he'd probably see new construction, but it didn't matter. Veriga had already broken the illusion.

"They'll put something new here, Jarel."

"Yes, sir."

"That's nice, at least. Twins, I'm lucky Veriga's not here." He shook his head. "Did you know? That was all my fault. I didn't know they were fake. I should have known, I didn't know. But oh, boy, they knew *I* was. I was fake, Jarel. The costumes. All of it. Fake!"

The Descent monitors didn't know I was fake.

She *didn't know I was fake.*

"Mai help me, Jarel! I can't go to a Descent. *I'm* fake. No wonder Veriga hates me."

"Sir," said Jarel. "Please, be fair to yourself."

"You should hate me, too."

"Of course not, sir."

It was all clear, suddenly. Fake, everything was fake. "I've never had good sex in my life, Jarel. All that sex, and it wasn't real, and the one time it was, *I* wasn't. It will never be, unless I Fall. No one's going to ask me to."

She didn't respond.

"Varin's teeth. Nekantor sent police here. Where's the police station?"

"I believe there's one along the circumference and to the left, sir."

Pyaras got out of the skimmer. Walking along the sidewalk was a lot harder than walking out of the Society Club. His feet kept disobeying. Whenever he came near, Lowers dodged away, or crossed the street. And they were right, too; he could only hurt them.

"Yeah, stay away from me," he announced. "I got all those people arrested. I'm the *worst*. They should arrest *me*."

"I don't think so, sir," said Jarel.

The red lamp of a police station wavered up out of the night. Pyaras pulled on the door twice, and then Jarel pushed it, and he half-fell in.

"Sir," said an older Arissen woman in a police uniform, from behind the metal counter. "May I help you?"

"Rivai," he said. The name was so sad. One had been so beautiful—arrested and fined because of him. "The arrests at the Lake Club. Did you arrange them, from this station?"

She hesitated. "Sir?"

"I'm Grobal Pyaras of the First Family." He leaned one elbow on her counter. "Please find . . . a Lake Club employee, name, Rivai. I'll pay one's fine."

"One moment, sir."

While she looked, Pyaras leaned his back against the counter. He couldn't see the old Lake Club building through the windows, but there was a shinca tree out there, glowing silver.

A jingling sound behind him, keys opening a file drawer, sounded like bracelets.

Distracted tonight?

Sirin and Eyn, you're beautiful.

Get your clothes off.

"Sirin and Eyn," he mumbled.

"Sir," said a voice behind him. He turned around. The Arissen had a paper in her hand. "Arrest record of a Melumalai Rivai. Fine levied, four hundred orsheth, of which sixteen have been paid."

Pyaras blinked. "Are you serious?" He'd paid that much for drinks! "That's *stupid*."

The Arissen looked nonplussed.

"Find the rest," Pyaras said. "The Lake Club fines. I'll pay them all."

Bang-bang-bang-bang!

Ohhhh, owww . . . Pyaras turned over in bed and unstuck his eyelids, slowly. His head throbbed with his heartbeat.

Bang-bang!

Nobody knocked like that. Father hated it when *he* knocked like that—who could be knocking like that? Shouldn't his Jarel have answered the door?

Pyaras curled, slowly, and got his feet down on the floor. Standing up hurt, and his stomach didn't like him at all. He shuffled to the door of his rooms, and leaned on the handle to open it.

Veriga???

"It's seven forenoon," Veriga said gruffly. "We're going jogging."

"We are?" Pyaras blinked up at Veriga's pockmarked, scowling face. "Do you hate me?"

Veriga crossed huge arms. "Well? You coming?"

"Uh, yeah."

"In your pajamas?"

"Oh. Give me a minute."

His head and stomach still hated him, but he went and found his clothes. While he only had one leg in his pants, he found a glass of water held in front of his face.

"Sir."

"Jarel, I'm in a hurry." He turned, wobbled, and put his other leg in.

The water reappeared. "Sir, please."

Pyaras grabbed his undershirt and pulled it over his head.

There was the water again.

"All right, fine," Pyaras said, though right now he had less than zero interest in putting anything in his mouth. He sipped the water, which tasted just like the medicine Veriga had given him. "Ugh." But his Jarel was still looking at him. He drank as much of it as he could before his stomach threatened to rebel. "Thank you—ugh."

He stepped out of his room. Veriga looked him up and down, turned his back, and walked out through the house to the vestibule. Pyaras tried to keep up. Every step made his stomach lurch, but he made it out of the Residence. When they hit the gardens, Veriga stopped beside the pole at the edge of the gravel walk where they usually met up.

Evvi was leashed to the pole.

"Oh, Evvi," Pyaras sighed. "Hi, pup." Just to sit and hold her—his knees nearly buckled with the impulse.

Veriga untied Evvi's leash and attached it to his belt. With one glance over his shoulder, he broke into a jog. The tunnel-hound bounded at his heel.

Here we go.

Oh, urrgh.

Running made him slosh like an overfull bucket. Heile help him, this was *not* going to end well.

He did it anyway, for Veriga. If he could just make it to the arena by the Arissen Section, he might be all right. But ohhh the bouncing. He misstepped in the gravel, caught himself, and his stomach lurched.

Nope, not going to make it.

He ducked behind a bush, doubled over, and emptied his stomach onto the ground in three body-shaking heaves. He straightened slightly, shivering. At least he'd managed not to make a mess of his clothes. He tore a handful of leaves off the nearest bush and used them to wipe his mouth—their smell was strange and green.

"Sir." Jarel sounded exasperated. She pressed a silk handkerchief into his hand.

He wiped his mouth, then rubbed the handkerchief over the back of his neck. He was still shaky, but his stomach felt vastly improved. "Gods, where did he go?"

"He's gone to the Ring, sir."

Pyaras nodded, and started to run again. He spat once into the gravel to clear his mouth, but this time running was much easier. He was panting hard when he reached the Ring and ducked through the gap in the wall surrounding it. Veriga was waiting, sitting on the low barrier of the arena, with Evvi on the sand between his feet. He buffeted her head playfully with his hands.

Pyaras staggered to a stop. His mouth was still disgusting—he stuck out his tongue and rubbed it with the silk handkerchief.

"There's a drinking fountain over there," Veriga said, pointing.

"Ah." Pyaras flushed, but went and sucked at the water, and rubbed some of it over his face before returning to the wall. "Thanks. Much better."

The police officer grunted and nodded. "Pyaras, do you know what the Captain's Hand at my station says whenever I mention you?"

Pyaras braced himself. "What?"

"Nobles are like tunnel-hounds. You can't keep them past a certain age; they grow claws."

"Oh. How old is Evvi?"

"Well past that age. Some people would have given her to the ashers by now."

"Seriously? That's horrible!"

"I'm smart about *some* things," Veriga said.

Pyaras raised his eyebrows at the silent implication that he was one of the *other* things. He sighed. "I like Evvi a lot."

"I like her a lot, too." Veriga stroked her head gently, betraying the depth of his understatement. "That's why I keep toys and pumice wheels. And I give her a lot of my time."

Pyaras swallowed. "So . . . I'm a tunnel-hound."

"Sorry, no," said Veriga. "You're much more dangerous." He was silent for several seconds. Finally, he shuffled his feet against the sand. "You know, a friend of mine works at that station near the Lake Club."

Pyaras rubbed his hand across his mouth. "Ah." Maybe that was why he deserved to resume morning jogs. "Um, Veriga."

The police officer looked over. "Yeah?"

"You've always given me good advice. You were right about the Descent. I couldn't handle it." He glanced back to Jarel. "I'm sorry."

Veriga sighed. "I'm sure you are."

Again, a silent implication. Pyaras squirmed a little. "I should have met you, like you said."

"I'm not your father."

"True. Though I don't obey my father, either."

"Ha," said Veriga mirthlessly. "You really aren't all that Arissen, in case you had any doubts."

"The reason I didn't meet you was—" Sirin and Eyn, that thought flushed him hot every single time. "I met a woman named Melín. A Specialist."

Veriga raised his eyebrows. "And she was interested? Specialists are supposed to have sharp eyes."

Pyaras breathed a *ha*, opened his mouth to say more, and—*Melín climbing him, her mouth locking on his*—could only shrug.

"Well. Hard to resist when you find what you've been looking for all this time."

All this time. Something in his mind shattered, as if an enormous stone had fallen from above. For several seconds, he couldn't even speak. "So," he said shakily. "I have to go to work. Are we back to jogging in the mornings, then?"

"Meet you at the pole same time tomorrow," said Veriga, and stood up. "Goodbye, Imbati Jarel."

"The heart that is valiant triumphs over all, sir," said Jarel.

"To me, Evvi."

Once they were gone, Pyaras walked toward his office, very slowly. He tried to pick up the broken pieces of himself, but they escaped him. Empty as he felt, he still had important things to do—support Adon and Tamelera, work with Commander Tret, look for allies against Nekantor. He pushed open the door to the Arissen Section. When he walked into his office, his Jarel presented him with a large silk bag. Had she been carrying it all this time?

"A change of clothes before you see the Commander, sir."

"Thank you, Jarel."

He refused to consider whether he'd actually made a mess of himself without noticing, just quickly changed clothes in the Executor's private bathroom. He thought about sitting down at his desk, then imagined what he'd do if Nekantor walked in right now.

"Jarel, I'm going to talk to the Commander."

"Yes, sir. Permission to wait here, sir."

She asked every time, though it had quickly become their usual arrangement. "Of course."

He walked into the Arissen offices. The officers in the maze of desks no longer showed surprise to see him. He knew maybe five of them by name; more work to do. Duty rotation had taken away the Captain's Hand who first helped him, and it hadn't brought Melín here—but that was a worry more than a hope. He didn't know what he could say to her with the lights on.

He knocked on the jamb of the Commander's door.

Commander Tret looked up. Didn't smile to see him—he hadn't given a real smile yet—but at least he'd stopped making that other face, cranking up his mouth-corners. "Executor Pyaras. How can I help you?"

Look for allies. He took a deep breath. "Commander, I need to talk to you about something. The Heir Nekantor's been by four times in the last two days, with new demands he wants to place on the Division."

Tret tensed.

"Honestly, the demands that aren't unreasonable . . . are ridiculous. Do we have to obey?"

"Sir," Commander Tret said stiffly. "I'm not sure what you're saying."

He was about to break a bunch of rules—but he'd far rather have Tret as an ally than Nekantor. Maybe he'd have had more courage if he had anything in his stomach.

"Nekantor asked the Division to stage a parade," he said. "A fancy review before the Eminence. I've never heard of anyone doing that, and I don't see why we should do it just to make him happy. Taking the Division away from its duties isn't just frivolous. It's potentially dangerous."

Commander Tret stared at him. "That's true, sir."

"I haven't told you the worst one. He wants to increase paper yields, without any increase in medical spending. That's—"

"Not possible, sir," said Commander Tret.

"Gnash it, I knew it." Pyaras moved to a chair, and sank down on it. His hands were shaking; he closed them on his knees. "In every season's paperwork you've shown me, it's the same pattern. Paper goes up, medical goes up, regardless of what Our Precious Heir says."

Commander Tret shook his head.

"Well? Am I wrong?"

"No, sir."

"The thing is, he expects obedience. Can you help me figure out what to tell him?"

Commander Tret rubbed one broad hand across his mouth. "I'm not sure, sir. Can you speak to someone higher up the chain of command?"

"I can try." There was the problem of Herin being Third Family; there was also the question of whether Herin would think he was trying to wreck the delicate balance of the Great Families. But this wasn't a Family issue; it was about safety, and costs. Tret had access to information, and maybe he could find something there that Herin would find compelling. "From what I've seen, when paper yields increase, medical costs don't go up as far as paper costs come down. But I bet it drives up costs in other places."

Commander Tret said nothing.

"Commander, the thing is, I'm not sure *why* it happens, so I'd like you to explain that if you can."

Tret exhaled. "I can explain it, sir. Paper is the most hazardous crop in the Pelismar fields. The Venorai recognize two cultivars of the plant, one of which is native to this area, the other to the Safe Harbor region. Both are associated with a high occurrence of wysp sightings, even in fields with few to no shinca trees. In recent years, there's been a lot of pressure to use the higher-yield Safe Harbor cultivar, but that leads to more wysp attacks during harvest. Additional Specialist surveillance of each field becomes necessary. The number of burn victims nearly doubles. Disability pensions increase."

"Heile have mercy." *Burn victims.* He raised his fingers to his slowly healing head.

"I'll be honest, sir?" said Tret.

"Please do."

"It's Varin's teeth up there, sir. And I should also mention that committing more fields to paper reduces the number committed to grains and other food crops."

"Well, I *have* to say no, then. Trigis stand by us."

"Well, but—sir." Tret pressed his lips together as if unsure how to continue.

"Yes? Commander, I would like to hear your thoughts."

"This has not been the approach of previous Executors."

Pyaras almost laughed. "No, I would guess it hasn't. Can you imagine how Herin and Nekantor would react if someone said no to their faces?"

Commander Tret's mouth pulled slightly to one side. "I'd prefer not to imagine that, sir. I—we, in the Division, sir, would prefer that you remain our Executor."

That was sobering. "Excellent point, Commander. On the other hand, if Sirin is smiling, I can get Herin to understand a money argument. He wants costs down. If I can show him that increasing paper yields raises the total expense rather than decreasing it, that might work."

"I hope you're right, sir," said Tret. "Here's where I would look for the cost numbers: casualties, Arissen and Venorai; medical expenses, Arissen and Venorai; disability pensions; import costs; cost of doubling Specialist deployments."

Specialist deployments.

"Commander," he asked, "what's the job of a Specialist?"

"Specialist is short for Wysp Specialist, sir," Tret answered. "Specialists are sharpshooters who undergo special training. They survey the field, tracking wysp movements and agitation states. They assess the risk of wysp attack, and if that risk exceeds the risk posed by disruption—"

"Pardon me, Commander—disruption?"

"The explosion caused when an energy bolt hits a wysp, sir. As I said, if the projected casualties exceed those for disruption, they shoot." He pointed out the office door, across the wide area of Arissen desks toward the door where Pyaras had entered, and then held up his smallest finger. "A Specialist could stand in the entry foyer on the other side of that door and put a bolt straight through my fingernail."

"Wow."

"Yes, sir."

Pyaras shook his head. He could ask the Commander to find Melín. It wasn't even the first time he'd thought of it. But his gut just wouldn't let him do it.

"All right, Commander," he said. "If you can send me records, I'll work on this."

"Thank you, Executor."

Pyaras returned to his desk in his comfortable room. "Jarel," he said, "do you mind helping me go through the paperwork I've requested?"

"I'm at your service, sir."

"Here's the thing. We can't disobey Nekantor, so someone else needs to say no to him. We're going to figure out how to get the Eminence to say no."

"No!" said a voice, dramatically, and started chuckling. "That was easy."

Heile and Mai help me. Pyaras turned around; the Eminence Herin was standing just inside his door. Herin's Argun must have opened the door so silently he didn't hear it. How much had Herin just heard?

Not enough to dim his mischievous smile. The Eminence glanced about the Executor's office as if enjoying the paintings on the walls. "Very nice," he said, gesturing about. "You're fortunate to work in such comfort."

Pyaras swallowed. "Thank you, your Eminence."

"No; have a seat, relax," said Herin.

Relax, right. Pyaras obediently returned to sit in his comfortable chair.

Herin smiled again, maybe attempting to reassure him. "How are you enjoying your work?"

"Very well, thank you, your Eminence."

"I've heard about the expertise you're bringing to your position, and I'm impressed." That was a dramatic change of attitude, considering that Herin hadn't seemed to care about his most recent report. Had someone spoken to him about his 'expertise'? Herin's face was pleasant when he said it, but it could just as easily be read as an insult. "I can tell my Heir is taking some interest in you. Have you made any changes in the Division's deployments?"

"No, sir," Pyaras replied. "I can see no reason to question the Division Commander's priorities at this time."

Behind Herin, the door opened on a Captain's Hand carrying a heavy file case, who stopped short at the sight of them.

"Sirs," the young Hand said.

"You may enter, Arissen," said the Eminence Herin.

"Set that here, please, Hand." Pyaras waved the Hand to a spot to the right of his desk. The Hand approached, set down the case, briefly saluted, and left.

"You're very sensible, Pyaras," said Herin. "However, I'd like to propose something that might benefit everyone. The idea occurred to me this morning, and since it affects the Arissen, I thought I'd come by and share it with you."

"Thank you, sir," Pyaras replied carefully.

"The Variner government could pay a lot less for paper if we could produce more."

What? Pyaras only just managed not to stare. "Have you considered how such a request might increase costs, sir?"

"No, no. This is about raising the supply to decrease costs."

"Sir, permission to report to you on the precise change in costs before implementing such a proposal?"

Herin broke into another smile. "You're diligent! I appreciate that. Have the report to me this time next week."

Which would be fine, except if Herin treated this report like the last one, it would help nobody. "Actually, sir, if you'll permit me . . ."

"Yes?"

"May we discuss it over lunch? I haven't yet had the honor of admiring your lovely partner."

"Ha!" said Herin. "I like your initiative. And, indeed, my Falya is the most lovely woman in all Varin. Why not? We eat at Society Club Five. Argun, arrange it."

"Yes, your Eminence," said Argun in his deep voice.

"Thank you very much for honoring me with your visit, your Eminence," Pyaras said. But when they had left, he shook his head in dismay.

Herin coming in to propose some 'new idea' that Nekantor had just proposed yesterday, in this very office? That was disturbing. Most people had forgotten Nekantor's school-time gang behavior, but *he* hadn't—Nek had always been the one standing at the gang leader's ear, whispering schemes that Benél would later claim as his own.

What else was Nekantor whispering to the Eminence?

CHAPTER SEVENTEEN

Melumalai, Kartunnen, Venorai

One thing you could say about Melumalai—paper merchants, anyway—they loved to decorate for parties. Della, open-mouthed, struggled to take it all in. This warehouse room was filled with white paper in myriad forms that, until this moment, she could not possibly have imagined. Narrow, twisted lengths of paper hung over the entry door, so Yoral and Kuarmei had had to push them out of the way when she and Tagaret came in. Bright lights shone from behind discs of paper pierced with tiny little holes, casting white points on the floor. Other paper shapes, almost crystalline in their patterns, hung on strings from above. Far off there, in the side corner, what looked like stone columns were surely enormous rolls of paper, stacked almost to the ceiling. Amidst it all, the employees of Dorlis and Nenda, Melumalai, had gathered to celebrate the deal signed this afternoon, after a month of competition among the Selimnar paper companies, and another month of arduous negotiations with the Imbati bureaucracy.

They'd made it this far.

She'd made it this far, to this room full of noisy strangers in snug hats and shining castemark necklaces of silver and chrysolite. The Kartunnen Jaia dresses were still holding her in good stead, though Yoral had adjusted them many times. Tonight she felt less awkward than usual—physically, at least. And Tagaret kept telling her she looked beautiful.

"I don't know anyone here," she said.

Tagaret patted her hand on his arm. "I don't know most of them, either. I'm also having a hard time understanding what I'm looking at. The last time I was in this room, it looked nothing like this."

"It's amazing."

"Let's try at the end near the paper columns; I think that's where the office is. I'd like to introduce you to Dorlis and Nenda, obviously, and also to my bureaucratic contact Imbati Wenn, the purchaser. Don't forget, though, the Administrator in charge of the negotiations only knows me as the paper research assistant. I'm not sure if he'll be here tonight."

"Don't worry," she said. "I remember. I'm so proud of you." It was wonderful to see him succeed at what he'd been held back from so long. In the same amount of time, she hadn't accomplished nearly as much, but it was difficult when you kept having to nap, suddenly, at odd times. The Residence Household under Director Aimali had accepted her easily, and she now had several friends at the Lady's Walk, but no one below the level of the Kartunnen, unless you counted bakers.

An energetic Melumalai approached them holding a tray of finger foods; Della took something that looked like a stack of colored circles on a tiny slice of bread, and bit into it.

"Mm!" Selimnar food kept surprising her in delightful ways.

Tagaret chuckled. "What is it?"

"I don't know. Bread. Roasted roots? Cheese?" She cleared her throat. "Pepper? It's not like cling-pepper, it's—sharper."

Tagaret took one, too, thanked the Melumalai, and led her onward. The closer they got to the columns, the more their enormous size became evident.

"Tagaret," she said. "That is just—*so much*—paper."

"They have entire rooms filled with it," he said. He waved to someone in the crowd ahead. "Here we are. Dorlis? Excuse me, Dorlis and Nenda!"

Dorlis and Nenda stood with arms around each other, one with an arm draped over her partner's shoulder, and the other with an arm around her partner's waist. Each wore a brimless felt hat that almost matched the color of her hair. They turned in unison. Both wore heavy silver necklaces with chrysolite pendants, and stars made of folded paper at their shoulders.

"Grobal Tagaret, noble sir, deal day!" The shorter, brown-haired Melumalai grinned, and her round cheeks shone in the light.

"Deal day is a great day, so," Tagaret replied.

"You're learning!" Dorlis crowed. Nenda smiled, and quietly leaned her pale head against her partner's.

"So," said Tagaret. "I've been meaning to introduce you to my partner, Della. Della, Nenda and Dorlis."

"A pleasure to meet you, Melumalai," Della said, and offered her hand. She wasn't wearing gloves tonight, because Tagaret said merchants didn't consider gloved handshakes binding. Yoral had expressed concern, but her inoculations were up to date, and Tagaret had agreed the risk was not particularly serious.

"How many times may we shake your hand, noble Lady?" Dorlis asked.

Odd question. She glanced at Tagaret, but he only looked at her encouragingly. "Uh, twice, please."

Dorlis seized Della's hand between hers, roughened in odd places, and pumped it up and down decisively, one, two.

"Lady," said Nenda, and did the same.

"Congratulations," Della said. "Tagaret has been very grateful for your flexibility in the negotiations."

"Give a little way, win a little way, make a better deal for everyone, so," replied Dorlis cheerfully. "Here, have a paper sample."

Della took the small paper rectangle, a fine and flexible paper with a shiny smooth surface. "Thank you."

"Well," said Tagaret. "I'm just going to take her now and introduce her to Wenn."

Nenda spoke, suddenly. "Take care with Wenn, Lady. She's Imbati, so."

Dorlis nodded. "Ask nicely first, and she'll surely only ever let you shake her hand once."

"Thank you, I'll keep that in mind."

Tagaret led her onward. Glimpsing a Melumalai with a tray, Della waved him down and grabbed a cup that was also made of paper. It contained what appeared to be juice, and she drank it gratefully; the pepper had left discomfort in her throat.

"Those two are delightful," she said, after clearing her throat again.

"They know a lot about Higher castes," said Tagaret.

"Really?"

"Oh, yes. All of them, in fact." He winked. "Except Grobal. I think they think of us as fancier Imbati when it comes to handshakes."

"Ah, that makes sense."

Imbati Wenn was the single figure in all black amidst the white paper, standing alone beside a wall with steel doors in it. The bureaucrat's pierced oval had been tattooed between her gray eyebrows.

"Wenn, hello, and thank you for being here," said Tagaret. "May I introduce my partner, Della?"

"Pleased to meet you, Imbati," Della said. "Thank you for your service in this negotiation."

The elderly Imbati woman bowed. "So kind, noble Lady."

All at once, fatigue overtook her in a wave. Della squeezed Tagaret's arm. "I'm really sorry, but I'm going to need to lie down. Really soon."

"Wenn," said Tagaret, "is there anywhere we could find her a couch?"

Wenn moved immediately past Tagaret to open one of the doors. "Over here, noble Lady. I hope you'll find the negotiations room suitable."

Tagaret and Yoral between them supported her into the room, which was smaller and quieter than the warehouse party room, quite dim, and furnished at the near end with deep stuffed chairs and couches. The other end had a long aluminum table with stools on either side.

Her head started to spin a little, and there was an unpleasant knocking low in her stomach, the soulless interloper reacting to juice or pepper or both. She lay down on the nearest couch; her Yoral gently lifted her legs and gown and rested them on a pillow. The knocking hit her in the spine, so she shifted her hips to an angle until it moved elsewhere.

Much better.

"I'll just rest a bit," she said. Her eyelids felt heavy.

Tagaret crouched down, and his fingertips gently stroked her hair away from her face. "Are you all right, love?"

She nodded. "The usual. Plus, too much excitement, I guess."

"Are you sure you don't need me?"

"I'll be fine. I just need four minutes. Don't let me keep you from your business connections."

His fingers caressed her chin, trailed reluctantly up to her temple, then moved away. "I'll be back soon."

Della stared up into the dark. They'd settled into a strange kind of silence, as if keeping the secret from others meant they must remain careful and oblique even between themselves. Tagaret was unfailingly caring and solicitous about how she was feeling. When they were together, he stayed closer than Yoral, as if waiting to catch her if anything went wrong.

Which it hadn't. But it might still.

Mother Elinda, why must you put me through this?

She closed her eyes. She'd dozed for what felt like only a few seconds when a male alto voice said directly overhead, "You don't wear a castemark, so."

Della opened her eyes. A pale face was staring studiously down at her. Below it, a dangling chrysolite pendant on a silver chain caught the dim light.

She said, "Hello?"

"You're sleeping."

"It's all right, I'm awake now. I'm Grobal Della."

The young man nodded several times, but said nothing.

"What's your name?" she asked.

"Melumalai Forder, Product Quality Assessor Number Two."

She shifted, tried to push herself back against the pillow, but managed to move very little. Where was Yoral? Maybe he'd retreated, so he wouldn't startle her visitor. "Who's Product Quality Assessor Number One?"

"Mom."

"Oh?"

"Nenda."

"Oh!" On closer examination, she could see the resemblance. It was hard to tell how old he was. Something about him reminded her of her little sister, though the longer she looked, the more she doubted herself for thinking it. Forder was big, and Liadis was small. And Liadis was unconfirmed, so she wasn't allowed to have a job. "That's a very important job for someone your age."

"Fifteen, so. Parties are overly loud."

"Yes, they are."

"You're able to sit up? If you're able to sit up, I'll show you how to be a Product Quality Assessor at Dorlis and Nenda, Melumalai."

"I can sit up if I ask my nurse to help me. May I?"

"Yes."

"Yoral?" she called. Yoral came to her and helped her up to sit. He'd probably been sitting quietly in one of the deep chairs; she had to guess the young heir of a paper company had appeared out of another.

"Your nurse is an Imbati, so," said Forder. "Imbati: may your honorable service earn its just reward."

"Thank you, Melumalai," said Yoral.

"Selimnar Imbati use eleven thousand five hundred spools of grade eight paper in a single year, so," Forder declared. He unhooked a blocky case from his belt, and pulled a cylinder from his pocket. He sat down on the couch beside her and clicked something on the cylinder, which emitted a beam of white light. The case, he flipped open to reveal an extensive collection of paper samples.

"You have a great many grades of paper," said Della.

"Eighty, so," Forder said. "You prove them by reflection, weight, opacity, silk content." He picked up a sample and shone the white light on it. "Reflection." He rubbed a corner between two fingers. "Weight." He lifted the sample and shone the white light through it. "Opacity." Then he flipped his cylinder around, clicked it again, and shone a bluish light through the same sample. "Silk content."

"I can see you're an expert," Della said. "Dorlis gave me a sample a few minutes ago."

"Mother," said Forder. When Yoral produced the sample, he rapidly ran through the steps he'd just shown her. "Grade forty-seven, so."

Della blinked. That was impressive; no wonder he was already Number Two. "I'd love to show you a piece of paper I brought from Pelismara, but I'm afraid I don't have it with me tonight. Maybe you could come see me sometime, at the Residence."

Forder dropped both hands into his lap, instantly intent. "You came out of Pelismara."

"Yes, with my partner Tagaret."

"You're Grobal Della, out of Pelismara, partner of Grobal Tagaret who has negotiated an extremely great deal, so."

Della swallowed. Had she upset him? "Yes."

Forder grinned. "So grateful ever! How many times may I shake your hand?"

Della had just set out for a morning walk when running footsteps came up behind her. She turned and found Tagaret arriving, slightly out of breath.

"Darling," she said, "is everything all right?"

"Oh, yes." He caught up her hand. "I just thought, with my negotiations finished, I could join you."

She smiled. "Please do." She resumed her path along the bridge, allowing him to tuck her hand under his elbow, and leaned her head against his shoulder. She'd finally given in and purchased a hat; it really did make the chilly air more comfortable. Just look at them, walking along with this magnificent view of the Selimna cliffsides. From here, you could see traffic on the road in places, and the Ride cars moving up and down, and even glimpse the roofway. "Come to the bakery with me?"

"I'd love to."

Music was playing at the Lady's Walk. They crossed through the Ride station and approached the bakery. The front entrance had the name of the shop, Bread in Hand, rendered sculpturally as if it were formed from twists of bread. When Tagaret's Kuarmei opened the door for them, a bell sounded.

"Greetings of the day, noble Lady," the proprietor called from behind the counter, where she was pushing a tray of buns into her display case. "Noble gentleman, too, today, so. Welcome."

"Greetings of the day, Seu," Della replied. "My usual morning bread, please. Tagaret, what will you have?"

"What's your usual morning bread?"

"Tea, and one plain bun, and one herb bun. It's just, they're so delicious that I've fallen into a habit."

"The same, please, Melumalai," said Tagaret. He sat across from her at the small front table, considering her with an odd expression on his face. "Clearly, I should have been coming here with you more often."

"Clearly."

Della looked over toward the counter. Seu's brother Beu had emerged from the back, and they were working on something side by side, though their hands were out of sight. "Greetings of the day, Beu. Did you get your garbage issue resolved?"

"So kind to ask, noble Lady," Beu said. "We did, so."

"I'm glad it worked."

"What worked?" asked Tagaret.

Seu placed a steel tray on the table between them. She'd set each of the four buns on a decorative leaf, and positioned the steel teacups with their rubber handles toward each end.

"So grateful ever," Della said, picking up a bun and holding it warm against her lips. The aroma still brought tears to her eyes. She lowered her voice. "There have been troubles with garbage and recycling pickup since Alixi Unger's 'cleanup' initiative. Akrabitti are afraid they'll be arrested for doing their jobs. I was hoping to speak to the workers, but only managed to speak with the neighborhood police officer. It appears to have helped a little."

"Mercy of Heile." Tagaret rubbed his face with both hands. "I've been too focused on Dorlis and Nenda. And if it's bad here, imagine what it's done in the rest of the city."

"I know. I particularly worry about the Up-Bend medical center, since Unger was paying so much attention to it. I should go and see whether there have been any effects."

"Iyemmelim Medical Center," said Tagaret. "We could both go, and if we pretend we want you to be seen, that would give us a chance to talk to Kartunnen Iyemmelim."

Della pulled her bun closer to her chest. "We could pretend that, to fool a Kartunnen, Tagaret. Or to fool me."

Tagaret winced. "I didn't mean that."

"What did you mean, then?"

He glanced at the Melumalai behind the counter, and lowered his voice. "I admit I think it would be a good idea for you to be checked by a doctor," he said. "It's just that I worry."

Talking about it gave her a cold feeling, as if Mother Elinda were looking over her shoulder. "When you were busy, you didn't worry. Please don't assume Yoral hasn't been checking me every day."

"I'm sorry. I'm sure he has." He inhaled deeply, and took her hand. "I'll try not to worry. Let's find some new areas of the city to explore."

"All right," she said. "In the meantime, I'll take Yoral with me to Iyemmelim, and the two of us will investigate who has access to his services."

"Keep her safe, Yoral," Tagaret said, and took a bite of his bread.

"Yes, sir, of course."

Della ate her bread, and drank her tea. Tagaret really did mean to be helpful. Perhaps, in his mind, he believed if he was always close by, he could bargain with Elinda for two souls or one. She knew it was one or none, and that Elinda did not bargain.

Going to the medical center made her stomach jittery. Remember: no subversive plan could be complete without tackling the question of medical care . . . As shields against panic went, the thought felt too flimsy, but Della carried it with determination.

Household Director Aimali had given Yoral the directions. They took the Ride up to the roofway; Lower passengers, mostly Kartunnen and Melumalai, allowed Della to sit at the window for the view. She should have talked to them. But how was she supposed to talk to people who cringed every time she tried to make eye contact? Of all her conversation pieces, only the paper card had received any interest, and she hadn't been carrying it when she needed it.

They passed through several stations where other passengers boarded or disembarked. She spotted the green buildings of the University, and then the track headed into the Bend's dramatic curve. She recognized one of the rooftop restaurants from their previous tour.

"We should eat there afterward," Della said, pointing.

"I'll try to arrange it, Mistress," said Yoral.

The station at the river confluence, where their previous tour had stopped, was very busy. Della started to get up in spite of the bumping, moving bodies, but Yoral stopped her, saying it would be less crowded and just as easy to access Iyemmelim from the next station.

He was right, at least about the crowds. Only a couple of Melumalai remained on the car as it continued. The roofway curved rightward, toward the waterfall above the mist zone, and stopped at a station by the entrance to the Venorai tributary. As they exited, they found themselves at the far end of a station deck so long it felt like a curving, widening corridor. Della walked along it cautiously, grateful that Yoral was close by and on the alert.

The farther they went along the curve, the more it was busy with Venorai. These people were strikingly different from one another, despite the uniformity of their broad castemark belts. Some were young, some old; some were short, some tall; some were wiry and some vast; some were pale, some golden, and many were sunmarked in a wild variety of patterns. Many wore hats of leather or animal fur. Eventually she and Yoral found their way to the Ride, which opened directly off the roofway deck, and boarded.

This Ride car was not made of delicately braided metal. It was a giant metal box, as if the cases in which their luggage had traveled to Selimna had been expanded to fit people. People, and freight. They rode downslope alongside five Venorai, including a splotchy-skinned older man with a cap of speckled gray fur and a wheelbarrow full of mushrooms. The smell of them was enough to make her head spin. Della covered her nose with a handkerchief. Thank Heile, Yoral nudged her to disembark at the second stop.

Outside was a narrow alleyway between high walls, just wide enough for a cargo skimmer. The air here was distinctly chill and damp, maybe from its proximity to the mist zone. She pulled her gloves tight and tugged her hat down over her head. The ground under her feet was a roof—you could tell because, while the left side wall had doors in it, the right side wall had skimmer-sized railed alcoves, each one labeled with a name in twisting bright neon, and containing a metal panel like the elevator she'd accidentally ridden by the Residence. There was no view here at all.

"Let's walk quickly, Lady," said Yoral.

She lifted her skirts and did as she was told. The alley curved, a single continuing wall on either side with no splits or turns. A group of Venorai emerged from a door on the upslope side, and Yoral defensively moved ahead of her, but they passed by without greeting or incident. Somewhere on the right, an elevator hummed. Who was coming up? She tried to push her feet even faster.

At last she glimpsed the lighted green globe of the medical center ahead on the right. Desire to get out of the alleyway propelled her into the elevator, which hummed and descended. Of course, halfway down, the fearful place in her mind remembered this was a medical center. She took a slow, shaky breath.

Oh, blessed Eyn, let me return home from this place.

The elevator deposited them in a large room with a row of reception windows along the opposite wall. Low aluminum chairs were arrayed all around the edges of the room, and three islands of back-to-back chairs stood in its center.

Every chair was full. She could hear crying, coughing, the occasional moan.

"Yoral, could you give me my notepad and pencil, please?" When he handed them to her, she began tallying the population of the room.

One of the chair islands was entirely occupied by Kartunnen, another by Venorai, and the third by Melumalai. The chairs around the edges of the room were similarly segregated, but with a bit more randomness. There were a few Imbati groups closer to the reception windows, a long row of Melumalai, a few Venorai and then more Melumalai again. No Arissen appeared to be here at all. Where the end of the row abutted the elevator, a single individual in a dark charcoal hood sat, both hands wrapped in a bloodstained towel. Between him and a Venorai woman with a bawling child on her lap was a single empty chair.

Della considered the chair, gulped, and looked around. *I should sit there. I should talk to that man.*

A Kartunnen nurse in a long gray coat emerged from a door beside the reception windows.

Della startled and took a step backward; she felt Yoral's hands press against her back reassuringly.

"Greetings of the day, noble Lady, may I aid you?"

Her throat tried to close up. "H-help him," she stammered, gesturing at the undercaste man with the end of her pencil. "He's bleeding and he needs help."

"Noble Lady?"

"That Akrabitti is bleeding, Kartunnen. Help him."

The nurse looked confused, but said, "Yes, noble Lady." She went to the man with the bloody towel and took him into the back.

What in Varin's name had she just done? She wasn't here to talk to Iyemmelim, not really—she was here to learn. She hadn't encountered a mixed-caste place like this since their arrival, but instead of taking advantage of her opportunity, she'd panicked and sent the Akrabitti man away. Where was her courage? Why couldn't she just have sat next to him?

Get yourself together. Just be brave enough.

Della braced herself and sat down beside the Venorai with the crying child. Yoral quietly took the chair that the undercaste man had vacated. The Venorai woman had a leather hat like a pot lid, with graying hair curling out from underneath it, and was too large to shrink away from her effectively. She started murmuring to her child, who looked to be under ten years old and had somehow hurt her arm. The child's cries subsided to whimpers.

"Noble Lady, may I aid you?" came another voice.

Della looked up. This was a different nurse: a young man with a friendly face. "Not now, thank you," she said.

"Kartunnen," said Yoral, "Please allow my Lady to sit until she feels ready to speak to you."

The Kartunnen bowed. "May your honorable service earn its just reward, sir." He glanced at the Venorai woman—would another opportunity vanish? But the nurse didn't call the woman in; he walked away and called an Imbati instead.

"Venorai," said Della, "how long have you been waiting?"

The Venorai woman startled, and her child yelped and started to cry again.

"Forgive me," Della said. "I didn't mean to scare you. I just—"

"Noble Lady, three hours."

"Three hours? Oh, I'm sorry!" The last thing this woman needed was an interview with a Higher. When the female nurse who had first greeted her emerged from the back, Della waved her down.

The Kartunnen bowed. "Noble Lady, may we aid you?"

"This Venorai child is in pain and has been waiting here for three hours. Why haven't you treated her?"

"I'm sorry, noble Lady," said the nurse. "That's confidential, so." She hesitated for a second, as if wondering whether she'd be punished for leaving Della's presence, but then moved away and called in a different Venorai.

Clearly, caste wasn't the issue.

Minutes passed. An Imbati patient emerged from the treatment door and approached the elevator; when the doors opened, a pair of Melumalai joined the waiting room crowd, and the Imbati left.

Della took a breath and let it out slowly. She was going to figure this out. She glanced at the Venorai woman. "What happened to your daughter's arm?"

"Broke, noble Lady," the Venorai said cautiously. "She made a dive, so."

"Heile's mercy, she's been sitting here for three hours with a broken arm?"

The Venorai nodded. "Noble Lady, are you here for the child you're carrying?"

Della shrank, and her neck prickled. "No." Was it that obvious?

"Noble Lady, Sirin bless you." The Venorai made some kind of warding gesture. "I didn't mean to offend."

She tried to smile. "That's all right."

The next time the door opened, two nurses came out: the young man, and one she hadn't seen before. The new nurse summoned a Melumalai into the back. The young man . . .

Yes, he was coming this way. Della's stomach clenched.

"Noble Lady, perhaps you'd agree to tell us what brings you here?"

"I'm evaluating your facility," she said. "And, to be honest, I can't figure out why you would leave a child here for three hours with a broken arm."

"Noble Lady," the nurse said. "Please come into the back if you wish to discuss our services."

"I don't think so." She shook her head, incredulous. "Why won't you help her?"

"Excuse me, noble Lady," the nurse said, and disappeared back behind the door.

Della found herself shaking—maybe from the Venorai's discovery of her condition, maybe from the outrage. She pulled her gloves tight again, and tried to slow her breathing.

"Carrying will tire you so, noble Lady," said the Venorai. "My sympathies."

Della glanced at her. "I wish I hadn't said it. I've never had a living child. Miscarried every one."

"Oh, noble Lady," said the Venorai, reaching out as if to touch her belly, but stopping before making contact. "That's a grief will tear your heart. May the Mother bless you. I never miscarried, but I've had children die. Our boy Lussy died last year, so."

"I'm sorry."

"Iyemmelim tried to help him. Failed, so. Wouldn't believe it was the wysps."

"What?" Della asked, shocked. "Wysps killed your baby?"

"Noble Lady, Lussy was no baby. He was eighteen, so. Firehead, and it killed him, the idiot."

"Heile have mercy!"

"Noble Lady," said a new voice.

Della looked up and found another Kartunnen here, a broad-faced man with a rounded gray hat and a University pin affixed to his gray medical coat. "Doctor Iyemmelim," she guessed. Well, she was *not* going to let him take her on a tour. She pointed at the Venorai child. "Is that girl's arm broken, or not?"

"Please, noble Lady, come into the back."

This was ridiculous! "Fine, on one condition."

"Name it, noble Lady."

"This Venorai and her daughter are coming with me."

He looked affronted. "Not Castremei. She lies."

"Not about a broken arm, Doctor. I insist." Stubbornly, she added, "So."

The doctor looked infuriated, but didn't refuse. "Bring her," he said. The Venorai obeyed, setting the small girl on her feet and guiding her forward as the doctor passed through the door. Della followed, grateful for her Yoral's supporting hands against her back.

The hall inside, with its rows of treatment rooms, made her heart flail against the inside of her ribs, and the soulless interloper picked up on her panic. The doctor waved significant fingers at nurses they passed, and they sprang into action. Scowling, he led them into a room where you could see a large machine through a window, and set the nurses to placing the child in it. The Venorai woman clung to the edge of the window, watching as the nurses emerged, returned and shifted the girl, emerged again.

"Noble Lady," the doctor said. "May we speak outside?"

She didn't trust him. "Yoral," she whispered, "give the Venorai your card and tell her to contact us if she doesn't receive proper treatment."

"Yes, Mistress."

Once she'd seen the card handed over, she allowed the doctor to lead her out into the hall.

"I'm here to evaluate your facility, Doctor, and after this, I'm not sure I'm impressed."

"I hope you'll understand," Iyemmelim said placatingly. "Venorai often make use of our facility. They're not a very careful people, and they breed infections due to their animal-like living conditions."

Della stared at him. "What are you saying?"

"We're doing the city a service, keeping them from harming others. But they overtax our facility, considering our level of funding, so. If you could consider having a word with the Alixi on our behalf."

She wasn't going to say what she really wanted to. It would obviously be no use asking him about Akrabitti. She smiled at him deliberately. "I'd be happy to, Doctor, but first I'd like you to send along records of which castes get treated here, in what numbers, for what kinds of complaints. To Lady Della at the Residence. And thank you for helping my neighbor. Castremei, was it?"

"Castremei was excluded from care because she lied about her son's drug dependency," said the doctor. "Firehead is a real scourge among the Venorai. It causes brain damage, so."

"That sounds terrible," said Della. "But I don't think it has anything to do with a broken arm."

He held his breath for a second; he looked like he was trying to control his temper. "Noble Lady," he said, "I began my career at the

Residence Medical Center, and have a great deal of experience with noble ladies, so."

"Oh?" She raised her eyebrows at him. She was not going to finish his sentence for him.

"So I would prefer, if you wish treatment, that you bring your partner with you. Our center is unprepared for legal action he might bring if we treat you without him present."

Her heart immediately started pounding hard enough to make her dizzy; her skin flushed hot. "I won't be asking for any treatment here, ever, thank you very much. Yoral, let's go."

CHAPTER EIGHTEEN

Into the Cohort

Orange was a horrid color—a color for ass lickers and fungi. But she couldn't put off wearing it any longer, because the medic had cleared her for duty, provided she taped her ankle every morning. That she should see the day! Just looking at the trousers made her head hurt. Melín belted on the handheld bolt-weapon in its holster, and buckled the short knife to her belt sourly, remembering her stolen blade.

She still had to get it back. Somehow.

That blasted Karyas!

Karyas wouldn't have returned her blade to the Division; it was registered to her, and she was supposed to return it herself, so if she didn't, Captain Keyt would know something was wrong. Karyas might have thrown the blade away, or had it destroyed.

She wouldn't, though. A blade like that had uses.

In Karyas' hands, not good ones.

Melín punched herself in the thighs a few times to stop the twitching, and put the orange jacket on. Gnash it, gnash it—the helmet had no crest, and no brim against sunblast. Nekantor and his pet might as well have pinned her under a rock. She'd never get back up there, to the one fight that really mattered.

Today she had to march in a review.

Fantastic.

Her ankle gave her almost no trouble down the level-rampway stairs. Credit to the medic for that. He'd been pretty blasted frustrating, in that Kartunnen way, insisting on the proper exercises, and the proper taping technique. But she didn't blame him for the nightmares, even though more than a few of those nightmares had involved him taking her ankle apart. No; bad dreams came whenever she was off the fields.

Today's order from Commander Abru had been to report to the Ring. She had no reason to think it was false. By Sirin's luck, she found the place busy with mates—dressed in orange, but what can you do—and unclenched her teeth a little.

Everybody had gathered outside the tall outer wall, because inside, Grobal were waiting. There was a lot of talk and shoving in the crowd. Talk, she didn't care, but shoving was a pain when most people's shoulders were at the level of her head. She moved through the group, calling sharply, "Watch it, seni!" when elbows got too close.

Someone behind her said, "Wysp!"

Melín whipped around, reaching down for a bolt rifle that wasn't there.

"Made you look," a tall man sneered. "You scared of wysps, seni? 'Cause I'm not."

She narrowed her eyes at him. He sounded suspiciously like that ass, Helis.

"I can handle them just fine, seni," she said. "If you try to mess with them, I'll fix your face for you."

The man laughed.

Waste of her time. She was supposed to be finding her own eight. It seemed like she'd have to ask where to find Crenn, and hope he'd make no attempts to fix her face when she found him.

His face needed fixing first. But not today.

She pushed for some distance from the wysp idiot, and nudged one of the nearest elbows.

"Hey, seni, where's—"

"Aren't you the one the Heir picked out?" A big pale woman with the rank pin of a Seventh bent down into her face, chin jutting forward. "How much did he pay you for your loyalty?"

"Better ask the Heir that question," said Melín. "Where's First Crenn?"

"You *would* say that, carrion breath. No respect where it's due."

What in Plis' name? She snorted. "Plenty where it's *due*."

"I should report your lack of loyalty to the Eminence," said the pale woman. "Or I could just—"

The pale woman's fist came at her face.

Melín ducked fast. She spun and tried to slip away into the crowd, but the woman shoved after her.

Gnash it, gnash it, kick and blast it! That woman might be a Seventh, but Helis had been an Eighth. Docked for insubordination on her first day . . . ?

Two backs parted ahead, but before she could escape through the space between them, she found First Crenn coming the other way.

My ass. Docked, and now decked by her own First . . .

"Touch our Eighth and you'll regret it," Crenn snarled.

Was he on her side now?

All right, then.

It wasn't just him, either. Sahris was here, too. Melín took the risk of giving them her back—and found not just the pale woman, but two more guards lining up with fists ready.

This was some bigger dispute, older to the Cohort than she was.

If Crenn wanted to defend her, though, she wasn't going to stop him. Even if his sudden about-face made no sense. She backed around him to a spot where, to reach her, the woman and her mates would have to attack Crenn first. Then she stood her ground.

A whistle sounded across the crowd. Most basic signal she knew, meaning 'line up.'

Good timing. Instead of leaping in to fight, the pale woman spat toward Crenn's feet, and walked away. Melín cast a glance toward Crenn and found the rest of her eight had joined him; relaxing slightly, she moved around to the line's end. This was basic stuff, same as they'd learned at Norendy.

Of course, line up didn't mean move. There was always the standing-around part. Pointless. Dragged-out. Don't-shift-your-feet-but-don't-lock-your-knees. With her heart aching for sunblast, reminded of her loss by each throb in her head and twitch in her thighs, it became a special form of torture.

Finally, they marched. Row by row, into the Ring. Easy stuff, minimal planning or commitment, and no fancy maneuvers to keep up with. Just line up in a block eight by eleven, and salute, right hand to left shoulder, in front of the Heir and the Eminence beneath their metal canopy.

She studied their smug Grobal faces. The Eminence was a ridiculously pretty man in a ridiculously pretty suit. He'd probably turn a beautiful brown if he ever stared Father Varin in the face. He looked over them with a brilliant smile that was probably intended to make them feel—rewarded? like family?—for safeguarding his life. The pale, narrow-faced Heir eyed them like targets. His eyes flicked constantly face to face to face.

Gods, did she ever feel like a perfect tool.

In the corner of her eye, weird shadows shifted. Wysp shadows. She focused on peripheral vision without moving her eyes. There it was: a wysp had come up out of the ground by the mate in front of her, and now drifted upward at a weird inconstant angle. Agitation level zero—but it was agony to watch.

What was she doing here, when she should have been in the sun?

Someone gave a singsong whisper. "My shot."

Rage whited out her vision.

"Eminence Herin and Heir Nekantor!" she shouted. "Thank you for the honor of nomination to your Cohort. But whoever shoots that wysp now will cause an explosion that will kill the Heir, the Eminence, and most of this Cohort. As a certified Wysp Specialist, I'm informing every one of you: I will personally deactivate you if you try it!"

Every member of the formation turned on her. For a split second, she thought she might be crushed.

"Cohort!" Commander Abru barked, and the implosion froze around her. "Attention! Eyes front!"

The Cohort returned to its previous position.

The Eminence Herin stood up.

Melín braced herself—maybe Plis would smile, and he'd be angry enough to expel her back to where she belonged.

"Thank you for your valiance, all of you," said the Eminence. "I can't imagine whose idea it was to shoot wysps underground where they cause no harm, but—" His voice hardened. "This ends. Now." He pointed a finger and waved it across the group. "Anyone attempting to shoot wysps will be immediately expelled from my Cohort."

The Heir stood up beside him. "Is that clear?" Nekantor demanded.

Melín snapped her heels together. The sound of eighty-eight pairs of obedient boot heels echoed across the ring, followed by the voices. "Yes, sir!"

Thank Heile. Melín exhaled.

What a bunch of pathetic tools.

You're upset, Melín," Aripo said. "Did you break somebody today?"

"Nah." Melín punched her fork into a bite of kelo mushroom fry. The tines protested against the metal plate. When she put it in her mouth and chewed it, the outside was crisp, the inside meaty and just slightly sweet. Maybe it even eased her headache slightly. "Thanks for making this."

"Gotta look at me when you say that."

Melín closed her eyes, tempted to roll them, but Aripo was right. Better to have beauty in her head than images of the Eminence and Heir cycling over and over. She looked up from her plate at Aripo's face. Aripo was leaning her chin on her hand, gazing. She had deep, incredible eyes. Incredible hands. Incredible everything.

Yeah, that did feel better.

"Isseni." Melín took a deep breath. "Thank you for making this."

Aripo smiled until her lips parted. "You're welcome. So, you gonna tell me how it went?"

Melín spiked another fry, considered it, and bit off one end. "You shouldn't have to bring your work home."

"That bad, huh?"

"He took me off the *fields* for this!" A quick stab-stab-stab cleared the rest of the fries off her plate. She shoved them in her mouth and ground them between her teeth, like Varin should the Heir. The Eminence, too, for that matter.

"Hmmm, and how does that make you feel?"

That croon was deep and comforting. Aripo had used it with her before, back when Melín was just her Division client, to coax her to talk about her problems. Now it made her stomach tingle.

Melín played with the ring in her left ear. "The Cohort's weird, Aripo. Something's off."

Aripo gazed and nodded silently. Twins, did she have beautiful eyes.

"Were they always like this?" Melín asked.

"They always loved their connection to the Eminence, if that's what you're asking."

"I don't think that's it." She scowled at her empty plate. "Gnash them all."

"Put your fork down, isseni," said Aripo. When she did, Aripo pulled her hand across the table and started playing with it. Aripo's strong fingers pressed into the meat of her thumb, and between her fingers, massaging, stretching . . .

Ooh, that felt good.

"Isseni, you're making me jealous of my fingers."

Aripo chuckled. "Jealousy is so unbecoming. What would Drefne say?"

"He'd say it was their turn."

"He actually might." Aripo twined her fingers through hers, and stood up, walking closer around the table. Melín loved the way the movement wrapped her own arm across her chest; Aripo, behind her now, found her other hand to hold, and bent down.

Heat surging in her tender places, Melín turned her head up for a kiss.

"Don't get ideas now," Aripo murmured. "You still have to tell me about your day."

"Traitor. Take me to bed."

"Will do." Aripo pulled her hands away, leaving Melín grasping after. Aripo hauled her up by the underarms.

"Hey!" A toss, and she was draped across her isseni's arms. Melín reached for Aripo's neck.

"I'll drop you."

"Isseni!"

"I know you, isseni. You have the headaches. You've had the nightmares. You're not facing your traumas. Do I have to wring words out of you?"

Melín wriggled. "Oh, yes. *Wring* me." She went for a kiss.

Aripo dropped her head.

"Aaaa!" A sharp grip at her knees stopped her upside-down. She punched Aripo in the thigh. Oh, look at her magnificent thighs . . .

Aripo hauled her across the apartment into the bedroom, swung her up and tossed her on the bed. "Words."

Melín gazed up at her, panting. Wanting. Aripo's breasts stretched the fabric of her white shirt; she could imagine holding them in her hands, and—

Plis' balls, words. All right.

"I hate the Heir for trapping me underground."

"Good start. I'll give you . . . a shirt." Aripo peeled the white shirt off, and tossed it in the corner.

"Oh, holy Twins . . ." Melín's hands closed on their own, and she licked her lips. Swallowed hard. "There's no reason why my eight shouldn't have hated me today, just like the day they tried to break my ankle. But they defended me." That had to be enough words. "Come here, seriously, I need those nipples."

Aripo laughed aloud. "Only if you turn on your stomach and keep talking."

"I'm going to kill you. I could go to the Cohort's therapist, you know."

"You won't. What are the Cohort's traumas, anyway?"

Melín turned over on her stomach. She could feel Aripo coming closer; she rubbed her knees together for the friction that ran all the way up her thighs. "The Heir's the trauma. I think he's doing something. He doesn't look at everyone. He—"

Aripo's hands landed on her ass and pushed her down, all of that godly weight behind them. The hands moved up, pressing into the small of her back, then higher, pressing the tension out of her with her breath—oh, yes—and then Aripo's knee pressed in between hers, nudging upward.

"Uhnnn," she said.

"I couldn't understand that," said Aripo, closer now. Her hair was down, tickling deliciously between Melín's shoulder blades.

"They might—" She gasped as Aripo's hands sneaked under her hips, grasped her inner thighs, and then pulled back out again.

"Might what?" Aripo asked.

"Hahh—uh. They hate me. My eight."

"Yeah?"

"But they hate me less than they hate that other woman. The woman who accused me of disloyalty to the Eminence." For an instant, she forgot everything else, even the woman behind her. "Because everybody knew the Heir had picked me. Holy Mai help me, the Cohort's split into factions. I hope I'm wrong." She turned on her elbows and looked around at Aripo. "I'd better be wrong."

"I love you, Melín." Aripo reached down to her.

After that, everything was right.

CHAPTER NINETEEN
In the Shadow

This morning, Della's body felt different. It wasn't the first time something about her pregnancy had changed overnight, but today she struggled so much to hold her stomach in that even the idea of a day gown was exhausting. Unfortunately, this happened to coincide with Household Director Aimali making an unexpected visit. Della received her in housecoat and slippers.

"Greetings of the day, Aimali."

"Noble Lady." The Imbati bowed, and handed her a letter with Adon's handwriting on it.

"Tagaret," Della called. "Adon's sent another letter!"

Tagaret came out to the vestibule, thanked Aimali, and scanned the letter. He smiled. "Adon's wishing me happy birthday a few days early."

"Congratulations, sir," Aimali said. She didn't immediately leave.

In fact, she never brought the mail.

"Director, is there something else?" Della asked.

"Noble Lady, there's been some disturbance, so. You'll excuse us, I hope."

"Disturbance?"

Tagaret dropped the hand holding the letter to his side. "What kind?"

"Noble sir, a Venorai came here with a child, seeking Lady Della. Claiming they had spoken, so. We told her to leave. You must understand, noble sir, Venorai are known to lie. But she gave us the card of your Yoral, so."

"Venorai Castremei!" Della exclaimed. "Is she still here? Can you bring her to see me, please?"

The Household Director hesitated. "I believe we've given you shame, noble Lady . . ." She bowed to the floor.

"No, please, get up, Aimali," Della said. "I'm so sorry; I should have told you. I'm trying to understand your city by speaking with people of every caste. I was remiss in not informing you I might have a Lower visitor."

Aimali got to her feet, though concern remained in the shape of her crescent cross tattoo. "May I escort her to you, then, noble Lady?"

"Please do." Once she'd stepped away, Della turned to Tagaret apologetically. "She'll be afraid, but I'd like you to meet her . . ."

Tagaret gently kissed her cheek. "I'll let you take the lead."

Venorai Castremei arrived in their fancy sitting room, wide-eyed, clinging to her daughter. Her brown leather hat and gray curls were the same, but it looked as though she'd dressed specially for her visit; today she wore a green skirt beneath her castemark belt, and a silk shirt with a stylized pattern of brown spiders. The girl was in blue trousers and shirt, but her brown leather vest had the same spiders stamped on its lower edge. Her arm was in a cast. She kept glancing over her shoulder at the Household Director as if the Imbati might bite her.

"Thank you so much, Director," Della said. "You are excused."

"Noble Lady." Aimali bowed and left them.

The young girl's focus shifted immediately to Tagaret, though he'd taken a seat on a blue stuffed chair so he would look less tall.

"I'm so sorry for the trouble you had reaching me," Della said. Her belly felt like it was bulging visibly, but if she tried to support it, she'd develop a habit that would eventually draw the wrong people's attention. And if their secret came out, their suite neighbors might try to send them back to Pelismara. "I'm glad you're here. This is my partner, Tagaret."

Castremei didn't exactly smile. "Noble Lady, we only came to say, so grateful ever." She glanced at Tagaret, and then back, anxiously.

"You're welcome." Della gave her a gentle smile. "I hope you got the care you needed. I wasn't much impressed with Doctor Iyemmelim."

"Nor I, noble Lady, nor I," the Venorai agreed. "But Sind needs an arm, for work, so."

Della tried not to wince as she studied the girl, and the brown belt that looked too broad for her. Venorai were destined for work. And if you were destined for work, not working would be worse. "I hope it doesn't hurt too much, Sind."

Sind bobbed her head. "Eased, now, noble Lady."

"Noble Lady, we're not able to repay you," said Castremei. "Except I brought you this, for your hat." She held out a long, iridescent green feather.

Della went to her, and took it carefully. "Thank you. It's beautiful. I've seen these feathers on hats in the city. What bird do they come from?"

"That's from the tail of a male beyfrull, noble Lady."

"You're so kind. I don't need any sort of repayment, really." But with them here, brave enough to come miles along the Arzenmiri and face down the Household Director, maybe . . . "I do wonder—would you be willing to teach us about your people?"

Castremei narrowed her eyes, and pulled Sind closer to her waist.

"I don't mean to frighten you," Della said. "Please let me explain. Tagaret and I haven't lived in Selimna long. We're trying very hard to be kind and polite to the people we meet. Whenever I visit Up-Bend, though, no one will take me near the Arzenmiri tributary. I fear we haven't had much of a chance to meet Venorai, until I met you."

"Don't worry, noble Lady, you're kind, so."

"You and Sind are the only Venorai I know."

Tagaret spoke suddenly, but softly. "I got a letter from a cousin of mine recently, and he told me something I found shocking."

Castremei was wary again. She shuffled her boots on the silk carpet.

"He said the more paper we use, the more of your people get hurt. I can't believe no one ever told me that before."

Castremei grunted. "That's true."

"But that's terrible," said Della. "How awful that we could know so little, that we could hurt you without knowing it." She kept her face open, pleading, hoping Castremei wouldn't give her another one of those narrow-eyed looks.

The Venorai woman eyed her up and down, chewing on her lower lip. She studied Tagaret, and then looked back at her. "Noble Lady, if you mean it, you ought to come home with me."

Go home with her! Della gulped. "Are you sure we can't just talk?"

"Noble Lady, if I told you, you wouldn't believe me, so."

"I would believe you," said Tagaret. "I promise."

Della shook her head. Any objection she might have voiced died before it reached her tongue. *Venorai lie.* Doctor Iyemmelim had said it, and Director Aimali, too. "Yoral," she said. "How long will it take us to get ready?"

"Wait," said Tagaret. "I'm not comfortable with this. Yoral, don't you think it's too dangerous for her right now?"

Della turned to look between them, and caught Yoral blushing.

"I don't know, Master Tagaret," he said.

"I need to—I just—" Tagaret didn't finish his sentence, but stood abruptly and left through the door into the back room.

Yoral followed him.

What?

It took a second before she could control her voice and speak calmly. It was inappropriate to leave a guest unattended, but what those two had done was much worse. "Castremei, I'm sorry. Please excuse me for a moment."

She stormed into the back.

"You!"

Tagaret and Yoral had obviously been talking in low voices; they looked up, startled. Della struggled to compose herself; it was hard to get a deep enough breath.

"Tagaret, you had better have an *excellent* reason for this."

Tagaret held out both hands, conciliatory. "I'm sorry. I don't think going home with a Venorai is a good idea."

"What's not a good idea is *taking my servant from me.* And making me leave a guest unattended in order to get him back. Yoral, at your station, please."

A devastated look flashed across Yoral's face, and he lowered his gray head. "I'm sorry, Mistress." He returned to his place behind her shoulder.

Della glared at Tagaret.

"Love," said Tagaret. "It's clear she's not inviting me; only you."

She snorted. "Do you really think I'm likely to be attacked by so many people my Yoral won't be able to defend me?"

Tagaret swallowed and lowered his voice. "Della, how the Venorai live . . . please, think. They are where Kinders fever originated."

Oh, so animal-like living conditions? Fury blazed inside her, but she held herself back. Of course Tagaret would be afraid; Kinders fever had almost killed him. "Please, listen to yourself," she said. "You told me not to wear gloves to Dorlis and Nenda, Melumalai, so we could be properly polite. You were fine with me visiting Iyemmelim. But with Venorai, you won't let me do what I need to strengthen this relationship? We talked about this. I'm inoculated against Kinders fever. I'll be all right."

Tagaret bit his lip.

"Tagaret, I know you're scared. But please, remember what we're here for."

"All right." He rubbed his face. "I'm sorry. Let me hug you before you go?"

She took as deep a breath as she could manage, and let it out slowly. "Of course." She wrapped her arms around him; he rubbed her back. "I love you, Tagaret," she said. "Could you please go out to Castremei, apologize, and tell her I'll be right out? I need to use the bathroom, and change into proper clothes."

Everyone knew the rumors. *Venorai lie. Venorai never go anywhere alone. Venorai are dirty. Venorai spread disease.* There were rumors about every caste. How could you know which were true or false without seeing for yourself?

More importantly, how could you make changes if you didn't know what needed to change?

The way to the Venorai tributary was perfectly familiar. It led through the same roofway station they'd used to reach Iyemmelim Medical Center. This time, instead of walking away from the highest concentrations of Venorai on the deck, Della followed Castremei and her daughter straight into them, counting on Yoral to keep the crowd from closing in too tightly. Her heart raced.

I promise to believe what I see.

The Venorai exit from the station led them to a broad walkway across the roof of a huge building; it looked like it would lead directly to the opening of the tributary where the waterfall came down.

"We won't go over there, noble Lady," Castremei said. "You wouldn't see near as much, so." She beckoned them instead to the entrance of a steel-railed enclosure beside a sign reading 'Union and Houses.' The entire floor of the enclosure proved to be an elevator plate. Every person who boarded the plate with them was Venorai, and most of them were watching her. The plate descended slowly. She watched the roof pass upward beyond the rail, and then the space opened up. With it came noise, and a smell so intense she could almost see it thickening the air. After a moment's struggle, she gave up and decided to breathe through her mouth. Covering her mouth with a handkerchief would surely offend the watchers.

The elevator stopped at a metal deck overlooking an enormous warehouse, at least four times larger, and far taller, than the space occupied by Dorlis and Nenda, Melumalai. The floor was distant below, seething with people and animals—so many it was hard to comprehend. She tried to make sense of which areas were enclosures, and which were meeting places, and which were storage areas for stone blocks, grain, or food.

"Castremei," she said. "What is this?"

"The Union, noble Lady," the Venorai replied. "We came for the view, but we won't stay. We're going to the Houses, so." She turned away, and with Sind following, headed toward the exit tunnel. Della shook her head at the chaos, and went with them.

The smell in the exit tunnel was a diminished version of the smell inside the Union: musty, sweet, sour, musky, oily, a blend she couldn't fully describe. Easier to breathe, at least. A thin line of lights ran along the low ceiling, and crowds of Venorai moved around them in both directions. In one section, there was bright light from the left. She watched between the bodies of passing Venorai, and realized the stone wall there had given way to window glass, showing nothing but white rushing water. Then the bright light vanished again and the thin line of lights showed the tunnel starting to slope upward.

"Sind and I are Spider House, so," said Castremei.

"Oh!" said Della. "Is that why you have spiders on your clothes?"

The Venorai woman flashed her a proud smile and held out one arm. "This is Spider House's proprietary silk, noble Lady."

"Oh, well, then."

"Houses have their stairways along here, so," said Castremei. "In the house, some will be sleeping, so we'll watch our steps, noble Lady, and Imbati, sir, won't we?"

"We'll watch our steps," Della agreed. "Won't we, Yoral."

"Of course, Mistress."

The Spider House stairway was on their left. It had spiders carved into the rock beside it. As they entered, Della asked, "Are there many Houses, Castremei?"

"Most of a hundred, I'd say, noble Lady."

"That many!" Not much like the twelve Great Families, then.

The stairs lifted them up into a new mix of smells, and quite a din. Definitely more noise than she'd expect for a place where people were sleeping. But this didn't look like a house—they were on an unremarkable railed metal walkway overlooking a river.

Della looked up, expecting the stone roof of the branch cavern, but instead, there was a ceiling overhead: heavy steel girders and concrete, with occasional lights.

Wait, did the whole tributary river run through the building? Or was this only a diverted section of it?

Castremei and her daughter didn't pause by the river. They turned away to the opposite side of the walkway, which was lined with hanging panels of leather stamped along their edges with spiders. Sind disappeared between two panels without hesitation, and Castremei ducked through after her. Della considered the panels, but by the time she'd mustered her courage, Yoral had already come and pulled one forward, opening a gap.

She stepped through.

Elinda help me, look at all the children!

The huge room was full of them. They were running, crawling, playing, yelling, crying, laughing, held in each other's arms. The sight hit her straight in the chest, and her knees weakened.

"Oh, Castremei," she breathed. "Oh."

"These are our Spider babies," said Castremei fondly. "Too tiny for work, or too breakable, so."

"Are they?" She searched as they moved through the crowd, but none of them looked over ten. And as Venorai, they'd be larger than Grobal of the same age, so they might be even younger, around eight or nine. A great many were grimy or snotty, and one large group of them was, appallingly, chasing and hitting each other with short lengths of rope, in an uproar of laughter. Was that what some people called animal-like? Some of the children were sitting in circles with their feet packed into the center, playing with actual furry animals. Limerets, she recognized from their slender bodies, and there was also another type, dark-furred, fist-sized, and plump. But she could find no disgust for these children in her heart, only awe and yearning. A few older, sun-marked and wrinkled people sat about chatting on stuffed leather cushions, caring little for the chaos. As they reached the edge of the open play space, she discovered a zone of children sleeping. Some were on the floor in patterns of four, using each other's stomachs as pillows. Others were just sleeping all over each other.

She watched her step.

"Mama!" A boy ran up to Castremei and flung his arms around her waist. He stared suspiciously at Della. "Where's Sind?"

"She's gone her own way, so," Castremei replied, grabbing his ears and wiggling them affectionately. "Find her as you like."

"Castremei, how many of these are your children?" The question popped out, but she knew instantly it was a mistake. Even if the answer were only 'two,' it was bound to hurt. Her hand moved unconsciously toward her belly, and she forced it down by her side.

"Why, noble Lady, every one."

"What? *All* of them?"

That was not any answer she'd expected; also, it was quite obviously impossible. Castremei only chuckled at her confusion.

"Noble Lady, Spider babies belong to all mothers and all fathers in Spider House."

"They do? But aren't there some who are your own? I mean, your very own."

"Noble Lady." Castremei shooed the boy on his way, and lowered her voice. "Venorai share; we don't hoard. Especially not feelings. That's unfair, so."

"Oh? Oh. I'm sorry." The apology was only reflex; it still didn't make any sense. Della frowned, but followed her guide out of the sleeping area into an enormous steel-fixtured kitchen. Here were even more very young Venorai, every one of them busy at something: pounding, rolling, chopping, mixing, grinding. The smell in here was sharper than it was in the main room. Greener, and dizzily fresh.

How could you pretend to be mother to children who weren't your own? Even setting aside the importance of a noble Family's gifts to the Race, how could you minimize your own precious treasures to 'share feelings' with someone else's? Much less *everyone* else's!

Would she feel better about her failures among people so willing to share? Or just more guilty for claiming something that was theirs?

How could Venorai think that way?

"Rooms are upstairs, but they're private, so," Castremei said. "Some are for partners' time. Some are for Union business."

"Union business?" Della asked. "Shouldn't that happen in the Union?"

Castremei smiled. "The Union is the House of all Houses, so Union business can happen anywhere. We're all threads, and the Union winds us together, so. In the Union, everyone owns a voice to choose the ways of the Venorai, by vote."

"Everyone?"

"At seven years, you're able to speak your mind. You're able to dig, weave, chop vegetables, spin silk," Castremei explained sagely. "So, you're able to vote."

"You let seven-year-olds chop vegetables?"

"You saw them just now, noble Lady." Castremei leveled a look at her. "By twelve, most are on mines or fields or spider tunnels, so. If you're able to lose a finger, an arm, or a life, for your labor, then you're able to speak for yourself in the Union."

Della needed several seconds to control an overwhelming urge to find Doctor Iyemmelim and slap him. 'Not a very careful people'? What about 'people forced too young into dangerous work'?

Varin only knew, he was probably wrong about firehead, too.

"Castremei, excuse me for asking this question, if it's too personal."

"Noble Lady?"

"What's firehead?"

"Oh, noble Lady." Energy drained from Castremei's hearty frame. She glanced at the floor, and sank down cross-legged. "I'll just take a seat here, so."

She couldn't reasonably stand while her host was on the floor, so Della sank down, too, pressing the air out of her gown. Yoral remained standing.

"I'm sorry," Della said. "I shouldn't have asked. You don't have to answer."

"No, I'll answer," Castremei sighed. "Wysps carry fire, right? They're fire, so."

"Yes."

"In the fields, and even in the mines, wysps are dangerous. We're in their house, see?"

"Are you?"

"So we need to lure them away from where we work. Some of us are able. Wysp lurer is high-paying work, and paid in orsheth, not just in kind, so. But luring's so much more dangerous, see, because what if wysps *do* follow?"

She started to see it. The boy, Lussy, must have been trying to help himself, maybe also his mother and all of Spider House by luring wysps away from the fields, and earning orsheth. But wysps were made of fire, and dangerous on the surface; naturally they'd burn if they got too close.

"I understand," she said. "I'm sorry."

Castremei scowled. "Excuse me saying so, noble Lady, but only Venorai understand. Look up."

Della blinked. "Look up . . . ?" She lifted her eyes.

Her heart fell into shadow.

Above their heads, the entire ceiling was hung with spirit globes. Each glass globe contained a tiny dim light: a remembrance for the dead whose souls had been taken to the stars by Mother Elinda. Growing up, Della had known the four that hung in the library of their home, each engraved with a name. Here, in this single House, there were thousands—so many that they didn't hang with their own electrical wires, but had been plugged into cheap strip fixtures. She glimpsed the truth, then, and her throat closed up.

How many orphans lived in Spider House? How many partner-lost?

Would she have dared ask this woman of the children of her own labor, if she'd known the next question must be 'How many has Elinda taken from you?' And after that, 'How old were they when they died?'

As a parent, could you refuse to love a child bereft? And what child could refuse to love a parent gutted by grief?

In the shadow cast by the mourning moon, who would refuse to share everything?

Tears welled in her eyes. "Oh, Castremei," she whispered. "Forgive me."

The shadow refused to leave her, even as Yoral escorted her home afterward. Della rubbed away her tears with a handkerchief, but more came after.

How was it possible for there to be so much suffering? Against this ocean of pain, all their careful plans seemed insubstantial. How could they possibly change this? How could they begin to help?

"Yoral," she said, "did you see it, too?"

"Yes, Mistress," Yoral answered. "It was nothing like what I was taught about Venorai. You were right to go. I was remiss."

"What can we do, though?"

He didn't immediately answer. "I'm sure you will find something,

Mistress. Don't imagine you've failed if you can't save them all. Even one life saved would mean something. Even one broken arm healed means something."

He was too kind. "I—" More tears trickled down her cheeks. "I think maybe I should lie down."

But luck wasn't with her. Tagaret's Kuarmei intercepted them as they walked into the curtained vestibule. "Mistress," she said, "we have a guest. Melumalai Forder arrived some minutes ago; Master Tagaret is with him."

Della swallowed. *Pull yourself together.* It wasn't the first time that social concerns had demanded precedence over her own comfort. She spread her handkerchief across her hands and pressed it to her face. After a moment, she crumpled the handkerchief and tucked it, and her tears, into her sleeve.

"Thank you, Kuarmei." She took several breaths and then walked into the sitting room.

Tagaret was sitting on their striped couch beside the big Melumalai boy; he looked up in relief. "I'm so glad you're home safe," he said. Deeper emotion hid in between the words. "Forder and I have been talking about paper."

She didn't doubt that for a second. Paper was young Forder's life, even as it was the Venorai's death. And three months ago she'd scarcely given it a thought. Such a small thing, to wind together so many people's lives.

"Greetings of the day, Grobal Della," said Melumalai Forder. "You're home, so."

She nodded. "Indeed I am."

"Grobal Tagaret is very kind," said Forder. "He's nice to speak to."

"He is," she agreed. "Scoot over, Tagaret, love, I'd like to sit next to you."

Tagaret made a space for her. She wrapped both hands around his upper arm and leaned against his shoulder, willing his warmth to ease the weight of the shadow.

"I want to go to Pelismara," said Forder.

That was a surprise. "Really?" Della asked. "Why?"

"Business, so."

"He's been telling me," said Tagaret. "It's apparently something encouraged for young people of the major merchant families, to create business connections in other cities. Dorlis and Nenda had thought he wouldn't be able to do it, but with the deal we just made, they've encouraged him to approach us about sending him over."

Business connections seemed such a lighthearted thing. "What an interesting idea," she said.

"Yes," Forder agreed. "Nenda came from Pelismara when she was fifteen, the same age as me, so. And when she was eighteen, she met Dorlis."

Della managed to smile. "That did turn out to be an excellent business connection."

"They fell in love!"

"Yes," she sighed. Bless Forder for his frank good nature. It really helped. "I shouldn't forget," she said. "That card I mentioned to you at the party—would you like to see it?"

"Definitely, yes please."

"Yoral," she said, "do you mind?"

Yoral quickly stepped out into their private rooms, returning with the pretty card, which he delivered to Forder. The Melumalai stared at it intently for a long time.

"What do you think?" Della asked.

"That's gold on one edge and two corners, so. It makes the paper very heavy."

Della shared a glance with Tagaret; he smiled at her.

"I believe this is pure silk," said Forder.

"Is it?"

The boy took her polite comment as a serious question, and leaned forward, looking at her around Tagaret. "Of course, I should check." He reached into his pocket and pulled out his light-cylinder, which, apparently, he kept always at the ready. He shone his bluish light on the card, and a wrinkle formed between his eyebrows.

"Pure silk, then?" Tagaret asked.

Forder moved abruptly, sliding off the couch and walking on his knees to the low marble table. He held the card by its gold edge and shone the bluish light on it again. He growled in his throat, a sound that made Della's chest tighten.

"Forder, what is it?"

"It *is* pure silk. Also, it casts a shadow. Barell and Ensindim."

"What?"

"Grobal Della, you take a look, so."

She stood and went to him, but had to kneel to see properly. The bluish light shining on the paper cast a shadow on the white marble, but unevenly; across the center of the shadowy rectangle, more light slipped through, tracing a pattern of bluish loops and dots. The words were quite clear.

"Barell and Ensindim." Saying it aloud put dread into her blood.

"Barell?" Tagaret asked. "Isn't that a circumference on Pelismara's fourth level?"

Dread crystallized into horror. "Wait, Tagaret—the paper casts a shadow. The Paper Shadows!"

Tagaret paled. "Gods help us, are you sure? Arbiter Lorman gave me that card. Surely Lorman wouldn't be telling me to hire an assassin!"

She shook her head. "Think of what he said. He said your father would know the right way to respond to the atrocity." Lorman's manner had been so strange and suggestive; she couldn't doubt he'd known exactly what he was saying. "What if Lorman wanted us to go to Barell Circumference and Ensindim Radius, and hire Paper Shadows to retaliate against the Fifth Family?"

"We didn't, though," said Tagaret. "Because I'm not like my father; Nekantor is. And Lorman wouldn't have contacted them without us."

"He didn't know who'd done it."

"Nekantor did. He was certain it was Grobal Innis who had attacked us."

"Grobal Tagaret, someone attacked you?" That was Forder, who sounded baffled.

"Not me, Forder," Tagaret said gently. "My little brother. I'm sorry, but give us a minute to think, please, all right?"

Della sat back on her heels and pressed her hands together over her nose, trying to remember. Adon and Pyaras had been attacked, but not Tagaret. That felt important. Even at the time, it had felt like part of a much larger plan. And Nekantor had seemed so sure the attack had come from Innis of the Fifth Family, sure enough to challenge him to that Imbati Privilege competition. The competition where Tagaret learned Nek had chosen Unger for Alixi of Selimna.

"Do you remember what happened to Grobal Innis of the Fifth Family?" she asked. "We thought he might have come here to threaten us, but he never did. We thought he might have been trying to escape retaliation from Nekantor, but Nekantor never retaliated."

"You're right. I haven't heard anything about retaliation, either from Pyaras or from Adon. And I should have. Nekantor doesn't let things go."

"Innis spoke to Unger about it in the Ride car," Della said. "Remember? He said something like he didn't think Unger should have accepted the position when Nekantor made him Alixi."

"Unger said he'd forced Nekantor's hand, and Innis said no, he hadn't."

Forced his hand, and hadn't. Like she thought she'd changed his mind, and hadn't.

"Innis was behind the attacks," she said. "You told me he was, when you came home from that Privilege competition. So that's why Unger believed he forced Nekantor's hand. But forced him to do what? To give Unger the appointment?"

"It can't be that. The appointment happened before the attacks."

She could feel that all of it was connected. She looked down at the card again. The Paper Shadows were supposed to bring about retaliation.

"Retaliation," she whispered. "Tagaret, what if the *attacks* were the retaliation?"

"For Unger's appointment? Why would you retaliate for an unexpected promotion? Unless—"

"Unless it wasn't one." Della shook her head. "Unger saw it that way, but Innis didn't; he wanted Unger back in Pelismara. Wait—" She pressed her eyes closed, imagining the freight section of the Ride car, the men speaking above, something about how this was not Unger's particular accomplishment . . . "Satenya. Who is Satenya?"

An unexpected voice spoke: Tagaret's Kuarmei had emerged from the private rooms with an intense look on her face. "Mistress, Satenya of the Seventh Family is the new Alixi of Peak," she said. "He passed through Daronvel Crossroads the day before you did."

"And left his glove!" Della exclaimed. "I remember now. Two new Alixi, both under thirty. One from the Seventh Family and one from the Fifth, passing through Daronvel within days of each other, because . . . because . . ." Her whole body went cold. "Oh, mercy, Tagaret, it was because Nekantor wanted them *out of Pelismara*, and had the power to send them wherever he wanted. He had the power to send *us* wherever he wanted, too. I gave him the idea. We wanted to keep him from seeing what *we* were doing—but he wanted to keep *us* from seeing what *he* was doing!"

Tagaret's voice shook. "And what he was doing—"

"He was sending promising young men of other Families out of Pelismara. It was supposed to look like promotions, but Innis saw it for what it really was—an attempt to remove potential Heir candidates. So he retaliated. Which means Nekantor is planning an Heir Selection. The Eminence Herin is in danger. Heile's mercy, he might already be dead!"

"No," Tagaret protested. "That can't be it."

"Of course it can."

Tagaret shook his head vehemently. "But you weren't there, at the Privilege competition. Innis' Brithe asked that question. He asked whether Nekantor was planning to assassinate Herin, and Dexelin said 'no.'"

Sweet Heile, how she wanted him to be right! But already, she knew the answer. "Dexelin *didn't know*, Tagaret. Your brother can't stand Imbati; he wouldn't have told Dexelin his most dangerous secret."

"Not in his first three weeks on the job." Tagaret shook his head. "But if Nek was planning to kill Herin, shouldn't he have done it already? He's always had his eye on Adon; why not do all this when Adon turned twelve?"

The answer to that had just arrived in the mail this morning. "Because of you," Della said. "In three days, you'll be thirty-one. You won't be eligible. So when Lorman chooses the First Family's candidate for Heir, he'll have to pick Adon."

"This is bad." Tagaret stood up. "We have to stop it. Warn Herin, somehow. A letter is too slow. And surely Nekantor will have spies watching the radiograph stations."

There was only one solution. Della moved her skirts out of the way, braced both hands on the table, and stood up slowly. "Sorry to keep you waiting, Melumalai Forder," she said. "Would you like to go to Pelismara?"

"Yes," said Forder. "Today?"

She nodded. "Right now."

CHAPTER TWENTY

A Special Mission

Some problems were for your therapist; others, you had to take to your Captain. Melín approached the door of her former Division adjunct substation before dayrise, with her fingers twitching. Hopefully her memory of Captain Keyt's habits wouldn't let her down.

The lights were off inside, and the glass door was locked. She tried the handle twice—shook it, just to be sure.

Varin's teeth.

She turned her back and leaned against the glass door. Why had she even come? And what if Captain decided to demerit or fine her for failing to turn in her blade?

She should go before someone she knew showed up and sneered—but the sooner she went to work, the sooner she'd end up posted on one of Eminence Herin's gods-forsaken doors.

Someone knocked on the glass at her back.

Melín turned around and found a pale Eighth staring at her—practically a child, with prominent ears and eager eyes. She motioned at him to open the door.

The young man opened it by a crack. "Seni, we're not open for an hour."

"Specialist First Melín reporting to Captain Keyt," Melín said sharply. Words she hadn't uttered in months—they felt strange in her mouth. She could feel his skeptical eyes taking in her orange uniform with its rank pin of Eighth. Rage and hate flashed. Let them burn these vile clothes from her body! "It's urgent."

He drew himself up. "We're not open for an hour."

She spoke louder. "Specialist First Melín. Reporting to Captain Keyt. It's urgent!" What if Captain wasn't here? First a tool, and now a fool . . .

The young man set his jaw. "I can take the Captain a message."

"That's my message. Please take it to her now."

"Seni. We're not open for—"

"Stand down, Eighth." A short, powerful figure appeared in the shadows of the office, beside a bright open door. The weights room.

Captain. Thank Plis!

"I bring a report, Captain," Melín said. "It's urgent."

"Come. Report." Captain vanished back into the weights room.

At last, the officious young Eighth stepped aside and swung the glass door open. Melín marched through without looking at him. When she entered the weights room, she found Captain back in the cage, out of uniform and sweaty, pumping legs.

"Melín," said Captain Keyt.

"Captain." About to launch into a report, she stumbled on her own rank. The last thing she needed was for Captain to argue on that point. "Melín, reporting. I've discovered a potentially dangerous problem in the Eminence's Cohort."

Legs straight, weights suspended in air, Captain Keyt fixed her eye on her. "What type of problem?"

"Divided loyalties, Captain. Part of the Cohort appears loyal to the Eminence Herin, and part to the Heir Nekantor."

Captain Keyt slowly bent her legs again, allowing the weights to click down on the stack. "What brings you to this conclusion?"

"Lack of discipline, sir," Melín said. "Infighting. Loyalty contests, a new ranking system, guards getting paid outside the usual channels. Dangerous behaviors like risky dares. I had to call out wysp-shotting in front of the Eminence and the Heir yesterday. The Eminence immediately forbade it on penalty of expulsion, but I'm not even sure that will be enough."

Captain raised her eyebrows. "You're still wearing a Cohort uniform."

"Captain, I wasn't lucky enough to be expelled. Everyone still thinks I'm on the Heir's side."

Captain swung her booted feet to the floor and stood, grabbing a towel from a bar on the cage and wrapping it around her neck. "Specialist, in my office."

Specialist?

Melín followed her across the darkened station. Captain Keyt entered the office, but didn't go behind her desk.

"Close the door, would you, Specialist?"

"Yes, sir." She pushed the door shut. This wasn't normal. She should not have been called Specialist. She should have been asked about her missing blade, at the very least.

"Specialist Melín," said Captain Keyt, still scrubbing the back of her head with the towel. "Since your departure I've had several—let's call them troubling—interactions with Commander Abru of the Eminence's Cohort. One of the first was when he told me about your ankle injury, but refused to give details, as if it were unimportant."

"Sir." Captain had been asking after her?

"After the second of these interactions, I decided to report to Commander Tret." She dropped her towel on the corner of the steel desk. "He told me he's had reports of the Cohort's behavior becoming increasingly erratic. Commander Tret and I don't believe there's any danger of increased wysp attacks in the city-caverns, provided that wysp-shotting can be kept under control. All this is to say, your report adds clarity to what I've already been investigating. Commander Abru appears to be in denial about the seriousness of these problems, and there isn't much recourse to be had in the chain of command. None, actually, if what you're saying is correct."

"Sir," Melín said. "I could be wrong, sir."

"You also happen to be in a position to determine whether you're right." Captain bent and opened a squeaky drawer. "As of now, you're back in the Division under my command. I'm promoting you, whether you like it or not."

Hand of Plis! Melín instinctively snapped to attention. "Sir!"

Captain Keyt straightened. Shorter than Melín though she was, her power and energy lent her stature. "Melín, you are hereby promoted to the rank of Captain's Hand."

"Yes, sir. Thank you, sir."

"I'm assigning you a special mission: return to the Eminence's Cohort and learn what you can about the factional divisions you describe, the risky behaviors, and their consequences. Report any findings directly to me."

"Yes, sir."

Captain Keyt held out the silver rank pin of a Captain's Hand. "Keep this hidden. The change in your assignment and rank must be considered protected information."

"Captain," said Melín. The word felt right on her tongue again, the way it always used to—thank Mai for justice! "I must inform you that my Division blade has been stolen. First Karyas of the Eminence's Cohort took it from me the day they attacked me and injured my ankle. I fear how she may intend to use it."

Captain Keyt scowled. "Put that among your investigative priorities, Hand."

"Yes, sir."

"Dismissed."

"Thank you, sir." Melín tucked her new rank pin into an inside pocket as she left the office. She said nothing to the young Eighth who had tried to bar her entry. She was an Eighth, so far as the world or the Cohort knew.

But by Mai's hand, the right had been partially restored. And she now had an excellent reason to look forward to reporting for work.

With twenty minutes still remaining before she'd be expected to report to First Crenn, she might as well start investigating now. You had to watch out for a piece of carrion like Karyas anyway, but today she could start tracking her rather than avoiding her. When Melín entered the station, lights were on, but not that many mates were here yet.

If someone like Crenn was reporting directly to First Karyas, this seemed like an obvious time for it. She stuck her head into the Eights ready room. Lights on, but nobody was here.

Maybe farther in. She entered the desk-workers' area. It wasn't empty; a couple of mates were getting an early start. She sauntered down between the desks toward the private offices. Commander Abru's office was locked and dark. The second office door was open, but the lights were off. The third office—

"I'm not happy with your results, Crenn."

Karyas' voice, from the darkened second office. Too easy. Either Karyas was stupid, or just stupidly confident. Melín walked a couple more steps at the same pace, and sat down at one of the desks as though it belonged to her. Maybe she'd get to hear what they were planning.

"I'm sorry, sir," said Crenn.

"I don't understand why you haven't fought her yet. Not scared, are you?"

The word 'her' put a bad feeling in Melín's stomach. This sounded less like mutiny, and more like a personal problem.

"Sir," Crenn objected. "The Eighth is not soft. When we broke her in, I lost my Sixth and Third to medics for over a week."

"Against a flimsy Specialist. Pathetic."

"Sir—"

"We need her managed."

"She's ours, though, sir. She was hand-picked—" Crenn grunted, as though Karyas had hit him.

"Don't talk to me about her skills, Crenn. Until she's managed, she's a danger. Assign her to the Eminence's dining room."

"Sir—"

"Do it. If she breaks, that solves our problem. If she gets fired, or dies, that also solves our problem."

"Yes, sir."

Footsteps! Melín ducked quickly below the level of the desk. Her ankle twinged.

The boot sounds emerged from the office . . . and immediately turned in this direction. Sickened, Melín realized she'd nudged the rolling chair.

Karyas burst out laughing. "Eighth Melín, you little sneak! Stand up."

Melín gritted her teeth and stood.

"Congratulations." Karyas licked her teeth. "I'll tell you now: it doesn't matter what you heard. You'll take your assignment because there's nothing you can do about it."

Crenn emerged behind her, smirking. "Reporting for duty, Eighth? You're assigned to the post at the door of the Eminence's dining room."

Melín looked between them, controlling her breathing. "Yes, sir."

"Go."

Of course, that meant she spent the entire morning trying to figure out what was so dangerous about the door outside the Eminence's dining room. She memorized the blond stone floor, the Grobal-green carpet, the ceiling vaults, the curtains along the walls, the entrance of a spiral stairway, and the Maze entrances where Imbati were likely to appear.

Really, there were only two unusual things about this hall. One was a small foyer outside the Eminence's private library, which had two guards and a window overlooking the gardens. It was not directly visible from her position on the dining room door, and on the third floor, no one was likely to access that window from the outside. The other unusual thing was that the hall ended at the grand rotunda, a bright column of space beneath a flattened dome of milky white glass. Across that column of air was the rich foyer that housed the entrance of the Eminent Chambers. Curved marble staircases from the lower floors ended there, and walkways led around the edge of the rotunda to give the Eminence access to this hall.

In four hours of standing, she glimpsed the Eminence Herin only once, when he left his Chambers and walked down the stairs with his manservant and his slab of a Cohort bodyguard.

Regardless, Karyas and Crenn clearly thought she might die here.

Her thighs twitched.

At noon, she was relieved, and took her break in the nearest guard room on the second floor. Four mates sat on stools around the table, eating mushroom or compressed fruit bars from the machine in the corner. They didn't seem much bothered by her joining them, but she stayed on the alert while she took a stool. "Seni."

"Seni," they replied.

"Mind if I ask . . . is there anything dangerous I should know about the third floor?"

Two of the four chuckled. "Not really," said the man beside her. "Unless you count the Eminence or the Heir. They eat dinner together sometimes."

She most certainly did.

The woman on her other side said, "Watch out for Lady Falya, the Eminence's partner. She won't take any nonsense."

Yeah, sure. But nonsense wasn't exactly her worry.

Over the course of the afternoon, the Heir made no appearances. As the dinner hour approached, a party of five climbed up from the rotunda. It was just the Eminence Herin and Lady Falya, their Imbati, and the Cohort bodyguard.

Was she being set up to be abused by them, somehow? No; that wouldn't be deadly.

Lady Falya's Imbati came to the front and opened the dining room door. The party passed by her without a word. There was nothing but faint murmurs under the door for an hour, and then they left, circling the rotunda to return to the Eminent Chambers.

Nothing dangerous.

When her relief arrived at the end of the day, Melín held professional stance just long enough to march out of the Residence. Then she shifted onto one leg and stretched her injured ankle a couple of times;

and when that was done, she leaned her head side to side, trying to get the ache out.

Plis and Mai, where are your blessings when I need them?

For a moment, she closed her eyes and imagined sunblast. The fields. The thrill of receiving a whistle signal. The battle they had to win, and were so close to losing while these pompous idiots strutted in silk and velvet.

She would get back there. Today she'd taken the first step.

I'm Division now. Nekantor can't change that if he never finds out.

Night fell as she walked along the gravel path back to the Cohort station. The atmospheric lamps on the cavern roof lowered to a dim, fading glow, and the path lamps came on. For some reason, a group of twenty or so mates had gathered in two clumps outside the station door. She started to walk between them—and they collapsed on her.

Punches flew. Melín ducked and dodged, trying to get to the door. A pair of mates wrestled into her path—this wasn't just about her, then—she laid hands on them enough to dodge around, jumped a trip, ducked again, and made it to the door. She flung it wide and bellowed,

"Commander Abru!"

The Cohort Commander did not appear. She did, however, get the attention of a number of the fighters. The nearest ones laid off each other and turned toward her with fists at the ready.

Varin's teeth.

"Don't think I'm just gonna let you jump me," she snapped. "The door's right here." She scanned over the group; two or three from her own eight were here, not that she was about to lay down her neck for them. On the other hand, "Fifth Sahris will support me, won't you."

Fifth Sahris grunted. "Yeah."

Good enough.

"You carrion-eating tunnel-hound," said a dark-haired man with a blunt nose. "You come in here with the Heir's favor and think you can push us with no consequences."

She snorted. "Not really."

The blunt-nosed man pulled an orange handkerchief from his pocket and threw it on the ground. "Knives, to blood. Right now. At the Ring."

A duel? Oh, my ass.

Melín picked up the handkerchief. "Fine, but forget the Ring. I'll fight you right here and now. With seconds."

"Sahris seconds Melín," called Sahris immediately.

Another voice came from the back of the group. "Drenas seconds Xunir."

The shape of the group shifted. People separated, back to the groups she'd seen before the fight started. She scanned the faces, sorting them. Best guess, these were the Nekantor partisans on this side. And on the other side, the blunt-nosed Xunir was backed up by none other than the Eminence Herin's slab of a bodyguard, so those would be Herin's people.

Hard to be sure, since no one was shouting slogans.

Xunir pulled his knife.

Melín drew hers. Too blasted short. Plis, she missed her blade. Xunir also had the advantage of reach. A loss here wouldn't be like jumping off a cliff, but gnash it! She wasn't in the mood to bleed. Or see the medic again so soon. She hung back, stance low, dancing foot to foot, waiting for him to make a move.

Xunir leered and jabbed.

She dodged, swinging her blade out to catch him behind the elbow.

Missed.

Too blasted short!

And he was still coming. *Watch out, watch out!*

A tearing sound—she sucked in her stomach with all her might, spun, sliced decisively across his shoulder.

Xunir roared in rage.

Drenas laughed.

"Blood!" Sahris cried. "Victory to Eighth Melín!"

Really? Melín pressed her hand to her side—and found a cut in her uniform. She sneaked a finger through it, feeling her side to be sure.

No blood.

"Crown of Mai," she said. "Thanks, Sahris. Wanna get out of here?"

"I gotta report this to First Crenn. But I'll clock you out."

Melín studied the other woman for a second. Whether Crenn had it out for her or not, Fifth Sahris was starting to look more like an ally. "All right. Thanks; tonight's my night to meet my isseni for dinner, and I'm already late."

She walked toward the exit of the grounds cautiously, because the duel had made her ankle tender. By the gate, she stopped and checked her ankle tape, and made sure to clean her knife-tip on her handkerchief.

Not a lot of blood; she'd done well.

Whenever it was time for Aripo to go and Drefne to stay awhile, Melín would meet him at the Riverside. It was right at the end of the Trao river's controlled path across the second level. The Trao ran swift here, between railed banks, heading out past the targetball arena and beyond the city's edge. She'd patrolled the adjuncts out there before. Out of sight of cityfolk, the river ran through a generator, powering this neighborhood on its way down to the third level. But here, in the space between the river and the giant targetball players depicted on the arena walls, the ground was paved with geometric tiles, offering benches and fountains. The best thing was that Melumalai food stands popped up here like mushrooms.

Drefne waited in the glow of a street lamp near their favorite skewer place. Dressed in red, not orange—handsome, and *safe*. She jogged toward him, bracelets jingling, and didn't stop until she felt his body bump hers. When he bent down for a kiss, his hand pressed her side. Mercy, the exact spot where she'd almost been sliced with a knife! She shuddered and flung her arms around him, squeezing so hard he wheezed a laugh.

"Whoa, isseni, were you planning to bed me before dinner? 'Cause I'm kind of hungry after slopping through adjuncts all day."

"I'm hungry too, isseni," she said. "Just happy to see you."

Drefne cupped her under the ear. "Happy to see you, too. And to be the one walking you home tonight."

They fished coins from their pockets for the Melumalai, a girl who reached around the steam from her red-glowing grill to hand them long metal skewers. Clustered near the end were steaming chunks of grilled oryen and vegetables.

Gods, that smelled like heaven.

"Mf!" Melín tore bites off with her teeth, one after the other, as they walked between the circles of orange light. "Dref—" she swallowed, and dropped her empty skewer into one of the collection bins. "Can you do a repair for me?"

"What kind?" She must have made some kind of face, because he frowned, still chewing. "Isseni, did you get yourself in trouble again?"

"Not my*self*," she said. "Cut in my uniform. You can sew it closed, right?"

He stared at her. "I can't believe you!"

"He started it."

Drefne puckered his lips disapprovingly.

She put her hands on her hips. "What? He should have known better. Don't throw down if you can't handle a few stitches."

"I'm starting to think Aripo's right, you know. You had your fight stolen from you, so you're looking for one."

"I didn't do anything. Mai's truth! The Cohort has it out for me. They're sick."

Drefne stopped on one leg, angling his hips in that way he had. He really had no idea how sexy it was. Or maybe he did. "I've changed my mind, isseni. You need to do something fun. We're buying ices and I'm taking you to targetball."

"Targetball? I thought the final was tomorrow night?"

"Tonight's the under-nineteens final. We're late, so they might be into the second quarter—you know what? We're not discussing this." Drefne hopped over a bench and jogged toward a stalagmite-seller. When Melín caught up, he'd already made a purchase. He handed her a deep red ice spike in a flexible insulated holder. She licked it—marshberry.

"Thanks, Dref."

"So, targetball," he said. "The Cave-Cats under-nineteens have a new center, and you have to see her. Last week she hit target from the quartermark, upside-down with her legs in the ropes."

"Wow." But she hesitated. In the corner of her eye by the river rail, a pair of figures stood together, talking.

One was the veteran assassin Treminindi. The other was someone she wanted to drive this ice spike into. They didn't seem to have seen her, so she took Drefne's hand and walked away at a steady, not hurried, pace. She didn't feel safe until she and Drefne had crossed all the way to the arena and started up the ramp to the entrance.

Treminindi had been talking with First Karyas.

She might just have found her danger.

CHAPTER TWENTY-ONE

Desperate Measures

There was nothing worse than being tied down and kicked internally for thirty solid hours. Escape from the seatbelt was incredibly welcome, but Della's legs wobbled, and she was out of breath by the time she and Tagaret reached Lady Selemei's office. Tagaret pushed in the door without knocking; she followed him and leaned against one of the desks in the outer office, panting.

Lady Selemei's son Corrim gave a sort of yelp and dashed for the inner office door, crying, "Mother! It's Tagaret!"

Lady Selemei's voice echoed from inside. "Tagaret?" The Lady rushed out with her Ustin behind her shoulder. "Tagaret! Della—what are you doing here? What's wrong?"

"Lady," Della began, but couldn't manage another word before her unwelcome resident cut her short with a vicious kick under the ribs.

"It's an emergency," said Tagaret. "We think Nekantor's going to try to assassinate the Eminence Herin. Today."

"*Today?* Why?" Selemei dropped one gloved hand into her jasper-striped skirts. "Holy Sirin, Tagaret, it's your birthday. You're thirty-one. I should have thought of it before."

Della finally found enough breath. "The question is, what can we do to stop it?"

"Imbati first." Lady Selemei turned to the tall servant behind her. "Ustin, every manservant and every member of the Household must know about these suspicions immediately. But you haven't heard this news from us."

Imbati Ustin smoothly bowed until her head touched the floor. "My heart is as deep as the heavens. No word uttered in confidence will escape it." She stood swiftly and leapt out the door.

"That's not enough, is it?" Della asked.

"It might be," said Lady Selemei. "But the Luck-Bringer's hand is not always kind. We need to take other steps. For one thing, people will soon realize you've come home, and wonder why."

"I've thought about that," said Tagaret. "I've come home because I couldn't bear to be away from Adon on my birthday."

Selemei nodded. "It'll do, for most people's purposes—but let's think ahead. Say we do manage to save Herin from your brother's plan; Nekantor must not suspect that you've acted against him."

Della swallowed. Already her fingers felt cold, her stomach uncomfortably hot and full. In her panic, she'd forgotten to put on her gloves. "We can go home," she said. "We want to see Tamelera and Adon anyway. Tagaret, we'll make sure that you're in plain sight of people who can vouch for you."

Tagaret nodded.

"Keep in contact, please," said Lady Selemei. "I'll get working on contingency plans, in case we fail."

In case of Heir Selection. The memory of last time washed over her with a sickening rush. Death, panic, traps, extortion . . . "Mai help us," Della whispered.

"We can't fail," Tagaret said. "We just can't."

"Let's go home," said Della. "The sooner we get there, the safer you are. And we should take Forder with us. We shouldn't leave him waiting in the floater for an hour while we figure things out."

On their way to take Forder to the suites wing, they sighted several members of the Household standing on the alert. Not in customary locations, so Ustin's message must already be traveling fast. It was reassuring.

A little.

Leaving Forder to wait by the door of their suite, Della and Tagaret entered. Lady Tamelera half-screamed at the sight of them. She ran and clasped them both tightly in her arms. "Oh, my loves, my darlings! And Tagaret, love, it's your birthday, congratulations . . . not seeing you was killing me, and now, and now!"

"I love you, Mother," Tagaret sighed, leaning into her shoulder. "I missed you so much."

"I love you, too," Della said. It was weird to be back here so suddenly, and discover so many things exactly the same as before.

"Here I haven't prepared a single thing to celebrate . . ." Tamelera stepped back from their arms. "Serjer, contact Kartunnen Vant and tell him to come right away. We must at least have music."

"Right away, Mistress," said Serjer. "I do believe we have a guest?"

"Forder, please come in," Della called. Forder walked in, looking about with wide eyes. "Forder, this is Tagaret's mother, Lady Tamelera. Mother, this is our friend Forder, the son of the paper merchants Tagaret wrote to you about. He'll expect to shake your hand. You should tell him how many times."

"Oh, well," said Tamelera. "Perhaps I'll curtsy, and you can bow, Forder. It's a pleasure to meet you."

Forder crossed one forearm across his stomach and bowed. "Greetings of the day, Lady Tamelera."

"I do hope you like music, Forder," said Della. "It's one of our family's favorite things."

"Yes," said Forder heartily. "I own a player machine and one hundred and thirty-four recordings, so."

"This will be an excellent gathering, then," said Tamelera.

"It will," Della agreed. "But I don't think it will be perfect until you call Adon home from school."

She'd tried to say it lightly, but Tamelera was too smart. She looked between her and Tagaret, blue eyes piercing. "What is it? Is Adon in danger?"

Oh, gods, that question. *Was* he in danger? Mercy! If Herin fell, he would be. Selemei's youngest son and oldest grandson would be. Pyaras would be. Every boy between twelve and thirty was eligible . . .

Not yet. *Not yet!* They could still stop this.

"No," she answered.

"I'll explain when Adon's here," said Tagaret. "How about I go get him? He did say in his letter that he wanted to see me. That would make a lovely surprise."

"Of course, love," said Tamelera. "Adon will be thrilled."

"I'll be back soon."

The moment he left, here she found herself—face to face with Tamelera. Despite Forder standing by, it felt like being stripped naked. She was instantly certain Tamelera knew. And of course the interloper chose this moment to start knocking on her spine. In Pelismara, being pregnant came with expectations, and consequences. Della tried to smile, but the sheer weight of *everything* threatened to crush her.

"My lovely Della," said Tamelera gently. "How can I make you feel comfortable? You've been on the Road so long . . . are you hungry?"

That question felt like a trap. Her throat went dry. The problem was, she *was* hungry. Very. "I—uh, I wouldn't mind something to eat. Forder, are you hungry?"

"Yes," said Forder.

"Maybe we could have something when Tagaret gets back?"

The corners of Tamelera's mouth curved upward. "Oh, I have to ask you. Did you enjoy the bread in Selimna?"

Della startled, and a smile sneaked onto her lips. "Yes!"

Tamelera nodded. "All these years later, and I still remember it so clearly. When I was there, I couldn't stop eating it. My figure changed entirely."

Della blinked at her. *That wasn't true at all.* Not that Tagaret had ever mentioned. But, staring at Tamelera, she realized her partner-mother *did* know . . . and had just handed her a shield. Her eyes felt hot. "M-my goodness, I believe it," she stammered. "I went to the bakery every morning."

"Well, you're home now. Please, try to relax. Forder, have a seat. I'll ask Keeper Premel to get us some drinks."

Forder dutifully went to a chair and sat in it.

The couch also looked very comfortable, but before she could sit down, a kick hit her in the bladder. "Mother, and Forder, will you excuse me for a moment before we eat?"

"Of course," Tamelera said. "Take your time."

Della walked back through the familiar double doors, and into her former rooms. To the bathroom. Yoral, who had silently accompanied her, helped her lift her skirts.

"Mistress, call me if you need anything."

"Of course, Yoral." She held her smile until he closed the door, and then bit her lip as she sat down.

The fear was back.

Every hour of the voyage, she'd become more conscious of the struggle to hold everything in—her bulging stomach, her feelings, her tears, her urine, everything. She'd felt like she was getting up to go to the bathroom constantly, and she'd wobbled into things at least three times. There was a bruise on her forearm, and probably one on her knee. The worst bruises, though, were inside—injuries of repeated sharp blows under her ribs, inside her hips, assaults where no one could see.

Now that she was here, the bulge felt like a disaster, a cavern lake heavy with too much water, moments away from the inevitable collapse that would flood everything underneath. In nightmares, she'd re-experienced the horror of the failure to come: a lake of blood, and at the center of it, a twisted corpse with hair and teeth.

Not now, not now, not now . . .

But the longer the waiting lasted, the worse the end would be. How could she beg for it not to be now?

Heile have mercy, have mercy on me . . .

Apparently, it would not be right now. Della stood, stepped away from the toilet, rearranged herself, and washed her hands. Took a deep breath, though breaths weren't deep enough any more. She opened the bathroom door, and gave Yoral a nod that meant, *not yet.*

He nodded back. He'd been counting the weeks, the months, the fifths; she hadn't, and didn't want to ask. Mother Elinda's eyes felt cold on the back of her neck.

She was still here. Still putting one foot in front of the other.

When she emerged into the sitting room, she found Serjer holding instrument cases. Vant was standing in the vestibule.

"Vant!" She almost ran to hug him, but he wouldn't have appreciated it.

He smiled, and bowed. "Lady Della."

"You came so quickly. I've missed you—have you met Forder?"

"I hadn't yet had a chance to introduce them," said Tamelera.

"Well! Kartunnen Vant, this is my friend, Melumalai Forder. Melumalai Forder, Kartunnen Vant."

"Kartunnen," said Forder, standing up. "The focused mind is the sustainer of life."

"It's a pleasure to meet you, sir," said Vant. And immediately blushed so red that the burn scar on his left cheekbone stood out.

"You have a scar on your face!" Forder exclaimed with delight. "I have one, too. Not on my face. Here; look." He held out his left hand to the musician. "A paper cutter sliced off the tip of my finger, so."

"Oh, ouch!" said Vant. "I'm so sorry." Sympathy seemed to snap him out of his embarrassment.

"Please, both of you, make yourselves comfortable," said Tamelera. "Vant, do have something to eat with us before you have to start working."

"You're kind, Lady, but I'm happy to play."

Vant took a wooden chair from the gaming table, set up in the corner by Tagaret's office, and played a series of beautiful songs on the pipes while they sat together, drinking juice and tea and eating crackers.

Forder seemed to love the music, and after a time he abandoned his food to go and stand near Vant, watching his fingers on the pipes.

At last, Tagaret returned. He looked quite solemn, though he smiled whenever he looked down at Adon.

Adon had changed as nothing else had. He'd filled out the green velvet suit he'd received for his birthday, and looked very grown up; his dark hair was longer, almost in his eyes, and he was at least an inch taller. Della went to him and started to ask for a hug, but already he was flinging his arms around her.

"Oh, Adon," she sighed. "I'm so happy to see you."

"I can't believe it," Adon said. "I can't believe you came home, for *me*."

Della looked to Tagaret and saw him swallow, anxiety bobbing in his throat.

"We are so happy that we can be with you today," Tagaret said, then lowered his voice. "I wish celebration were the only reason."

Tamelera drew closer, closing her fists on her skirts. "I had a feeling."

Adon sighed. "So did I. There are too many Household in the halls today. And too many guards."

"I'm not surprised you noticed." Della mustered her courage to say it aloud, but hesitated, glancing at Vant and Forder in the corner. "Adon, we won't keep secrets from you, but we'll be in danger if we're ever identified as the source of this, so you mustn't speak of it outside the house."

Adon's eyebrows rose into his hair. "In *danger*—?" He shook his head. "All right. I won't say a word."

"We think Nekantor will try to kill the Eminence Herin today."

"Wh—Varin's teeth!"

"Adon," said Tamelera reprovingly. Her back had stiffened, though she'd scarcely moved. "I assume you're sure, and have a good reason to be telling Adon."

"This is about him, Mother," Della said. "Nekantor wouldn't have picked today unless it were."

"I can't compete with him any more," Tagaret explained. "You remember how Nekantor placed Unger of the Fifth Family in Selimna, when we were expecting him to send us? That looks like it was part of a larger plan to place prominent young men from other Families outside of Pelismara. We only recently realized what it meant."

"Innis of the Fifth Family figured it out first," Della added.

Tamelera hissed in a breath. "Of course he did. And we know what his answer was. So what do we do now?"

"Well, we have outside witnesses who can place me here at home," said Tagaret. "I can probably go out, so long as I'm publicly visible. Unless we hear of arrests or violence, we need to keep trying to stop it. There are people we need to reach out to."

"Yes," Della agreed. "I'm going to go out with Forder and find the murder shop."

What did a murder shop look like?

A shop with shelves full of human bones?

A dirty alleyway where bloodthirsty Arissen would skulk out of sight?

A hidden drinking spot allowing Arissen to numb all compassion with alcohol before they did terrible deeds?

Heile have mercy!

By the time her Yoral pulled the skimmer to a stop at Barell Circumference and Ensindim Radius, Della was trying hard not to panic. This neighborhood wasn't ill-lit or unclean, however—quite the opposite. One corner of the intersection was occupied by an irregular stone cascade with a bright shinca piercing through it; the others were shops typical of those you'd expect anywhere along this road, fancy specialty places run by Melumalai. Neither she nor Melumalai Forder looked out of place here, even if no one would have expected them to arrive together.

Which meant she might be right in front of a murder shop, with no idea how to find it.

"Grobal Della," said Forder, "why do you need to find this place?"

Della blushed, and stood up with one hand on the edge of the skimmer seat; her balance was weird again. "I—I'm not sure," she admitted. She'd brought Forder because he'd seen the shadow of the card, but as for why *she* should be here? It wasn't as though she could find assassins and say 'Don't kill Herin, please' for best results . . . "I guess I'm tired of feeling like killers are out there and we don't know who they are. I've been through this once before, Forder."

"When did you go through this before?"

"About fourteen years ago. The Eminence died, and when that

happens, suddenly everyone starts walking around with guards, fearing shadows."

"Paper Shadows?"

"Yes." She nodded and pushed her hair behind her ears. "Paper Shadows are Arissen with weapons. They tried to kill Tagaret. And his brother Nekantor. They did kill one of the other young men . . . but no one ever tries to find them. Why would no one ever try to find them? Why would no one hold them responsible?"

"Hm," said Forder. "Recycling, so."

She turned to look at him, and wobbled; her Yoral caught her elbow. "You're right." Adon's assassin had been caught, and then killed. If the Paper Shadows were ever held responsible, *they could no longer be used.* "Varin gnash them all," she spat. "The assassins, Innis, all of them." Any divine retribution would have to wait until they died, though, and right now it seemed like this was a dead end.

Herin still didn't deserve to be killed.

Do something.

"No. Crown of Mai, I'm not giving up. Yoral, let's just walk and look into a few of these shops."

"Of course, Mistress." He offered her his arm.

"Forder, you can look around, if you'd like. I'm sorry I took you away from the music on a chase into the dark."

Forder only beamed. "This is a tour, so," he said. "Mom said Pelismara was flat, but it's so very very flat! I need to make notes on the layouts of stores, anyway."

"Well, please do. How about we meet back here in twelve minutes?"

Forder readied a pad of paper and a pencil from his pocket, and wandered off.

Della started looking. There was a Kartunnen-owned jewelry store across from the shinca; it shared a front wall with a restaurant, and across the street was a small theater that advertised a singing competition. Both restaurant and theater were closed at this hour. On the fourth corner were a clothing shop and a shop with silk and wood items. There was no shop on the shinca corner itself, but the nearest building was an empty storefront with paper in the windows.

Paper in the windows seemed promising. She tried to peer through a crack at the side of it, to no avail.

"Excuse me, Mistress," her Yoral said. "May I look?"

She stepped back, while he placed one foot on the sill of the papered window and hopped up to look through a larger gap nearer the top.

"What can you see?" she asked.

Yoral hopped back down. "It's construction," he said. "I don't think this is what we're looking for."

She sighed. "We came all the way out here."

Yoral reached into a hidden pocket and extracted the card that had brought them. "Mistress," he said, considering it, "I don't believe the Paper Shadows should want to make their contacts difficult to find."

"May I see?" A normal business card would have a number on it. She took the card and flipped it over. Nothing written on the card, and there'd been no numbers in the shadow, only the name of the intersection. The only other feature the card had was its gold edge, and gold corners. Which, come to think of it, were asymmetrical, which was odd. They might be intended to signify something. A gold edge might be a number one. Gold-dipped corners, though? She held the gold edge in her hand, imagining it as a number one drawn between the upper and lower edges of the card. "Yoral? Do you see a store numbered one and six, or six and one?"

Yoral walked back toward the intersection, looking at the numbers. Suddenly he stopped, and ran back to her. "It's one and six, Lady. This way."

She held his fist, to make it easier to hurry. He led her back across the intersection to the shop called Silk and Wood. Its front window displayed several kinds of paper and envelopes, as well as wooden trinkets—rings, trays, bowls, and bottles.

Forder was already inside, taking notes.

Yoral opened the door for her, and a bell rang somewhere; Della walked in warily.

"Hello, Forder," she said.

Forder turned around. "This isn't a silk and wood shop, so."

How in Sirin's name had he figured that out? "Let's not talk about that for now," she said. "All right?"

"All right."

A blond Melumalai with a cute upturned nose came out from the back.

"Welcome, Lady," the cute man said. He gave a wary glance at

Forder, who still stood in the center of the shop, but then returned attention to her with a smile. "You realize, of course, that our paper is very expensive. Would you like to consider our selections?"

"Yes. Melumalai . . . ?"

"Melumalai will do, Lady." He bent down behind his counter as she approached it, and for an instant she really thought he might come up again with a tray full of human skulls. Instead, what he came up with was a tray made of glossy wood, with four short stacks of paper on it. Each type was embossed with a number, and two of the stacks had gold-dipped corners. One type had gold on all four of its edges.

"Wow, look at these, Forder," she said. To the nameless Melumalai, she smiled. "The embossing looks very nice."

"We do specialty embossing," the man said. "You can put your name on the paper—any name you like, in fact."

Forder arrived beside her elbow. "Castemate, you wear a heavy chain, so."

The nameless Melumalai gave a strained smile. The castemark necklace he wore was thick silver, with ten stones in it. Showing off his wealth, at least compared to Forder with his simple pendant. Forder was most definitely not poor.

"That's praise in Selimna," said Forder. "Is Pelismara different?"

"Thank you, Castemate," said the man. "Lady, perhaps we should speak of your needs in our private office. Whose name you would like stamped, and when you need the delivery. We can deliver by today, if your need is urgent."

"Oh, it's not—"

Forder hooked the corner of the wooden tray with one finger and pulled it decisively toward him. His notepad was gone, and now he held his blue light. Why hadn't she guessed he would always have it with him? By the time the blond man had blinked twice, he'd run checks on three of the paper stacks.

"Castemate, don't touch the merchandise!"

"Oh, don't worry," Della said. "He won't damage it. He's a friend of mine."

"What? Lady—"

"Forder," she said, "I think you should stop."

"But, Grobal Della," Forder objected.

"Please. Let me finish talking with this man."

Forder frowned. "Well, don't buy anything."

"Don't worry." She smiled at the Melumalai. "Do I have any way of meeting the delivery personnel?"

The Melumalai smiled back. "That's not part of our service, I'm afraid."

"Can you give me prices now, or only after we've settled on the embossing details?"

"We'll need to have a private meeting, Lady." He shot a pointed glance of disapproval at Forder, who was now realigning every sheet to its original position. "What's he doing?"

"Why, he's sorry and wouldn't want to leave your display disarranged, of course," she said. "I'm not in a hurry with my order. I'll speak with you soon, when we can meet privately."

"Thank you, Lady. We'll be happy to do business with you."

"Come, Forder, let's go." As she went to follow Forder out the shop door, an idea stopped her. "Melumalai, what's your cancellation policy for existing orders?"

The cute man had disappeared beneath the counter with his tray, but now he stood up again. "With refund, Lady? One week."

"Without?"

"Sixty-six hours for a provincial delivery. Two hours for a delivery in Pelismara."

"Can I buy out an existing order?"

The cute man blinked at her. "I'm sorry? I don't understand."

"Never mind. Thank you, Melumalai."

She held her breath, walking out. She joined Forder in the skimmer, while Yoral took the controls. Hopefully they didn't look too wary of being shot. Yoral engaged repulsion, and they drove down the Circumference. Only then did she dare exhale. She turned to Forder, whose short brown hair was ruffled by the wind of their passing.

"Forder, how in Sirin's name did you know that was the shop we were looking for?"

"Easy," said Forder. "Silk and Wood, but only silk paper was displayed. No silk handkerchiefs or scarves. Wood items, but no woodwaste paper. No sensible wholesaler would offer a client only half their merchandise, so."

"Clearly, we should have asked you first, then."

"Mistress," said Yoral, "I'm certain that Melumalai's offer to emboss names was code for identifying a target."

"He's protecting killers," Della said. "You can't actually speak to the Paper Shadows, just to a Melumalai who won't give his name."

"Yes, Mistress. He's also protecting himself from his own clients, who expect to stay anonymous."

Forder snorted scornfully. "That man doesn't know paper at all. He's an orsheth-eater, so."

Despite the deep disapproval in Forder's voice, she couldn't stop a laugh at the image of the cute man crunching down on a stack of orsheth coins. "What? They eat money?"

Forder shook his head. "I don't know Pelismara's way to say it. High price, way over base cost because the item value means nothing. Their true deal isn't legal, so."

"Shadow-sellers," Yoral said. "That's what they're called here."

"Ugh," said Della. "And now we know why. Let's get home and see if there's been any news."

So, the news," Della said. "It's not bad?"

Tagaret stopped pacing the sitting room, came to her, and wrapped her in a tight embrace. "Thank Eyn you're back. It's not bad, love, but it's not good either. It's nothing."

She rubbed his back, and the unwelcome resident gave a kick she was sure he'd also felt. "That's about as much as we learned, too." Who knew what would happen if she reported Silk and Wood to the Pelismar Police? They might disturb the Melumalai, and the store might be shut down, but surely it would just pop up elsewhere. She couldn't imagine it would make any difference in a delivery scheduled for today. She sat down on the couch, relieved to be off her feet, though any relief could only be temporary.

"Grobal Tagaret," said Forder, taking a seat farther down from her. "'Nothing' means no Arissen shooting, so."

"That's true," Tagaret agreed. "At least, so far."

"We appreciate your help very much, Forder," said Della. "Are you hungry?"

"Yes."

"Me, too."

"I'm hungry, too," said Adon, who sat beside Tamelera on the couch opposite. He was flipping the edge of his green velvet jacket against his knee. "This isn't how I imagined this day would go."

"Let's ask Keeper Premel to get lunch on," said Tamelera.

"I don't disagree about lunch," said Della, brushing down her skirts decisively to distract from a series of internal thumps. "But what do we do next? Walk up the rotunda stairs to the Eminent Chambers and tell Herin that his Heir is trying to kill him?"

"Grobal Della," Forder announced, "I don't want to talk to the Eminence, so."

"Oh, Forder, we wouldn't ask you to. That would be unfair."

Forder glanced toward the corner. "I liked the music. Why did Kartunnen Vant leave?"

"I'll ask him in again, I promise," Della said. "For now, would you like to get in contact with your cousins?"

"Yes, please," said Forder. "Their shop is on the third level, close to the Trao parks."

"Serjer," Della called. "Could you please arrange a ride for Forder?"

"Of course, Mistress Della," the First Houseman answered.

"As far as talking to the Eminence," said Tagaret, "I already sent my Kuarmei to request an informal audience. She was sent straight back. Herin isn't interested in speaking with me."

"Name of Varin." Adon sprang up. "Hey, Herin, do you want to chat with someone from the First Family or do you want to die?" He reversed his stance with a twirl that flared his jacket, and poked one finger to his chin, mockingly. "Oh, I don't know, I'm just too *handsome* to decide, maybe *die?*"

Della winced. "We could just barge in on him, if we knew where he was."

"The Household Director would know," said Tagaret. "But I don't think we could convince her to tell us."

Adon dropped his mocking pose. "I know."

"Adon, please don't joke," said Della.

The boy's cheeks flushed. "I'm not joking. Pyaras met Herin for lunch at Society Club Five a few weeks ago."

She stared at him.

"I guess he might not eat there every day."

Della looked at Tagaret.

"Sounds like a good idea to me," said Tagaret.

"All right," she agreed. "So long as we haven't heard that all is lost, we might as well give this a try."

Pelismara was such a cage—the feeling was worse because she'd just lost Selimna's grand views. Della's stomach muscles ached, alternately tensing and releasing against their burden. On either side of them, her Yoral and Tagaret's Kuarmei walked warily, scanning the streets for killers as they approached Society Club Five.

Would killers really lie in wait in the street, though? That didn't seem like Nekantor. Much as he enjoyed making a scene, his bigger plans tended to be covert and complex. If she had to guess, she'd pick something more subtle than Innis' assassin-in-the-Grobal-School ploy. Something like—poison.

They crossed the sidewalk and entered the front door of the windowless club. As it thudded shut behind them, she felt more and more certain.

The headwaiter at the club was a gray-haired woman with the crescent-cross tattoo of the Household. Tagaret approached her to inquire about a table for lunch. Della scanned for the Eminence. The stripes of brown and white leather that covered the walls distracted somewhat from the diners' faces, but maybe that was the point. Maybe Herin wasn't here at all.

If he wasn't here, she was definitely going to sit down and eat before going anywhere else. The juice and crackers she'd had earlier weren't going to hold her much longer.

Wait—there. Herin sat at a small table with his back toward the corner, looking out across the entire dining room. He was wearing a dark brown suit with white lace today, and his hair lay in tight perfect curls against his head. He was already eating quite happily, conversing with his pale-skinned partner, Lady Falya. Lady Falya's gold-and-brown hair was twined up onto her head, held there by sapphire-studded pins that matched her gown. Their manservants stood by, as did the huge Arissen bodyguard who had so disturbed Imbati Serjer at Adon's birthday party.

"Tagaret," she murmured. "I see them." She twined her gloved fingers into Tagaret's, all the while watching Herin's fork move from his plate, to his mouth, and back. "We could wait for a table, or you could just take me over there directly. Before he gets a bad bite."

Tagaret's head snapped around and his brown eyes stared down at her in dismay. Then he nodded and said to the headwaiter, "Please excuse us for a moment, Imbati."

Holding her hand in the crook of his elbow, Tagaret drew her into the dining area. Della squeezed his arm. People turned to watch them as they threaded in among the tables.

Hello, everyone. Yes, we're back. Much as I wish we didn't have to be.

They didn't get very close. Herin's Argun moved away from his Master, intercepting them when they were still two tables away. He inclined his head to them politely, but blocked the way forward.

"Sir, and Lady," he said in his deep voice. "The Eminence is having a private meal, and must not be disturbed."

"This is important," Della said.

"We would like to speak with him privately, Imbati, please," said Tagaret. "Just for a few moments, about a matter of grave importance."

"I'm afraid I can't allow that," said Herin's Argun. No slightest sign of concern on his face, not even a wrinkle in his tattoo.

Della could have screamed in frustration, but she managed to hold one more thing inside. "This is about *keeping him safe*, Imbati," she pleaded. "Why wouldn't you concern yourself with that?"

Lady Falya looked over her shoulder and frowned.

Della met her disapproving eyes, hoping to find some understanding there, but then the headwaiter appeared beside Argun, blocking them.

"Sir, Lady, I'm sorry, but we have no tables currently available."

She knew what *that* meant. They were being asked to leave.

Well, she wasn't going to stand here and wait to be physically encouraged. She turned and walked out of the dining area—managing, naturally, to bump through the corner of one of the tables with her thigh. She flung open the front door and stomped out. On the sidewalk she stopped, panting, digging her fingernails into her palms. She wanted to hit somebody.

"Mistress," her Yoral said from behind her, with concern, "are you unwell?"

"Gnash it, I've hardly slept, I've been running around pointlessly, I'm hungry, and I've just been kicked out of a restaurant!"

"I'm sorry, Mistress." Yoral reached into a pocket and passed her something small. It was a Selimnar treat—a compressed cube of dried fruit in a thin, dry grain wrapper that melted when she put it on her tongue. Instantly, it brought tears to her eyes.

She mumbled through the delicious stickiness, "Why did we even come back here?"

Gentle arms wrapped around her. Tagaret . . .

"Tagaret, we shouldn't have come back. How can there be nothing we can do?"

"Sweet Della," he murmured. "I'm sorry. I'm sure we've done the right thing. Herin's Argun probably stopped us because of the warning we sent out across the Imbati this morning."

"But we still don't know if Herin will walk out of that restaurant alive! I should just take the risk. I should go back in there and make them listen."

"Darling, please don't."

"Mistress, I don't suggest it," said Yoral.

"What are you saying?" she demanded.

"Let's trust Herin's Argun," Tagaret said. "He's a consummate professional. Besides, if we try to approach again, the others in the club will take more notice of us."

"Of you."

"Sure, of me. But I don't want there to be any chance of you," he glanced down at her stomach, "getting hurt."

She wanted to shake him. She looked up into his eyes. "Tagaret, you realize we're being careful. I can guarantee you that Nekantor won't do the same."

"Della, you're more important to me than Herin."

She bit her lip. *Why did we even come back here?*

"Mistress," said Yoral. "Please. We'll think of something else."

"I'm not comfortable just wondering if—"

"What if I ask my Kuarmei to stay?" Tagaret asked. "She can tell us if anything happens."

Della glanced at the small Imbati woman. Didn't Tagaret realize he wasn't just putting Herin at risk, but potentially his Kuarmei also? Just in the name of getting *her* to go home?

Della took as deep a breath as she could manage. "Fine," she said. "Let's go."

Her appetite was stronger than her fear, but with every bite of lunch, she kept thinking about Herin—how the Eminence held that fork in his shapely golden hand, white lace swaying as he moved it up and down from his plate.

Whenever she looked up from her food, Tagaret seemed to be

watching her. She loved his brown eyes. She loved the way he gazed at her, as he had ever since Yoral had first given him permission, as if he never wanted to stop. She wanted him to be doing it, preferably in bed, in their private suite in Selimna.

Footsteps approached the dining room door, and she held her breath.

Tagaret's Kuarmei entered with a short bow. "The Eminence has left the restaurant, Master and Mistress."

"Thank Heile," Tagaret exclaimed.

Della exhaled, but a voice in her mind muttered, *If he survived lunch, he certainly won't survive dinner.*

"All right, then," she said. "What do we do next?"

Adon, who was sitting across from her, set down his fork. "Talk to Nekantor?"

"No!" Della cried. Tagaret and Tamelera echoed her at precisely the same moment, turning it into a general shout.

Adon shrank in his brass chair and raised both hands, shaking them apologetically. "All right, all right."

"Sweet darling boy, I'm sorry," said Tamelera, "but if you told Nekantor not to kill Herin, he'd know we suspected him of planning a murder. And then, if his plan failed, he'd blame us. He'd punish us."

Adon squirmed a little. "But haven't we tried everything else?"

"Not quite everything," said Tagaret. "Kuarmei, can you reach out to Lady Selemei and ask her what she's learned?"

"Right away, sir." She ran out.

Half an hour passed, and Kuarmei did not return. At last Tamelera sighed and retired to her rooms so her Aloran could brush her hair.

"Della," said Tagaret. "Would you like to play dareli? How about you, Adon?"

Cards, at a time like this?

But they had to pass the time somehow, so she nodded. Tagaret and Adon gave her first choice of the pretty wooden chairs at the gaming table in the sitting room. Adon got the second one, and Keeper Premel brought a metal stool for Tagaret. Tagaret dealt out the cards. While sorting her cards into families, Della glanced up every few seconds toward Imbati Serjer by the front door. The First Houseman looked back at her with sympathy.

The next time she looked, Serjer had disappeared.

She stood without thinking, and nearly tipped over her chair. "Serjer?"

Serjer reappeared. "Master, Mistress, Lady Selemei is at the door."

Tagaret calmly set down his cards. "Ask her in, Serjer, by all means."

"Heile have mercy," Della whispered.

The Lady entered grim-faced, followed by her Ustin. She didn't even begin with a greeting. "Well, we're ready for whenever it happens."

To hear Lady Selemei say it—not *if,* but *when*—was terrifying. Sickened, Della hugged herself. "Gods help us."

"What did you do?" Tagaret asked.

"I had a serious talk with Speaker Fedron, and we decided to tell Arbiter Lorman we were testing the Family's readiness for an emergency." Lady Selemei looked meaningfully at one of the couches.

"Oh, I'm sorry," Della said, and gestured at the couch. "Please, do sit down."

"Thank you." Lady Selemei sat, leaned her cane against the couch arm, and arranged her striped skirts. "Fedron and I demanded a rehearsal of our strategy for evacuating First Family boys from the School and offices. I'm afraid it was an indelicate approach. If we're wrong, we've terrified a great many people for no reason, and I'm sure I'll hear something from the Schoolmasters about disrupting classes."

No one said anything.

Adon, who was still holding two hands full of cards, heaved an exasperated sigh. "What are the chances of that?"

"Low," said Tagaret.

Lady Selemei frowned. "I take it you haven't had any success in counteracting him."

Tagaret swallowed. "We've put people in a position to counteract him."

"We did that this morning," Lady Selemei said.

Gnash it, they'd done next to nothing.

"We tried," said Della. "We tried to talk to Herin, but his Argun wouldn't let us near." Plis help them, they had to *do something!* "I could try to talk to Lady Falya. If she weren't out in public like she was at lunch, or if I could find her alone, she might not perceive me as a danger. And then *she* could warn him."

"Della, love," said Tagaret, "that's a pretty big risk."

Della raised her eyebrows and stared at him. "Maybe it is. So?"

Tagaret pressed his lips together, with a glance at her Yoral. "Could Lady Selemei do it?"

Lady Selemei looked between them suspiciously. "I'm not the best person for that," she said. "As a member of the cabinet, I'd surely be perceived as more of a threat. I don't think Lady Falya would consent to see me."

"Gnash all this!" Adon smacked down his cards on the gaming table and sprang out of his chair. "Is talking all we can do? I can't stand this anymore." He shoved through the double doors farther into the house.

"I'm sorry, Lady Selemei," Tagaret said. "It's been a tense day."

"I understand; don't worry," the Lady replied.

"I'll go talk to him," said Della.

Tagaret smiled at her, sadly. "He'll probably be changing clothes."

He probably would be. She could have left it alone, but it seemed unfair not to acknowledge the discomfort that they all shared. She walked into the back.

The quiet here was different from the tension in the sitting room, and something of a relief. With Lady Selemei visiting, Tagaret wasn't likely to mention her pregnancy explicitly, but she could feel him holding back. If they started arguing, it might slip out—and she just wasn't ready to be compared to a woman who'd borne five confirmed children. Not today. She walked down the hallway to Adon's door, and knocked.

"Adon, are you all right?"

Adon didn't answer.

"I know this is hard. Can I come in and talk to you? Or are you getting changed?" She tested the door handle; it wasn't locked. She cracked the door open and peeked into the soft, colorful space full of Adon's fabulous clothes. "Adon?"

No sign of him. Was he hiding? Heavens, had she opened the door on him half-naked? She quickly ducked her head back out.

"Adon, are you getting dressed? I'm sorry if I startled you. I just want to make sure you're all right."

No answer. With a twisting feeling in her chest, she peered back in. The room was empty, the bathroom dark with the door open. Adon's gloves were in a neat pile on the floor.

Oh, no.

The window was open. She hurried to it and looked out, but couldn't see Adon anywhere. What was he doing? How could he have gone out when he knew every eligible boy in the First Family had been evacuated to their homes for their own safety?

Unless . . . was he trying to get to Nekantor?

The twisting in her chest worsened, and she panted, clenching her fists. He would be all right, though, wouldn't he, if he went to Nekantor? Nekantor would never hurt Adon, not if he wanted Adon to become his Heir.

Would Adon know not to implicate Tagaret in trying to stop him?

There was no way to know. And now that he was already out, no one could stop him from doing . . . whatever he planned to do.

The real question was, what did *she* plan to do?

Something.

But she knew what would happen if she went back to the others.

Before she knew it, she found herself assessing the height and width of the windowsill. She stood before it and lifted her skirts, gathering them into a bundle and shoving them in a pile on the stone. The window-casing was metal, and she could hold onto it with her fingers . . . if she could get up there.

"Mistress," said a soft voice behind her. "Please, don't."

Yoral. In Selimna, he'd tried to stop her from going with Castremei. At the restaurant today, he'd tried to get her to go home.

"I'm going to warn Herin," Della said, without turning. "Somebody has to. If you want to stop me, you'll have to restrain me. If you want to keep me safe, you can help so I don't get hurt when I jump out."

"Oh, Mistress."

"I'm not joking. I swear by the crown of Mai."

"I know you aren't."

She turned around; her pile of skirts slid off the windowsill and cascaded down over her feet. Her Yoral was standing with his head leaned to one side. She knew him well enough to know there was emotion hiding in his expression. Sadness, maybe. Kindness, too. "I'm not ordering you to help me, Yoral. I'm begging you. You know how important this is. You said even one life saved means something—and if I can save Herin, it will save so many others. It's just that I don't think Tagaret will let me leave by the front door."

"Mistress," said Yoral, "he might want you to stay, but I don't believe he would fight to keep you here."

"I don't want to fight him," she said. "I don't want to discuss it. There's no time."

Yoral inclined his head solemnly. "Mistress, if you'll stop in Adon's bathroom before we go, I'll just fetch you a step-stool so you won't struggle to climb. I think it would be safest if I caught you in the garden."

"Yes, please," she said. Her heart raced. Finally, they could do something!

If she'd hoped to find Adon by chance in the gardens, her wish went unanswered. In silent agreement, she and Yoral hurried across the grounds and into the central section of the Residence.

"Mistress, perhaps we should avoid the grand rotunda," Yoral said.

Della frowned a moment, then shook her head. "No; I think we should use it. We might see Herin there."

"We might also see the Heir Nekantor there, Mistress."

She pressed her lips together. "I could handle that. I could just pretend I was looking for Adon."

They crossed rooms decorated with statues of former Eminences until they reached the rotunda. This was a gorgeously bright space: white marble stairs curving upward on both sides along white marble walls punctuated with bright sconces and falls of Grobal-green curtain. There was even some daylight filtering in from outside through the dome of milky glass. Not a soul was here except themselves.

Della couldn't hurry on the stairs. When she tried, she grew short of breath, and the unwelcome resident thumped her under the ribs. The first flight of stairs delivered them to the opening of the second-floor hall that led toward the back of the Residence. Unfortunately, this put them in plain view of the Heir's suite, should Nekantor chance to come out. She started to climb again before she'd fully regained her comfort.

I could handle him, but I really don't want to . . .

Somehow, she made it to the top. These stairs ended right in front of the Eminent Chambers. In the foyer before the Chambers door, six Arissen of the Eminence's Cohort stood guard. Della paused for breath while they watched her. Even huge Arissen were small compared to the nude male figures in white marble who held the lintel of the Eminence's door on their shoulders, and lighted globes in their hands.

"Arissen," said Della, when she found enough breath to speak, "is Lady Falya in?"

One of the men clicked his heels. "No, Lady."

Think. Where would Lady Falya be at this time of day?

"Yoral, should we try the library?" she asked. But then it hit her: dinner. "I know what to do. Thank you, Arissen."

She walked around the rotunda's edge and into the third-floor hallway. The guards at the entrance of the Eminence's private library took no notice of her. There was a short, sunmarked guard standing beside the dining room door, who accosted her the moment she stopped moving.

"Lady, may I ask your business here?"

Della swallowed. "Of course, Arissen. I'm here to see Lady Falya. I contacted her earlier today, but at the time she was busy and we didn't have a chance to speak as we should. I thought I might catch her on her way to dinner."

"Lady Falya is not here, Lady."

"I'll just wait, then. If you don't mind, I'd like to sit. May I go in?"

"Yes, Lady."

Of course, it was too early for dinner. The Eminence's private dining room was empty. Yoral pulled out one of the chairs that faced the entry door, checking it thoroughly before he sat her in it. Then he left her and searched the room, checking each of the stalactite-brocade curtains in the corners, the kitchen entrance, and the curtain over the Maze entrance. He also checked under the edges of the silk carpet, and even vanished for some minutes under the table, which couldn't have been comfortable for him.

"Have you found anything?" Della asked.

Yoral's head came up on the other side of the table. He emerged, straightening his black silk suit. "Nothing, Mistress, I'm afraid. I suppose we can comfort ourselves that anyone thinking to set traps will find it difficult now, with us here."

"I imagine so."

Yoral moved behind her, so she turned in her chair and watched him check the opulent wooden sideboard, searching all of its carven crevices. Above it was the service curtain that allowed the Household to hand food through from the kitchen. Yoral lifted each panel one by one, giving a nod to someone on the other side.

"This room is clean, Mistress."

Clean. If they were wrong, this was going to be very embarrassing. But they couldn't be, could they? What else could they do but assume the worst, to prevent the worst from happening?

Della sat, absently rubbing the cold brass of the table. It wasn't comfortable, thanks to occasional knocking on her inner bruises. She watched the door to the hall. *Lady Falya, come in. Please come to dinner.*

No one came in the hall door. After they'd been sitting for what felt like forever, a woman of the Household entered from the kitchen.

"Lady," she said. "I'm going to have to ask you to leave so we can set the table."

Dismay melted her remaining confidence. "Imbati, please let me stay. You must have heard of the danger today. I need to warn the Eminence."

The woman's face didn't even twitch.

"Has someone else spoken to him, then? Did the Household tell him something bad might be coming? Can I trust him to protect himself without my intervention?"

"Please, Castemate," said Yoral.

The woman gave a short nod. "You may wait here, Lady. Provided that you stand in the corner."

"Thank you, Imbati." At least she wasn't being sent home again. She stood when Yoral pulled out her chair; her belly stubbed on the table. She pressed hard against the pain as she walked to the corner. She leaned into the stone and watched the Household lay out a long white tablecloth with pressed napkins, and silver- and glassware at each place. Yoral didn't seem to find anything amiss with the preparations.

The Household withdrew again.

If she had to wait much longer, she'd have to leave for reasons of personal discomfort. "Yoral, do you have any more food?"

The door to the hallway opened. Della jumped upright.

"A Lady and her manservant are here, your Eminence," said the sunmarked guard's voice. "She has been asking to speak to Lady Falya."

They were here.

First to enter was Lady Falya's servant, a slim pale-skinned woman with a look of deep disapproval in her eyes. Lady Falya, dressed in a beautiful silvery gown, stopped just behind her.

"Lady Falya," said Della, curtsying.

The Lady's fine brows drew together. "Why are you here? Again?"

"I'm sorry to inconvenience you, Lady. I need to speak with you, please, just for a moment. It's life and death."

"You've been following us."

The Eminence Herin looked in behind his partner, and a frown crossed his beautiful face. He was flanked as usual by his Argun and by his enormous Arissen bodyguard. Someone else was approaching behind them. Who?

"I have an important Family meeting scheduled," Herin said. "Your presence is inappropriate."

"I'll go, I promise. Just please, Lady, just give me two minutes."

The Lady's slate-gray eyes narrowed. "I'll permit it," she said. "Herin, dear, I'll only be a second."

Falya stepped to one side, and her servant returned to her shoulder; that opened just enough space for Della to slip through with a quick curtsy to the Eminence. The person who had just arrived behind them was an older man who didn't seem dangerous at first glance.

"Arbiter Plist and I want to include you in the meeting, darling," Herin protested. "Why are you taking this Lady seriously?"

"We can spare her for two minutes," said Arbiter Plist. If they knew him and considered him safe, he would surely be from Herin's Third Family Council.

"This *won't* take two minutes," Falya said meaningfully, and marched off down the hall. Della panted to catch up. When they reached the rotunda, Falya took the curving, stone-railed walkway on the right. Her servant opened the door to the Eminent Chambers between its guards in orange, and its bearers in white stone. Della followed her into the vestibule, where the two of them were enclosed by purple curtains. "All right, then," Falya said. "What is it?"

"I'm Della of the First Family. I think your partner is in danger. We have reason to believe that his Heir is plotting to take action against him today."

Falya glared. "The Heir is First Family, and so are you."

Della gulped. "Nekantor might advance his Family politically, but we don't trust him. If you've met him, you might understand why."

"Yes, of course I've met him. We've been coping with him for years."

The way she said 'we' was fascinating. Herin's desire to include her in his political meeting suddenly made more sense. "Please," Della said. "At least let me explain why we think there's a danger."

Falya was slightly taller; she considered Della sourly down her nose. "Go ahead."

Blessing of Mai! "We've realized Nekantor was placing very young men of powerful Families in positions outside of Pelismara, like Unger of the Fifth Family, and Satenya of the Seventh Family. The Fifth

Family detected a pattern and has already attempted to retaliate using the Paper Shadows. As for why today, we know that Nekantor wouldn't want competition in an Heir Selection from my partner, his brother Tagaret—but today Tagaret has aged out of eligibility."

"We've been on the alert most of the day," Falya said severely. "What makes you think you're any help? Why should I consider you anything more than a dangerous distraction at a critical moment?"

A critical moment? Della bit her lip. *Oh, mercy!*

CHAPTER TWENTY-TWO

Between Arissen

It's life and death.

Even after the copper-haired Lady had left with the Eminence's partner, her words still rang in Melín's ears. Whoever that Lady was, she'd waited almost two hours to deliver her message. Life and death.

What did she know?

One thing was certain: something bad was coming. Something that could kill her, too, if she wasn't ready. She kept her eyes on the rotunda where the Lady had vanished.

Thud.

Behind her.

Melín whipped around.

Farther down toward the end of the hall, First Karyas stumbled backward across the corridor. She wheezed as if she'd just been winded—punched, maybe, by someone behind the Imbati access curtain?

Karyas swung her arm back so she wouldn't hit the wall. A bulge showed there, under her arm.

Plis' balls, that was her blade!

The blade—Karyas—her threats—Treminindi—*life and death*—!

Melín charged down the hall.

She lowered her shoulder and drove it into Karyas' ribs, slamming her into the wall. Karyas slid to the floor. Melín grabbed for her jacket and tore it open; two buttons flew off and pinged against the stone. Yes, there was her blade in its scabbard—the strap was buckled around the First's shoulder. Melín raced to unbuckle it, then grabbed the blade, scabbard and all.

Down the hall came a high, terrified yelp.

Melín looked up. A dark-haired Grobal boy in green and black stood staring at her, seemingly paralyzed with fear.

Karyas came to life. She surged up, snarling in Melín's face, and shoved her backward. No way to stop—Melín kept her grip on her blade, rolled legs-over-shoulder onto her feet, but Karyas was still coming too fast. She lost balance and landed on her back. Karyas came at her neck with both hands. Melín twisted sideways, whipping the scabbard strap into Karyas' face, and scrambled away toward the boy—or where the boy had been a second earlier. There was no sign of him now. She shifted the blade, trying to free her stronger hand.

Karyas tackled her in the small of the back.

Melín fell. Her hands hit the ground and the blade shot out of its scabbard. Karyas grabbed her by the helmet and yanked her head back.

Sirin help me, she's going to slit my throat . . .

Cold pain, under her left ear.

Karyas whispered, "I knew you were soft, you little—"

"Arissen Karyas!" a high, imperious voice commanded. "Release her!"

Karyas' grip loosened slightly.

"Do it now! Or my servant will make you. Yoral?"

"Ready, Mistress." An Imbati's threatening voice.

Karyas growled and let go. Melín scrambled to her feet and backed sideways, looking for her blade in Karyas' hand. No; that was Karyas' dueling knife.

Where was the blade?

It wasn't in Karyas' hand. It wasn't under her coat. It wasn't anywhere on the floor.

Where was it?

Melín had no choice but to look at her rescuer. It was the copper-haired Grobal Lady who had been begging to speak to the Eminence's partner. Her black-suited manservant was over fifty, but his arm was cocked to throw one of the eyeball-sized metal rounders that Imbati used for ranged attacks. You could count on him to take out your eye if he decided to hit it—and Karyas quite obviously knew that.

Melín took three steps toward the Lady, to get more distance between her and Karyas. "Lady," she said. "Thank you."

"Both of you are now off duty," the Lady said. "Leave the Residence immediately."

"Lady Della," First Karyas objected, "this guard was—"

"Enough!" Lady Della snapped. "Do you think I don't know

you, Karyas? Leave, now." She called over her shoulder toward the rotunda. "Arissen! I'm sure the Eminence would like to see a guard on this door."

Here was some good luck, actually—one of the two men who left the complement at the Eminence's chamber door was Gul, a reliable First she'd seen fighting against one of her own eight yesterday. Which meant his loyalty to the Eminence was not in question.

"Thank you, Lady," Gul said, while his companion moved to the door of the dining room. "First Karyas, Eighth Melín, follow your orders. I'll be reporting both of you to the Commander for this."

Between Gul, his companion, and the Imbati, that should be enough to make Karyas obey. Still, Melín held her breath.

"Yes, Lady," said Karyas.

"Yes, Lady. Yes, sir," said Melín. She waited only long enough to see Karyas commit to the rotunda stairway, then ran for the other spiral stairway near the end of the hall. She took the spiral fast, bolting through the nearest outer door as fast as she could and cutting at an angle across the gardens, so Karyas had no chance of finding or following her.

Lady Della showing up really *had* been a matter of life and death.

Her whole body felt numb with shock.

Check yourself. If she'd been injured, she wouldn't necessarily know.

She shook her hands, bent her knees, swung her arms. Last, she rubbed her hand down from her left ear and across her neck. Swallowed hard. Looked into her palm.

The faintest streak of wet.

That was way too close.

CHAPTER TWENTY-THREE

In the Maze

Oh, mercy of Heile, that was a big knife.

It lay only inches from Adon's toes, on the near side of the curtain over the narrow door where he stood peeking. Had he made a terrible mistake bolting in here? Had the fighting Arissen seen him enter? Too late to worry about it now; he was already here. He could only follow the Headmaster's rules as best he could, and that meant he couldn't go back out.

He couldn't stay here, though. That knife was staring at him. Its blade was broad, not quite straight, with a single sharp side that curved into a pointed tip. Deadly—and it made him imagine terrible things the fighting Arissen had intended. No, he should try to find his way to some Imbati. They could help him.

He turned his back on the crack of bright light and started into the dim, narrow corridor. There were delicious smells here. Brighter light came around a corner. He turned in through the doorway.

It was a kitchen, and very busy. He now stood amidst clouds of marvelous scent, surrounded by chopping and stirring and sizzling. The workers here were Household, wearing black suits and white aprons, and they worked in silence. Only two voices spoke, out of a speaker on the wall: one a stranger, and the other more familiar.

"I wonder where Falya has got to?" the familiar voice asked.

"Don't worry, your Eminence, I'm sure she'll be here soon."

Wait, was that the Eminence Herin? Talking to someone?

It felt acutely uncomfortable to be overhearing the Eminence's dinner conversation, but he had to follow the Headmaster's rules. Adon quietly leaned back against the wall beside the door so as not to be in the way, and waited to be noticed.

The Household was assembling food on three plates that they had arrayed on a metal table on the far wall, just below a long opening with a paneled curtain across it. Seared meat, and slivered mushrooms, berries and green nuts that must have been the first of the season.

His mouth started watering.

Then Nekantor's Dexelin walked in the door beside him. The huge knife was in his hand.

Adon gasped.

Dexelin took one look at him and his eyes went wide. He hid the knife behind his back. "Young Master. What are you doing here? You can't be here. Not now!"

"Please, help me," Adon pleaded. "The Arissen were fighting, and I didn't know what to do. Please don't get me in trouble with the Headmaster."

The stranger's voice spoke again through the wall speaker. "Herin, if you wish, we could begin our planning for this week before Lady Falya returns."

"That First Family Lady has no manners." Herin's voice was annoyed. "She came to cause trouble."

"Oh, mercy," said Dexelin. "Oh, mercy, there's no time; I have to take care of this, first." He found his way to a sink full of soapy water and sank the knife into it, washing its blade and handle.

"What are you doing?"

Dexelin pulled the dripping knife out and doused it in a neighboring sink of clear water, then wrapped it in a towel. He opened his coat and slid it awkwardly into an inside pocket. "I can't have this in the equation." He fastened his coat closed again.

"Equation?"

A sudden fit of coughing issued from the speaker, as if one of the men behind the curtain had inhaled some of his food.

Dexelin looked at him with pain in his face. "I don't want this, young Master Adon. It's just that I can't stop it."

"What?"

"Plist?" the Eminence's voice cried. "Plist, what's happening?"

Dexelin's eyes filled with horror. "Oh, no . . ."

Suddenly, a huge voice roared, so loudly you could hear it through the speaker, through the curtain over the window, as if it could echo all the way to the heavens—and then came a sound, the worst sound in the entire world.

Zzap!

Shouts. Screams, cut off by—

Zzap! Zap-zap-zap! Zap!

"Gods help us!" cried Dexelin. "He's shooting! Everybody out before he realizes we're here!"

Every member of the Household team dropped their tools and ran. Adon stood frozen, breathless with terror. Then Dexelin's hands grabbed him, lifted him—he found himself bent in half over the servant's shoulder. He clutched at the Imbati's arm, bouncing helplessly as Dexelin ran into the dark of the Maze.

CHAPTER TWENTY-FOUR

Bodies

Cheers, jeers, shouts—the heat and smell of thousands of bodies packed together—dim light on a seething crowd—bright lights on the game.

Melín breathed in chaos and life until the numbness eased.

The cut by her ear didn't hurt as much as she'd feared. Her ankle was sore, though.

She should sit somewhere.

She scanned down along the rows of metal benches. Wysps floated here and there in the air, common when you got a big enough crowd. Her ears throbbed with the din. Down in the targetball cage—not really a cage when you played at the professional level, but a long, rectangular room with polyglass walls and ceiling—the game had just started. The magnified excitement of the commentator came over the speakers, talking about leaps, swings, dodges, passes. This obstacle layout of ropes and stones was new, the commentator said approvingly, and a great challenge to the players of the Pelismar Cave-Cats and the Herkethi, since none of them had ever seen it before.

From here, Melín couldn't see more than half of the players, much less the ball, though huge suspended mirrors gave a view around some of the obstacles. The glow of the targets at either end of the cage was clearly visible. She hated watching a game from the stairs. But she'd never get a decent seat.

She should have been at the Cohort's station reporting First Karyas to Commander Abru, instead of following her feet.

But here she was.

It was too hot in here. She took off her helmet and coat, and draped them over her arm. The scabbard of her blade hung empty over her shoulder. At least she'd recovered her old Division rank pins.

Varin's teeth.

She trudged down into the layers of noise until she reached the first crossway path, and started moving to the right, keeping her eyes on the players in the cage.

"Seni, don't block the play!"

"Don't make me punch you," she shouted back. She kept moving.

"Melín!" someone shouted.

She turned, searching for the voice. The buzzer sounded and the crowd leapt to its feet with a roar. She turned back toward the cage—the Cave-Cats had scored, their target was flashing, and she'd missed it.

"Gnash it!"

The roar died down. An official with a new ball climbed to the top of the cage, readying herself to drop it through the chute. A man and a woman hung from ropes below, waiting to leap for it.

"Melín!"

"Where are you?" she bellowed.

A man in a white shirt and dark trousers separated himself from the crowd and ran up with the most amazing look on his face—so obviously wanting to grin, but not sure he could get away with it.

"Pyaras!" She grabbed him by both elbows and shook him. Something like a scream rose in her throat, but what came out was, "To life!"

"To life, Melín!" He flung his arms around her.

Oh, the feeling of him surrounding her . . . Tears welled in her eyes. His chest under her cheek smelled sweaty and delicious. His arms were strong, his body hot, and he was definitely excited to see her. Tempted to touch him, she breathed hard, and leaned into him instead. Lust coiled and burst, a splash of fire in her stomach.

Voices shouted, "Get down!"

She shouted back at them, one thumb hooked in her helmet strap and Pyaras' belt loop. "Fine, fine!"

"I'm here with my friend Veriga," Pyaras said. "Want to sit with us?"

"Yeah!"

He led her two rows up. Veriga was a big scarred man with knotted shoulders, who greeted her with a nod and a short, "Seni."

"Seni," she said. They could talk after the game, maybe, when it wasn't so loud. She arranged her scabbard inside her coat, folded it, and put it on top of her helmet underneath the bench. Seating was tight. She tucked herself in at the end of the bench, but if she wanted to stay on, she had to press her hip hard against Pyaras. She wanted to press him harder. Gnash it, no point pretending for some police officer she'd never met before. She wrapped her arm around Pyaras' waist, startling his nearer arm up into the air.

The crowd roared. People all around leapt up, even Veriga. Pyaras didn't stand. He lowered his arm around her shoulders, squeezed her arm, stroked it. *Oh, yes.* She shifted her arm, so his hand slipped in against her breast. She clamped her arm down, holding him there.

Pyaras gulped, staring at her.

She held his gaze. "Yes?"

He nodded.

She already had her arm around him, so she tickled up the hem of his white shirt and sneaked her fingers in, to the skin of his side. His hand moved on her breast. *Gods, yes.* Him, definitely. And definitely at a targetball game. There was a wet throb between her legs—the kind you had to do something about, one way or another.

She was alive. Here. Now.

She looked up at him.

Pyaras was breathing hard, his mouth half-open.

She mouthed at him, *I want you.*

He nodded.

Melín stood and started climbing back up the stairs. At the top, she looked around. Where was private in a crowd? Bathroom? Gross. They were nowhere near home, or the barracks. Where?

Was he even coming?

Yes, here he was, running up the stairs. The top of his head was almost healed now, and he swooped up and kissed her. Gods, she wanted to eat him up—she tried, and got in deep, a drink of his throat, a bite of his lips, not near enough. Her whole body vibrated.

He was panting, quivering. "Not here?" He asked like it was a question, like he'd actually have her on the dirty steps in front of six thousand people. Gods, the idea that he could want her so badly! But she wanted him with no one watching.

Then she spotted the ladder against the arena's back wall.

"Follow me," she said.

The crowd roared again. She climbed the ladder, intensely aware of every sliding movement of her thighs. At the top was the walkway where they serviced the lights and mirrors. It was flat. Narrow, but wide enough. It had wire mesh safety barriers on both sides, and through them you could see down into the crowd below.

Pyaras climbed onto the walkway and came out toward her. His eyes took in the safety barriers, and the closeness of the steel ceiling beams. "Sirin and Eyn," he said.

She grabbed him, pulled him to her, pulled up his shirt and yanked on his waistband. Why did he have to be wearing a belt? He groaned and reached under her shirt. She pushed her breasts into his hands—aah—and then pulled herself tight against him, pressing her face into his chest, biting at his nipple. His hands moved on her back; one went up to her neck, while the other went down into her pants. Her knees buckled. He held her up.

"Gnash you, isseni," she gasped. "How dare you be so delicious."

She pulled away and went for his belt. Loosened her second buckle of the day even faster than the first, and slipped her hand in where she'd wanted to before, to the root of his excitement. Pyaras fell to his knees on the walkway.

She had the height advantage, now. She pulled her pants down to her ankles and fell on him, covering his mouth with hers, wrapping her arms around his shoulders and seizing his hips between her bare knees. He surged up at her, cushioned her as she fell back onto the walk, and then came down over her. Into her.

Oh, Sirin and Eyn!

The crowd roared.

The walkway dimmed in the sensations of pulse, rub, pull, gasp, moan. She buried her fingers in the hair at the back of his head, and he stroked up her side from knee to breast, and when he was spent thank the gods he still didn't pull away, but rocked with her, nuzzled her, nibbled her, stroked her until she screamed out everything she had into the noise.

Then he pulled away, and fell onto his back on the walkway, chest heaving up and down.

She curled and got onto her knees. "Pyaras. Again."

He laughed as he panted, mouth open. "Give me—just give me a minute."

She walked forward on her knees. They were flying, untouchable above the thousands.

But something below caught her eye through the mesh. She swiveled fast, and instinct sent her into a crouch, pulling her pants up and fastening them before she could even put words to what she'd seen.

"What?" Pyaras asked, pulling himself together in a messy hurry. "Melín, what's wrong?"

The Eminence's bodyguard, Drenas, had just entered the arena and plunged down into the crowd.

Alone.

"Danger!" she hissed. "Danger!"

CHAPTER TWENTY-FIVE

Other Bodies

Danger!"

"What is it?" Pyaras asked, breathless. She was unbelievable. How could she could go from abandon to readiness so quickly? He buttoned his pants and knelt beside her, staring down through the mesh barrier while he fastened his belt. What was she seeing in the shouting mobs of Arissen?

"Drenas is here, alone," she said, pointing. "Can you see him? He's in uniform. He's gone down to the second crossway, and—" She hissed. "Someone's following him. If that's who I think it is . . ."

Drenas was a name he should know. He'd heard it before. Who was Drenas? Too many Arissen names lately; it wasn't coming to him. Following the second crossway with his eyes, he found a big man in uniform pushing along it, away from their position. Easier to see because his uniform included an orange helmet, and because he'd just passed by one of the drifting wysps. Several body-lengths behind him was a woman, also in an orange helmet, whose jacket looked unbuttoned.

The woman reached for her hip. He'd seen that gesture before—it drove him to his feet.

"NO!" he shouted.

The woman widened her stance and hesitated, almost as if she'd heard him. But then a bolt flashed—

—and disappeared into a bloom of white fire that expanded—

—expanded—

—vanished—

Every person within reach of that fire fell, as if they'd been hit by mining explosives. Then the screaming started.

"Varin's teeth!" Melín cried, and bolted for the ladder.

"Heile's mercy." His brain wouldn't comprehend it. "Heile's mercy! Heavens help us!" Then he realized Melín was gone, and ran after her.

He couldn't get down the ladder fast enough. When he arrived on the ground, the air of the arena felt closer and more unpleasantly hot than before they'd climbed up. He spotted Melín several rows down, hopping from bench to bench to get closer to the hit area. The stairs were crammed with people mobbing the exit, though a number were also climbing benches.

"Veriga!" he shouted. "Veriga!"

What if Veriga had been caught in the explosion?

No, it couldn't be . . .

He looked around frantically. The maintenance walkway had been almost directly above their seats, and they'd been seated near the first crossway. Drenas had been in the second crossway, visible from the walkway, moving away.

That meant, unless he'd abandoned their seats for some reason, Veriga wouldn't have been hit. So he would be somewhere here, taking charge like he always did.

Pyaras stepped over the bench at his knees, onto the next concrete row level, and then did it again, moving down toward the disaster area. The exit aisle was a wall of people. He hesitated when he reached it, then remembered the Descent and pushed into a tiny gap. Arissen pushed hard, carrying him upward, but he kept his feet on the ground and shoved sideways, a little farther, a little farther—

He popped out on the other side. Here, he was still two rows above the crossway that Drenas had used, but the disaster area was straight ahead. It smelled of blood, smoke, horror. Melín was going into it. And there was Veriga on the edge of the circle of burned bodies, directing people who came to help.

Pyaras' stomach roiled. Heile help them all. Those people had done nothing but come to see a game. Now they were dead, or would be if they didn't get treated immediately. They needed doctors. Medics—probably some of the people helping were medics, but they wouldn't necessarily have supplies.

The Pelismar Cave-Cats would have team doctors, though.

Pyaras turned and started climbing downward again. The farther he went, the more the spectators seemed scared and confused.

He found a man in the yellow-green vest of event staff, who was turning in circles helplessly in the face of the mass rush for the exits.

"Arissen." He stopped the man with one hand on his arm. "Where are the locker rooms? Can the team's doctors be summoned?"

The man gaped at him.

"Arissen. Take me to the locker rooms."

"Yes, sir." They made their way farther downward, fortunately not all the way to the cage. The man hopped a barrier and dropped into a sloped concrete walkway. Pyaras hopped after him, remembering to bend his knees as he landed. They ran up the slope and into a door on the right.

The Cave-Cats locker room. He could see where the events man was going, a glass door on the right side of the main locker area. He leapt after him.

The events man pushed the door open, startling a team of Kartunnen in gray doctors' coats. "Help."

"There's been an explosion," Pyaras said. "At least a hundred casualties, lots of burns. We need you right now. Bring whatever supplies you can."

The doctors scrambled out of their chairs. Pyaras scanned them as they went for the cabinets, and assigned himself to a woman near an open cabinet door.

"Let me help you."

He took the supplies she handed to him, but it was going to be too much to carry. He dashed out to the locker area, grabbed a stray sports bag, and dumped its contents—shoes, clothes—out on the ground. Once he'd returned to her, he filled the bag with water bottles, clean cloths, everything she gave him. When she ran out the way he'd entered, he followed, counting on the others to come when they were ready.

The crowd was thinner now. The air was thick with the smell of death. The Kartunnen doctor waded right into the disaster area. At its edges, people sat curled around their injuries, but farther in people were writhing, moaning. With no idea how to help them, he just carried the bag and handed the doctor whatever she asked for. He couldn't bear to look toward the explosion's center, where there was no movement at all.

Two rows up from him, he spotted Melín talking to Veriga. Veriga appeared to be writing down what she told him in a small book.

Thank Sirin that Veriga was safe. There wasn't time to speak with him, though, not when so many people needed help. His throat felt tight, and his stomach hated him, but he kept moving, kept handing things to the doctor.

"Pyaras."

He looked up from the latest victim, a child who had been partially shielded by her dead parent but had severe burns all over her legs.

His friends were standing beside him. "Veriga?" he asked. "Melín?"

"You need to leave," Veriga said.

"What?"

"That was a wysp explosion," said Melín. "It was caused by First Karyas. I saw her take the shot."

He'd seen the shot, too. First Karyas—that woman in the orange helmet had been Nekantor's favorite Arissen? And she'd just shot Drenas.

Oh, dear gods help him, he remembered the name, now: Adon's birthday party, the Eminence Herin waving proudly toward the huge Arissen in the vestibule. *Imbati make fine bodyguards, but there can be no finer specimen than Drenas, here. We must keep safe every way we can . . .*

Veriga shook him and pushed something into his hand. "Pyaras! Get out of here. Go home, *now*."

"Melín, I'm sorry." But he didn't have to be told a third time. The main exits were still too busy to be safe, so he hopped down the benches and over the barrier again, then ran up the slope into the locker room. Thank all the gods that the exits were clearly marked. He pushed through a door, ran through a hall, jogged around a corner, down another hall, and out.

This was the Riverside. He stood, legs shaking, inhaling the scents of river and food. There were still a lot of people here, and more still emerging from the exits of the arena. The bridges over the Trao were busier than they should have been. The vendors here clearly knew something was wrong, even if they didn't quite know what.

He hadn't brought his Jarel with him. Stupid, stupid!

He looked down at his hand. Veriga had given him the key to the skimmer. It seemed like days ago that they'd driven up together from Veriga's place. The skimmer was parked just on the other side of the third Trao bridge.

He had a few minutes of safety, probably. Nekantor wouldn't target him, even if he had spies overseeing what happened. He started to walk, fast but casually, fist closed tightly on the key in his hand. It didn't feel fast enough. Other Families would be reacting, as soon as the news got out.

If the news was what he thought it was.

Drenas had come alone.

He reached for the iron bridge rail and pulled himself faster, into a jog. His legs wouldn't take much more of this. For a second he couldn't remember which skimmer was Veriga's, but then he found it. He pushed the key in, and pressed buttons. The skimmer hummed and lifted.

He was leaving Veriga and Melín behind.

But right now, it was more important to be safe.

He drove fast. Arriving at the Conveyor's Hall, he delivered the vehicle to the Household with embarrassment, requesting that they hold onto it because he needed to return it to a friend.

He didn't have to ask for an escort. Three members of the Household fell in around him and escorted him across the Residence grounds, all the way to the door of his suite.

When he walked into the vestibule, his Jarel emerged from the First Houseman's door.

"Bad news, sir," she said.

"The Eminence Herin is dead."

"Yes, sir, but that's not all. The Cohort bodyguard Arissen Drenas shot dead every person in the Eminence's dining room, including the Eminence Herin and his Argun, and Arbiter Plist of the Third Family and his Rowyeth. While they were at dinner."

That didn't nearly complete the list of deaths, but when he tried to form words for what had happened at the arena, they refused to come. "H-have you told Father?"

Jarel inclined her head. "Sir, I thought you might prefer to tell him yourself."

Name of Elinda. To take the news to Father . . . that thought brought reality crashing in as nothing else had. His knees quivered, but this was necessary. He walked, shaking, into the back of the suite, and knocked at Father's door.

"Come in."

He pushed the door open.

It looked like Father had just been getting tended, because a rolling stand of medical things was out and visible in the room. However, the care appeared to have been completed, and Father was fully dressed. A pair of his caretakers gently helped him to sit up in bed.

Pyaras felt dizzy and sick. This shouldn't be happening this way. There should have been a messenger coming to speak to Father, and Father should have been the one rushing in to bring him bad news, like it was before. The quivering reached his throat.

"F-Father, there's—there's s-some news. It's bad."

Father winced.

Pyaras glanced away instinctively from his father's pain, but forced himself look back up. "The Eminence's Arissen bodyguard shot Herin and three others to death at dinner tonight. Nekantor of the First Family is now Eminence of all Varin."

Father gaped at him for several seconds. At last he swallowed with some difficulty. "Pira . . . that's very bad news. Four people! Elinda keep them."

It wasn't four people, though. It was so many, many more. *Gripping the bag in his hand, smoke and death in his nose, the doctor's hand reaching, the victims, the wounds . . .* Tears rose suddenly in his throat. He gulped hard. "Elinda." He had to gulp again. "Elinda keep them all." He rubbed his face with both hands. His knees weakened.

"You must be respectful of your cousin," Father said.

Pyaras looked up, blinking. He couldn't mean Nekantor. "What?"

"Young Adon needs to be the First Family's candidate for Heir, not you. I don't want to hear you arguing."

Maybe he should have felt insulted, but he didn't. He couldn't imagine putting himself through such a nightmare. Besides which, he couldn't possibly give up the Pelismara Division—not now, when he had just started being able to help them.

"Don't worry, Father," he said. "I'm not eleven anymore. But I have to go now. I need to make sure Adon is all right."

CHAPTER TWENTY-SIX
Witness

How can you be alone when you've witnessed something terrible?

You can't. You just can't.

Adon curled in a ball on the couch in the private drawing room, with Mother's arm around him on one side, and Aloran's on the other. Tagaret and Della were here, too: Tagaret was folded into the other couch, and Della sat straight-backed on the chair. But he felt alone anyway. He pressed his face into his knees until his cheekbones hurt.

The memories cut. They tumbled in his mind like sharp stones that would never wear smooth.

When they'd reached home, Nekantor's Dexelin had—brokenly—told Mother and Aloran the basics of what happened. At least he'd been able to speak again by that time. How, Adon had no idea. His own tongue might as well have been permanently glued down.

"How could you?" Tagaret's voice cried. "How could you have left? And through the window, of all things?"

"Tagaret," said Mother, above his ear. "It's not a good time to ask Adon questions."

"I meant Della."

Della snapped, "At least I was doing something!"

"Both of you, hush." Mother's hand moved on his back, rubbing gently.

There was a change in the room, and a new voice—Imbati Serjer's voice, at a carefully gentle pitch. "Masters, Mistresses, Lady Selemei has come asking after your safety."

"Do let her come in," said Tagaret.

Aloran's arm slid down off his back, and his weight lifted off the couch. With him gone, it was too easy to hear voices echo in the waiting silence.

Plist! Plist, what's happening? Oh, no . . . Zzap! He's shooting! Everybody get out . . . Holy Mai help me, what he's turned me into, help me, oh holy Mai!

Plist, what's happening? Oh, no . . . Zzap! He's shooting! Everybody get out . . .

Adon groaned aloud, so a real sound might break the awful loop just for a second.

"Would you like to go into your room, love?" Mother asked.

But he couldn't be alone. He reached one hand across, over his shoulder, and felt for Mother's fingers. When he found them, he held on tight.

"All right, don't worry," she murmured. "Of course you can stay."

"Good evening," said Lady Selemei's voice. "I'm sorry to disturb you."

"No; we're sorry," Tagaret replied. "We happen to be in something of a state at the moment."

"It's understandable. Were you all here when it happened?"

"I was here, and so was Mother," Tagaret said. A hint of anger crept into his voice. "Della and Adon were not."

"Young Adon," said Lady Selemei, "thank Heile you're safe."

Safe. Was he safe? He was, of course he was. Mother was here holding his hand, and Aloran was standing near, and they were deep in the house. There was no safer place in the world. He lifted his head by a hair's breadth, but the voices tried to echo in the space between his face and his knees. He pushed his face down again.

"Our apologies, Lady," said Mother. "Adon's not ready to speak quite yet."

Lady Selemei seemed to think about that for a few seconds. "Della, where were you?" she asked.

"The Eminence's dining room," said Della.

"Oh, Bes save us!" Tagaret burst out. "That very room?! What if he'd killed you?"

"My Yoral was with me the entire time," Della said. "He checked it for traps and found none, so I stayed until Herin and Lady Falya came for dinner, to warn them. Herin told me to leave, but Lady Falya took me aside to the Chambers for a minute. When I came out, I found Arissen Karyas trying to kill the guard who had been posted at the dining room door. I thought Karyas was the killer trying to reach Herin, so I stopped them and sent them away."

Adon twitched. The First Family Lady with no manners was *Della?* She'd seen the fighting Arissen? Suddenly he wasn't alone with those particular echoes. He raised his head just enough to look at Della through the fringe of his hair.

"What?" she demanded irritably, in response to some look from Tagaret that he hadn't seen. Her back was straight as a shinca. "I thought that was it; how could I have known?"

"I'm surprised at you, Tagaret," said Lady Selemei. "None of us knew. And of course Della wanted to take some kind of action. You had come all this way. And you were personally constrained, but she was not."

"It's just that—!" Tagaret broke off, and crossed his arms.

"It's not fair to imagine anyone could have anticipated this," Lady Selemei said. "Nothing like it has ever happened."

"Something doesn't make sense," said Della. "This doesn't seem like Nekantor. I have no doubt that he arranged it, but shooti—" She broke off, with a remorseful glance toward Adon. "I mean, but, the thing that actually happened? I can't imagine him arranging it. It's too chaotic."

"Mistakes," Adon mumbled.

"Adon, darling?" asked Mother.

The moment was gone, though. Because he'd spoken, now a dead man was back, choking in his memory, another dead man's voice speaking in his ear, *Plist? Plist, what's happening?* It stole the breath out of his lungs.

"Lady," said Imbati Aloran. "May I have your permission to speak with young Master Adon alone for a few moments?"

Mother leaned close and squeezed him. "Would you, love?"

Adon nodded. It was hard to uncurl; his stomach felt like it might pour out horrors if left unprotected. He managed to get his feet on the floor and stumble into Mother's bedroom when Aloran held the door open for him. Instead of stopping by the lounge chairs, though, Aloran passed the bed and opened the Maze door behind the curtain on the far side.

"Please, come in."

Aloran's private room was small. It had a single window onto the gardens, like his own. Unlike his own, it was spare, and scrupulously tidy. He was almost embarrassed to muss the bed by sitting on it. The only way *he* could make a bed so well would be not to sleep in it at all.

He'd been wrong, earlier. This was the safest place.

Aloran sat down beside him and looked him in the eye.

Adon wanted to speak—truly, he did. He took a breath, but it only came out again as a shuddering sigh.

"May I ask you a question, Adon?"

He nodded.

"Is your information dangerous?"

He nodded again. Tears prickled in his eyes.

"I could swear an oath to you to protect the information," said Aloran. "But if I did so, it might be more difficult for us to solve this crime. I take it you might wish it solved."

Adon swallowed, and glanced away toward the windowsill. On it stood a row of books, and a portrait-frame containing an icon of holy Mai the Right in armor. From this angle he could see Mai's female embodiment, which looked an awful lot like Mother. She gave him the words he needed.

"Yes. Nekantor must be brought to justice."

"Do you permit questions?"

"Yes."

"Did you see Lady Della while you were out?"

"No," Adon admitted. "But I saw the fighting Arissen. They scared me, and I hid." He gulped. "They didn't see me go in, I swear."

"I believe you. So, as I understand, you entered the Maze quite near the Eminence's dining room."

And there was a knife. He could almost see it where it had landed, by his toes. He couldn't say the words.

"Kitchen," he said.

Aloran's eyes widened. Then he controlled his expression and held out one hand between them, palm up.

Aloran never did that anymore. But he wasn't about to question it. Adon put his hand on top of Aloran's, so they were palm to palm. Then the faithful servant gathered him into his lap and put his arms around him.

Wrong again; *this* was the safest place, though he'd grown large for it. Adon rested his forehead against Aloran's hair and took a deep breath beside his ear.

"The Arbiter died first," he whispered. "Coughing."

Aloran's arms tightened around him.

"The Eminence was scared. And then someone shouted—loud as a rockfall—and then there was the shooting. The Household ran."

"Did you count the shots?"

"There were—many. More than four."

"Did you run?"

"Nekantor's Dexelin carried me."

Aloran started stroking his head. "When did Nekantor's Dexelin come into the kitchen?"

"After me. Before . . . before."

"Did he say anything?"

"He said something about an equation. And he said, 'Oh, no' when he heard the Eminence's voice. And then he said to run. And then—" Adon breathed out, in a shudder. "Aloran, he's in trouble."

Aloran sighed. "Yes, he is. And he's so young. It's so hard when you're newly Marked."

"He fell down under me. He was—" He held Aloran tighter. "It was like he couldn't hear me. He was shaking. And praying to Mai."

"Where?"

"I don't know where. In the Maze. Aloran, I don't know what Nekantor is doing to him. I don't know how to help him."

Aloran squeezed him again. "I don't know, either. You may need to consider that there may be no way to help him."

"There has to be some way," Adon insisted. "He saved me. Again."

"It is only his duty as a bodyguard," Aloran said firmly. "You are his Master's brother. He is marked to the First Family, as I am."

Adon pulled back slightly and considered the beautiful, curving tattoo that covered most of Aloran's forehead. "Aloran, if the police come, will you talk to them?"

"Yes. I won't let them interrogate you."

Love and gratitude bubbled up in him. Adon flung his arms back around Aloran, and pressed their cheeks together.

"Are you ready to go back out?" Aloran asked.

Of course this safety couldn't last. Adon sighed and looked down, blinking to push back tears before he looked up again. "Yes. I'm ready now."

CHAPTER TWENTY-SEVEN
Saving Lives

Della sat very straight while her unwelcome resident battered her inside. *No sign of you, now. It's only me, being very obviously home and safe.* But since Adon and Imbati Aloran had stepped out, Tamelera had dropped her face in her hands, and the resulting silence invited someone to pounce.

Tagaret was angry with her—and it would not take many words for him to reveal her secret to everyone present. As kind as Tamelera had been, a sick feeling too high in her gut said the bread excuse wasn't going to fool anyone.

No. She had to pounce first.

"We all need to agree on something, Lady Selemei," she said. "Adon cannot be the Family's choice for Heir, no matter what Nekantor says. He's been through too much already."

Lady Selemei nodded sadly. "Poor young man. I hope he starts feeling better. You realize, Nekantor will be hard to dissuade."

"Your son Corrim could represent the Family," Della said. "Or Pyaras could, maybe."

"He participated in your evacuation today, did he?" Tagaret asked. "Pyaras?"

Lady Selemei frowned. "I can only assume—Arbiter Lorman was in charge of that."

Della squirmed. A horrible feeling seized her, hearing the word *assume* applied to Pyaras. No one had much chance to express their worries, though, because the door to the master bedroom opened. Adon looked a little better—moving, walking—though she would never have wished to see such a haunted expression on a child's face. Tamelera jumped up and ran to him.

"I've spoken to young Master Adon, Lady," said Imbati Aloran. "We should make sure to reach out to the investigators."

"Thank you, Aloran," Tamelera sighed. "Oh, Adon. My sweet, brave boy."

"I love you, Mother," said Adon.

Then the door from the sitting room cracked open, and the First Houseman looked through. "Mistresses and Masters, before you concern yourselves terribly about Master Pyaras, I should inform you that he's approaching us at this very moment."

Della caught her breath. "Is he?"

Tagaret asked, "How do you know?"

"I just asked the Household Director, sir, and was told he'd left his suite two minutes ago, so I checked the hall. Under the circumstances, it seemed best. I shall most certainly invite him in." Della didn't like the tilt of his head, though. Something bad was coming.

The look on Pyaras' face, when he arrived, was dreadful. Tagaret jumped up and wrapped an arm around his cousin's shoulders. Pyaras reached across, patting him as though to make sure he was real. The drawing room was becoming quite crowded, and they had some rearranging to do; Serjer and Premel brought in a pair of extra chairs, and Lady Selemei asked for hers to be placed beside Della's, while Pyaras remained under Tagaret's arm and joined him on the couch. For fear of drawing notice, Della kept her gaze away from Lady Selemei's, and held very still.

"I'll save you the trouble of asking where I was," Pyaras said sharply. "I was at the targetball arena on the second level. The Eminence's bodyguard must have thought he'd get lost in the crowds there after escaping the Residence, but Nekantor's pet, Karyas, found him. She shot a wysp and caused an explosion that killed him. Along with more than twenty innocent Arissen spectators. I helped the doctors treat the wounded."

All the breath vanished out of the room.

Della caught herself about to say '*what?*' as if, by making him repeat it, she could fix a tear in the fabric of what was possible. She hugged herself. Most of the others were just staring.

The fear of something just like this was why they had dropped everything and come back from Selimna. But, against disaster of this magnitude, they'd managed so little . . .

Tamelera was the one who found words. "Pyaras, have you eaten anything tonight?"

Pyaras seemed startled. "I don't know." He gulped, eyes shining, and started blinking fast. "I was—busy, helping."

Tagaret pulled his cousin's head tight against his cheek and shook him gently. "I'm sure we can find something for you to eat."

"I'm so sorry," Lady Selemei said suddenly. "I believe I've stayed too long. This should be your time."

"Not at all," said Tamelera. "Please, Cousin, we consider you family. Do join us for dinner. We can stay right here, if Premel wouldn't mind bringing the food in."

Lady Selemei relaxed. "Thank you, I would like to," she said. She glanced over; Della blushed at the attention. "I'm sure we're all hungry."

Unfortunately, before food could arrive, Serjer announced more guests—this time, the sort of guests who could put her off her dinner. Speaker Fedron she didn't mind so much, but Arbiter Lorman had her wrinkling her nose in disgust before he'd done more than walk in the door. Her unwelcome resident had just settled down; she'd hate for something to disturb it again. Lady Selemei stood to greet Speaker Fedron; he squeezed her gloved hand.

"Selemei, thank you so much for everything you did today," Speaker Fedron said. "I don't know where you got your intuition to evacuate the school and offices, but I'm certain you've saved lives."

"It's kind of you," Selemei replied. "But when it comes to saving lives, the real credit should go to Pyaras, who helped the doctors at the targetball explosion, and to Lady Della."

She hadn't expected that. "Me?"

"You," Selemei said. "You stopped Arissen Karyas from killing the guard at the dining room door. And, whether you meant to or not, you saved both Lady Falya and her Suril. Without you, they would have walked into the dining room with Herin and Plist and their servants, and never come out."

I saved lives. Was that Sirin's blessing, for luck, or was it—by any chance—Elinda's? *Turn your eyes softly on me, holy Mother of Souls . . .*

"We'll need to make some kind of statement," said Speaker Fedron. Selemei's words appeared to have shaken him. "So many people have been affected. I'll call the cabinet together. We must honor the Imbati's sacrifices, and the efforts of the rescuers."

"Speaker, but, so, so," objected Arbiter Lorman, twisting one side of his whiskers, "I don't think we'll have time for that. So, we have to prepare for the Accession Ball, and there are the security concerns—"

"Don't be ridiculous, Lorman," said Speaker Fedron. "Emergency meetings can be convened within an hour. This will be easy. I'm thinking the day after tomorrow, so we can compile a list of people to invite."

"So, but, Speaker, you'll tell me Pyaras must attend, and right now everyone across the Families is scrambling to concoct plans and arrange assassination attempts—so it's hard enough just planning for the Ball . . ."

Della glanced at Selemei, who gave her a smile of sympathy. Her belly felt uncomfortable; she shifted slightly, trying not to draw attention, but it only got worse—her insides had turned into a large stone—

It hurt . . .

She winced, and hissed in a breath.

"Della," said Tagaret. "Are you all right?"

"Fine," she said. But it got worse. "Tagaret—I don't know—" Her heart started pounding.

"Oh, Elinda help us!" Tagaret exclaimed. "You did this to yourself! Why did you put yourself in danger when you know you're in no condition—"

"Tagaret!" She cut him off, but too late; everyone was staring. Her fingers went cold.

"What? Are you telling me she's pregnant?!" Lorman demanded. "Tagaret, I can't believe you could be so irresponsible!"

Della cowered. The stone in her stomach wouldn't relax. Her heart cut off her breath.

Selemei stood up. "Lorman, calm yourself."

"They came back from Selimna as soon as they knew," said Tamelera.

"But Lady Della has a *history*," said Lorman. "A history of—"

"A history of tragedy and grief," Tamelera interrupted. "Which you're now making worse."

"A history of failure," Lorman snapped. "Of medical weakness. She should never have been brought into the Family."

"No," Della said. "No . . ." She couldn't breathe, and the pain was getting worse.

Tagaret stood up. "Tell that to Nekantor," he said, red-faced. "He made the arrangement."

"You can't tell anything to Nekantor!" Lorman shouted. "None of you understand the importance of this—do you think the decline is some kind of game? Nekantor threatens me if I offer him a partner, Tagaret can't produce an heir, and Adon's about to have everyone in Pelismara try to kill him! Gnash it, we are looking at the *end of Garr's line*, and not one of you seems to care! What about the Race?"

"Tagaret," Della moaned, "Tagaret . . ." She clutched at her stomach. Was it happening again?

"Heile help us!" Tagaret cried. "Serjer, call the Medical Center!"

"No!" Della shook her head. The pain had leveled out, but she couldn't get enough air to shout. "Tagaret, no . . . It's getting better, please . . ."

Tagaret stared at her, frozen, for several seconds, then dashed out the double doors.

"You think you're so smart, when really you're a liability," Lorman snapped. "Going out and putting yourself in danger . . ."

"Lorman, stop," said Fedron. "You're making it worse."

"Someone had to try to save Herin," Della insisted. "I saved lives."

Lorman glared at her. "Well, time to save another life." He shoved out the double doors.

Speaker Fedron shook his head. "I don't know what to say. Lady Della, I'm so sorry." He went out after Lorman.

They were gone, finally—but so was Tagaret, and so was her safety. "Tamelera, Selemei, help me. Don't let them. Please." If she could just get enough air, surely she could make the stone inside her release, but she couldn't control her breathing.

Tamelera came and wrapped an arm around her. "Della, I love you. But with the terrible danger to you, and to your child—don't you think caution would be best?"

"It's not a child," she said. "It's nothing. Lorman's right, I'm a failure, and that means there's nothing to save . . ."

"But, love, what if you're wrong?"

"What if *you're* wrong? What if Tagaret is wrong?"

"The doctors will know what to do," said Tamelera. "That's what they're for."

Lady Selemei sat down in the chair beside her. "Della, I understand your fear, but I don't know what we can do. What doctors have you been seeing?"

"Yoral," she said. "He's been watching, looking after me. Yoral? Yoral, I need you."

Yoral came out from behind a curtain. "Lady, breathe into this." He handed her a silk handkerchief. "What are you experiencing?"

Putting her attention on it was a mistake; panic tried to throttle her, and tears started trickling down her cheeks. "M-my . . . it's . . . hard, I g-guess . . ."

The doctors came suddenly. Four Kartunnen in gray medical coats rushed in the door as if they'd been told she was dying. Della tried to jump to her feet, but her stomach hurt, and she couldn't stand up straight. She caught herself on the arm of the chair. She couldn't have run. What would she do, climb out a window?

"I'm not dying," she cried, clenching her fists to try to sound calm. "I don't have bleeding. I don't have anything. You can leave me alone."

"Lady," said one of the male doctors. She knew that one. He'd seen her many times, and his eyes were knowing, filled with the unquestioning certainty of every bloody moment he'd ever witnessed beside her bed. "Just come this way, please, so we can evaluate you."

"No. Selemei, tell them no."

Selemei winced. "Doctors, you should be able to evaluate her here."

"Lady," the male doctor said, "that would be highly indiscreet."

Yoral spoke in her ear. "Please, Mistress. Just let them do the checks, for your own safety."

"You've done the checks, Yoral," she said. "How many more will you allow? Will you protect me?"

He didn't reply.

"Tagaret!"

He came out from behind the doctors, speaking gently. "Della, my love, my darling, I forgive you for endangering yourself, all right? Don't work yourself into a state, or everything will be worse. I'm here for you, no matter what you have to go through."

"Go through! I shouldn't *have* to go through—"

One of the doctors grabbed her arm. She spasmed in terror, trying to pull free, but another one grabbed her from the other side.

"No! You can't—can't let them do this. Oh, gods—help me, someone—help me!" She tried to hold onto words like a rope, but no one would catch the other end and pull her to safety. The Kartunnen were strong, and dragged her into her bedroom. "Help me!" she shrieked. No one came.

"Lady, please get in bed now."

She couldn't answer. She could only sob. She glimpsed Tagaret, talking with Yoral and one of the doctors outside the door, but she couldn't hear what he was saying.

"Tagaret!"

"Lady, please, just get in bed."

The doctor who had been speaking with Tagaret came in with a frown. "Lady, you're overwrought. You'll endanger yourself and your pregnancy. We're going to need to ask you to get in bed and lie still. If you fight, or harm yourself, or try to climb out any windows, we'll be forced to take steps."

There were no windows in this room. There was no escape, and there would be no rescue. Della sank to the bed, wracked by silent sobs, with hot tears streaming down her face. A Kartunnen woman pushed her shoulders gently but implacably, forcing her down. And then there were two of them on her arm, and a needle, and tubes, and tape, and it was all happening again.

Coercion invaded her veins, cold as ice, and the fog rose until everything drowned in gray.

CHAPTER TWENTY-EIGHT

Gains and Losses

Waking up alive was an incredible gift. Waking up with Drefne on one side and Aripo on the other—indescribable.

On the schedule, last night had been Drefne's night, but then he'd told her he'd also escaped the targetball game. That definitely called for a therapist, so they'd stopped by Aripo's and asked her over. The three of them had stayed up late talking, and talking, and talking.

They'd both stayed.

Drefne was breathing against her forehead. She felt for his knee with one hand, shifted her hips slightly, and lifted her other hand to feel Aripo's long, sweet-smelling hair.

"I love you," she murmured.

The alarm had gone off already. She had reports to make and acts to answer for. She'd prefer never to leave this spot.

Drefne sighed and opened his eyes, stretching one muscular arm far out toward the wall. "I'll make breakfast."

"Breakfast?" said Aripo clearly, as if she'd already been awake for a while. "Wow, come on my nights any time." She nudged Melín. "No offense, isseni, but you're a terrible cook."

"Ha," said Melín. But maybe Aripo was joking around so they couldn't return to thoughts of yesterday. She turned over and put a kiss on her strong arm. "Dref, I'd better skip. Reporting early this morning."

Drefne flung both legs high in the air, then rolled back down and straight up onto his feet, launching himself out the bedroom door. Gods, did he know how to move.

"Nope, no skipping," he called back.

"Bet you can't finish it in time."

"Bet you dinner out that I can. Aripo, I hope you like eggs and grani."

Aripo gave a delicious laugh. "Sure."

That wasn't a bet she really cared if she lost. Most days, she got dressed before breakfast, but now she went out in top and shorts toward the sounds and smells of Drefne in the kitchen, walking carefully to protect her as-yet-untaped ankle. Drefne was bare-backed, heating a mess of grani strips in oil in one pan, and the eggs in another.

"Put an apron on, isseni."

He shrugged, a beautiful movement, but didn't move toward the apron, so Melín grabbed it off the hook and wrapped it around him, which also meant wrapping her arms around him. She leaned into his warm skin, feeling muscles move in his back.

"Can't get this over your head from here, Dref, come on."

"Fine." He hooked it with the hand that wasn't stirring, and pulled it over. Behind them came the sound of Aripo's slippers by the electric kettle.

"I'll make tea?" Aripo said.

"Don't tell me that's the thing you know how to find in this place," said Drefne.

"Of course it is."

He chuckled. "Yes, of course it is."

Melín closed her eyes to focus on the sounds of them, but her mind brought back a different voice: *Melín, I'm sorry.*

I'm sorry, too.

Pyaras shouldn't have left. He should have stayed, so they could talk afterward, and get through it together. That was a new kind of thought, and serious. The kind of thought that meant she should try to find him, and make sure she succeeded this time. It meant something else, too.

She took a deep breath and let go of Drefne. "Dref? Aripo?"

"Isseni, you all right?" Aripo asked gently. "I might be able to excuse you from early report if you need to talk some more."

"It's not that," she said. "I just—I need to tell you about someone, before it turns into a secret."

"Aww," said Drefne. He combined his two pans, grabbed three plates down from the shelf, and started heaping food on them. "Sit down, and you can tell us. Oh, and you owe me dinner."

"How serious?" Aripo asked.

Melín shrugged as she took a chair at the table. It was snug with three; Aripo, who was the tallest, sat on the aluminum step-stool Melín used to reach top shelves when neither of them was around. "I don't know. I've met him twice. And twice he's really surprised me with his instinct for dangerous situations." She started shoveling food into her mouth. "Drefne, this, mm."

"You're welcome. Is he a fighter?"

She shook her head and swallowed. "Strategist."

"Does he know about us?" Aripo asked.

She felt her cheeks grow hot. "Not yet. We haven't done a lot of talking."

Both of them burst out laughing.

"All right, isseni, all right." She set down her fork. "But also, we stopped a Cohort hound from shooting a wysp outside the Descent. And he was there, yesterday. He kept his head. He was the one who thought to look for the Kartunnen and their medical supplies in the locker rooms."

Neither of them was laughing now. "He really is a strategist," said Aripo. "I can see why you'd be impressed."

Drefne nodded seriously. "If you get a chance to talk to him, let us know how it goes."

The thought of that conversation put a knot in her stomach, and not the pleasant kind she usually got when thinking of Pyaras. It wasn't like she could avoid it—not everyone was a team player. But you didn't end up with isseni like Drefne and Aripo by hiding things; you had to lay your heart on the table, and see who had the courage to pick it up.

Pyaras, how brave are you?

She had a lot to report to Captain. It felt insulting to walk into the adjunct-local Division station wearing Cohort orange after the massacres two Cohort traitors had caused. Every step felt tense; her mates might well jump her if she showed her face. But the adjunct-local Division station was quiet. Too quiet. It should have been full of mates readying packs and supplies for their adjunct routes.

Captain was not in the weights room, or in her office.

Eventually she found everyone: they had packed themselves into the assembly room, standing somber and silent while Captain Keyt addressed them from a podium on a raised platform at the front. Melín slipped in the door and moved sideways against the wall.

Captain was reading names.

The chill of the moon ran down her back. Those were the names of the Division dead.

Her throat tightened, and the headache that had held off this morning started up again. Why hadn't she killed Karyas when she had the chance? In her place, Treminindi would have done it.

Sickening thought.

How in Varin's name had she gotten sucked into this? Why couldn't she escape the reach of meddling noblemen? Give her back the adjuncts! She'd happily spend four hours listening to Fourth Luun rave about his favorites for the targetball final—

Oh, no.

Was Luun now among the dead? She hadn't heard his name, and now Captain came to the end of her list.

But she'd come in late.

Gnash it all. *Be alive, Luun. Watch your favorites compete another day.*

A Captain's Hand walked in among the crowd. He was carrying a wire basket full of moon-yellow mourning armbands. Melín snagged one as he went by, and pressed it to her lips. Behind her closed eyes flashed a vision of the blast area. The injured. The dead, Elinda keep them. She opened her eyes again. Mates broke from their positions and began moving toward the rear and side doors. Melín pushed toward the front platform, and Captain's position.

Captain Keyt was putting on an armband. Her face wasn't as firm as usual. She took up a paper from her podium, nodded to Melín, and turned away. Melín followed her, pulling her own armband up over the sleeve of her uniform. When they reached the office, Captain Keyt sat down in her chair and set the paper on her desk. She closed her eye.

That paper was the list of names the Captain had just read. Hard to read upside-down, but impossible not to try.

"Thank you for your patience, Hand Melín," said Captain Keyt, and opened her eye again. "Report."

But then Melín found Luun's name. A man she'd barely known, but her throat closed up anyway. She couldn't report. She couldn't pretend. She took a deep breath.

"Permit me to speak my mind, please, Captain?"

Captain sighed. "This is a good time for it."

"Sir, I acted too slowly. Nekantor has suborned the Eminence's

Cohort. I'm sure he's behind the assassination of Herin. And I suspect, because I chose to fight his favorite, First Karyas, I may be discharged." *Or worse.* "In fact, I would be lucky if he only discharged me."

"I hope he doesn't," said Captain Keyt. "If he wanted Herin dead, it would have been simpler to go to the Paper Shadows."

"Respectfully, sir, they don't always complete their missions."

"True. But if he's suborned the Cohort, there's likely more to this. It's more important than ever for you to observe him for his next plans."

The thought of spending another day as a nobleman's tool! She swallowed. "Captain—"

"Hand, you told me you'd called out wysp-shotting in the Cohort. Please tell me you didn't give First Karyas any ideas."

"Crown of Mai, Captain!" She controlled her voice. "Based on the things she's said to me, I believe First Karyas is a failed Specialist. Last night, I was at the targetball game. I saw her take her shot. It was . . . unprofessional. Her aim was accurate, but she miscalculated the distance, and had to be taken in by the medics with severe burns to her hands."

"And what about the assassin, Drenas? Did he strike you as stable?"

"Sir, I didn't know him well, but he seemed like anyone else. The Cohort had split into factions, and I thought he was on the Eminence's side, but clearly I was wrong. Maybe he was unstable, though, sir. It makes no sense to me how he could so completely undermine his stated mission."

"People have failings," said Captain Keyt. "I'll need to see what I can learn about First Karyas. The police will have trouble laying hands on her, I suspect. Commander Tret and I may need to bring these concerns to Executor Pyaras."

Melín blinked. She had to have heard that wrong. "Sir?"

"We got lucky in our Executor, for once," said Captain. "He's not stupid. He keeps his hands off our operations, and unlike most of those idiots, he actually listens. For example, the Heir tried to raise paper quotas, and when the Commander explained the risks, Pyaras actually went to the Eminence Herin and convinced him to change his mind. That's something I didn't think was possible."

"That's—not possible," Melín said. Then realized what it sounded like, and added, "Usually, sir, I entirely agree." But it really, *really* wasn't. It had to be some kind of weird coincidence. Some name-lines did show up in more than one caste.

"Thank you for your report, Hand," said Captain Keyt. "And for your honesty. These are dangerous times. Please keep me updated on anything new you learn."

Melín saluted, right hand to left shoulder. "For so long as I remain in the Cohort, Captain."

"You're dismissed."

She walked out, shaking her head. Her Pyaras couldn't be Grobal. He wasn't scrawny, selfish, or whiny; he was sexy, considerate, and playful! And *sensible.* Certainly a better strategist than a good many mates she knew.

Gnash his police friend—that scarred, knotty-shouldered guy who'd been gathering evidence. Why had he sent Pyaras home? If Pyaras had stayed, she could have gotten to know more about who he really was, and this wouldn't even be a question.

She had other worries to deal with, however, now that she was on her way to the Residence Cohort station. With every rampway down, she became more convinced that today was going to stink like carrion. When she arrived, she nodded a quick 'seni' to the night-shift guards at the grounds gate and jogged across the grounds. Then she saw the deserted station entrance.

Had the Cohort also met early for a memorial? Was she late?

Did being late even matter when the Eminence probably thought she'd acted against him?

She pushed in the fancy bronze door; the door into the Eights ready room was cracked open and she could hear a voice, reading a long list of names. Too many to be the dead. And worse, she knew the voice.

Nekantor is here. Looks like I'll get my ass handed to me earlier than I thought.

"Now," came the haughty voice from beyond the door. "All of you. Get out."

There was a roar, a chaotic mix of triumph and outrage. No time to get into the ready room; Melín hit the wall to one side of the door as a crowd of people burst out shouting, some screaming in rage. Another group of Cohort guards followed them into the foyer. Organized, this second group was, with a frightening determination in their eyes. Sahris was among them, and Fetti and the others of her eight. They drove the members of the first group out through the bronze door.

First Crenn, as he came out, looked to the right and found her.

Now she was going to get it.

Plis and Sirin help me.

"Eighth Melín, you're late. You'll answer to the Eminence."

"Yes, sir. Sorry, sir."

Crenn had no idea the things she'd be asked to answer for. The fact that she hadn't been run out the door after the others looked very bad. Maybe Nekantor would demand worse than firing. As she walked in through the inner door, the back of her neck prickled, and her thighs started to twitch.

The Eights ready room was a mess. Benches had been knocked over; lockers had been opened and their contents dumped on the floor. Even mourning armbands lay shockingly abandoned amid the mess. Nekantor stood on the Commander's low stage, beyond it all, with his long-haired Imbati manservant at his back. He was staring fixedly at the watch on his wrist, and both of his fists were clenched.

Melín found an empty spot of floor, stopped and saluted.

"Your Eminence! Eighth Melín reporting for duty." Or death.

The Eminence's eyes snapped up, and latched onto her like a grip. "You're late, Arissen," he said.

"Yes, your Eminence, sir. I'm sorry, sir."

"Make sure it never happens again."

"Yes, sir."

Nekantor glanced at the floor, made a face, and his fingers fluttered over the buttons on his silk vest. "You should know something, Arissen Melín. The one thing I won't stand for is disloyalty."

"Yes, sir." She understood what she'd just seen, then, and certainty turned her stomach cold. They were all gone. Every one of the Herin loyalists, or every one he could find. He really *had* suborned the Cohort, and now with a perfect excuse to expel potentially unstable or dangerous guards, he owned it completely.

"I placed my trust in you. You were to do your duty, Arissen, and instead you acted against me."

Down this path was the crevasse that would swallow her. Suddenly she became very aware of First Crenn, standing behind her, too near. He might grab her any second. Or shoot her. Her mind raced. This was a risk, but every word was a risk, and it was the only thing she could think of.

"Your Eminence, sir! You did not place your trust in me, sir. If you had, you would have told me First Karyas' role in putting you in your rightful place. I would have known not to delay her."

She braced herself for a sentence, a blow, a weapon bolt.

"First, take off that armband," the Eminence snapped. "This is not a time for mourning. I want readiness."

"Yes, sir," she said, automatically. She forced herself to pull the armband down to her wrist. *The Eminence permits no human feeling for death.* The thought was disturbing, but it explained why so many armbands had been thrown on the floor. She hid her dismay, and dropped the armband.

Now Nekantor laughed in what sounded almost like relief. "That's better. You're lucky I enjoy your bad manners, Arissen. And you're quite correct. If I had trusted you more, this would have been so much more—" He shuddered and flicked dirt off his hands that she couldn't see. "—tidy."

A shiver ran down her spine, and her head throbbed. She tried to stand straighter.

The Eminence smiled. "That means you deserve to be rewarded."

"Thank you, sir." A wave of sick anticipation rushed over her. Another reward, from this man? What form of torture would it involve?

"I'm missing a bodyguard at a critical time. The Accession Ball and Heir Selection will begin before Karyas can hold a weapon, much less fight."

Stinking carrion. She'd have to spend days *by Nekantor's side?* She forced herself to answer, "I'm honored to guard you, sir."

Nekantor gave a smirk. "Not me," he said. "My little brother. He's going to be the First Family's candidate for Heir, and he's going to win."

CHAPTER TWENTY-NINE

Heroes

It was awful every time Veriga put himself in danger. Pyaras watched Tagaret's office door, rubbing his temples anxiously. Veriga was in there right now, in his capacity as police investigator, interviewing Imbati Aloran.

Pyaras paced around the couches, the chairs, the fancy gaming table. Again. He touched the top of his head where the hairs were growing back. The skin there still felt strange and fragile.

Veriga interviewing Aloran, by itself, wasn't so disturbing. However, it meant the investigation had reached the First Family, which was bad. Veriga would be safer in the midst of a deadly ongoing disaster.

At last the door to the office swung open. Aloran emerged first, blank-faced and moving like a machine—an Imbati defensive formality you saw all the time, but unusual for Aloran. Being interviewed by an Arissen couldn't have been easy for him. At least he got to be questioned by someone who wasn't a stranger.

Veriga's hand appeared on the doorjamb, then his arm in Arissen red, crossed by the moon-yellow of a mourning armband. Last came his face, somber beneath the edge of his round police helmet. "Pyaras, come in here for a minute, please."

"Oh. Sure, yes, of course."

Since every noble suite had a room with the same function in precisely the same location, he felt odd walking into Tagaret's office. The office in his own house was an uncomfortable place, ostensibly his but still largely Father's. This place was just the opposite, with a thick carpet, a couch, and a warm lamp. The desk had a player machine for musical recordings sitting on one corner, which was very, very Tagaret. If his cousin hadn't just been in Selimna, the walls would probably have been full of art.

Thank the Twins Tagaret and Della had come back.

Poor Della. May Heile keep her safe . . .

"Shut the door," Veriga said.

Pyaras shut the door. "Something's wrong, isn't it. Are you in danger?"

"Not immediate danger," said Veriga. "But yes. I'm handling some very sensitive information that I will need to deliver directly to the Chief of the Pelismar Police."

"Sensitive information," Pyaras echoed, and shivered. Assembling evidence to implicate Nekantor in all of the deaths was potentially deadly.

"That's not what I called you in here for. Early this morning I was asked to produce a list of the people who aided the victims of the arena explosion, and a basic description of their contributions. When I delivered it, I was informed that the list would be forwarded to the Speaker of the Cabinet. The heroes will be called before the cabinet at four afternoon today to have those contributions recognized."

"Did that list include me?"

"I am pleased to say that it did."

"And you."

"Yes."

"And—oh, gods help me."

Veriga stared at him levelly. "Yes. It also included Arissen Melín. I thought you should know."

Pyaras gulped, and his heart pounded. He'd sworn never to cross-mark again, so he'd worn only a casual white shirt and gray trousers to the game. Melín hadn't seemed to notice or care. But he'd been in an arena full of Arissen, sitting with his friend who was an Arissen. As honest as he'd thought he was, it wasn't honest enough.

He couldn't wear casual clothes to a cabinet meeting. Even if he did, he could no longer hide his name.

Sirin and Eyn, he didn't want to!

But the abyss in his stomach told him that Melín wouldn't see it as honesty.

"Thank you for telling me, Veriga," he said.

"Young nobleman, I suspect you've got some decisions to make."

The big decisions were impossible; he focused on smaller ones. He knocked at the door of his cousin's rooms. "Adon? Are you in there?"

Adon didn't answer.

He knocked harder. "The Arissen investigator is gone, Adon, please, I need to talk to you."

A muffled, grumpy voice came from behind the door. "Gnash it, Pyaras, why are you always so *loud?*"

About to bang on the door again, Pyaras quickly pulled his hand back. "I'm sorry, all right? I need your help. I have, uh, an event. And I don't know what to wear."

A second later, the bronze door cracked open, with Adon's eye behind it. "You swear you're not messing with me."

"I swear by the Twins," Pyaras said. "I have to go before the cabinet with some people." *Before Melín.* The more he thought about it, the harder it was to stand still.

The door opened by an inch. "Why?"

"Uh, because they think we're heroes?"

"Well." Adon leaned out, one shoulder on the door and the other on the jamb. "You sure aren't dressed like a hero now."

Pyaras looked down. This pink suit was one he liked, but he was ready to admit it wasn't the latest style. He opened out his hands. "Come to my house?"

"Not without bodyguards."

"Of course not." He'd brought his Jarel with him; he wasn't making that mistake again. The problem was, with an Heir Selection coming at them fast, Tagaret had gone out to strategize with the First Family Council, so his Kuarmei wasn't available. And even if poor Imbati Aloran hadn't needed a break after his interview, Lady Tamelera never lent him to anyone. That left only one bodyguard they could conceivably make an arrangement with. "We have to ask if we can borrow Della's Yoral."

Adon's face crumpled slightly. "Yoral is really upset right now. But I guess we can talk to him."

They went and knocked on the other bedroom door. After a second or two, Pyaras knocked again. Unexpectedly, Adon's hand slipped into his. He almost jumped, but then squeezed his cousin's fingers.

Della's Yoral opened the door, blank-faced. "Sirs, my Mistress is indisposed and should not be disturbed."

"May we speak with her?" Pyaras asked.

Yoral's face twitched. "No, sir. I'm sorry, sir."

She'd seemed fine until just before the doctors arrived. He rubbed his hand across his mouth. Della shouldn't have become an unrecognized casualty of yesterday's events.

Also, if Yoral was too upset to leave, Adon wouldn't be going out.

"Yoral," Adon said, "would you be willing to come down the hall with us for a few minutes?" Yoral didn't answer. "If the Kartunnen can be trusted?" Adon waited again, while Yoral said nothing. "Aloran is an excellent nurse. If he came in to see her, maybe he would know what to do."

Yoral inclined his head. "If you would please ask your mother to come for a visit, young Master."

"Perfect. I'm sure that will help." Adon pulled his hand away and ran off across the private drawing room.

"Yoral," Pyaras said. "I'm . . . sorry." Words didn't seem weighty enough to convey what he meant. He tried to find something else to say, but then Adon returned, carrying a small case, followed closely by Lady Tamelera and her Aloran. They went straight in.

Yoral stepped out and bowed. "Just a few minutes, please, young Master."

"Of course," said Adon.

His young cousin did have a gift for understanding Imbati. The three of them walked out together through the sitting room to the vestibule, where Imbati Jarel joined them. Pyaras found Adon's hand sneaking into his again as they walked down the hall.

"So, Pyaras . . . I brought some things. I'm going to make you look great."

"You'd better." Oops, that sounded terrible. Pyaras shook his head. "Adon, sorry, I'm just nervous because of . . . the people I'm going to see." It was more than just Melín. "Nekantor, for one."

"Nekantor doesn't care what you look like," said Adon.

"The rest of the cabinet will." And Nekantor would hate seeing him in a line of Arissen, no matter what he wore. He let go of Adon's hand for the spiral stairway to the second floor.

Pyaras pressed his hand to unlock his front door, and greeted the First Housewoman as they entered. Escorting Adon past Mother's colorful pouf in the sitting room and taking him back into the private areas of the house, where Father was resting, brought the blood rushing into his face. It was the weirdest feeling to have his cousin here—wonderful, yet it made him ache.

Adon was looking around. "Do you get the whole master bedroom to yourself?"

"Yes."

"Lucky. Why in Varin's name do you spend so much time at *our* house?"

Pyaras shrugged, opening his door. "I don't know; I just always have."

Adon took charge of the room immediately. He set down his case, went to the framed-glass wardrobe against the left wall, and opened its tall doors with a flourish. After a second, he cast over a skeptical look. "You really don't have a lot to work with. Maybe we should start with the ruby velvet."

"No—not red." The last thing he wanted was to look like someone pretending to be Arissen. "But, actually, Grobal green isn't much better."

Adon raised his eyebrows. "So we're left with variations on sapphire, beryl, and feldspar-gray. Are you serious?"

"I'd let you take me shopping, except it's this afternoon."

Adon looked at him and sighed. "Also, if we go out, people might try to shoot at us."

"Again."

"Right?" Adon looked back into the wardrobe and pushed some things to one side with dissatisfaction. "You're wearing tourmaline now. I suppose we could just add a few things to it?"

"I'm not sure."

"Ooh, wait, what about this one? It's not red or green, and it's not as overly popular as sapphire velvet. I could work with this." He pulled it out: it was blue-gray matte silk, finely tailored, with matching piping along the seams, and no other embellishments at all.

"Oh." Pyaras winced. "That was my dad's."

"So, it doesn't fit?"

"Well, we did have it altered."

Adon flashed him a look.

"All right, all right." He excused himself and put it on in the bathroom. The fit was just fine, but it still felt awkward. He braced himself for Adon's assessment.

The boy's eyes lit. "You look basic, Pyaras."

"Ugh."

"In a good way, though. We can add things." He picked up his case, crossed to the foot of Pyaras' large bed, and opened it out. There were pretty things inside—neck-scarves and handkerchiefs and jewels. "Let's use these button covers," Adon said, plucking out some that looked like diamond. "And this scarf, I think. I'll tie it for you. You're going to have to supply your own gloves."

"All right."

When Adon was finished with him, he was afraid to look in the long mirror that hung inside his bathroom door. But when he did, he had to admit his cousin had an eye. He didn't look forty, as he might have feared, probably because Adon had tied his neck-scarf in the latest style. The jewels glinted on his buttons, and the tint of his pale gray gloves provided a subtle contrast to the color of the suit.

Adon peeked in at him. "Now, you look like a hero."

"If you say so."

Gods help me, I don't look like a hero. I look like a nobleman.

But it was only the truth.

Pyaras walked into the central section of the Residence in an anguish of dread. This was a dangerous time, and his Jarel was here to make sure Paper Shadows didn't target him as a potential First Family Heir candidate, but he was far more worried about Melín. At every turn, he half expected her to appear out of nowhere and knock him out cold.

Every movement felt wrong. His breathing was tight, and his buttons were heavy, and his cheeks burned. He tugged at his neck-scarf with one gloved finger, but it didn't help much.

"Sir," said his Jarel from behind his shoulder, "you may not want the Eminence to see you fidgeting."

"I may not want the Eminence to see me at all."

"I'm sorry, sir."

"It's not your fault, Jarel. It's mine." He thought of Melín again, and stopped as his rib cage tried to close down on his lungs. He just couldn't breathe like this. *Sorry, Adon.* He pulled the stylish knot of his scarf until it came undone. "Can you take this, please, Jarel?"

"Of course, sir."

He started walking again. There might be people waiting in the hall when he reached the central section. And he'd just wrecked the top anchor of his look. He stopped again.

"Do I look unbalanced?"

"No, sir."

"I'm just going to do this anyway." He clicked off his button-covers, and handed them to Jarel.

"I'm sorry, sir."

Stupid as he felt for panicking, he couldn't just tell himself not to panic. He forced a deep breath into his lungs, tugged his gloves straight, and started walking again.

There were people outside the cabinet chamber when he arrived. Sixteen, at least, standing around talking in hushed voices.

At least half of them were Arissen in dress uniforms, some wearing the front-brimmed, low-crested helmets of the Division, others wearing the smooth round helmets of the Police. A few faces turned when he arrived, but he wasn't about to start searching for Veriga. Mai's truth, it was probably safer for Veriga not to publicly align himself with a nobleman.

There was also a clump of Kartunnen who had to be the Cave-Cats' team doctors, because he recognized the woman he had followed. She wasn't dressed as a doctor today. She'd painted her lower lip dark green, and she wore a long, flowing dress coat in the regulated pale gray of her caste.

He couldn't see Melín. She would be here, though. Probably just hidden somewhere behind the tall, Arissen-red backs. He wanted to go looking for her, but it would disturb everyone. He shouldn't force her to be seen with him in public.

Or tempt her to knock him out cold.

Movement. Over the heads of the group, the door to the cabinet chamber had opened, and people started moving through. The Manservant to the Eminence was the only Imbati permitted in the chamber; that much he remembered.

"Thank you, Jarel," he said. "I'll see you afterward."

"I'll wait right here, sir."

Pyaras hung back long enough for all the others to enter. He gritted his teeth. Then he pinched at the fingers of his gloves, and pulled them off. He stuffed them into his jacket pocket as he walked in.

The cabinet chamber was just as he'd always heard: Grobal-green carpet under his feet, a big brass table with tall matching chairs, stone walls filled with heavy wood-framed portraits of former Eminences. A beautiful portrait of Herin had already been added, low near the front of the room where Nekantor now sat in the Eminence's chair.

So Nek had finally got what he'd always wanted for the First Family. He was wearing his usual simple light brown suit: clean lines and buttonless coat over a three-button vest and a white shirt. His back was straight as a pole, his eyes were hungry, and his face was . . . pleasant. Which meant he'd decided this meeting was a performance.

Fair enough. Everyone here was performing.

Pyaras looked away along the assembled cabinet members before his cousin's restless gaze could meet his. He gave a nod to Lady Selemei. Ah—there was Veriga, standing proudly behind Kaspri of the Fifth Family. Where was Melín?

"I call to order this meeting of the Pelismar Cabinet, and serve as a reminder of the Grobal Trust," said a young voice. Nekantor's Dexelin, newly the Manservant to the Eminence, had begun speaking. "Giving to each according to need, the hand of the Grobal shall guide the eight cities of Varin."

Speaker Fedron of the First Family stood up.

A sharp hiss of shock jabbed into the moment's silence.

That had to be her. Pyaras turned his head.

Oh, Sirin and Eyn, *Melín.* She stood behind Amyel of the Ninth Family and Tass of the Tenth. She wasn't wearing a uniform, but a high-necked, formal white shirt with long sleeves and an embroidered over-tunic of Arissen-red silk. Her hair was oiled, she wore gold rings and diamonds in her ears, and even the sunmarks on her face made her glow brighter than everyone around her. Desire electrified him; he flushed hot all the way to his feet. She was so beautiful he couldn't breathe—

—and she was so, so angry.

"Welcome," said Speaker Fedron. "Thank you all for joining us. We asked you here today because Varin has just experienced one of the most tragic days in its history. We wish to honor the sacrifices of those who died, and to honor all of you, the heroes whose intervention prevented the casualties from being so much worse."

Pyaras tried not to glance toward Melín, but he couldn't really help it. Speaker Fedron was speaking of the impact of needless deaths—both those inside the Eminence's dining room and at the arena—and watching Nekantor feign concern made his skin twitch. Once when he looked over, Melín was glaring at him, her eyes wide and her lips pressed together. He looked away.

With ceremony, the Manservant to the Eminence produced a dark cylinder and unrolled it down the brass table. It was paper, black as the home of Elinda, upon which the names of Herin's Argun, Plist's Row-yeth, and the thirty-six Arissen dead had been written in gold. An appropriate recognition for people who had suddenly been stolen away to take their places among the stars. Spirit globes would hang in their homes; but now, they could be remembered in death by something glimmering and beautiful that could be seen by all. Nekantor's Dexelin slowly read the entire list aloud, name after name, in the silence of the crowded chamber. When he finished, he bowed.

Murmured prayers flitted among the assembled people. "Elinda keep them," Pyaras whispered.

Nekantor coughed.

"These names will hang in the Eminence's Library in perpetuity," said Speaker Fedron. "And beside them will hang the names of the heroes who saved lives on this terrible day. *Your* names."

Now Nekantor's Dexelin unrolled a second scroll, this one black ink on white paper. Easier to read, fewer names. Pyaras found himself there, the longest name in the list: Grobal Pyaras of the First Family. Then he found Arissen Veriga, and Arissen Melín. There were also the other Arissen, and the Kartunnen. One of those names would belong to the doctor he'd helped.

He sneaked a glance at Melín, and found her frowning—not at him this time, thank Sirin and Eyn, but at the paper on the table.

The Manservant to the Eminence spoke. "Now, I will call out the names of the heroes to be heard and recognized by the Eminence of Varin. When you hear your name, please come to the front and receive a pin."

Nekantor stood up from his chair and thoroughly straightened his clothes, betraying some impatience. His Dexelin set a small silver tray of pins on the table in front of him.

"Kartunnen Mohemei," Dexelin began.

Pyaras watched Nekantor. Under normal circumstances he would love to see his cousin make some mistake and show his true character, but the people here deserved better. As each one approached the front, Nekantor took up a pin and dropped it into their palm. One by one they walked up and then proceeded out the main door.

"Kartunnen Yaleni . . . Arissen Budrien . . ."

Yaleni was the doctor he had helped. Her face was sober and professional.

Maybe he didn't belong here. All he'd done was hand her things. And now Melín hated him. But why shouldn't she, when he'd been false all along?

"Arissen Melín . . . Arissen Veriga . . . Grobal Pyaras of the First Family."

He didn't fit. It was excruciatingly obvious. He walked along the backs of the chairs and got in line behind Veriga. Melín didn't look at him. She walked to the front with as much formality as if she had been in uniform, and accepted the pin from the Eminence's thin hand without a word. Veriga accepted his with a click of his heels. And then it was his turn.

Nekantor was smirking at him. Gnash this whole thing, he wasn't going to dignify that look with comment. He held out his hand, and Nek dropped the pin into it.

"Pyaras," Nekantor said.

"Thank you, your Eminence," said Pyaras. He turned to the cabinet members. "Thank you, to all of you." Then he turned away and walked out. He didn't look at what he had in his hand until he reached the hall outside.

It was an Arissen honor pin, like the kind Commander Tret wore on the collar of his uniform. He was going to keep this, even if it had come from Nekantor's hand.

"Hey. Grobal Pyaras of the First Family."

Oh, no.

He looked up from the pin in his hand. Melín was standing right in front of him, every part of her body stiff with anger, as striking and as painful as sunlight.

He tried. "I'm sor—"

"I am never going to see you again."

CHAPTER THIRTY

Broken

No one should be allowed to hold a party three days after a murder.

Adon walked with arms crossed, chin pressed to his chest, staring at a spot on the floor in front of him so he could ignore the yellow mourning scarf tied to his arm. Shoes were flickering in and out of that spot: the suede-soled leather boots that belonged to Tagaret's Kuarmei. Their silent, regular movement was comforting. He didn't want to see the mob of the First Family surrounding him. Most of them were chattering and gossiping as if the world hadn't already been broken.

Mother was the sensible one; she'd told her Aloran she had a headache and she needed to be treated for it at home. It wasn't fair that she could get out of this so easily. She probably didn't really have a headache—but he was developing one.

Xeref and Cahemsin had attached themselves to him, ignoring the fact that he wasn't speaking. Occasionally, they darted back and forth to tug on other people's mourning scarves. At the moment, the two of them were arguing about whether Arissen Drenas had been a monster, or just out of his mind.

He was neither. He was just a guard who would kill for Nekantor. The new Eminence.

The fact that Drenas was now dead made it even less likely that his victims would ever see justice. And Nekantor would be at this party. Which meant Adon would have to smile, or something, and pretend Nekantor wasn't a murderer.

Mai help me.

There was so much security. They met a whole orange wall of it in the hallway leading to the Residence's central section. Tunnel-hounds lolloped about on the ground, and some of his cousins shied away; Arbiter Lorman shooed them forward.

"You're not nervous about tunnel-hounds, are you?" That was Pyaras, on his left. "They don't make good pets, but they're smart, and very sweet."

Adon shrugged. "They're just—big? And kind of weird." The dark animal snuffled at his feet and knees with its wide, soft snout. Its paws looked too big for its body, and part of him couldn't help wishing it had eyes.

Not that everything needed eyes, but fish generally came on a plate.

As weird as they were, tunnel-hounds were easier to trust than armed guards. A big Arissen in Cohort orange carried a tunnel-hound in among them to sniff for poisons and weapons as far as their shoulders. When he came near, Adon accidentally looked into his eyes.

Arissen eyes, gray, and thoroughly bored. You couldn't tell what the man was thinking. There was no way to know if he was another one who would kill for Nekantor.

Adon straightened his gloves.

"Thank you, Arissen," Pyaras said, and they went through.

Most people were moving toward the main door of the Hall of the Eminence, but Tagaret and Lady Selemei took them up along a side corridor to a private entrance peopled by even more guards. These guards were questioning everyone to be sure they were all members of the Eminence's family. Adon stuck close to Tagaret and Pyaras. Already he wanted to go home and change clothes. The tight mourning scarf made his arm feel numb.

At last they were passed through.

This was a roped-off passageway along the stone wall at the head of the Hall. There was an opening in the ropes just this side of the stage steps. They turned left into the First Family's audience area.

In the rest of the room bubbled the chaos of the Pelismara Society—people, people, and more people. They wore yellow scarves, to be sure, but all were dressed in jewel-toned fashions, adorned with the finest accessories, eagerly waiting to see the accession of the new Eminence as if they weren't properly in mourning at all. Their gossiping voices echoed up to the ceiling vaults, among the stars of a mosaic sky.

A false sky, with no gods to judge them.

The new Eminence, himself, was quite close by, sheltered from general view by a column embedded in the wall. Nekantor stood with his back pressed against the stone, scowling down at the gold watch on his wrist. He wore a regal-looking white suit, with no mourning scarf, and no gloves. His Dexelin had assumed bodyguard stance between him and anyone who might approach, causing Family members to keep away and fill other parts of the enclosure as they arrived.

Adon tried to meet Dexelin's eyes, but the servant wouldn't look at him.

Soon, Lady Selemei and her Ustin came, and also Speaker Fedron with his Chenna. Arbiter Lorman was accompanied by his Oidi. All the eligible male cousins old enough to command manservants kept to the edges, while the younger ones milled about in the center. Adon put distance between himself and Nekantor before it became too crowded to move. If he could stay close to the ropes, it would be easier to escape into the ballroom afterward.

Of course, here, there was no one to protect him. He hugged himself, and shivered.

"Adon," called Tagaret. "Hey, can we stand by you?" He'd brought along Pyaras.

"Yes, thank the Twins." Adon sent a nod to Tagaret's Kuarmei and Pyaras' Jarel. This was much better. Safer. He nudged his toe into the white and green carpet, breaking the loops of the Grobal insignia.

A sound of swishing silk caught his ear. He looked over; two priests had entered through the side door and now walked nearer along the passageway.

The Voice of Varin was a man wearing light blue silk robes, with a gold sun-disk hanging down his chest on a heavy chain. He carried a length of white and gold cloth over one hand. Unexpectedly, he came into the First Family area, and made his way past them toward where Nekantor had hidden himself by the wall.

The Voice of Elinda, meanwhile, processed toward the stage. She was a tall, gray-haired woman wearing a silver moon-disk. Her moon-yellow funereal cloak draped over rich layers of deep blue silk. There was something about her—her stature, her grace, her dignity as she climbed onto the stage—that made you feel like the Mother of Souls was real.

Adon's throat thickened. He heard Herin's voice again—*Plist! Plist, what's happening?*—and burst out in a gasp.

Tagaret squeezed his shoulders. "Adon, are you all right?"

Adon flung his arms around his brother's waist and held on tight. "Tagaret . . ."

"Don't worry, I've got you."

The Voice of Elinda started to sing. Her clear voice penetrated the safety of Tagaret's embrace, ringing into his ears, bringing tears to his eyes that he pressed into his brother's jacket. "All with eyes in this place, hear me, gaze and turn your faces upward! Though ages pass, the heavens still show us the inevitable way: the silent sister spins and circles beneath our feet, and her holy siblings dance with her around our great Father."

"Father Varin, source of all life," the crowd responded.

Tagaret's voice said softly from above him, "It *is* the inevitable way. Gods help us."

"Today we honor Herin of the Third Family," said the Voice of Elinda. "He rose in brightness, and grew to glory, Eminence of all this land which takes our great Father's name. Nightfall came too quickly upon him."

A poke. "Adon."

Adon didn't look up. Tagaret didn't poke him again, but tugged at his arms until he couldn't stand it any more. He let go, sniffing with irritation.

"Come on, raise your scarf."

Fine. Adon tugged the scarf off his arm and held it up. Tagaret was holding his own as high as he could. Arms were raised everywhere around.

"All honor to Herin of the Third Family as he sets in this life," said the Voice of Elinda. "Let him find his way to our great Mother's arms, and take his place among the stars."

"Honor to Herin of the Third Family," the Pelismara Society rumbled.

"Herin of the Third Family, we release you into our Mother's care."

"We release you."

Tagaret's scarf fluttered downward. Adon let go of his own. For the tiniest moment, he was caught in wonder as scarves fell everywhere.

Then Nekantor pushed past him.

Once out into the clear, roped path, Nekantor gleamed with confidence. Focused on the stage, he looked like a ruler. Untouchable. Not a sniff of attention for the Voice of Varin, who had passively followed behind him.

That priest wasn't Father Varin.

Father Varin would stand forty times Nekantor's size. Father Varin would bring Mai the Right to gaze into Nekantor's soul and sentence him. Father Varin would open his mouth upon teeth of fire. Father Varin would consume Nekantor, and gnash his soul in the flames.

The Voice of Varin only sang him up the stage stairs.

When Nekantor came to stand before the wooden throne, the Voice of Varin wrapped the long white and gold cloth around his thin shoulders. Nekantor shuddered once, as though it were heavier than it looked, but then he stood tall.

"The day of the Eminence Herin has ended," cried the Voice of Varin. "The day of the Eminence Nekantor has begun. All hail the Eminence Nekantor!"

The room roared. "All hail the Eminence Nekantor!"

Nekantor smiled amid the shouts. But when those shouts faded, so did his smile. There was a bright ring on the little finger of his left hand; he began to rub it with his thumb. Then he spoke.

"Thank you all. Now I wish to dedicate myself to my people."

The Voice of Elinda and the Voice of Varin moved to places on either side of the throne. The throne was carved from wood, ancient, gnarled, and twisted. Nekantor sat down in it.

Adon heard a click, and turned. The outside door had opened again, and in walked a big Arissen with a chest like a keg. He wore a white leather strap across the front of his red jacket, and a crested helmet topped with red kanguan feathers.

"Oh," murmured Pyaras. As the Arissen neared, Pyaras said clearly, "Commander."

The Arissen gave him a nod. "Executor."

The way the Arissen spoke to Pyaras was friendly—and, to be honest, there was something totally different about an Arissen in rust-red instead of orange. But once the Commander had passed by, you could see the white strap on his jacket was connected to a scabbard in the back. A scabbard containing a huge knife.

That knife, next to his toes. In Dexelin's hand. In Dexelin's coat.

Where was it now?

Adon shivered and looked away. By the outside door, the Headmaster of the Imbati Academy had appeared, quietly awaiting his turn.

A big Arissen voice rang out behind him. "I am Tret of the Pelismara Division and I speak for the Arissen. I give my people into your Trust."

Adon kept his eye on the Headmaster. Moruvia glanced over, a silent greeting in his eyes. Adon sucked in a breath, and his stomach flipped. How could he thank him for his protection? How could he explain what had happened when he'd claimed it?

There was no chance for better connection. The Headmaster walked with silent steps onto the wooden stage. When he spoke to Nekantor, his calm voice felt like a memory from long ago.

"I am Moruvia, Headmaster of the Imbati Service Academy, and I speak for the Imbati. I give my people into your Trust." Moruvia then went and signed something at a table near the back wall before returning to stand beside the Arissen Commander.

The next Lower didn't look at anyone, only stared piercingly into space. She was a Kartunnen with a purple-painted lip, voluminously robed in pale gray University regalia. From what Adon could see of her trousers, she was wearing hand-painted silk underneath. As she climbed, the back of her robes draped in angles over the stairs.

"I am Wilven, Chancellor of the University, and I speak for the Kartunnen," she said clearly. "I give my people into your Trust." She, too, went and signed at the back table.

Next, a muscular man leapt up the stage stairs. He had a thick brown belt and about a million sunmark spots over every exposed area of his skin. He swept his gaze across the room as though it were nothing more than an intimate gathering. "I am Leader Bestec of the Venorai Union, elected to speak for all of us. I give my people into your Trust."

The Melumalai representative had already started up the stairs, moving slowly, with a cane. He had gray hair and a heavy necklace of large chrysolites set into teardrops of silver. Venorai Bestec returned from the back table before he even reached the center of the stage. "I am Odenli, chairman of the Melumalai Banking Syndicate," he said, in a quavering voice. "I speak for the Melumalai. I give my people into your Trust."

Melumalai wasn't the last caste, but no one followed Odenli. Before the old Melumalai had returned from giving his signature, Nekantor stood impatiently.

The Eminence shifted from foot to foot, thumb still playing with the ring on his little finger. He was taller than any of the Lowers who stood before him, and he didn't really look at them, but over their heads, off into the distance. When Odenli was finally in his proper place, Nekantor said to the far corners of the ceiling:

"With the spirit of the Great Grobal Fyn as my guide, I pledge myself to the Grobal Trust. Giving to each according to need, the hand of the Grobal shall guide the land of Varin."

The two celestial Voices called together, "All hail the Eminence Nekantor!"

"All hail the Eminence Nekantor!" the crowd roared back. Then their noise split into a thousand chaotic noises of celebration, protest, anticipation. Adon found that the cousins around him had started moving, pushing him against the ropes.

"Well, holy Twins, here we go," Pyaras muttered. "I hate this next part."

Adon shook his head. "The Ball?"

"The Heir Selection."

"This way," said Tagaret, leading them toward the exit. "Now everyone moves to the ballroom. Keep your gloves on and your eyes open, Adon. Nek will be here any minute wanting to take you around to meet people, and most will not be your friends."

Adon shuddered. "What if I don't want to meet people with him?"

Tagaret's mouth pulled sideways. "Trust me, you'll meet people even if Nek has to drag you, so don't make him. Pyaras and I will stay by you. Pyaras, you need to think very hard about impressing people here, because we need you to be the candidate for the First Family in spite of what Nekantor says."

"Really?" Adon asked. What a relief that would be. "You have a plan to convince him?"

"Well, not yet."

"I'm not doing it," said Pyaras. "I have the job I want."

"Regardless," said Tagaret. "You're still sticking with us, because there's no way we're leaving Adon unprotected right now. Say yes."

"All right, fine, yes."

People started moving. Adon shuffled his feet to stay in the midst of the First Family crowd, but as close as possible to Tagaret and Kuarmei, and to Pyaras and Jarel. Slowly, they all crossed the aisle and passed under the archway into the tunnel that led to the ballroom.

Halfway through the tunnel they found Nekantor, standing with his back against the wall. He was closing and opening his hands, muttering angrily under his breath. His Dexelin stood beside him, just out of his Master's arm's reach—a distance that looked distressingly deliberate.

Adon stopped walking.

Tagaret squeezed Adon's arm, speaking low and quickly. "I need to talk to Nekantor; stay near and listen. Pyaras, you stick here with Adon. Let the others go around us." He walked up to Nekantor, and said loudly, "Congratulations, Brother!"

Nekantor's head snapped up.

Tagaret made a deep bow. "Or I should say, congratulations, your Eminence."

"Ha," said Nekantor. He looked down at his watch. "Yes, actually, you should say that."

"Look how far we've come, thanks to you," Tagaret said. "Look what you've accomplished for the First Family. We're all indebted to you. It's what Father would have dreamed of."

Adon blinked. His first thought was that Tagaret was an incredible liar—but when he thought about it, nothing he'd said was technically untrue. More than that, the praise had an immediate positive effect on Nekantor's mood. He stopped muttering. His hands, instead of closing and opening at his sides, floated to the buttons of his vest, touching them one by one.

"He dreamed of it," said Nekantor, looking at Tagaret again. "But Garr didn't do this."

"No, he didn't," Tagaret agreed. "You did. Now we get to celebrate you, and work toward the Heir Selection. I hope you'll help me."

"Help you? You'll be helping *me*."

"Yes, of course," said Tagaret. "This is all your plan. I just want to make sure I remember it right. I believe you said you wished to approach the Second Family first. Did you want to take both Fedron and Selemei with us?"

"Gnash it, no." Nekantor stood away from the wall. "Tagaret, you're hopeless at politics. We've discussed this. Fedron and Selemei will stay in the First Family's area with the other eligible boys."

"I know we can rely on my Kuarmei and your Dexelin while we walk, but I think a bit of extra security might be a good idea. Can we bring Pyaras' Jarel?"

"Yes," said Nekantor. "Pyaras is no threat. Are you ready to go, Adon?"

Adon startled at the sound of his own name, and cleared his throat. "Yes."

"Hurry up, then."

Together, they walked into the ballroom. The huge space was quickly filling with people whose eager talk echoed up into the vaults of the ceiling. There was no more sign of sadness or mourning. Nekantor took them straight to the First Family's area, to the right of the entry arch. Tagaret had definitely changed his mood—by the time he'd greeted Speaker Fedron, Lady Selemei, and Arbiter Lorman, he seemed as confident as when he'd first stepped up onto the stage. He demanded that Adon prepare to tour the room immediately.

Ugh, of course.

At least they would have manservants with them. Imbati Dexelin, Kuarmei, and Jarel arrayed themselves in defensive formation all around, and the seven of them moved out into the crowd beneath the glittering crystal chandeliers. Adon tugged his gloves tight and kept his eyes open.

"Tagaret," he whispered, "I don't know what to talk about."

Nekantor snorted. "Nothing yet. Just look healthy."

"Just be ready to answer questions about your health and studies, if you get them," said Tagaret. On his other side, Pyaras walked along looking stiff and unhappy.

"Your Eminence!" A man with long hair and a beautiful suit of gray silk with emeralds came out of the crowd. It was Tagaret's friend, Gowan. "Tagaret, and Adon, and Pyaras, nice to see you."

"Gowan," said Nekantor, and pulled a smile. "Do you have any possible candidates to introduce us to?"

"Of course," Gowan said, gesturing a boy forward. "You already know my cousin Igan."

Hey, Igan. Adon met his friend's gaze, but this wasn't like it had been at his birthday party. Igan was a rival now.

"Give our best wishes to your father," Tagaret said.

When they walked away again, Adon tugged his sleeve. "Who's Gowan's father?"

"Amyel of the Ninth Family," said Tagaret. "He's always been kind to me."

"He's also in the cabinet," said Nekantor. "If we're nice enough, he might vote for you."

The next people they met were from the Second Family. Adon faced his friend Nayal like a stranger and tried to keep smiling while Tagaret and Pyaras spoke with their friend Menni, and Nekantor spoke with Menni's father Boros, who was bald with a booming voice and was also in the cabinet. It wasn't hard to imagine the calculations in Nekantor's head.

"Tagaret," said Menni suddenly. "Have you been to see the Fifth Family yet? You'll never believe who I saw arguing with Arbiter Innis."

"Really, who?"

Menni shook Tagaret's arm. "*Unger.*"

"What? He came back?"

Adon pushed up to them. "Who's Unger?"

"The Alixi of Selimna," said Tagaret. "He shouldn't be here."

"No, he shouldn't," Nekantor agreed sourly. "But don't worry, Adon. Forfeiting the position of Alixi to become an Heir candidate won't exactly make him look like a competent politician. You'll beat him easily."

Adon swallowed. "I don't know . . ."

"Forfeiting!" Tagaret exclaimed. "Sirin and Eyn, I have to tell—" He broke off, and his face fell.

Della. Adon squeezed Tagaret's arm.

"All right, no time for that," said Nekantor. "Let's go."

They didn't actually try to talk to Arbiter Innis or Unger of the Fifth Family. Nekantor was more interested in the Eighth Family—specifically, in an old man with eerie bulging eyes named Caredes. Eighth Family also meant his roleplay bully, Venmer. Adon stuck close to Tagaret and Pyaras to avoid him, but that meant having to join in the adult conversation.

"Adon of the First Family." The old man scowled at him. "Any new diseases?"

Ugh. "No, sir," said Adon.

"Caredes," said Nekantor. "Let me introduce my brother Adon. He's perfectly healthy, as I'm sure you already know. Adon, this is Caredes of the Eighth Family. He was at your birthday party last year."

Caredes pointed a finger at Adon's face. "You should have invited me this year. It's your mother's fault. Is she here?"

He didn't slap the finger away; he didn't step backward. "I'm sorry, sir, she's not."

"And I see you're also dragging your cousin around. Pyaras, you still a muckwalker?"

Adon winced and glanced at Pyaras.

"Oh, Caredes," said Pyaras, with a beaming smile. "I'm happy to say that my muckwalking days are over. I'm now the Executor of the

Pelismara Division, fully licensed to interact with Arissen—and finding my past experience quite useful."

"Are you, now?" Caredes looked surprised. "Clever choice, Nekantor. I might be interested in an alliance, if it comes to that."

"Thank you so very much," Nekantor replied. "I wish you good evening."

By the time they had circulated through the entire ballroom, everything started mixing together in a big unfriendly blur. No one felt near as dangerous as Nekantor, though. The biggest surprise was how much fun Pyaras seemed to be having; his big cousin had grinned wider with every attempted insult, and flashed his Executorship like a shield.

"Fah," Nekantor said, as they arrived back to the First Family's area. "Don't be too happy with yourself, Pyaras." He walked off to Arbiter Lorman and started pulling at his shoulder, talking in his ear.

Adon looked for a place to hide, just for a few seconds' break—but he'd scarcely taken a breath when Lady Selemei and Speaker Fedron walked up. The Lady took Adon's shoulder.

"How did that go?" she asked. "Are you feeling all right?"

Adon shrugged. "Not terrible, I guess."

Speaker Fedron nodded. "It's an ambitious crowd. I'm sure you did well."

In one corner of his eye, Adon could see Nekantor giving Lorman a lecture; and in the other, Tagaret was speaking seriously into Pyaras' ear. Pyaras scowled, and his voice cut through the noise of the crowd.

"I don't care how well you think I did, Tagaret. I'm still not doing it."

CHAPTER THIRTY-ONE

One Life

Gentle rocking, rocking, rocking . . . a boat, floating through the gray. And somewhere in the mist, a thread of melody, pulling . . .

Rocking, rocking, a voice now . . . a song of mm, oo, so and how does this work, oo, sustainer of life, la, so, I want to talk to her, so, mm . . .

The melody, stronger . . . billows in the gray . . . the rocking, the pulling, so, oo, me, lu, ma, la, i . . . what are you doing, mm, rocking, rocking . . .

No more melody now, voices, and rocking, castemate, listen, listen, it's just music, why shouldn't she listen, listen, and the pipes are louder now in the mist . . .

Don, don, don . . . drums on the inside . . .

Oww . . .

Into the gray pierced a single perfect note on the triscili, that curled into a melody.

A voice spoke quietly beside her ear. "Now you're able to hear the music, so. But keep your eyes closed, all right?"

Forder.

Della kept her eyes closed. The light coming through her eyelids was dim red-orange, and there was knocking in her belly. In her ears, there was music—

For Della.

Vant was here, too.

More of her body came into focus. Her head and back felt heavy, and her feet light, as if she were on a slope. There were warm covers. In her stomach came a weird, stretching movement.

Still floating in the melody, she remembered why she was here.

Tears welled up, escaped, warm lines on her temple cooling as they reached her hair. Questions surfaced in her mind.

Where are the doctors? Where's my Yoral? Where's Tagaret?

Am I safe?

Forder and Vant had awakened her, somehow. She wasn't supposed to be awake. If the doctors found out, they might make her sleep again. But she couldn't learn any answers with her eyes closed. She cracked them open just slightly, praying for Sirin's luck. This wasn't her usual bed; she'd been moved. It was a hospital bed, shoved up against the wall. Forder was sitting beside her head, watching her, intent and serious. Her ears told her that Vant was somewhere down by her feet. She couldn't see any of the people who had put her here, but Yoral would be somewhere in the room.

Yoral had the authority to make the doctor stand down, if he was on her side.

He should have been.

He would be, so long as Tagaret didn't come in.

Yoral.

She practiced his name silently. Her tongue felt heavy. Whenever her eyes closed, she felt the drift again. When she was reasonably sure she could say the word intelligibly, she took the risk.

"Yoral."

"Shhh," said Forder. "Grobal Della, shhhh, don't speak."

But she'd been right. Through the crack in her eyelids, she saw a black silk shape arrive just on the other side of Forder.

"Mistress," Yoral said. "There's been some mistake—"

"What vow . . . did you swear?"

"Oh, Mistress . . ."

A new voice spoke. "Wait, she's not supposed to be able to—Melumalai, what did you do—"

Rage flared inside her, burning away the gray. "Kartunnen, you will not touch my friend, Melumalai Forder. Yoral, if you remember your vow, send the doctor away now."

"Doctor," Yoral said. "You are excused. I will take charge of the Lady's care from here."

A few seconds' silence. Then, "May your honorable service earn its just reward, sir." And the sound of the bedroom door, opening, then thudding shut.

"Mistress," said Yoral. He knelt on the floor. "I'm so sorry for what I did."

Della took a breath. It felt shallow, pressed by the weight of her belly. "You were supposed to protect my person. You let them detain me."

"Mistress, I was selfish," he confessed. "You had put yourself at risk. But I betrayed you. I put my own worries about your physical safety ahead of your will and your wellbeing, when it was only a minor contraction."

She turned her head. Yoral had bowed so low she couldn't see him any more. Forder was still standing by her bed, using his body to block access to a suspended bag of fluid that was attached to her arm with a tube. She shuddered, and tears welled up again.

"I love you, Yoral. I want to trust you."

"I'm so sorry."

"I'm going to have to forbid you to discuss my care with Tagaret, unless I give you express permission."

"Yes, Mistress. Shall I call him to speak with you?"

"No." Saying it made the tears come faster. Her belly felt warm and uncomfortable. "I'm not ready to speak to him. Disconnect me." She couldn't bear to hear him hesitate, so she pushed on. "I promise not to hurt myself. I promise to stay in bed if you give me what I want, and give me no reason to get up again. Now, disconnect me."

"Yes, Mistress," said Yoral. "Melumalai Forder, will you please step out?"

"Imbati: may your honorable service earn its just reward, sir," said Forder. "Don't injure her again. She's my friend, so." He frowned, and his hand patted Della's hair gently. Then he vanished from her side.

"Vant may stay," Della said. "He's not blocking your access."

The music made it easier for her to endure the removal of tape, and the press-and-pull of Yoral disconnecting her from the tube. Yoral kept pressure on her arm for half a minute, and finally bandaged her. She lay for more than a minute, breathing, hovering at the edge of exhaustion.

"You may go now, Yoral," she said, when she found energy to speak. "Please turn off the service speakers for half an hour. I want to listen to music, alone."

"Mistress," said Yoral, in a miserable voice.

"Vant will call you if there is any emergency."

She lay there for a long time, bathing in the music. Disappearing into melodies had always been one of her favorite methods of forgetting herself. But the knocking inside her wouldn't let her escape. And there was also the misery of knowing she couldn't trust the ones she had always trusted. At last, she gathered her energy and turned onto her side. She could see Vant sitting on a brass chair near her feet, wearing his fine gray coat over a blue silk shirt.

"Vant?"

The musician stood, placed his triscili gently on the seat of the chair, and walked over to her. "Lady Della, I'm so glad you're awake," he said softly. "How are you feeling?"

"Tell me . . . have you seen my family?"

"I saw them this morning," he said. "Your parents are well. Your sister is in good spirits. She and I are learning a new piece together, for yojosmei and triscili. I'm trying to convince her to learn the triscili part to get a new perspective on the piece, but she doesn't always listen."

"No, she doesn't. Especially when she's lost in music she loves."

"Especially then," he agreed.

"I'm glad she has you," Della sighed. Tears rose in her throat, and she struggled not to sob. "I love your music, Vant. You've been s-such a gift to my whole family. We—we've been friends for a long time, h-haven't we?" Would he object to her calling him a friend? She reached out and touched his sleeve, but didn't have the energy to hold her arm up.

Vant laid his hand over hers. "We have, Lady."

Oh, bless him. She turned her hand to his. He seemed startled, but allowed her to hold it. To think a musician was the only person here she really trusted . . .

"I do still want to send you to Selimna," she sighed. "You would love it there. They would love you."

"You're so kind to me, Lady. I can't go."

"Liadis would miss you, but it wouldn't be forever. The travel isn't so bad. Everyone there would support you."

"Lady, it's not safe for me to leave Pelismara. Please understand. I'm only an apprentice. Kartunnen Ryanin . . . requires things of me."

Something in the way he said it sent cold suspicion through her. She turned her head to look up into his face. "Vant, what is it?"

He turned his face away.

"Is your master abusing you?"

His face twitched.

Mercy, he *was*. "How bad is it? Maybe I could get help for you—my cousin has a friend in the police—"

"Lady, no," Vant cried, suddenly in a panic. He tried to pull his hand away, but she didn't let him. "Please, no—that would be so much worse!"

She gulped. What a turn this conversation had taken . . . "I'm sorry. Vant, you're important to me. You saved me, today. I can't *not* try to help you, there has to be something . . ."

"I'm—I'm breaking the law," he stammered.

"*What?*"

"I'm not Kartunnen." He tried to pull his hand away.

"Don't." She pulled his hand closer to her face. "Vant, I don't understand. You're a composer. You play yojosmei, shiazin, pipes, and triscili, at *least*. You're the most brilliant musician I know. And how long have we known each other? Since I was thirteen?"

"I've been lucky," he said. "I haven't been caught. But, can't you see? It doesn't matter what Ryanin does, you can't help me. Arissen will kill me for what I've done."

Every word out of his mouth made it forty times worse. "Trigis and Bes, now I *have* to help you! Sixteen years, and you suffering secretly all that time? You just saved my life. How can I not save yours?"

"You can't," he said. "Anyway, you won't want to."

"You're my friend. I love your music, and I love you. I don't care what else you are."

"I'm Akrabitti."

She blinked at him, stunned. Then he tried to pull his hand away again. She gathered wits enough not to let go.

"Vant," she whispered. "You are, aren't you." That look on his face, when he'd accidentally called Forder *sir* . . .

He wouldn't meet her eyes.

"I've never told you what Tagaret and I are trying to do in Selimna," she said, slowly. "We went there because we hope to understand the city, and the people who live there. All of them, Highest to Lowest. We want to change things. Little things at first, but little things add up to big things over time. I met Forder there. I've learned so much from him. I met a woman named Venorai Castremei. I tried and tried to think of a way to meet an Akrabitti, but I never once managed it. And here you are, and you're one of my oldest friends." She sighed. "And it seems that I know almost nothing about you."

Vant looked at her, sadly. "You have my secret, now. What do you want to know?"

"Who are the Akrabitti?"

He stood silent for a long time. "We're the Patient Folk," he said at last.

"Are you waiting for something?"

"The fires of heaven, I suppose. To burn away the pain from our souls."

The misery in his voice—she couldn't stand it. And she couldn't stand to be making it worse.

"Wait," she said. "I have an idea. Could I take you away from Kartunnen Ryanin? You could be my personal musical attendant, and write songs for me, and live in your own apartment so he couldn't reach you. And, you could help me understand your people, and how you see things. In whatever way you wanted."

Vant gaped at her. "Lady, you'd really . . . ?"

Lying down with your feet above your head was the worst possible position to convince someone from, but she tried to speak sincerity with her eyes.

Vant took a deep breath, and let it out in a rush. "Can my mother live with me?"

She'd never even thought about whether he might have a family. "Partner, too, if you want," she said. And made herself say the word, "Children."

"I don't have that kind of family," Vant said. "My life's not safe. My mother and I live in the Blocks. My father died of blood poisoning in Indal 6, and she can't work anymore, so I pay a Bargain to all the folk who support her while I'm working. Ryanin pays me more than I could ever earn at a trash center. But when he isn't happy with me, he threatens her. She always says she's close enough to the Gate that it doesn't matter . . ."

Had she imagined she would slap Iyemmelim? Ryanin deserved worse! But Vant's safety was more important. He must never, ever be forced to work at a trash center. "Of course she can live with you," Della said. "I'll need a few days to arrange it."

Vant's hand in hers moved again, but this time, he squeezed her fingers. "I'm so sorry you haven't been well," he said.

"I'm getting better now, I promise. Could you do me a favor?"

"Anything."

"Can you tell me what day it is?"

"It's Soremor fifteenth."

Della thought hard. Four days since Tagaret's birthday, when the Eminence died. That meant only two days before the Heir Selection began in earnest. Adon might already be the family's candidate. But he might not be, yet. And if he wasn't, there was only one person who could really stop it.

"Would you mind stepping out and asking my Yoral to summon Pyaras to me?"

"Of course, Lady." He pulled his hand gently out of her grip.

"Bless you, Vant. We'll talk again soon."

For a long time, she was alone with her unwelcome resident. She dozed, woke, shifted to her back again, and then to her other side. Finally, there was a loud knock on the door. Yoral, bless him, had done exactly as she'd requested.

"Come in."

Pyaras came in. His dark eyebrows pinched together when he saw her. "Della, hey. Look, I'm sorry I haven't come to see you."

"I wouldn't have known if you had."

"Oh, I'm an idiot. Sorry. I'm glad you're awake." He came over, and stood by her elbow. "How are you feeling?"

What a question. "How do you think I'm feeling?"

"Mai's truth. These days, it's hard—I won't lie, I've been wanting to run away from everything."

"Me, too," she said. "It's all a trap."

Pyaras looked at her, a glance that encompassed her, the hospital bed, everything. He winced. "Yeah."

Della gathered her courage. "Look, Pyaras. I need to talk to you about the Heir Selection."

He snorted. "Just when I thought people were going to leave me alone."

"I'm sure that would be nice. But you need to be the First Family's candidate."

"They want Adon."

"I don't care. It has to be you."

Pyaras shook his head. "Are you serious? Della, no. Even if I wanted it, it's not realistic. You know what people think of me; any approval I get will only come if I'm Executor."

"This isn't about what people think of you!" she snapped. He took a breath to object, but she cut him off. "It's not about the horrors you've been through, either. Adon has been through horrors, too, and that's not stopping anyone from laying candidacy on his head. It's not even about the idea of spending hours with Nekantor every day."

"What, then?" He sounded exasperated. "What do *you* think it's about?"

"Saving Adon's life."

"By risking my own? No thank you."

She grunted in frustration. "Listen, Pyaras! Adon's life will be in danger if he enters the competition. But if he wins, it could destroy the Family. It could destroy everything."

Pyaras frowned. "What in Varin's name are you saying?"

"Come here." She reached an arm toward him. "I'll tell you exactly why Adon can't be our Heir candidate."

He moved closer, but not close enough. She tapped one finger to her lips. "Put your ear right here."

Pyaras shook his head. He looked nervous bending down, as though afraid she would scream and break his ear.

Della pulled him close until she could whisper where no one else could possibly hear.

"Imbati Aloran is Adon's father."

CHAPTER THIRTY-TWO
Responsibility

"What!"

He couldn't remember shoving away from her, but Pyaras found himself staggering backward. He hit the side of the larger bed, almost toppled, and sat down with a thud.

"Pyaras, be careful, for Mai's sake!"

"Gods—gods!" He couldn't even untangle his thoughts well enough to swear properly. "Is *that* why he doesn't want to be chosen?"

"No!" Della pushed up on one elbow, eyes wide. "Adon doesn't know."

"He doesn't? How can he not know?"

She shook her head, and didn't answer.

Adon—half Imbati—and he *didn't know?* How was that possible?

But if he *did* know, maybe he would try harder not to be so graceful and quiet. He would never have dared start a fight with his cousin Cahemsin. And maybe, instead of being so comfortable with Aloran, he would try to push him away. He might try to hide from the Society entirely. Or Fall—gods forbid—which was what the Society would require of him if they found out.

No. No. Adon was best just as he was, colorful and quiet both at once.

His mind still struggled. Wouldn't you be able to *feel* it if you were half Imbati? Because the more he thought about it, the more obvious it became. It showed in everything Adon did. He had naturally excellent Imbati manners. He understood them so well. And he liked to be around them . . .

What did that say about *him* and Arissen?

His mouth went dry.

"Pyaras, please," said Della. "You have to talk to the First Family

Council. You have to try to take the candidacy instead. You're healthy enough."

"I *am* healthy enough." Just like Adon was. "Sirin and Eyn help me."

"Pyaras, tell me you'll talk to them."

"I'll talk to them, yes, of course I'll talk to them," he said. He stood up. "I'd just better go and talk to some other people first."

Della was looking up at him, confusion in her green eyes.

"I won't let them choose Adon, all right? I'll talk to them, I swear."

"It's so dangerous," she murmured. "If Adon ever took a position of such importance, there would be incredible attention focused on him. Someone would be bound to find out eventually, and then . . ."

"I get it. I won't let that happen. Thank you for telling me."

He closed her door respectfully, but then the hurry seized him. He laid his shoulder into the doors to the sitting room and excused himself from the house as quickly as possible. He ran upstairs to his own suite, cast a quick greeting over his shoulder to the First Housewoman as he entered, and hurried past the sitting room into the back to find Father.

He knocked on Father's door. "Father, may I come in?"

"Come on in."

Father was in the same position he always was, propped up on pillows and looking vaguely frustrated—but now he looked worried, too. "What's happened, my Pira? No more murders, Heile grant?"

Pyaras took a deep breath, and shook out his fingers. "Nothing like that, Father. Can I ask—I mean, can I talk to you for a minute?"

"Of course."

One of the caretakers brought a brass chair; Pyaras nodded thanks and sat down in it. Now that he was here, with Father, some of the anxiety drained away. Father's face was his face, if somewhat narrower: brows in the same strong arch as his own; mouth with the same set. When he was little, he'd been made much of, praised over and over for being so much like the admirable Administrator Vull.

He'd hated every second of it, right up until everyone decided he was part Arissen.

"Son, what's wrong?"

"Were you there when I was born?"

"Yes, I was."

That surprised him more than he expected. "What, you watched?"

Father's brows pinched. "Pira, that's not done. When the doctors let me in, my sweet Indelis was holding you in her arms." His voice quavered. "That was the happiest moment of my life."

"I'm so sorry, Father. I didn't mean to upset you."

Mother had died when he was three; she was a legend, embodied in phrases Father sometimes used, and in the colorful pouf in the sitting room. It was easy to forget she'd been a real part of Father's life. Pyaras leaned forward and laid his hand over Father's, oh-so-lightly so as not to hurt him.

"I love you."

"I love you too. Don't worry; I love talking about her. Indelis was so beautiful, and so full of life. Those were wonderful times." Father sighed. "I sometimes wonder where we would be now, if we could have stopped trying to have children. But Indelis wanted so badly to have as many children as Lady Selemei—all the Ladies did. At that time, no one had the slightest suspicion that Lady Selemei wished to stop, or that the strength of her wish would carry her all the way to the cabinet."

Pyaras had questions. But he didn't have time. "I'm sorry, Father. I'd love to hear the whole story, but I have to go."

"Do you?"

"It's Selection business," he explained. "I have to talk to Arbiter Lorman. It can't wait."

Father frowned. "You're being respectful of young Adon, aren't you, Pira?"

For a second, doubts thundered over him like rockfall, but he gritted his teeth. "Of course," he said. "I'd give my life for him. I'll talk to you later."

He'd scarcely made it out the door, however, when a voice spoke from behind him. "Master Pyaras, sir."

Pyaras turned around. One of Father's caretakers had followed him. "What is it?"

"Sir, I'm sorry if this seems rude, but if you wish for absolute certainty about your parentage . . . there is a way."

"A fast way?"

"I'm not sure what you mean by that, sir, but I'm referring to genetic testing. Kartunnen don't generally offer it to Grobal, but you could try requesting it if you so desired."

"Thank you. I had no idea."

"Sir." The caretaker bowed and returned to Father's room.

Pyaras stared at Father's closed door. Absolute certainty—imagine it! Why would the Kartunnen restrict access to it, when every Grobal he knew would leap at the chance to know the truth?

But maybe that *was* the reason. The more he thought about it, the more dangerous it seemed. Imagine if he were to find a doctor willing to deliver a test, and discovered that his grandmother, or great-grandmother, had a secret Arissen lover! Or, what if a test found his Grobal ancestry was pure . . . but then Nekantor found out you could request testing?

If that knowledge ever became public in the Pelismara Society, there would be a mob rush for testing, with disastrous consequences. Adon would be forced to Fall. Tamelera, too. Who knows what effect it would have on Tagaret, or Nekantor, or the First Family as a whole? And it wouldn't stop there. Every Family would rush to test, and suddenly everything would be exposed. Every secret dalliance. Every rape. Every flaw in the purity of every Family.

It would take the Great Families down like a wysp explosion.

Pyaras took a deep breath. No; if he wanted to protect Adon, he just had to have faith in Father, and in Mother, and in himself.

Returning to the vestibule, he asked his Jarel to double-check that he looked acceptable for a formal petition. Then he asked her to accompany him, and crossed the Residence to the office of the Arbiter of the First Family Council.

He wouldn't hide from Lorman again.

Lorman's Oidi opened the door at his knock. "Master," he said. "Pyaras of the First Family."

"Let him in."

Pyaras walked in. Lorman had his back to him, rummaging in one of two large metal filing cabinets that stood in the corners of the room. Lorman's gloves, with fingertips discolored by wax, sat in the center of his desk.

"Good afternoon, Arbiter," Pyaras said, hoping to take charge of the topic. "I'm here to propose myself as a candidate for Heir for the First Family."

Lorman stopped rummaging and looked over his shoulder. "Well. So, that's . . . not what Nekantor told me."

"I take it the Council hasn't made its final decision yet."

"So, that will happen this evening," said Lorman. "However. So, so, I'll be honest. I don't believe *you* are well suited for the task."

"I'm better suited than Adon," Pyaras said firmly. "Adon's not interested. There's the doom of your whole effort, right there. *You* know a candidate has to give his all to achieve success. Nekantor almost broke himself trying to become Heir, and Garr *actually died*."

Lorman looked at him skeptically.

"You don't want Adon to be our candidate, Arbiter; I know you don't. You're so worried about the end of Garr's line—you wouldn't want him to be killed in Selection."

"Well, so, what about you?" Lorman said. "You're the end of Vull's line."

How could he respond to that? He was right: Father was dying. Soon, the house would be empty. He would be alone . . .

Not now. He shook himself, and pushed the thought away.

"Fine, then Adon and I mean the same loss risk. I'm as healthy as he is. Not many can say the same. It would set me ahead of many candidates from other Families."

"All right, so, you've convinced me to listen," said Lorman. "So let's talk." He turned back to his filing cabinet.

"What about?"

"So, you need to think about something." The Arbiter pulled a slim folder from the drawer he'd been working in, shut the drawer, and brought the folder to his desk. "This is what our file on Adon looks like." He set it down, and gave an unpleasant smile. "So, just a moment."

Oh, boy. This was not going to be good.

Lorman returned to the cabinet and opened the drawer beneath the one where he'd previously been working. Pyaras didn't have to stand on his toes to see that the entire drawer was full of papers. Those drawers, and the drawers in the cabinet in the opposite corner, obviously held records on every single child of the First Family, from the last who-knows-how-many years.

Lorman leaned into the drawer with two hands, and pulled out a file fully four inches thick. "This one is you."

My whole life in paper. He'd been alive longer than Adon; clearly, he'd been followed by spies a lot more, too. What did they know? What *didn't* they know?

Lorman set the file on his desk with a thud. "So. Well. If you're willing to come and talk to us about this, you're welcome. But you'll have to be willing to come right now."

Now? With no time to prepare?

Pyaras considered the huge stack of papers. Was it everything he'd ever done? Then Sirin the Luck-Bringer could dance the silatunmi, because there was no way to prepare for that.

"Great!" Pyaras said. "Let's go."

Lorman sneaked several glances at him while putting his gloves back on. He patted his whiskers, and led the way out of the office, with his Oidi behind him carrying the files. They climbed stairs up to where a group of men and manservants waited outside a bronze door. Lorman nodded to them, and entered.

Pyaras took his time coming in with Jarel. This room wasn't particularly special, just your basic small meeting room with a brass table and chairs, two windows, and green curtains in the corners. Lady Selemei was already seated in a chair beside Speaker Fedron at the near end of the table. Imbati Ustin and Chenna stood against the stone wall behind, so Jarel joined them.

"Pyaras!" Selemei called, without standing up. "I'm glad you're here."

Speaker Fedron stood, and offered one gloved hand. "I hope this means what I think it means."

Pyaras shook his hand, smiling. "I'm here to propose myself for candidate."

"Thank Heile," said Lady Selemei. "I've been so worried."

"Good man," said Fedron. "Why don't you stand between us? This is going to be interesting."

The other members of the First Family Council took seats along the sides of the table, while their manservants stood by the walls behind them. Lorman set his files on the far end of the table.

Finally, Nekantor walked in. The look of satisfaction on his face immediately fell to a scowl. Pyaras gave him a deliberately pleasant smile. *Gnash you, Nek, I'm not going to let you intimidate me.*

Arbiter Lorman called the meeting to order, but Fedron interrupted him before he could announce any kind of agenda.

"Arbiter, I believe Pyaras brings us a pre-emptive order of business."

"So, indeed," Lorman agreed, with a smile that didn't reach his eyes. He stroked his mustache with one finger. "So, Pyaras, please explain why you're joining us today."

"I want to be the First Family's candidate for Heir," Pyaras answered.

Someone at the table started to laugh, but choked off amid the silence of the others. At least some of the men here believed he was serious. Maybe they'd seen him at the Ball.

"Fah," said Nekantor. "Don't be ridiculous. Adon is going to be our candidate; it's already been decided."

"By you, maybe," Pyaras said, before anyone else could speak. "But the Eminence doesn't choose his Family's candidate; the Family Council does. I believe the honorable Council members would prefer a candidate who's willing and able to fight through the Selection. We're not likely to win without a candidate who's willing to compete."

"Adon is healthy," said a bald man at the corner of the table.

"So am I," Pyaras said. "Lorman has all my health records."

"Pyaras is a muckwalker," Nekantor growled. "He's an Arissen."

"I'm not an Arissen." Pyaras looked across the Council members. "You all know my father, Administrator Vull. He can testify as to the circumstances of my birth." The thought made him shudder. Father needed to be cared for, not forced in front of councils.

"Councilmen," said Lady Selemei in a clear voice. "I will also testify to the circumstances of Pyaras' birth. His mother, Lady Indelis, was a personal friend of mine."

"So, was she, really?" asked Arbiter Lorman.

"She was. If you wish to pursue this, Arbiter, I'll be happy to invite the manservants and medical staff who were present at the birth to testify before the Council." Lady Selemei smiled. "Your Eminence, with respect, slurs against Pyaras are irrelevant to our discussion."

"They're relevant if the other Families take them seriously," said Nekantor.

Pyaras snorted. "Nek, if they do, that's your own fault. But they didn't seem to when we were touring the Accession Ball."

Nekantor growled, but Arbiter Lorman held up one hand. "Your Eminence, so. I believe our records are sufficient to disprove any specious accusations." Slowly, he lowered his hand until it rested on the thick file of papers on the table in front of him. "However, so, well, we should definitely discuss certain events in Pyaras' file before we proceed to make a decision."

Pyaras kept his eyes on Lorman without flinching. "Of course, Arbiter."

"So, so. To start with, Pyaras, you have a history of muckwalking with a man by the name of Arissen Veriga. So do you deny it?"

"I do not." There would be no point lying; the truth was right in front of him.

"So how do you explain your actions, which are beneath the dignity of a member of the Grobal Race?"

"Are they really?" Pyaras asked. "My father raised me to believe in the Grobal Trust, which gives us a responsibility to care for Lowers. Arissen Veriga saved the life of the Eminence Nekantor in the last Heir Selection, by eating poisoned food intended for him. I watched how he suffered for it. He deserved to be acknowledged for his sacrifice, but he received no gratitude from Nekantor, and no recognition for his heroism. I therefore chose to honor him with my own care, and in return he taught me about Arissen, a skill which not only allows me to better fulfill the Grobal Trust, but which the Eminence Nekantor himself has found useful."

"That's why you're Executor," said Nekantor sourly. "Not an Heir candidate."

"Well, so, we'll get to that in a moment," said Lorman. "And your—unsavory—activities with Arissen Veriga?"

He swallowed an uncomfortable wave of guilt, but there was only one plausible way to get the Council to set those aside. "Veriga teaches me about Arissen," he said. "I'm his student. I get to choose what I learn from him as much as my cousins get to tell their Schoolmasters what to teach."

Lorman's eyes narrowed, but some of the other council members were nodding. Maybe they didn't know what all he and Veriga had gotten up to. Or maybe they didn't care about his behavior as much as they cared that the First Family had a plausible story to tell.

"So. Arissen Veriga submitted a report to Speaker Fedron the day before the Accession Ball," said Lorman. "According to that report, you worked alongside an Arissen by the name of Melín. So, explain to the council who she is."

Oh, Sirin and Eyn, let him not be blushing! If spies had seen anything of his encounters with Melín, his chances were zero; he'd have to hope Veriga's report was their only source. "Arissen Melín is a Wysp Specialist in the Pelismara Division," he said. "And I am its Executor. I did encounter her at the targetball disaster, but I did most of my work helping Doctor Kartunnen Yaleni treat the wounded."

"One more question," said Lorman.

He tried to keep his voice level. "Certainly."

"So, recently, you were given an order, as Executor, to direct the Pelismara Division to increase paper yields. And so, well, not only did you not carry it out, you went to the Eminence Herin of the Third Family in order to countermand it. So how do you justify acting against the First Family in this manner?"

What? Pyaras tried not to stare. That wasn't at all where he'd imagined that question starting, or ending up. Not Veriga this time, or Melín, but his defense of the Division was being construed as some kind of betrayal?

"I was trying to protect my cousin Nekantor from looking like a fool," he said.

"Pyaras . . ." Nekantor growled.

Pyaras turned to face him. "What did you think, Nekantor, that I was just going to carry out an order that would get Division—" He carefully chose which word to use next—"*assets* maimed and killed, and waste thousands upon thousands of orsheth in medical costs, damages, and compensation? And make you look incompetent before you'd even taken the throne? How would that advance the interests of the First Family?"

"You're to do as you're told," Nekantor snapped.

"If you give me orders that aren't contrary to the Family's long-term interests, naturally, I will." Pyaras scanned the men around the table. Several of them were smirking. Very odd—but maybe some in the Council favored the idea of an Heir candidate who could stand up to Nekantor.

"Thank you, Pyaras," said Arbiter Lorman. He smoothed his mustache with one hand. "So, one last thing. We are willing to place you alongside Adon on our ballot for candidate, *only* if you can make us a promise."

Oh, Plis help me . . . He knew, with a sick feeling in his gut, exactly what Lorman was going to say.

"You must promise to remember your responsibility to the Grobal Race. So, by this, I mean, your time to learn from Arissen is over. You must never again have any social contact with them, beyond what normal interactions are expected between an Heir and his guards and Commanders."

Pyaras had clenched his teeth so hard his jaw hurt. How could he promise he would never speak to Veriga again?

He would be alone . . .

But the more power he gained, the more danger Veriga would be in, merely for associating with him. Veriga was in danger enough because of what they had in that enormous file of papers. And now it would be worse—because Veriga was working with the Chief of Police on the investigation into the Eminence Herin's murder.

Adon had to be protected.

And both Veriga and Melín were safer without him.

"No contact beyond expected official interactions," he said, though his tongue felt like paper. "I swear it. Jarel, please bear witness."

"Witnessed, sir," said Jarel tonelessly from the wall.

"Well, so, then," said Lorman. "Councilors, shall we prepare to vote?"

"FAH!" Nekantor exploded. He shoved away from the table and strode out of the room, with his Dexelin running to catch up.

"Lorman," said one of the men at the table, "does the Eminence need to participate in the vote?"

"So, I'll go talk to him," Lorman said. He smiled at Pyaras and preened his mustache. "So, so, Pyaras. Thank you. You may be excused."

CHAPTER THIRTY-THREE
To Choose

If you stayed in your own room, sitting cross-legged on your own bed, you didn't need to think about your big, stubborn cousin being the only thing standing between you and more shooting.

You didn't need to think about it.

Don't think about it.

Zzap! He's shooting—

No. Not that, either.

Adon stood up. He could change clothes again, but he'd already done that twice. The layers of colored fabric all around the walls were not as comforting as they should have been.

Then a quiet knock came on his Maze door, and his heart lifted. "Aloran? Is that you?"

Imbati Aloran came in, quietly shutting the door behind him. Maybe they could sit together awhile, in silence. That would be just perfect . . .

"Adon, I've received a message for you," Aloran said. "It's from the Headmaster."

"Oh?" He shook his head. "Why?"

"He's concerned for your safety," said Aloran. "He's also concerned that you're coming under pressure to accept a position as the First Family's candidate for Heir."

"Oh." Under pressure—that was one way of putting it. He was being crushed into a tiny box, unable to scream, or run. "Did you tell him I was trying not to?"

Aloran met his eyes reprovingly. "It makes no difference to the Headmaster if you're trying or not. If you become the First Family's candidate, it makes a big difference."

"Because more people would try to kill me."

Aloran sighed. "Yes. But also, if you were to accept the candidacy, the Academy could no longer offer you its protection. You could not enter the Maze again."

"Oh." Adon hugged himself. Honestly, he didn't want to enter the Maze again—he'd only ever gone in once, and look where that had got him. If Dexelin hadn't been there to carry him off, he probably would have been killed in spite of the Academy's supposed protection. And that protection obviously was doing nothing to help Dexelin. "I don't *want* to be a candidate, Aloran. But I don't know if I can make Nekantor and Arbiter Lorman listen to me."

Aloran didn't respond to that.

Adon glanced up, and found him struggling with emotion—fear? Anger? What?

"You're lucky, Adon," Aloran said at last. "You're Grobal. You get to choose."

You know Nekantor! he wanted to retort. But of course Aloran did. He looked down at his left hand. "I'm sorry."

"You were offered real safety. You refused it, as is your right, and so you got something less. A compromise. That compromise will disappear if you take the First Family's candidacy. Whether you *try* to take it is irrelevant. That safety is still there for you. But you have to choose it."

He meant their trip to the Academy. The Headmaster's offer to sponsor him, if he wanted to Fall. Aloran obviously saw it as a way out.

A way out of the tiny box—into another box. Did Aloran even hear himself? Did he understand that he'd just admitted Imbati weren't allowed to choose?

How did that help anything?

"Thank you for telling me," Adon said.

Aloran's face closed down instantly. He stood up, bowed, and left. Without him, the room became intolerable. Adon walked out into the drawing room. Mother was sitting on the couch talking with Tagaret; she looked up when she saw him.

"Adon, what's wrong?"

His throat felt tight. "I just spoke to—well, Aloran is upset."

Mother stood up. "What did you say to him?"

But he'd promised never to tell her. "I don't know."

Mother scowled, and her eyes flared. "I'll go talk to him." She strode away into her bedroom, and shut the door.

"That wasn't very nice, Adon," Tagaret said.

What was he supposed to say? He couldn't muster outrage to respond. He stared at the toes of his shoes, and shook his head.

"Hey," said Tagaret. "Want to see if we can talk to Della?"

"All right."

Tagaret crossed to the other bedroom door, and Adon straggled up beside him. Tagaret knocked. Imbati Yoral opened it, but his expression changed instantly from expectation to deep fatigue.

"Master Tagaret," he said. "Young Master Adon. I'm afraid my Mistress is indisposed at this time, and not receiving visitors."

That was strange. "But I thought she was awake," Adon said. "Melumalai Forder said she was awake."

"She's awake," Yoral conceded. "However, she's not receiving visitors."

"Della," Tagaret called. "Please, love, I need to talk to you."

There was some small sound from the space behind Yoral, but no more than a grunt. Yoral stilled his face. He stepped out of the room and shut the door behind him. "Master Tagaret, sir," he said. "She does not consent to see you at this time."

"But, Yoral. Why is she shutting me out? We're—we were—I mean, we're supposed to get through everything together . . ."

Yoral said nothing. Was he angry? Or guilty?

"I know how hard this is for her," Tagaret pleaded. "*You* know how hard it is to have to go through this. I'm here to support her, no matter how hard it gets. I need to be there. Yoral, I thought we understood each other on this."

"My duty is to my Mistress, sir," said Yoral. "Her wishes are my own."

Oh, no. Yoral had failed to follow Della's wishes, and been chastised. Adon cleared his throat. "Yoral, I'm so—"

"You're being unreasonable," said Tagaret. "What if I don't talk to her about her health, but just . . . talk to her? Can't you just let me in?"

"I'm sorry, sir, no."

"Why not?" Tagaret demanded.

"Sir, because I want her to trust me again."

Tagaret didn't say another word. He turned away and shoved through the double doors into the sitting room. Adon cast an apologetic look at Yoral, and went after him.

"Tagaret . . . ?"

Tagaret didn't even turn around. He walked into his office and shut the door.

Standing in the middle of the sitting room, alone, Adon took a deep breath and let it out slowly.

The latch of the front door clicked. The vestibule curtain was pushed aside. Adon recognized Dexelin a split second before Nekantor walked into the sitting room and said,

"Adon, we need to talk."

His insides seized; for a second he wanted to throw up. "No. We don't." He backed up until he hit the drawing room door, and stopped.

But did he really have to stop? Why stay under Nekantor's attention if he didn't have to? He took an extra step and slipped sideways into the private drawing room.

No one was here. He laid both hands on the double doors, but was forced to back up when they started to open toward him.

Nekantor winced as he entered. "Do you think I *like* coming here?"

I hope not. He didn't say it aloud, only shrugged. He glanced at Dexelin, who had followed Nekantor in; the servant looked utterly dejected.

"I'm here because I have to be," Nekantor said. "Adon, I need your help. I need an Heir, and you're the only one who can do it."

Adon backed up farther, down the hall toward his room. "That's not true."

"Maybe not, but there's no one else who could do it as well as you."

There was the handle of his door. Adon grabbed it fast, retreated into his bedroom, shut the door and locked it.

This was the place that was supposed to be safe. He couldn't go out the window to escape; there might be assassins out there.

A little tiny box.

There was a scraping sound, and the handle of the locked door began to turn.

Heile help me.

The door opened. Nekantor started to enter, but then he recoiled, backing across the hall. "You've turned my room into a disgraceful mess!"

"It's not your room, Nekantor."

Nekantor panted, staring down the hall toward the light of the window. His fingers flickered over his vest buttons. "Fine. Come out here and talk to me."

"No."

"I'm offering you a unique opportunity. You need to understand."

"I don't want to be Heir."

"This is about power, Adon. The pattern is perfect: with me as Eminence, you as Heir, Speaker Fedron and Selemei in the cabinet, and Tagaret ready to step up, the First Family can command this nation for a lifetime."

Adon steeled himself, and looked into his brother's eyes. "I don't want to."

"You do, though," Nekantor insisted. "You're only saying that because you're upset right now. I understand. Politics is a nasty business. But you could do so much, as Heir. You'd have the power of appointment. You could place anyone you like in any open position across Varin."

The eye contact was too exhausting. Adon glanced aside and found Dexelin. The servant's eyes were begging. Dexelin whispered, "You could command service."

"I want Dexelin to be my bodyguard," Adon blurted.

Nekantor seemed startled. "What?"

When the Eminence's Cohort struck, no special protections had been sufficient. It had been him and Dexelin. Dexelin had saved him when they stood against death together. The one power that being Heir could give him was the ability to save Dexelin back.

"I want your Dexelin. Give him to me, right now."

Nekantor stared at him for so long he could hardly breathe, but then, slowly, he said, "If I give him to you, you'll willingly enter the Selection for the First Family?"

Adon cleared his throat. "Yes."

Nekantor nodded. "Dexelin, you may go to Adon."

Dexelin looked guilty. He stepped away from Nekantor and came closer. Adon tried to reassure him silently, *I will protect you.* To Nekantor, he only said,

"Thank you."

"Oh, no, Adon," the Eminence replied. "Thank *you*."

I hate this so much.

Adon sat on the drawing room couch, staring at the contract on the glass-topped table. It was a very fancy piece of paper: the standard contract for a manservant, that he was supposed to sign. Serjer was here watching, and so was the Headmaster, and so was Dexelin.

Why do I hate this so much?

He swallowed hard, leaned forward, and signed it.

I did it. I saved him.

Serjer and the Headmaster moved the table slightly to one side. Dexelin sank down on his knees in front of Adon's feet, and lowered his head. His braids slipped forward onto the floor.

"Master," Dexelin said.

Oh, gods. He couldn't stand it. He had to sit still and listen to this? He'd rather crawl right out of his skin.

"The Mark upon my face I dedicate to your noble name. Thus I kneel before you to offer my duty, my honor, my love, and my life to your service. Upon your loyal servant pray you bestow a touch, the seal of your hand upon this, the vow of my heart."

Adon gulped. Tried to figure out what he'd just been asked to do. Touch. All right—

He held out his hand, palm up. Dexelin didn't notice.

"Dexelin," he said.

The Imbati looked up, blinked a moment in confusion, and finally put his hand on top of Adon's.

"Serjer as Household witness."

"Moruvia as Academy witness."

"Thank you," Adon said. "Now, can you please go?"

Both Serjer and the Headmaster bowed and excused themselves through the double doors.

"Please get up, Dexelin. Sit on a chair if you'd like."

"Yes, Master."

Adon squirmed. "Crown of Mai, please! Please don't ever call me that."

"Yes, sir." Dexelin seemed uncertain, but he did get up and take a seat in the nearest stuffed chair.

Here they were, now. Sitting side by side, and every second that passed felt easier. Most importantly, Dexelin wasn't working for Nekantor anymore, so he didn't have to suffer.

Adon caught the servant's eyes gratefully, and smiled.

CHAPTER THIRTY-FOUR

Respect and Insult

Why was she here, looking for a killer?

Melín scanned the fancy neighborhood that the business card in her pocket had brought her to. Daylights, rows of shops facing a busy circumference that crossed in front of her. Trunks of shinca, an occasional harmless wysp. Nothing like sunblast, and the fight all her nightmares reminded her she should have been fighting.

Treminindi knew what that was like; she shared that loss. For that reason alone, she deserved the respect of a warning.

The address couldn't be far. On the right side of the radius that had brought her here from the Residence was a neighborhood full of Imbati apartments, probably well-connected Household types who wanted to live as close to work as possible. The circumference, though, was a mercantile zone. She turned left, watching the numbers along the row of buildings, looking for 742.

The numbers were weird. She kept passing archways that led into courtyards full of shops, and every time she did, the numbers jumped higher.

Here, maybe?

She turned in under an archway on her left. No; this couldn't be right. It smelled too Kartunnen. The shops all had front walls of curved glass, and in the center of the courtyard, a fountain caught water from the cavern roof. Closest by was a fancy clothes shop, and the number 744; she'd skipped right over her destination.

Frowning, she turned around and walked back out through the arch. The building immediately to her right was 740. But this was the right street . . .

On the other side of 740 was a gap. She peeked in. It wasn't an Akrabitti trashway, as she'd assumed. It was actually a very short alley leading to a railed stairway, and the number . . .

There we go.

Melín jogged to the top of the stairs and found a landing across the back side of the upper story. She peered up at a peephole in the door.

The door opened.

"Well, if it isn't the best Wysp Specialist in the Division, come to see me." Treminindi gave a wry smile. "You're going to draw attention to me with that orange uniform. Hurry on in."

"I'm not staying," Melín said. This was a small space, lit by one bare ceiling bulb. It contained only a very old-looking metal desk with a stool on the near side. A chair sat between the desk and the large frosted window, which, if you could've seen through it, would overlook the circumference.

"Tell me you are, though," said the veteran. "You're a gift to me at precisely the right time. We're about to get very busy."

Melín shrugged. "It must be very inconvenient, with Karyas in the hospital."

Tremi gave an indignant snort. "That Cohort First belongs to the Eminence. She's not one of mine."

"No? Why did I see you talking at the Riverside, then?"

"I caught her following you. It occurred to me that if you saw us together, you might be tempted to speak to me."

Melín raised her eyebrows. "I was tempted to punch you. Karyas wasn't the only one following me."

The veteran shrugged, and sat on the corner of her desk. "I admit I haven't had the best aim, when approaching you. Doesn't mean you wouldn't do this job well."

"Look," said Melín, "I already have a job. I've just been made Selection bodyguard. They even promoted me to Third."

"So do I have to fight you, now?" Tremi sighed. "I gue—"

"Plis' boots, Tremi, no!" Melín took a deep breath, and spread both hands to show she wasn't about to grab for a weapon. "I thought you should know, though, since I may be shooting at your people. My plan is not to kill them."

"Fancy plan, Specialist. I can tell you've never done this before."

"Think what you like. I respect you, so I'm being polite. Let your people know at least one Selection bodyguard will be shooting to disable. Unless they want a change of career, they can leave Adon of the First Family alone."

"Coward," said Tremi.

"Nice word, seni."

"I can make you rich."

"No, thanks," she said, and turned back toward the door.

You're not going to make me a killer.

She'd figured out how to ignore Imbati—at least, gotten used to seeing them in the halls of the Residence. Door guard wasn't at all the same job as personal bodyguard, though. Today, she had to pass through the black wall.

That meant stepping carefully.

Melín presented herself at the office of the Household Director, just inside the main Residence entrance. The bronze door was open, and a pair of children in maroon uniforms stood just inside it: a tall, dark-haired girl of around thirteen, and a pale-haired boy who looked around seven. Both of them wore the Imbati child's black dot painted between their eyebrows. Director Samirya herself was a tall, thin woman with golden skin and dark hair pulled tightly back; she sat on a tall stool at a brushed-steel podium. At the moment, she was murmuring into a microphone while her hands flew across an ordinator keyboard. The wall above the podium held the largest ordinator screen Melín had ever seen, with what looked like an approximation of a map, in green on black, with names and blinking lights.

Not that the Household Director should catch her looking.

She stepped cautiously between the children and stood to attention. "Cohort Third Melín, assigned as Selection bodyguard to Adon of the First Family."

The Household Director ignored her.

Melín pursed her lips and glanced over her shoulder at the Imbati girl, who only stared at her stonily. She turned back just as Director Samirya slipped off her stool and walked over, long black skirts swishing. She was tall enough that Melín had to look up. The Household tattoo scored a severe line and downward-facing crescent between the Imbati's eyebrows.

Bet that had hurt.

The Director curtsied respectfully. "The heart that is valiant triumphs over all, sir. Please present your password and credentials."

The credentials were in her left inside pocket, while her maps and antidotes occupied her right. Nekantor himself had given her the password.

"Garr's legacy," she said. She pulled out three cards, separated out Tremi's, and passed over the other two.

"Thank you, Melín, sir," the Imbati said, returning a card to her, which she replaced in her pocket. "You will now be escorted to the home of Adon of the First Family, where you will present yourself to the First Houseman, Serjer. Do not leave your escort for any reason, or you will have to return here."

"The children? Are they the escorts?" she asked, considering the two beside the door. The little boy stared fixedly; the girl was fiercely intent. She couldn't help grinning. "Which one of you is going to take me?"

"First to answer shall escort Arissen Melín," said Director Samirya. "What was her password?"

"Garr's legacy," the little boy answered instantly, in a quiet voice; the girl was louder, but a half a word behind.

"Very good, Xinta. Four minutes. Check in with Serjer when you arrive."

"Yes, sir." The Imbati boy gave Melín the smallest formal bow she'd ever seen. "The heart that is valiant triumphs over all, sir. Please follow me."

Melín did, shaking her head. *Imbati are so weird.* Small as he was, the boy didn't get distracted, or hesitate at all. She stuck with him gamely through the fancy halls and into a corridor on the first floor of the suites wing. The door opened as they approached it.

Her small escort bowed to the Household man inside. "Arissen Melín has arrived, Serjer, sir."

"Thank you, Xinta."

"Thanks, small Imbati," said Melín. Her escort bowed again, and made his way back down the hall. She faced the First Houseman reluctantly; her escort had been amusing, but Serjer's expressionless face made her thighs twitch.

He bowed. "The heart that is valiant triumphs over all, Arissen Melín, sir. Please enter the vestibule."

She stepped inside, and the Houseman closed the door. This was a tiny rectangular space with green curtains on three sides. "So, Serjer—"

"Please repeat your password, sir."

"Uh, Garr's legacy."

"Show me your weapons, please, sir."

Melín frowned. She needed the First Houseman's goodwill if she could get it. She unholstered her bolt weapon and held it out on the palm of one hand. She offered the dueling knife the Cohort had given her in the other.

If the Imbati tried to touch them, this was going to get awkward.

He didn't. "I have your valiant word, Arissen, sir, that these are your only weapons."

"Yes. One ranged and one close combat." She tried smiling at him. "You have pretty tight security of your own, don't you, Imbati."

Not a twitch in his expression. "Yes, sir."

Serjer pulled back the vestibule curtain, revealing a rich sitting room full of art and curtains and plush couches and chairs. Melín slipped her weapons back into their places, and began by identifying the exits: the door behind her, a single door on her left in the near corner, a pair of double doors straight ahead, a single door on the right near the far corner.

"I'd appreciate a map of the suite," Melín said. "I didn't receive one."

Serjer nodded. "The heart that is valiant triumphs over all, sir. We have the suite covered. Our palm locks are intact on front and service doors. I keep lists of which members of the Residence Household are permitted to enter each room. These rules are enforced by me, by Household Keeper Premel, by Tagaret's Kuarmei, and by Tamelera's Aloran. You are currently permitted in the sitting room. If you encounter an unfamiliar member of the Household here, touch your thumb to your fourth finger and you will remain unmolested."

They really did have a security plan. "That makes my job easier, Serjer, thank you," she said.

"Please wait here, sir." Serjer disappeared behind one of the side curtains of the vestibule—a servants' door, or she'd eat a toad. And she'd bet there was a matching door on the opposite side.

"Sir," said a new voice.

Melín turned around. An Imbati woman about her height now approached, as the double doors swung shut behind her. This woman wore the complex tattoo of a personal bodyguard, and moved with taut menace. Her dark hair was graying at the temples. She stopped just outside knife range, and gave a short bow without ever taking her eyes from Melín's face.

"The heart that is valiant triumphs over all, sir. My name is Kuarmei.

My Master is Tagaret of the First Family, Master of this house and older brother of the Eminence Nekantor and of Adon."

Definitely a fighter. "I'm pleased to meet you, Kuarmei."

"When did you join the Eminence's Cohort, sir?"

"At the start of Heken, this year. Just over two months ago."

"Sir, you have advanced quickly."

I wish I hadn't. "I suppose I have."

"Why did you move from the Pelismara Division to the Eminence's Cohort, sir?"

They knew more about her than she'd thought. She could see no reason to lie. "The Eminence Nekantor forced me to, Kuarmei. It was not my choice."

"Please wait a moment, sir." Kuarmei exited the way she had come.

A tall man with a manservant's tattoo and long black hair stepped smoothly out before the door swung shut. This man wore more color than she usually expected from Imbati; his suit was not quite black, and dark red embroidery made a pattern on his chest. He had the same fighter's motions as Kuarmei, and a considerable reach advantage. She wouldn't have wanted to fight him.

She gave him a nod. "Imbati."

"The heart that is valiant triumphs over all, sir," the man replied, in a soft baritone. "I am Tamelera's Aloran. My Lady is the mother of Tagaret, Nekantor, and Adon."

"Hello, Aloran."

"I have two questions for you, sir."

"Go ahead."

"One. Do you have any current bets or betting debts?"

"No," she said, and then remembered Drefne. "Unless you count that I owe my roommate dinner out."

The Imbati nodded. "Two. What is wrong with Nekantor?"

"Wrong with him?"

What kind of question was that? In the home of his own family?

But maybe this was exactly where she should expect such a question—it would explain the First Houseman's lists, the hand code she'd been given, and this elaborate series of interviews. Nekantor's family knew him. Did they fear him?

Did they think she was on his side?

"Arissen Melín, sir," said Imbati Aloran. "Please answer the question."

"Of course." Melín swallowed. "The Eminence Nekantor permits no human feeling for death." She found herself reaching unconsciously for the place on her right arm where she'd worn a mourning armband. "His rewards are used for control. He can't be trusted." She risked a guess. "Even with his brother Adon."

The Imbati inclined his head to her. "I will now escort you into the private drawing room, sir. If you encounter unfamiliar members of the Household there, touch your thumb to your middle finger two times, and you will remain unmolested."

She tested the gesture. "Thank you, Aloran."

"Please come in and meet the family."

Hand of Sirin, she'd passed the black wall. She took a deep breath, and followed Imbati Aloran through the double doors.

This room was busier to her eye than the one she'd just left. The walls here were packed full of art, including paintings, and hangings of woven cloth.

Three people sat on a couch facing her. One of them looked startlingly like Nekantor, if maybe a bit younger, with no gray in his sandstone hair—that would be Kuarmei's Master, Tagaret. There was also an older woman with intricately braided hair and a colorful silk gown—Aloran's Mistress, Tamelera. Between them was the boy she was supposed to guard: a dark-haired young nobleman in a suit of green patterned silk, with lace at his throat and at the wrists of his white gloves. Grobal Adon of the First Family.

They looked exactly like you'd expect nobles to look, right down to their noses. Except there was one truly striking thing about them: they all looked grief-stricken, as though someone had just died.

Mai's truth, someone had.

A lot of people had—people who deserved to be mourned.

Maybe these three wouldn't be so bad.

Melín stood to attention and saluted, chopping her right hand to her left shoulder. "Cohort Third Melín reporting for duty, sirs, Lady."

"Welcome, Melín," said Lady Tamelera. The boy's mother. Also the man's—and the Eminence's. "We're deeply grateful that Adon will have your protection in the coming days."

"I'll do my best for him, Lady. I believe it would be advantageous for me to discuss security arrangements with your Household."

"They will be happy to assist you in your assignment," said Grobal Tagaret.

Heh—happy, right. "Thank you, sir."

The First Houseman looked in from the front. "Guests for the Round of Twelve are arriving, Masters, Mistress."

"Coming," said Grobal Tagaret. "Adon, you get to know Arissen Melín, and come out when you're ready, all right?"

Lady Tamelera kissed her youngest son on the top of the head, then rose and took Grobal Tagaret's arm. Together they walked out to the front.

The boy, Grobal Adon, sighed heavily. "All right." He got to his feet with unexpected grace. He was not yet as tall as she was. "Is there anything you'd like to know, Arissen Melín?"

"Sir," she said, "how old are you?"

"Thirteen." Grobal Adon looked down for a second, then cast a glance up through the fringe of his dark hair. "I'm going to ask you something, now."

"I'm happy to answer, sir."

"Why were you fighting in the hall with Arissen Karyas?"

Melín managed not to gape. The yelp she'd heard—the one that had distracted her and allowed Karyas to wrest control—this was *that* boy? "Sir," she said. "I believed Karyas intended to murder the Eminence Herin." She wasn't about to mention how.

"You were wrong."

"Yes, sir, I was."

The boy took a breath as if to ask something else, but then the double doors burst open and a man ran in, straight into Adon's arms before she could do more than blink.

"Twins, Adon, I'm so sorry, I tried to stop them—"

Gods, I'm supposed to be on duty! "Sir!" she snapped. "Some distance, please!" She grabbed the man by his coat and hauled him backward off Adon; he turned his face in shock.

It was Pyaras.

"Varin gnash your face!" she shouted, and flung him away from her. Her whole body flushed so hard she almost shook—anger, this was only anger, by Plis!

"Melín—oh gods . . ." Pyaras stumbled backward, hit the door, and fell through it.

"Lying carrion! How dare you do that to me?"

"Arissen Melín," said a cold voice from over Pyaras' head, beyond the now-open door. "Explain this behavior."

At least six Grobal were staring at her from the sitting room. Including Nekantor.

My ass. I am so dead.

She gulped, but couldn't make a sound.

"Oh," said Pyaras. He made a hoarse noise like a chuckle as he picked himself up off the floor. "Don't worry, Nek, it's my fault. I wasn't thinking, and I grabbed Adon without realizing she—our new bodyguard, that is—was on duty. I hope she treats anyone else who tries to touch him so . . ." He licked his lips. "Decisively."

Decisively. The way his tongue moved across his lips, or maybe the way he straightened his clothes, made her traitorous stomach turn over. Under the weight of noble eyes, she didn't dare move, not even to smack herself in the head.

"So, Pyaras, why—" This was another of the nobles, a man with a ridiculous curled mustache. "—would you allow a Lower to speak to you in this manner? This is not behavior befitting—"

"Lorman," Pyaras cut him off, "weren't you paying attention when I told you about learning from Arissen? There's a unique Arissen tradition. And it says that you're allowed to chastise a superior if that superior has given you a particular type of insult. And I'm afraid I really did give insult to our bodyguard. Entirely without meaning to, but there it is. Arissen Melín, are you satisfied with your redress?"

He was lying his ass off for her. Why?

With Nekantor still staring, she could only snap to attention and hope for the best.

"Yes, sir. Thank you, sir."

Nekantor snorted. "There's no such tradition, Pyaras."

"Oh yeah? Tell me how much you know about Arissen, Nek."

The Eminence only gave a low hiss.

Fury still bubbled inside her. *Why,* she wanted to scream. *Why would you lie for me? Why would you sit outside a Descent? Why would you crossmark? Why would you let me kiss you?*

No—that last question was too easy. Angry as she was, she still wanted to get him alone and do a *lot* more than ask him questions. Reminding herself that he was a pathetic nobleman wasn't working; she needed an ice bath. She'd better be very careful not to get him alone.

Lying piece of carrion.

"Arissen Melín!" the Eminence snapped. "Resume your duties!"

She saluted—"Sir!"—and returned to Adon's side. The boy was staring at her, but he couldn't see how her insides were shaking. He kept on staring, while Pyaras stepped out into the sitting room and the door with all the faces swung shut.

"Arissen Melín, are you all right?"

"Perfectly, sir. I apologize for my outburst."

The boy lowered his voice. "You know, it's natural to hate Nekantor, but Pyaras is a good cousin. Loud, but good."

"*Cousin?*" Her voice cracked. "Pyaras and you and the Eminence—your fathers were brothers? Sir?"

Adon's brow wrinkled in a frown, but then he exhaled and half-smiled. "No, of course not, Arissen Melín. Our grandfathers were brothers."

Right. Because that made it so much better.

CHAPTER THIRTY-FIVE

About Arissen

Imbati Dexelin—*his* Dexelin—came with him as they all left for the Hall of the Eminence. Adon imagined him: long brown hair in finely finished braids, wearing a black suit and suede-soled black boots. Black was the color of trust. Dexelin would keep him safe, and would keep the crowds from getting too close. The only sad thing was that, with Dexelin at his station, Adon couldn't see him.

Arissen Melín walked ahead. Her shiny black leather boots, under bright orange trouser-hems, had thick soles and chrome fittings: intimidation she would use on his behalf. Yes, she was Cohort, but the Household had approved her. That meant she was safe.

His own suit was Grobal green with a pattern of stalactites and stalagmites in raised velvet on flat silk, the only thing that had seemed appropriate for standing up on a stage in front of the entire Pelismara Society.

Tagaret walked on his left, and Nekantor on his right, with the rest of the First Family all around.

Nekantor whispered words down into his ear.

"The Round of Twelve has traditionally been a simple matter, Adon, but we can't count on that. Not after last time."

"Yeah," said Tagaret. "Because Nekantor made everybody panic last time."

Why was that not surprising? "Did he?"

"He decided to talk about how the Eminence had just died of Kinders fever."

Nekantor snorted. "It's not my fault they weren't prepared to talk about reality."

The more he heard Nekantor talk, the less he liked this decision. It would be so much easier if Mother were here . . .

I can't go with you, love. I've been through this before, and it's too much. I can't stand to watch you go up there. Into those lights. Under all those eyes.

Adon grunted. It wasn't fair that Mother wanted to stay home. The attention of the Pelismara Society was actually the one thing he'd been looking forward to. Finally his good health could be a real advantage, and not just something everyone resented.

Would people make a fuss if he asked Dexelin to walk where he could see him?

"You'll be the first one to speak," Nekantor said.

"All right."

"Memorize who your opponents are. You must be prepared to speak about recent events."

"Recent events?" Adon asked, frowning. The voices of dead men? A murdering brother?

Tagaret patted his shoulder. "Remember the Ball. This is more political, but it's not entirely different. The most important thing is speaking about something that makes you feel confident. Confidence will impress the cabinet."

"Recent events," Nekantor insisted. "The Great Families won't have forgotten that I confronted their fears in my speech last time. Their candidates will be prepared. If you have nothing of substance to say, you'll look foolish and weak."

"Great." Adon rolled his eyes.

"Arissen," Nekantor said. "Talk about the danger of Arissen."

Adon grunted again. *Arissen*, what a suggestion. What they really needed to talk about was that Nekantor was a murderer and every guard in orange worked for him.

"Fine," Adon said.

"What are you going to speak about, then?"

"Arissen."

"Good."

"Mercy of Heile," sighed Tagaret.

Adon tried to ignore the two of them, to focus farther back. "Dexelin, are you there?"

The servant's voice spoke at his left ear. "Yes, sir?"

Are you all right? I wish I could see you. He didn't say it. "Thank you."

There were crowds of Eminence's Cohort guards outside the ballroom entrance, and they endured tunnel-hound security all over again. Beside him, Nekantor kept making small disgusted noises under his breath as though the hound would soil his white suit. Adon shuddered, and tried to move away.

At last they were passed through into the ballroom, where the Families were preparing their candidates to enter the Hall of the Eminence. The space beneath the arches was mostly empty, now; the heavy chandeliers shone brightly down on tight clumps of people from each Family.

"So, so," announced Arbiter Lorman. "Here's where we have our spot. So we wait here until you're called to line up."

"Here's how it will work," Nekantor said. "The throne will have been moved to the far side of the stage. That's all right, though. It's all right. It's all part of the game. Only the chosen Heir may pass, when the game is done."

Adon flashed a look at him. "This isn't a game, Nekantor."

"It's the best game of all." Nekantor's eyes were bright. "The *real* game. Don't worry; no one will try to kill you until tomorrow."

The look on his brother's face made a horrid feeling crawl down his back. "Tagaret? Can I please talk with you for a minute?"

"I'm right here," said Tagaret. "Come on, Nek, give him a break."

"Your Eminence, sir," said a Cohort guard who was accompanying Nekantor today, "your place is ready on the stage."

"Yes, of course," Nekantor agreed. "Adon, don't forget, you need something to talk about."

Just leave. Adon closed his eyes in frustration. "Arissen, I know."

"He's got it, Nek," said Tagaret. "Don't worry. You can go take your spot."

"Arissen," Nekantor said. He stalked away beneath the arch that led to the Hall of the Eminence.

Mercy! Finally, Adon managed a full breath. "This is killing me."

"Don't say that, young Adon, please." That was Lady Selemei's voice. When he looked over, the Lady was gazing at him with concern in her dark eyes. Her gray gown glittered with flecks of crystal, a waterfall over stone that began at her left shoulder. "Don't call down Elinda's attention."

"Sorry." Wrong again. Nothing he did was right anymore.

"I'm proud of you, Cousin," said Lady Selemei. "Don't worry. You're going to do beautifully."

"Lady—"

She patted his arm with a hand in a gray glove that matched her dress. "I want you to remember that I'll be in the cabinet seating area, right below the stage. Just look down if you feel nervous, and I'll be right there."

"Thank you, Lady." When she was gone, he whispered, "Tagaret?"

Tagaret crouched down to him, resting both hands gently on his shoulders, and spoke in a whisper. "Adon, when Nek is here, I have to pretend that I want you to win. But really, you don't need to. A lot of people want you to, and I get that it's a lot of pressure, but it's so dangerous. People *will* try to kill you again, definitely more than once. There's no kind of power in the world that's worth your life."

Adon swallowed. "I wish Mother were here." *And Aloran.*

"Mother would say the same thing I'm saying. That's why she's not here."

Arbiter Lorman marched up. "So, so. Young Adon, time to line up."

Tagaret squeezed his hand, with eyebrows raised, a reminder in his eyes:

You don't have to win.

If he dragged his feet, he just knew Lorman was going to grab him. The candidates of other Families were forming a line near the broad archway where Nekantor had disappeared. Five of them were grown men, eyes full of hate, who seemed to have attention only for each other. The others were boys from school, and friends he'd seen at the Ball.

He didn't want to memorize the people in that line. He didn't want to look at them at all.

"So, off you go, young Adon," said Lorman. "Win our future for us. Make the First Family proud."

Half-sick, Adon walked into the shadow of the archway. The bright light on the far side drew closer, and then opened up: this was the same stage access aisle he'd watched people walk through at the Ball. He straightened his shoulders, tugged the hem of his coat, and raised his head.

Whether he hated every minute of this or not, he could at least look as good as his clothes deserved.

Step by step, the stage lifted him above the crowd, its colors, and its gossip. The broad, bright space of the stage felt strangely close to the crystal chandeliers. Wood vibrated under his feet, harder than carpet, softer than stone. He looked for Nekantor.

There he was: on the far side, wound into the throne as tightly as the vine pattern that had been carved into it. His hands gripped the wood.

No; don't think about him. This is not for him.

Adon looked down and found his spot, marked with a number 1.

Looking down was also how he should find Lady Selemei—and sure enough, she was right there. Light sparkled from the crystals on her dress. She looked up at him, and smiled.

Adon smiled back. *I can do this.*

Speaker Fedron was sitting beside her; now, he stood up and began to speak into a microphone.

"Ladies and Gentlemen of the Pelismara Society, welcome," he said. "Allow me to announce the candidates for Heir. From the First Family, Adon, age thirteen. From the second, Nayal, age seventeen . . ."

It seemed like ages since his birthday party. He almost wished Nayal had been wearing a bicolor jacket. But, as he had at the Ball, he was trying to look like a grownup: he wore a fashionably knotted scarf, glittering amethyst buttons, and matching purple gloves. Farther down the line, Igan of the Ninth Family actually *was* wearing something from the party: a black velvet cape with gold edges. His vest and gloves had gold buttons to match. Venmer of the Eighth Family wore sapphire. Out of fashion, but what did you expect from a bully and tunnel-hound with no sense of style?

The others would be trickier to remember. In the corner of his eye, Adon watched each candidate straighten as his name was called. The Fifth Family's man was named Unger, and had long waves of blond hair that shone against the shoulders of a dark garnet-red jacket. Some others—Preines, Gosek, Rorni—seemed to think nothing of wearing last season's button fashions as if they didn't care. The Twelfth Family had sent a twenty-year-old with black gloves and a snarling smile.

When the last candidate had been announced, Nekantor stood up from the throne. His white suit and drape of white and gold made him stand out like a shinca beside everyone else.

"Candidates," he said, staring at them each in turn. "Welcome. You have now joined in a tradition of dignity hundreds of years old. Your initial statements, please."

Adon took a deep breath and looked away from his brother's clutching gaze. *Talk about Arissen.* There were Arissen all around the edges of this room, and every one of them held a weapon. Out of all of them, only Melín was worthy of trust. To talk about them—gods, it made his chest feel tight. At least he couldn't see any wysps in the hall.

"Thank you," Adon said. "I'm proud to represent the First Family." He glanced at Nekantor again, and wished he hadn't. He turned instead to look across the line of candidates. "I wonder if you are all as scared as I am by the way that the Eminence Herin died. Because if you're not, you should be."

"Scared?" a boy near the other end of the line exclaimed, out of turn. "Maybe that's because you're only thirteen. You should leave this discussion to men who can handle it."

Men? Adon raised his eyebrows, but starting a petty argument onstage seemed like a stupid idea. He cast a glance to Nayal, beside him.

"You mean, sixteen-year-old 'men' who haven't reached the age of choice, do you, Rorni?" Nayal asked. "I agree that we need to talk about how the Eminence Herin died. We've allowed Arissen to carry bolt weapons through our halls for too long. It's time to disarm the Eminence's Cohort."

That suggestion sent murmurs through the assembled crowd.

"Bolt weapons were designed to be used against wysps," said the big man from the Third Family. "They belong on the surface, and not in the city at all."

The Fourth Family's boy had a high piercing voice. "If a single Arissen can cause an explosion that kills forty people, then we've given them too much power."

Adon scanned the Cohort guards at the doors again, his stomach in a knot. Nekantor had gotten what he wanted, because here they were, talking about Arissen. Did the guards care about being discussed like this?

"Such dramatic suggestions," said Unger of the Fifth Family, smoothly. "Have you forgotten how a member of the Eminence's Cohort used her weapon to save Adon of the First Family from an assassin? We need to improve their training, but tying Arissen hands would prove hazardous to our health."

"Training will never be enough," said Preines of the Sixth Family. "Arissen are violent. Violence is in their nature."

"We could require them to be examined by doctors," said the Seventh Family's candidate. "To make sure they're not insane."

You realize you're saying this to their faces? Adon couldn't help glancing toward the nearest Cohort guard, at the base of the stage steps. No way to tell if he cared, or even if he was listening.

"This is stupid," said Venmer of the Eighth Family. "It's just—stupid. Arissen are Arissen."

"Excuse me," said Igan of the Ninth Family. "If we're speaking of deaths caused by Arissen, I think it's time we discuss the Paper Shadows."

Muffled exclamations burst from the assembled crowd, quickly subsiding into a round of frantic murmurs. Adon had definite opinions about the Paper Shadows, but it wouldn't do him any good to speak now. He bit his tongue, watching for the man with the black gloves to have his turn.

"Paper Shadows?" echoed the boy from the Tenth Family.

"Assassins, Rorni," said Igan.

"Assassins should not be part of this discussion," said the man from the Eleventh Family. "We're losing focus. This is about the Eminence's Cohort."

"I'm not sure about that, Gosek," said the man with the black gloves. "Paper Shadows are as much Arissen as the Eminence's Cohort. Are we serious here, or not?"

His turn again, at last.

"We're not!" Adon cried. He looked out over the milling, uncertain crowd. "Here we are, arguing back and forth about Arissen responsibility, but we're erasing the most important thing. Orders! Arissen take orders! What about *our* responsibility? What about Nekantor's responsibility, for ordering the death of Eminence Herin?"

The entire crowd gasped.

Oh, holy Mai, had he really said that to the whole Pelismara Society?

But what if Nekantor deserved it?

Adon didn't dare look at his brother.

"First Family," said the Eleventh Family's candidate, "Are you suggesting that the Paper Shadows have infiltrated the Eminence's Cohort?"

"What?" several of the candidates exclaimed.

"Wait, wait," said Nayal. "Why are we using the Paper Shadows at all? If we twelve represent the best blood of the Race, how does it help the decline to kill any of us?"

"Exactly," said Igan.

"There is a legitimate discussion to be had about that," agreed Unger, calmly flipping a lock of blond hair behind one shoulder.

"Speaker Fedron," said a voice from a different direction. Below the stage, one of the cabinet members had stood up. It was a face Adon recognized: one of the Fifth Family men who had come to the Privilege competition at the Academy. "Given what we've just heard, we should put priority on obtaining the results of the investigation into the Eminence Herin's death."

"Not now, Kaspri." Speaker Fedron waved his hands before anyone could speak further. "Please. The candidates have made their initial statements. It's time to vote."

Fedron's Chenna moved around the circle of cabinet members below the stage, entering votes into an ordinating machine, and finally delivered it to her Master.

"We give thanks to all the Twelve Families for offering us their best," said Speaker Fedron. "Will the following four candidates please step down."

Adon held his breath. He probably should have thought harder about whether he would be disappointing Speaker Fedron and Lady Selemei by accusing Nekantor. By now it was too late.

You don't have to win.

"Preines of the Sixth Family. Venmer of the Eighth Family. Rorni of the Tenth Family. Gosek of the Eleventh Family."

The crowd in the Hall burst into cheers and moans, almost drowning out the sound of Speaker Fedron's voice as he congratulated the candidates, wished them luck in their interviews with the Eminence, and told them to reappear in three days for the Round of Eight.

Adon didn't want to turn his head back toward the throne. Nekantor was sure to be furious—

He sneaked a glance. Nekantor was walking straight toward him, not smiling, but not scowling either.

"You're through to the next round, Adon."

Adon swallowed. "Yes." It seemed too risky to say anything more.

"Better study up for your interview."

"All right."

"I can see you're not planning to go easy on me."

Heile help him. "Uh," he managed. "Well—"

Nekantor's mouth crept into a smirk. "I won't go easy on you either. I want an Heir, not a fool. Don't try that again."

CHAPTER THIRTY-SIX

Violence

Those noble slime-stains had some nerve, talking about her like that!

Melín fumed, watching Grobal Adon of the First Family and the others descend from the stage. The feeling in her gut was furious, sure, but also . . . queasy.

'Arissen are violent. Violence is in their nature.'

You didn't reach the age of eight without hearing that line. Hearing it from resentful Lowers was no big deal. From nobles? Totally different.

Sure, it was easy to laugh at pathetic, inbred Grobal while standing in line for a Descent. But it got less comfortable when one of them was about to be put in charge of you. In charge of everyone.

Tremi had been right about noblemen's tools.

Melín's head hurt. That wasn't a surprise; she'd walked in here expecting to stand around and wait while her body reminded her of a fight she was missing.

She hadn't expected to have opinions on who won.

Precious few of the candidates were worth a shred of hope. Adon, though, had just accused his brother of murder, and done it with conviction, in front of hundreds of people. He was worth keeping alive.

Convenient, that that was her job.

Security conditions for leaving the Hall of the Eminence weren't optimal. As far as she could see, the posted guards had relaxed as if their work was done, and most Grobal were counting on the dense crowds for protection. Nekantor *had* promised that no one would pull out weapons until tomorrow.

But she knew what his promises were worth.

"Sirs," she said, sharply enough so that all the First Family group could hear. "We may come under attack now that the event is over. Please ask your servants to prepare a strategy for the way home."

Grobal Tagaret looked at her with dismay in his eyes, but nodded.

"Good idea," said Pyaras. Soon, his Jarel was talking to Tagaret's Kuarmei, and they then spoke to the others. Imbati bodyguards moved to post positions, which cleared up the question of who was coming home with them—mustache man and event announcer man moved off separately, with their Imbati. It looked like Adon, Tagaret, Pyaras, and Lady Selemei were in their group. Two of the manservants took the front, and two the back.

Adon stood stiff, his eyes wide. "Danger? Already?"

"Young sir," Melín said, "perhaps not, but these precautions are to keep you safe. Please stay alert as we leave the Hall. Be ready to drop if I say."

The boy made an unhappy sound in his throat, but nodded.

They moved out. The bottleneck of the door into the corridor brought Kuarmei and Jarel together in front of her, black silk shoulders converging to block her view ahead for a split second—

—gnash it—

—then they parted, revealing the corridor.

Two Cohort guards posted. One wysp. No curtains and no crowds.

Melín exhaled, and continued forward. Just past the posted guards, the corridor opened out into a fancy room.

Four curtains. Four guards posted. No crowds.

It wasn't far, but still, there were a lot of obstacles between them and Adon's home. They turned left, toward the suites wing. Another big fancy room—curtains, guards in this one, and a young lady in a velvet gown with her manservant, who backed against the wall to let them pass.

A doorway, and then here they were in the long suites corridor: a pair of guards posted, curtains, deep-silled windows, a wysp, two ladies, three men. Bronze doors, which meant safety within sight.

Adon gave a hiss.

Look again—one of the men wasn't wearing velvet. His hand moved, pulling out of his pocket.

"Down!" Melín barked. Drew and fired.

Zzap!

The man screamed and crumpled to the floor. Nobles in the hallway bolted for safety behind their doors. A glance over her shoulder at her own group revealed the Imbati in ready stances, and every one of her noble companions crouched on the floor. Excellent.

"Imbati Dexelin, take Grobal Adon into the house, now," Melín said. "I need one Imbati to help, but everyone else should join him."

She ran forward, sickness growing in her stomach. That wasn't a wysp she'd just shot. The would-be assassin wasn't screaming now, but panting convulsively, curled around his injury. Still-curling smoke carried the smell of burnt flesh, but nothing appeared to be on fire. She shoved his shoulder, enough to see: caught him in the fingers, as she'd intended, and missed the weapon's power cell, which might have exploded.

Was it worth it? The money, in exchange for your fingers? She didn't ask him. If he was lucky, some of them might be saved.

Merciful Heile, what would Durkinar say?

Her face went hot. *I didn't kill him. I did my job.* But her head felt like she'd driven a spike into it.

"Imbati," she forced out, hoping one of them had followed.

"Sir."

"If we give him to the Eminence's Cohort, I doubt he'll survive the day. I want him delivered to the Pelismar Police."

"Jarel, get him to Arissen Veriga if you can."

Melín turned around. The powerful Imbati woman wasn't the only one who had stayed. Sirin and Eyn! She almost swore at Pyaras, but gulped it down. "*Sir,*" she spat. "What in Varin's name is it about Veriga?"

Pyaras didn't answer, just pressed his lips together as if she'd hurt him.

She looked away fast. "Imbati, understood?"

"Yes, sir," said Jarel. "The Household will get it done. The heart that is valiant triumphs over all."

Within seconds, three more Imbati appeared from behind curtains and joined them. They hauled the assassin up, claiming his weapon from a bloody spot on the carpet and sealing it in a plastic bag. He cried out again as they carried him away.

The door to the First Family's home suite still stood open. The First Houseman was there, watching; and farther back, through a gap in the curtains of the vestibule, so was Adon.

"Adon, sir," Melín said. "All the way inside, please, for your safety." He immediately vanished. Melín nodded to Serjer as she went in, and watched him until he'd pushed the door fully shut. "I'd like your approval to double-check the perimeter of the house," she said. "I bet more attacks are coming."

Serjer hesitated, then nodded. "You may, sir. The heart that is valiant triumphs over all."

"Can I get a map?"

"The servants' Maze encloses the house on both sides, sir," Serjer said. "Palm locks are on the front and service doors. You may wish to check the windows on the outer walls, however."

I sure may. "Thank you." She started to turn away, but then looked back. "If you take me to them, we can both be certain."

Serjer gave a tiny nod, and joined her.

They started in the suite's northeast corner, which involved walking through Lady Tamelera's bedroom and into one of the servants' doors. Serjer was obviously uncomfortable with her here, but attackers might not follow rules. She'd bet this was Aloran's room; he used the windowsill as a bookshelf, and kept an icon of Mai the Right. Serjer made sure of both window locks, allowing her to look past his arm to double-check. They checked the two windows in the Lady's bedroom, and then the one at the end of the hall out of the drawing room.

"The last window is in Adon's room, sir," said Serjer.

Of course it was.

Stepping in gave her an instant glimpse of what kind of boy she was guarding. Wow, did he take clothes seriously. Organized, though: the walls of hanging garments were neatly arranged. He had all his gloves laid out in a circular pattern on the deep windowsill, fingers outward.

She really didn't like that window. Locked or not, this was the first floor; anybody could break it if they tried hard enough. That would give them an easy straight shot.

"We're going to have to move him," she said.

Best option was probably the room next door, that she'd spotted as they'd come out of the master bedroom. She left Serjer locking the window, walked out of Adon's room, and ducked in the neighboring door.

"What are you doing in here, Arissen?"

The voice was female, and didn't sound particularly alarmed, but Melín froze anyway. A gray-haired Imbati manservant faced her, staring, with one arm cocked to throw.

I've been here before.

But she couldn't have; she'd never walked into this room in her life. She didn't shake her head, because that would give the Imbati an excuse to take her eye out.

She had a code, though . . .

Carefully, she sneaked her thumb and middle finger into his sightline and tapped twice.

There was no change in the Imbati's threat posture.

Her throat felt dry. She swallowed. "My name is Melín, Lady. I'm Grobal Adon's assigned Selection bodyguard. I can show you my credentials—"

"Yoral, you may allow her to show her credentials."

Melín exhaled. "Thank you, Lady." She fumbled the credential from her pocket and held it out. "I apologize for barging in. Grobal Adon was attacked just now, on the way back from the Round of Twelve. I was looking for a safer room for him to sleep in tonight, away from the windows. I intend no violence."

"Sorry for the misunderstanding, then," the Lady said. "Yoral, you may stand down."

"Yes, Lady." The Imbati lowered his arm. Even that motion was familiar . . .

Wait. Melín took her eyes off the manservant, and looked for the Lady, who lay in a medical bed with her feet higher than her head, looking miserable.

Copper hair. The Lady from the hallway.

"Lady Della of the First Family?" she asked, though she already knew the answer. This Lady had been missing from the cabinet meeting. The name Della of the First Family had been glaringly absent from the scroll of heroes. What was she doing *here?* "We—I—missed you, at the cabinet meeting. Did you have some accident?"

The Lady frowned. "No accident. What do you mean, cabinet meeting?"

"For the heroes, Lady. Those who saved lives. You called Lady Falya out of the Eminence's dining room. You saved me from Karyas."

"You're *that* Arissen?"

"My name is Melín." She tucked her credential card back in her pocket, then drew herself up and saluted. "Thank you for saving me. Crown of Mai! You should have been honored for that."

The Lady winced, and shifted in the bed, awkwardly, heavily. "I couldn't be at any cabinet meeting, Melín. I was put—well, I was here."

"*Put?*" The word popped out of her, propelled by outrage. She scanned the room. Hospital bed, double bed, bathroom through a door in the wall . . . It was just the Lady and her servant. Was someone keeping her captive here? That shouldn't be possible. "Why?" she demanded, then added quickly, "Lady?"

"Because I'm . . ." The Lady's face paled. "Pregnant."

"Lady, someone *put* you in bed for being pregnant? Mai help us, that's not a reason."

"It is for me. They always—it's to protect the child, so I don't lose—again . . ."

"But, Lady, you were just as pregnant when you saved me. If there was no accident . . . I don't understand."

Lady Della clenched fists on her covers and bit off her words. "Of course you don't. You're not of the Grobal Race. Arissen don't have the decline."

Outrage half-strangled her. "Another precious noble knows so much about Arissen!" she snapped. "What, you think our health is perfect and we don't ever miscarry?" Then she realized what she was doing and shut her mouth so fast her teeth clicked together.

The Lady should have been furious, but instead, she looked baffled. "Do you?"

"Lady." Deep breath; calm down, don't shout. "It happened to my mother, three times. She had a womb weakness. She got it treated by a medic, though, when she had me, and then my brother."

"A womb weakness," the Lady whispered. "Yoral, do I have a womb weakness? That would explain a lot . . ."

"No, Lady. Not to my knowledge."

Mai and Elinda stand witness! Melín turned on the servant and glared. "So let me get this straight, Imbati. You did no internal exam?"

He didn't answer.

"If you did no internal exam, you don't know if she has a womb weakness. And if she doesn't have a womb weakness, then why—did they *put*—her in bed?!"

The Imbati lifted his eyes to look at her directly. One thing was sure: he had courage. "You would have to ask Master Tagaret, sir. And perhaps also Mistress Tamelera, and Lady Selemei, who witnessed it."

Melín snorted. "You know what? I will. They're all here—I'll tell them what they've done." If she could get them to hear. "Requesting your support, Lady. I'm not sure the Master of the house will like my opinion."

"Wait a minute," said Lady Della. "You would fight for me in this?"

"You fought for me, Lady."

The Lady's hands, which had relaxed, tightened on her sheets again. "Yoral, can you bring everyone in to speak to us?"

"Yes, Lady."

Melín hopped out of the Imbati's way as he left. "Lady, can you tell me exactly what they did?"

Lady Della looked away from her. "I felt hardness in my belly," she said. "It hurt."

"All right. How many times?"

"Once. Tagaret called the doctors. They put me in bed. They . . . made me sleep."

I'm going to break somebody. "Lady, that's—terrible." It was the most polite word she could think of.

"Would you please . . . stand by me?"

"Happy to, Lady." Melín crossed to the head of the Lady's bed and set her back to the wall. Stupid risk, maybe, but did it *really* matter if she lost this job? Lady Della deserved so much better than this.

The others arrived all at once. Apparently, no one from this afternoon's event had yet gone home, because suddenly it was two against four: her and Lady Della over here; and over there Grobal Tagaret, with his mother on one side and Lady Selemei on the other, and Pyaras sneaking in behind. The only reason it wasn't twice that many was the small room couldn't fit all their manservants.

I hope Lady Della has some courage.

Grobal Tagaret sniffed and looked at her down his nose. "Arissen Melín. You wished to say something?"

"Grobal Tagaret, sir," she said. "I came in here on my security check, and I found Lady Della stuck in bed. She saved my life, sir, on the day the Eminence Herin died. And she told me what happened after that. You did—wrong, when you forced her into this bed against her will."

Gnash it, she'd backed off what she meant to say! Was it because Grobal Tagaret looked so much like his brother? She could have kicked herself. *Come on, forget who he is for a minute.*

Grobal Tagaret crossed his arms. "You're presumptuous, Arissen."

"So are you, sir. Thinking you'll prevent her from miscarrying by drugging her and forcing her down."

He scowled. "Varin's teeth! You know nothing about her."

"Neither do you, sir. She hasn't had an internal exam."

"She's my partner. I've lived through this with her for more than twelve years!"

She had no idea what to say to that. Had the Lady never had an internal exam in twelve years? Why, in Heile's name, why?!

"Tagaret," said Lady Selemei. "An exam could make certain."

His head snapped around toward the Lady. "Certain of what?"

"The health of her pregnancy," said Lady Selemei.

Melín clenched her fists. "Every pregnancy is different, sir. Maybe you knew she'd miscarried before, but without an internal exam there's no way to be sure why. I can't believe you decided it was fine to restrain your own partner based on nothing but guesses and fear."

"I did no such thing." But he looked away. Such obvious guilt!

"What did you do, then, sir?" she demanded. "Were you out of the house when strangers attacked your partner with needles and stuck her in a bed? Or were you here to watch them do it?"

"Enough!" Tagaret snapped. "You have no authority here. You have no manners. All you've done is prove that Arissen *do* have violence in their nature."

"Tagaret!" Lady Della exclaimed. "Tagaret, please."

"Go ahead, sir, fire me," Melín said. "You're absolutely right. We Arissen *do* have violence in our nature—enough to recognize violence when we see it done. Just because you didn't personally lay hands on Lady Della doesn't mean you're not responsible. Maybe if you'd drugged her and tied her down yourself, you might have realized what in Varin's name you were doing."

Grobal Tagaret flushed, and clenched his fists.

She had it coming, now. She braced herself. *Is your punishment as much fun as your brother's rewards?*

Lady Tamelera laid one hand gently on her son's shoulder. "Tagaret—how you remind me of your father."

Blood drained out of Grobal Tagaret's face. He turned to her in horror. "Oh," he whispered. "Oh, dear gods, Mother, what have I done?" In two long steps, he rushed across the room to Lady Della's bed and fell over her, his head on her chest. "I'm sorry, I'm so sorry. I was just trying to—I was angry when you ran away, and then—the pain, I was so scared, but she's right, I don't know anything . . ."

Lady Della's hand moved lightly to stroke his hair. "You might be right," she said. "If you are, and I need to, I'll stay in bed. But let's be honest." She hiccupped, clearly struggling not to sob. "Chances are better this is a . . . a growth, and not a child at all."

Dear gods, the despair in those words! Melín swallowed hard. "You may not have to grieve, Lady. And even if you do—be certain."

Lady Della nudged Tagaret until he stood up again, but kept hold of his hand.

"How?" she asked. "How can we be certain?"

"A medic could scan the child, Lady. Not that I know how to take you to one."

"Leave that to me." That was Lady Selemei. "I'll call my personal doctor."

Unbelievable. They had listened. They had changed. They were planning, now—and Pyaras was smiling. It wasn't like the smiles she'd seen on him before; it was triumphant, full of admiration and pride. Her insides melted, and her cheeks burned.

Time to go. Now.

"Lady Della," she said. "Please excuse me."

"Melín, wait." The Lady reached a hand above her head, and touched her arm. "Would you be willing to sit with me, when the doctor comes?"

"As my duties permit, Lady." She shook her head. "Why?"

The Lady smiled gently up at her. "I could use your courage."

CHAPTER THIRTY-SEVEN

Shinca

It seemed all anyone could do was argue. Nekantor and Tagaret, arguing over his head. Arbiter Lorman, too. Arissen Melín, yelling at Tagaret about Della. Maybe he could have handled it better if he weren't having to sleep in Tagaret's office.

At least he had Dexelin, now.

It was still weird and uncomfortable. He still dressed himself, because why wouldn't he? But Dexelin was in his room with him when he did it, in bodyguard stance, facing the window.

Whenever the curtains were open, he felt exposed, but when Dexelin closed them, he could feel invisible assassins gathering. Trying to let Dexelin feel included, he requested green gloves to match the green and black suit he'd gotten for his birthday—but then changed his mind after the servant had already handed them to him. If he'd been by himself, he wouldn't have felt guilty putting them back and changing to black ones.

Someone banged on his door.

He froze. So did Dexelin.

Please, please, don't be Nekantor.

Adon tugged his gloves tight, bracing himself to answer, then remembered Dexelin was supposed to do it. But if it was Nekantor, how could he even ask him to?

A voice echoed in from outside. "Adon, can I please talk to you? I promise I won't break your door down."

Oh, thank the Twins. Adon exhaled and opened the door himself. "Pyaras!"

"Adon, do me a favor?" His cousin's eyes were too wide. "Eat before you leave today?"

"What?" He looked at him harder. "What's wrong?"

Pyaras pressed his head between his hands, as if to keep it from splitting in two. "The thing is, they're going to expect your bodyguard to eat and drink for you, before you do. Don't let her. Please. Even if it means you don't eat at all."

"Uh—"

"Adon, *please*. Someone might try to poison you. How would you feel if she died?"

He gulped. "All right, I won't. I promise."

Pyaras deflated, sinking against the doorjamb. "Thank Heile for mercy."

"Is Melín here?" Adon asked. "If we're going to pretend-eat lunch, we should probably have more breakfast." He eyed his cousin. "Did you forget to eat again?"

Pyaras didn't answer.

"Come on." Adon caught up Pyaras' hand and pulled him out into the sitting room.

Arissen Melín was here, waiting beside the gaming table. Mai's truth, the more he knew about her, the less ordinary she seemed. She was hardly taller than he was, but radiated an explosive potential that made you want to keep your distance. Her skin was sunmarked brown, with darker pinpoint spots across her cheeks and nose; brown eyes sharp as daggers judged everything from under her orange helmet. Dexelin was definitely afraid of her.

He glanced up at Pyaras, and found him gaping as if he'd been hit in the head.

All right, then. "Arissen Melín," Adon said. "Are you hungry?"

She snapped to attention, so her heels clicked together. "No, thank you, sir."

"I'm serious. I won't be asking you to taste for me today, so Pyaras and I decided we should stuff ourselves up before we go. You should, too. Come on." He headed into the dining room, counting on her to follow.

The Household had clearly been listening behind the walls, because Serjer emerged with tableware as they entered, and Keeper Premel appeared a second later with a tray. He cast Adon a smile, and transferred to the table a basket of bread rolls, a plate of sliced meats, a pitcher of water, and a butter dish.

"You're so kind, Premel," Adon said. Pyaras took the chair next to him, and eventually, Arissen Melín sat down in a place across from them. She sat with her back frighteningly straight, and a blank stare on her face.

Adon turned his attention to layering a roll with butter and meat. Some seconds later, he looked up. Neither of them had made a single move for the food.

"What is it?" he demanded. "Go on, eat."

They both reached for the rolls at the same time. Melín got one; Pyaras shied off like the basket was hot.

Adon rolled his eyes. "I swear, why won't you talk to each other like normal people?"

Arissen Melín instantly popped her roll into her mouth and held it there with her sunmarked fingers, as if it could save her from having to utter a word.

"You wouldn't understand," said Pyaras. "You're too young."

Adon glared at him. "Are you serious?"

Pyaras shrugged as if he didn't care. But he *did* care, or he wouldn't have asked him not to eat lunch, and they wouldn't be here stuffing rolls in their mouths.

Never mind. Adon chomped on his first roll, eating with concentration until he'd finished it, and fixed himself another.

Halfway through that one, Serjer appeared at the dining room door. "I'm sorry to interrupt, young Master. The Eminence has arrived, with the Arbiter of the First Family Council."

Oof.

The bite of roll in his mouth felt suddenly dry as dust. He swigged water to get it down, left the other half on his plate, and stuffed a final roll into his pocket. When he stood up, Melín and Dexelin came to places before and behind.

Here we go. Nekantor was standing in the sitting room, looking at his gold watch. He wore a light brown suit—Heile knew he probably owned four identical ones, because he always looked exactly the same when he wasn't in fancy Eminence white. Arbiter Lorman was sitting on the couch. He looked to be taking on the day with fashion optimism, in lapis with fine jet stripes. He'd also trained his whisker-tips into loops. Lorman's Oidi stood beside the couch arm, but Nekantor's Cohort guards had remained in the vestibule—Adon could see their orange trouser-hems underneath the curtain.

"Good morning, young Adon." The Arbiter smiled. "It's a big, big day."

Adon forced himself to smile. "Good morning."

"Business," Nekantor announced, glancing up and then back to his watch. "We're meeting the Eighth Family today, for lunch, at Society Club Five."

"I won't be eating," said Adon. "So you know."

The Arbiter sat straighter. "Young Adon, that's not polite."

"It's fine," Nekantor said. "Just look enough like you're eating to keep them satisfied. They're going to see what they can get out of us in return for a vote. I have some plans for that."

Plans—an uncomfortable thought. "What kind?"

"Several, which you don't need to worry about. Caredes of the Eighth Family has a history of alliances with our departed father. They'll expect you to talk about him."

Talk about this, talk about that. Always the impossible. How could you talk about someone you'd never met? Someone who was Not Spoken Of, whose mere mention could break Tagaret?

Of course, Lorman saw his reaction, and smiled. "So, don't worry, young Adon. I worked as Garr's assistant for five years. So, I'll help you."

"Thank you," he said, though he didn't really want help.

Arissen Melín snapped audibly to attention. "Sirs. We should discuss our route to the club."

"It's already decided." Nekantor waved a hand. "We'll walk to the Conveyor's Hall and go from there."

"Respectfully, sir, we won't," said Arissen Melín.

The Eminence scowled.

"Your Eminence," said Melín. "Attacks started yesterday, earlier than you predicted. That suggests the chances of attack today are extreme. Skimmers won't offer us the protection we need. I've planned a walking route. I'll show you the map."

"Walking!" Nekantor snapped. "We'll be shot at. Skimmers will keep us out of range."

"Bolt weapons fire faster than sight, your Eminence. The only thing skimmers can do is make risky maneuvers to confuse a shooter, which makes crashes a serious risk. I can show you my proposed route. If we leave within the next four minutes, we should arrive in plenty of time."

"Arissen . . ." Nekantor's tone was low and threatening. "You'll do as I say."

But she'd taken on Tagaret and won. Adon knew in his gut she wouldn't back down. It was reassuring.

Arissen Melín saluted. "You, sir, may travel in any way you wish.

I promise you, the route I've chosen will be safest for Grobal Adon of the First Family, given the high probability of shooting attacks."

Nekantor pointed a long, thin finger toward her face. "He'd better be there. On time."

"Yes, your Eminence."

"Lorman," Nekantor said. "Make sure of it."

"Of course, your Eminence," said the Arbiter.

Adon held his breath until his brother and the two Cohort guards had departed, then let it all out in a whoosh. "Melín?" he asked, shaking his head. "What's so special about this route, that you think we can walk it safely?"

"One thing, sir. The best precaution against weapons fire," the Arissen answered.

"What's that?"

"Shinca."

You didn't exactly go through life counting shinca. They were just all around, here and there, sometimes in a room or a wall, or in the street. When you paid attention, though—like Melín obviously did—there were a lot. None in the hall outside the suite, but there was one in the wall of one of the guardrooms. And one right outside the exit Melín chose to use.

"Grobal Adon, sir," she said. "Here's how this works. You stand with your back against the shinca. It'll feel hotter the longer you lean on it, but it's safe. And I promise it won't damage your fancy suit." She winked.

He'd already inhaled to ask. He exhaled, blushing.

This shinca was medium-sized, about the same diameter as his thigh, though it was as unimaginably tall as any other—the ends of it were lost far below and above. He put his hand on it first. The surface felt like glass, not so hot he had to pull his hand away, but hot enough his palm started to sweat and slip. He turned his back to it, and nodded.

"Perfect," said Melín. "That's your safe spot, so don't move from it unless I tell you to. No matter what happens."

"All right."

"Imbati Dexelin, your job is to stand in front of Adon and keep him from being hit by projectiles or physical attacks."

Dexelin didn't say a word, but moved immediately to the spot she indicated.

"Grobal Lorman, sir, if you'll be participating in Grobal Adon's protection, I'll ask you and Imbati Oidi to walk side by side behind him, when we're moving from one shinca to the next."

Melín herself, it turned out, was the scout. She ranged ahead into the garden, checking behind shrubs and borders and scanning along the gravel paths before returning.

"Our next destination is at the border of the City Garden."

They walked fast, Melín adjusting her position in response to dangers he couldn't detect. The new shinca was as narrow as his arm, and wasn't even the only shinca in this section of the gardens, but one of the others was growing through a bush, and another would have forced him to stand in the water of a fountain. Adon let warmth tingle along his spine, and waited for her to identify their next destination. It felt like a strange game of table-tag. Run run run run *safe!*

"Our next destination is over there, at the edge of the path."

"Our next destination is there, beside the grounds gate."

"Our next destination is just around that corner, in the wall on your left."

In the public streets, it was hard to ignore how weird this must look to everyone walking by. Hop. Hop. Hop. Once, beyond Dexelin's elbow, Adon spied a Melumalai boy blinking up at the glowing trunk above their heads, as if he'd only just realized there was a shinca there at all.

And now Melín returned.

"Our destination is around that corner to the right, in the middle of the circumference. I'll block traffic."

This one was awkward, because the hum of skimmers was all around them, and sometimes Dexelin slowed so abruptly Adon almost bumped into him, and then speeded up and forced him to jump forward off a back heel to catch up. By the time they reached the center of the street, Adon was panting with nerves.

This was seriously the weirdest possible way to hop around Pelismara. So far, they were safe—if for no other reason than because attackers were confused by their choices.

"Our destination is right there at the gutter. Ready, and—WATCH IT!"

Dexelin spun, grabbed Adon by the arms, and flung him into the street. Adon stumbled, nearly fell, but kept his feet under him and flung his arms around the glowing white trunk that emerged from the gutter. The hot glassy surface pressed against his cheek. *Safe . . . ?*

A crash behind him, splintering, clattering.

He looked back. A skimmer had smashed into the shinca tree, right where he'd been standing. Broken composite and glass were scattered all over the road; a few skimmer parts bounced, rolled, and rattled to a stop. The front of the skimmer was utterly wrecked; the tree showed no ill effects at all. Arbiter Lorman stood in the lee of the trunk, dazed but seemingly undamaged, with his Oidi beside him. The skimmer driver was slumped over the handlebars of his vehicle, and Dexelin . . . where was Dexelin?

Adon held his breath for several seconds, but then Dexelin's head appeared on the other side of the crash.

Arissen Melín came around the twisted skimmer, pointed Dexelin at Adon, and then went back. She hauled the driver from his seat, nearly disappearing under him until she laid him out, face-up, in the unnaturally clear, silver-white shinca light.

"Gnash you," she said. She tied his hands and feet together and left him there.

They had to get back into formation, but Adon couldn't take his eyes off the assassin. He shivered. When everyone arrived near him, he looked up. Lorman's mustache had come untwirled, and Dexelin had blood on his face.

"How far is it?" Adon asked. "We have to—"

There was a glint of light, and a soft popping sound. Melín whirled around and zapped a shot across the street. A high-pitched scream echoed off the cavern roof, and Melín winced.

Adon gasped, "Mercy!"

"We're here," said Melín. She pointed to an entrance eight feet away, just on the other side of the sidewalk. "The sooner we get in, the better off we'll all be."

The metal door opened as they hurried toward it. An Imbati marked with the Household's crescent cross greeted them inside, and shut the door behind them. Adon shook out his hands, and smoothed out invisible wrinkles in his green velvet coat.

"Your room is this way, sirs." The Imbati escorted them quite calmly into the club. The hallway smelled like food. When their escort stopped by the door of a private room, Adon realized Nekantor would already be in there, and stopped dead.

"Young Adon, it's all right," said Lorman. "You're here, and we're safe."

"I'm not worried about that."

"Your brother is expecting us."

Well, exactly. "Arbiter, you can tell him we've arrived," Adon said. "I need a minute." Lorman took a breath, but he cut him off. "Just—tell him. I'll be right in." When Lorman had gone and the door had shut, he whispered, "Dexelin?"

"Adon, sir?"

"Are you all right? You're bleeding."

"A piece of glass hit me, sir. It's minor."

Adon waved one of the Imbati servers nearer. "Can you help him, please?" She nodded and approached Dexelin with a towel and water. That felt a little better. "Melín?"

"Sir?"

"Talk to me, please. I thought shinca were supposed to protect me."

"From weapons fire, sir. You were shot at only once, just before we came into the club."

"I was? I only heard your shot."

"I disabled the assassin, sir, but she shot first. That was the popping sound we heard. Imbati Dexelin was to protect you from physical threats, and he did."

"Did he ever." And behind this door was not a physical threat—or shouldn't be.

"Yes, sir, he did well," Melín agreed. "I'm happy to answer any questions you have."

"Thank you." He nodded to Dexelin, who—thank Heile—had cleaned his face and no longer appeared to be actively bleeding. The servant opened the door, and Adon stepped in.

Everyone inside the room turned and stared. Worst was the old man with bulging eyes who had asked rude questions at the Ball. Of course, after a second or two Adon realized he was staring back, coughed, and said, "Good afternoon, gentlemen."

"Good afternoon, young Adon," said a younger Eighth Family man with dark brown hair. "We're glad to see you in good health."

"Thank you." The automatic response, though his queasy stomach reminded him that this time, it wasn't normal or expected. There was still glass all over the road outside, and an assassin tied in a knot. He looked to the walls where the manservants stood, each face careful, calm, with a beautiful tattoo; it helped a little. But Nekantor had two Cohort guards behind him. It would only take one of them to kill everyone in the room. "How may I help you today?"

"Please, join us," said one of the Eighth Family men.

Adon sat down in a chair that his Dexelin pulled out for him. There was a plate of food in front of it; the thought of food made him ill. "Thank you." Caredes was still staring at him; he tried not to squirm.

"I remember your father," said Caredes. "Your father was a great man."

"Oh." Adon swallowed, glancing at Lorman and back. "Uh, thank you."

"He's also dead."

Name of Elinda. Hopefully, he'd managed to hold his face still.

"Let's get to the point," said Nekantor, who was also totally ignoring his food. "You said at the Ball you would be interested in an alliance."

Caredes snorted, playing with his fork. He appeared to have started eating before Adon walked in. "I thought at the time you might be bringing me Pyaras. Healthy! Robust! Not a child too young for betrothal. What can you offer us in return for our vote?"

"You need new blood," said Nekantor. "Don't deny it." One of the Cohort guards behind him handed him a portrait; he placed it on the table. It was a painting of a young Lady with white skin, smiling, with sapphires in her bright orange curls.

"Wait," Adon said. "That's Lady Pelli. Lady Selemei's daughter."

"You're correct," said Lorman. "Nineteen years old. So, she would make an excellent addition to the Eighth Family."

Adon tried not to squirm. No one had explained this—maybe because he'd been avoiding it, and hadn't asked? But had they even discussed this with Lady Pelli? Or Lady Selemei? They must have, mustn't they? How else would Nekantor have gotten the portrait? The thought made his insides twist.

Caredes didn't move, but the younger Eighth Family man took up the portrait, studying it closely. He gave a nudge to another man beside him, who joined him looking at it. Adon didn't like the looks on their faces.

"Sure, we'll take her," the second man said. He sounded like a Melumalai.

"Excellent," said Nekantor. "Lorman, draw it up. Caredes, the deal will be final when your final vote is cast, not before."

"I'm not stupid, Nekantor." Caredes waved his hand, and his manservant removed his half-empty plate. "Also, you should know something. There's no news."

Adon glanced at his brother. He hated the idea of asking for Nekantor's instruction, but it felt awful to know so little. Everything around him felt wrong. "No news? What does that mean?"

Nekantor waved off the question, his attention still locked on Caredes. "Not since we arrived?"

"Not since the Round of Twelve." Caredes shifted his stare to Adon, pronouncing doom. "None. At all."

Adon swallowed, and nodded. He looked at Lorman. *Would someone please explain it?*

"So, it's unusual, is what Caredes is saying," said Arbiter Lorman. "Usually, the day after the Round of Twelve is full of news about assassination attempts."

"No," Nekantor snapped. "It's not unusual; it never happens. It's wrong."

The old man smirked. "You have the Eighth Family's vote, Adon—if you survive to get it. May Sirin stand by you, for luck."

"That's enough," Nekantor said. He shoved back from the table. "We're leaving." He grabbed Adon's arm and dragged him out into the hall.

"Let go of me!"

"It's all wrong, don't you understand?" Nekantor leaned into his face, panting. "No news means the other Families aren't trying to kill each other. They're only trying to kill *you*."

He gulped. "Heile have mercy."

"There were supposed to be attempts on *everyone*, not just on you. This is a different game than I thought." Nekantor released him and paced off down the hall so fast it looked like he was planning to slam into the wall at the end of it, but then he snapped back around and returned. His hands opened and closed. "If we're going to get you to the center of the game, I need to find the new pattern."

"But I got here safely," Adon said. "Imbati Dexelin and Arissen Melín kept me safe."

"Everyone cheats," Nekantor said, as if he hadn't heard. He wheeled and paced away again. "If this is an alliance between our enemies, it's temporary; it won't last. They'll want me to take the interviews seriously. I'll look like I'm taking them seriously." He turned and paced back. "I'll have to speak to Amyel of the Ninth Family, and to Secretary Boros of the Second Family, and make sure of them. There must be a way to find the pattern. To *control* the pattern. No more mistakes."

His intensity was frightening. Adon hugged himself. "I need to go home, Nekantor. I want to be somewhere safe."

Nekantor stopped and whipped a pointing finger at Arissen Melín. "Do it, Arissen. You got him here. Get him home. Don't fail me. No more mistakes."

She saluted. "Yes, your Eminence." She held the salute while Nekantor paced past them. His guards joined him, and they vanished into the front lobby. Then she said, "Come, Dexelin. And Oidi, with your permission, Arbiter Lorman, sir."

Adon waited several seconds before walking out to the front. It was safe here, in this windowless club. At least, now that Nekantor had left. But as many times as his mind insisted, his body hadn't had time to agree, and now they had to go out again. Just the five of them.

"I wish Pyaras were here," he said. "And Jarel."

"Me, too, sir," said Melín. "I'd even appreciate Veriga."

"Veriga would be great," Adon sighed. "Police support would be great."

"So he *is* police, then. That's good, at least."

Adon wrinkled his nose at her. "Of course Veriga's police. You didn't know?"

She looked at him, and her mouth pulled sideways. "I figured. He acts like it. But I wasn't sure . . . some people have lied to me."

It clicked together, suddenly. "Pyaras *lied* to you. That's why you're so mad."

She looked away fast. "We should go."

"Wait," Adon said. "You don't know how Pyaras met Veriga. Do you."

"So, so. Young Adon," said Arbiter Lorman. "Delaying won't help. So we're going to have to do this one way or another."

"Veriga was in the Eminence's Cohort," Adon persisted. "He got assigned to bodyguard Nekantor in the last Heir Selection."

Melín had started toward the front door, but now she stopped and turned around with horror on her face. "Oh, gods help him."

"That's right. Veriga got poisoned, right here, at this same club. And Pyaras sat by his bed until he got better, and after that, they were friends. Veriga joined the police later."

She seemed to think about that. "Thank you, sir. I believe we should go."

"Oh, and you should know. Pyaras came to me this morning, about ready to tear his hair out, begging me not to let you eat for me."

She stared at him.

"But if we're going to have to go, what do we do about the crashed skimmer?"

Melín shook herself. "I'll check ahead." She disappeared out the front door, and returned a few seconds later with a short nod. "Good news. They took the main part of it away, and the first thing you have to do is just get across the sidewalk to the corner of the club. Arbiter Lorman, sir, are you ready? Adon, sir?"

Adon's throat closed up and his chest tightened, but he nodded. *Sirin give me luck. Eyn help me get home.* He kept close behind Melín, one step, two, three, four, until they reached the shinca in the gutter. He slid into position, leaning into its heat while Melín ranged farther ahead. The circumference had been closed to traffic in the few minutes they'd been inside. The assassin with his crashed skimmer was gone, though the street was still full of debris. At least ten red-uniformed police moved about here and there, which—probably made them safer?

Melín returned. "Shinca in the middle of the street. Go."

He gulped a breath and followed her as quickly as he could. Broken composite crunched under his shoes.

"And the next one. Go."

"Go."

"Go."

One of the gaps was longer than the others, and he found himself gasping at the end of it.

"Adon, sir, this next gap is also a long one," Melín said, brusquely but kindly. "Please remember to breathe while you walk."

He blushed and nodded. "Sorry."

"Around the corner to the left, middle of the sidewalk. Go."

He walked fast, forcing himself to breathe, trying not to look for dangers, just watch Melín's black boots.

"Varin's teeth!" she swore suddenly. "Run!"

She loosed a shot—*zzap!*—and broke into a run ahead of him, weapon in her hand. He tried to keep up and follow. Around the corner to the left she'd said, and there was the corner, coming, here now—turn left—and there was the shinca, the white glow of safety! He flung himself at it.

A flash—sudden heat at the edge of his right ear, and that weird sound, *pop!* He half-fell into the shinca's smooth surface. Dexelin arrived two heartbeats later, sliding into place in front of him. Adon straightened, with the shinca warm against his back.

Where had Melín gone?

Another bright flash, another pop. And then pop—pop—pop! Were those weapons shots? The flashes hurt his eyes; he closed them for a second—

It got ten times worse.

Pops and crackles assaulted his ears. The surface against his back grew hotter. When he opened his eyes again, the air itself was boiling—street, buildings, flashes of fire, distorted and near-unrecognizable. The silver-white light from behind him flickered and brightened. Then the screaming started.

Oh, holy Eyn . . .

The shinca got hotter—hotter. Was this what was supposed to happen? It hurt! Melín had said the tree wouldn't burn him, but he couldn't bear it any more. How far could he move away and stay safe? He leaned forward, crouched down where the tree met the sidewalk, and wrapped both arms around his head.

In the tiny space between his knees, it was only as hot as his own body, but he couldn't shut out the sounds. The screaming got worse, coming from more directions. Slowly, the weird popping and crackling diminished, and then finally it stopped.

Adon sneaked a look up. The air shimmered, slowly returning to normal, but it smelled of smoke. The shinca was still too hot, too bright. And there was still screaming.

"D-Dexelin?" he quavered. "Are you all right?"

"Here, sir." Right beside him, also crouched low.

"What was that? Did you see what happened?"

"Sir, assassins shot at us. We took . . . a lot of shots. Maybe as many as eighty. But Arissen Melín has stopped them, and we should get you home. Just a few more hops."

"I don't think—" His voice broke, and he cleared his throat. "I don't think I want anyone to know—what just happened."

Dexelin bowed his head. "My heart is as deep as the heavens. No word uttered in confidence will escape it."

Adon stood up. His legs shook. Melín came back, jogging across the radius with guilty discomfort on her face, but seemingly uninjured. Arbiter Lorman and his Oidi appeared to have been caught behind the corner, and have missed most of it. Lorman's face was aghast.

"Elinda's blessing," Lorman said, taking up Adon's hand and patting it incredulously. "I thought you were dead for sure."

"A few more hops," Adon said. "We're almost there. Melín?"

"Ready when you are, sir," the Arissen said. "We'll keep to the plan, but with those five deactivated, we shouldn't face such a barrage again."

Adon swallowed hard. "I hope you're right."

CHAPTER THIRTY-EIGHT

No Lies

Pyaras couldn't stand sitting and waiting. But there was no better place to do it; whatever news there was to be had about Adon and Melín, it would reach here first. He wanted to pace, but this was Tagaret's house, and Lady Tamelera was sitting on the next couch.

Watching the door was agony. Watching Tamelera was worse. Her Aloran stood behind her, quiet as usual, and outwardly calm. If he watched her with more attentiveness than was appropriate, it was impossible to tell.

They're waiting for their child.

He couldn't condemn them for it. After all, what was *he* doing here?

I'm waiting to glimpse my Arissen lover's hair.

A terrible confession. And, oh! the thoughts that came with it. Her breath, her kiss, her grip, her energy—they conquered him like she always did. He doubled over in a flush of acute embarrassment, and clutched his head in his hands.

Thank Heile for mercy, Lady Tamelera seemed too preoccupied to notice.

She was the lucky one. Every Lady was constantly attended by a manservant, so no one could reproach Aloran for the care that was his duty anyway. Adon had inherited his mother's very Grobal face, and since Tagaret's father had been dark-haired in his youth, even that could pass unremarked. Every detail conspired to spare Aloran from accusation. He was safe.

Melín, though, was glaringly visible to everyone, and in danger of death every second she was near this family. They were probably shooting at her right now.

The doorbell rang.

Lady Tamelera sprang up from her seat. "They wouldn't ring the bell." She turned toward Aloran. "It can't be—holy Eyn look down on us! Elinda forbear!"

"Lady," Aloran murmured. "I'm here."

Pyaras quickly turned away, and pretended he hadn't been looking. The prayer echoed in his head. *Blessed Eyn, look down on us—bring them home safe. Bring Melín here so I can tell her to stay away from us forever . . .*

Serjer looked out from behind the vestibule curtain. "I'm sorry for your alarm, Mistress. Lady Selemei is here, accompanied by a Doctor Kartunnen Wint. They say they are here to see Mistress Della."

"Oh—oh, mercy of Heile, do please ask them in."

This was none of his business; maybe he shouldn't have come here in the first place. Still, Pyaras stood up politely as Lady Selemei came in.

Lady Selemei handed her cane to her Ustin, and took Tamelera's hand in both of hers. "Tamelera, it's good to see you. This is such a difficult day for everyone. Have you had any news?"

"None," Tamelera sighed. "We're waiting for Adon to return from a lunch meeting."

"My heart aches for you," Lady Selemei said, shaking her head.

"It really doesn't feel right," Pyaras remarked. "I remember the day after the Round of Twelve being nothing but news and rumors pouring in all day. Isn't that how it's supposed to work?"

Lady Selemei turned and looked at him. "Yes. It worked that way last time, and the time before. This isn't normal." She turned back to Tamelera. "How is Della doing?"

Tamelera shook her head. "She's awake. She's scared. No change in her condition."

"Ladies, pardon me," said the doctor, an older Kartunnen woman in a gray medical coat, whose hair was tied back in a red-and-silver knot. "If I'm correct in understanding that Lady Della has been abused by doctors in the past, and hasn't suffered any bleeding with this pregnancy . . ."

"That's correct, doctor," Tamelera said.

"Then I would like to invite her to begin by speaking with me in a public room."

"Serjer," Lady Tamelera said. "Could you ask them to come out, please?"

"Right away, Mistress."

Pyaras crossed his arms in frustration, then realized what he was doing and uncrossed them. He forced himself to admit that it made no difference whether Serjer walked away from his station; nothing would make Adon and Melín come home any faster. He tried sitting down, but it was unbearable. He stood up again.

Then Della and Tagaret walked together out of the back rooms. Tagaret had one arm wrapped around Della's shoulders, and supported her hand with the other. She was in a dressing gown, and her beautiful copper hair had been brushed. She looked far better than she had lying in bed. She seemed both scared and worried—Mai's truth, so did they all. Della glanced toward the doctor, and then quickly looked away. "Maybe we could just wait for Adon with all of you?"

"Fine by me," said Pyaras.

Tagaret nodded. "Thank you for asking us to come out, Doctor. This is a scary time. Please, make yourself comfortable."

Della glanced at the doctor again. "Don't make me."

"Lady, we don't need to do anything you're not ready to do," the doctor said. "Perhaps we could just have a conversation today."

Della pressed her lips together for several seconds. "It's that—Mother, can you stay? I don't want to be alone right now."

"Oh! Oh, my love . . ." Tamelera went to them, silk gown swishing, and enfolded both Della and Tagaret in her arms. "That's perfect, because we don't want to be alone either."

I certainly don't. Yet he felt more alone than ever. "I don't know if you want to hear this, Tagaret," Pyaras said, "but there's been no Selection news yet. Bad or good."

"What?" Tagaret asked. "No news at all?" He looked over at the First Houseman, who had followed them out. "Serjer, nothing from the other Families?"

Serjer bowed. "No, sir. I'm afraid not."

Tagaret shook his head. "Something's wrong."

The front door burst open. Adon wobbled in first; then came his Dexelin and Arbiter Lorman and his Oidi, and finally—

"Melín," Pyaras breathed, though he wanted to shout it. "Thank all the gods."

"Shut the doors." Melín's face was severe. "Check all the windows." Imbati Serjer ran off at once.

Whatever had happened, it was bad.

"Adon," Lady Tamelera cried, running to throw her arms around him, "Adon, love, are you all right?"

"S-sort of," said Adon. He looked drawn and exhausted, so pale his skin was almost green.

"What's that smell?" Della asked. "Smoke?"

Tamelera lifted her hands from Adon's back. They were black with ash. "Oh, love, what happened? Did someone shoot you? Your new suit . . ."

"Oh, gods!" Adon jerked away. "I—I think I'm going to be sick." He ran off into the back, with his Dexelin close behind.

"Can I do anything to help?" Pyaras asked. They ignored him.

"Doctor," said Lady Tamelera, "Adon may be injured. May I trouble you to come with me for a moment?"

"Of course, Lady." The two of them went after Adon into the back of the house.

"Arbiter Lorman," said Tagaret. "Are you well? Shall I get you a drink of water?"

The Arbiter demurred, then seemed to notice that his hands were shaking, and said, "Yes, please."

Tagaret strode off toward the dining room door.

Pyaras found himself alone with Melín, Lady Selemei, and Arbiter Lorman. Hopefully Lady Selemei could handle Lorman right now, because he had to ask:

"What happened? Are you hurt?"

Melín tensed. "Why should you care, *sir?*"

Sirin and Eyn, how he despised that word. "Why shouldn't I care about what happens to you? When my own family has put you in danger?"

She gritted her teeth and didn't respond.

"I knew it," said Arbiter Lorman.

"Knew what?" asked Lady Selemei.

"Pyaras," Lorman hissed, pointing at him with one shaking hand. "You have no manners. No honor. Your muckwalking is compulsive!"

"Lorman," Lady Selemei scolded. "That's a terrible thing to say. I realize you're upset, but this is not the time."

"No, Lady, this is the perfect time," Lorman said. "Look at what he's doing. He couldn't keep a promise if his life depended on it."

Something inside him snapped. "Varin gnash you, Lorman, that's enough!" Pyaras roared. "How dare you talk to me about promises? Do I look like the First Family's candidate for Heir? No? Oh, that's right, the actual candidate just ran out with his new suit half burnt off after *you* failed to keep your promise to *me.* You shame me, twist me into becoming a tool for the Family's purposes, and then drop me when I'm less than convenient? I'll talk to whoever in Varin's name I like!"

Lorman gaped at him.

Blast all of this. Pyaras turned to Melín. "Go. Please. Quit this horrid, dangerous job. Get away from my stinking family. Stay away from me and never speak to me again."

Tagaret had just emerged from the dining room; he stood blinking, glass of water forgotten in his hand. Selemei had been shocked into silence.

"Pardon me, everyone," Pyaras said. "I'll be going now."

He walked out the front door and slammed it shut behind him.

This was the way he would wake up forever: a black abyss inside, aching with confused dreams of a life that might actually mean something. And one day—maybe even tomorrow, in barter for a vote to make Adon Heir—the First Family would find him useful enough to offer him a partner. Some pretty, fragile girl who would fear him and do as she was told.

Gods, what he would have to do, so that she might bear him sickly children for the gods-forsaken Race!

Mechanically, he got himself out of bed, cleaned up, and got dressed, with his Jarel's help. It was pretty early; Father wouldn't be awake yet.

Halfway through a bite of morning mushroom tart he remembered he was allowed to see Arissen, now. He dropped his fork to the table.

"Mmf! Jarel, jogging—" He gulped down his food. He hadn't been out with Veriga since the day the Eminence died. "Is it too late?"

"I don't believe so, sir."

It better not be. He pushed away from the table and ran for the front door, flinging himself down the stairways and into the gardens. Maybe Veriga had stopped coming, when everything got crazy. He wouldn't have blamed him.

But when he reached their usual meeting spot, he found Evvi tied to the pole.

"Evvi, pup!" The tunnel-hound recognized his voice, and started wiggling joyfully. Pyaras fell on his knees in the gravel and took her in his arms, rubbing his face against her velvety head. "Where's Veriga, huh, pup? Why isn't he with you?"

"Because I was looking around for you."

Veriga. It suddenly hit him how close he'd come to never doing this again. Pyaras hid his face in the tunnel-hound's fur until he could face his friend without choking up.

"Hey, uh, sorry. We had a dangerous few days, there."

"Me, too. Can't talk about it." Veriga bent and untied Evvi from the pole. "Let's run."

Running felt unbelievably good. Breathing, moving, the crunch of gravel, Veriga running ahead of him. They circled out past the Ring and around the Arissen section and back, twice. Veriga brought them into the Ring to finish up, like he always did; Pyaras grabbed a drink of water from the fountain, then joined him sitting on the low wall around the sand.

"You said something about danger?" Veriga asked, leaning elbows on his knees with his hands hanging. "Anything new I should know about?"

"No one's making any of the usual Selection attacks," said Pyaras. "They're only attacking Adon. Thank Heile you're not a part of that. Nekantor's had Melín guarding him, but she might have quit."

Veriga grunted. "All right."

"Also, the Round of Twelve turned out to be all about Arissen. Paper Shadows were mentioned. And Adon publicly accused Nekantor of murder, so, yeah."

"Hmph. Did anything happen after that?"

Pyaras shook his head. "Not to Adon. There was a cabinet member who seemed interested, though. Fifth Family. He wanted to talk about the investigation. You haven't heard anything from him?"

"Not me," Veriga said. "Chief of Police might have; I wouldn't know."

Pyaras looked at him, over his shoulder. "You're staying safe, right?"

"Best I can."

"Nothing you can tell me about the investigation?"

"Not and stay safe."

Pyaras nodded. "Run again tomorrow?"

Veriga slapped his knees and stood up. "See you then."

If Melín was gone, that was for the best. She hated him now; and she was safer out of his reach. He had Veriga. He had the Division, and Commander Tret. Of course, when he'd shown up at work Tret had given him a look like he was crazy, and told him to check back in when the Selection was over.

Which was fair.

Pyaras knocked on Tagaret's door.

Imbati Serjer opened it. "Good morning, sir."

"Good morning, Serjer. Does everybody hate me now?"

"Of course not, sir. Do come in. The family has decided against going out today."

"Thanks. Sounds very sensible." He pushed through the vestibule curtain. The sitting room was empty.

"I can call Master Tagaret for you, sir," said Serjer. "He's in the back with Lady Della at the moment."

Pyaras shook his head. "Don't bother him if he's busy. I can sit by myself awhile. I live here half the time, anyway."

Serjer answered with a slight smile. "You are always welcome, sir."

Pyaras wandered to the nearest couch. He could still feel the warm effort of the run in his muscles. He'd just started to sit when Melín walked in through the drawing room doors.

He jolted to his feet.

She stared at him. The intensity of her attention stopped his breath. He couldn't hide the tears that leapt into his eyes. Couldn't hide the guilt, either. He looked down at his own hands, and eventually managed enough breath to speak.

"Melín, please. Please, may I talk to you?"

Her reply was wary. "No lies."

"The truth, I swear. Or Mai strike me."

She hesitated for a second. Then she crossed the room, buckles clinking on her boots, and pushed open the door of Tagaret's office.

Pyaras followed her in. The office was as comfortable as ever, soft carpet, soft chairs, warm light. Tagaret had hung a few paintings back on the walls. For some reason, a tidy daybed had been set up on the floor. His thoughts leapt instantly to the things the two of them could do on it.

Shut up, you.

"Adon is sleeping here," said Melín, who'd obviously noticed. "His bedroom isn't safe."

"Ah." His heart pounded; if he looked at her, he couldn't trust it not to break. He kept his eyes on a shadow the desk cast across the thick carpet. "Good idea. You're an excellent bodyguard. Not that I'd expect anything else—you're magnificent—but it's killing me and I wish you would stop."

"Because of what happened to Veriga."

He couldn't help looking up. She'd taken off her helmet and set it on the corner of Tagaret's desk. Her hair, shorn close to her skin, made his fingers tingle to touch her; her gaze pierced him to the core. His next inhale was an effort. "How did you . . . ?"

"Adon told me," she said. "But I don't think he told me the whole story."

"You want—"

"No lies."

He swallowed. "All right—uh, I was eleven. One day I sort of beat up one of Nekantor's friends, and he started calling me Arissen. I hated it, and I hated him, but I was an ignorant child, so decided I hated Arissen."

He almost looked at her, but a wave of shame forced his eyes back down. He wiped his lip with one hand.

"The Eminence died, and Tagaret was supposed to become the First Family's candidate for Heir. He heard me insulting Arissen, and got angry, and told me to talk to his Selection bodyguard."

"Ah," she said. "So that was Veriga."

"Yes." It hurt to think of him, young and still unharmed. "It went bad fast. Tagaret and I got sick with Kinders fever. I thought Tagaret would die. Nekantor stole the candidacy, and next thing I knew, Veriga had been poisoned."

"Thank Heile for blessing him with healing."

He nodded. "I—sat with Veriga, while—" He couldn't say it. Already the memories of the medical center came rising, trying to overwhelm him. He raised both hands and pressed them to his head.

"Hey," said Melín.

He looked at her.

"You don't need to tell me that part. Sit down for a minute."

"Yeah." He skirted the daybed to the couch, and sat. She didn't join him, but leaned on the edge of the desk, considering.

"Here's something I don't get," she said. "Why would you still see him?"

"I probably shouldn't," he admitted. "My father hates me seeing him. Arbiter Lorman keeps an enormous file on all our unsavory activities. I don't know—Veriga's my friend. His tunnel-hound likes me. He takes me jogging. He takes me to targetball."

Melín's gaze sharpened. "Did he take you to the Descent?"

"I wouldn't have known what a Descent was if he didn't take me. He meant to teach me a lesson that night. But I lost him in the crowds, and it didn't turn out like either of us had planned."

"Ha," Melín said, mirthlessly. "Obviously not."

"I have a talent for doing stupid things, I guess. Veriga did crossmark me, but he couldn't have done it if I didn't consent. He wanted me to see how Arissen live—to humble me, so I could learn not to be so pushy." He picked at the arm of the couch with his fingernail, and sighed. "Not so I could learn that everything in my life up to that point had been false."

She frowned. "No lies."

"I'm not." Clubs and restaurants and prostitutes—all the pointless orsheth he'd spent on Lowers' bodies that he'd never cared enough to tell apart . . . it was sickening. He couldn't explain it. "I promised I would never crossmark again, after that. I wasn't crossmarked at the targetball."

She thought for a long while before speaking again. "So why did you tell me somebody shot you?"

"Somebody did." He glanced up at her. "A Paper Shadow."

"Plis in a mist! Your family begs for weapons fire."

"I guess we do."

"Why did you kiss me?"

That question aroused him instantly. He crossed his legs and looked away toward the office door, so he wouldn't look at her—or worse, at Adon's bed.

"Y-you said you w-wanted to," he stammered. "And I w-wanted to. Nobody ever—I didn't expect—I mean—I thought it was for fun. I never expected to see you again."

She snorted. "That makes us even. I didn't expect to see you again either. That's what Descent nights are for: leave your lovers at home and explore a bit. Try something new. Celebrate being alive."

He turned to look at her. "Lovers?"

Melín narrowed her eyes. "Veriga lives alone, does he?"

"Uh, yeah." He swallowed. "With his tunnel-hound. He got her for medical reasons." The word *lovers* bounced around awkwardly in his head.

"So maybe he's not interested in sex. Or maybe he's a team player, and his lovers take turns staying over."

"I have no idea." Here he'd thought he knew so much about Arissen. How had Veriga never talked to him about lovers?

Stupid question. Veriga had a way of responding to undue curiosity: 'Enough, young nobleman.'

But the questions that spun in his head right now eroded a thousand things he'd thought he was certain about. Did Veriga really hate brothels? Was he just uninterested? Or did he have real lovers, before whom paid professionals looked flimsy as paper?

Pyaras shook his head. "Melín, all I know is, it doesn't matter what I meant to do that night. I—" It was hard to breathe with her looking at him like that, but he had to say it. "I can't stop thinking about you. You are more real than every lover I've ever had. You gave me something I never imagined I was looking for. For one night, I knew how to celebrate being alive—and now I don't know what to do."

For a second her eyes widened, and her lips trembled. Then she barked, "Gnash you! Why do I even care?"

He gulped and sat back against the couch cushions.

But her anger vanished as quickly as it had come. She rubbed her face with both hands. Then, slowly, she walked closer and sat down in the other corner of the couch, keeping a careful distance between them.

"I don't think you understand," she said. "Descent lovers are real, but I've had more than twenty."

"Oh." He couldn't bear to consider what that meant.

"I was never lacking love. Drefne started as my barracks lover, then slowly got to know me, and lately he's been a rescuer. He cooks the best breakfasts. Aripo was my Division therapist until she transferred me to someone else and when I asked why, she said she was struggling to keep her hands off me. I told her she didn't have to try. She makes the tea."

That didn't make sense. "They're both your lovers at the same time?"

"They're not just my lovers, Pyaras, they're my *foundations.* After each Descent lover has been forgotten, I go back to them. I was supposed to go back to them this time, too. Except I kept thinking about you. You were at that cursed targetball game. And after all the deaths, when Drefne and Aripo and I went home to nurse our injured hearts together, I wanted you there." Her fists knotted on her knees. "I *told* them about you, gnash it! Do you have any idea what that means?"

The only thing he could be certain of was that he had no idea at all. And no foundations—she'd always stood on rock, and here he was on sand. His heart screamed that she couldn't mean what she was saying. Maybe this was some Arissen thing? Because if it wasn't—

She leaned closer. "I was ready to share everything with you! And then I found out." She lowered her voice, but spat the words out. "It was a lie. I was nothing but your tool."

"No," he moaned, shaking his head. "You're not, Melín, you're not—there was only one lie. Crossmarking was my mistake, and I'm so sorry. You're not my tool. You shouldn't be anyone's. All I want—"

There were no more words he could say. His heart screamed, *I want you to be mine!* But she wasn't his. She never had been. He'd intended to play with her, and she'd intended to play with him, and whatever had happened afterward meant nothing. He had responsibilities. And she lived an Arissen life, one where she was fulfilled—one he could never understand.

He cleared his throat painfully. "All I want now is for you to go away, somewhere you'll be safe from my family."

"I get it, I do. But it's not that easy. Nekantor stole me from my work in the Division to put me in the Cohort under his personal control. He's put me in charge of keeping Adon alive until the end of the Heir Selection. Both times, he called it a reward."

"Gods," he said. "I hate Nekantor."

"Unless you can keep me safe from him, then I'm trapped."

A terrible thought struck him. Nekantor had clearly made Melín a favorite, next to Karyas. If Nek somehow got the idea that *he'd* made some claim on her, whatever he'd put her through up to this point would be nothing.

"No," he said. "No—Melín, my seeing you, and talking to you, is putting you in danger. So if you can't stop, then I have to. I'm sorry. I'm going to leave now."

He stood quickly, without looking at her face, and walked out into the sitting room, toward the front door.

"Pyaras! Thank all the gods; I was looking for you."

Pyaras turned around. "Tagaret?"

His cousin had just emerged through the double doors, and his face was unnaturally pale.

"What's wrong?"

"You have to help me, I can't do this."

"Uh . . ."

"That doctor's back. She's in the room with Della, and she asked me to leave, but Della asked me to stay, and—I can't say no if Della wants me there, but they're going to take her clothes off!"

"What?" Pyaras blinked at him.

"To examine her, and the—you have to come with me."

Pyaras shook his head, vehemently. "You can't be serious. Della won't want *me* to see her like that! She's your partner, you've . . . seen her before. You need to do it." Now Tagaret was staring. "What?"

It took a second before he realized Tagaret wasn't staring at him. He turned around. Melín had come out of the office. She looked absolutely disgusted.

"Grobal Tagaret, sir, if you're correct that Lady Della has requested your presence, you should be there. You're not the one getting your parts looked at. You started this. The very least you can do is show up when she asks you to. Besides, you might see your child." She didn't wait for a response, but marched past them into the back.

"Mercy of Heile," Tagaret said. "Our child. So many things could go wrong. So many already have—Pyaras, I'm scared."

Staring his own best future in the face, Pyaras could hardly breathe. He put his arm around his cousin. "Della's scared, too. She needs you. I'll take you as far as the door."

CHAPTER THIRTY-NINE

The Unwinnable Game

"I'm scared."

Della sat with her feet dangling over the edge of her bed. Her body felt too warm, flushed behind the ears. Her belly was a heavy knot of horror that folded against her upper thighs, and moved all on its own.

"Would you feel more comfortable if I took off my coat?" the doctor asked.

"I don't know." There was a rolling stand with medical things on it by the foot of her bed, and she wasn't wearing underwear, so feeling comfortable was just not going to happen.

The doctor's name was Kartunnen Wint, and she sat in a brass chair at what distance the small room allowed. She had wrinkles at the corners of her eyes. Her expression was kind. They'd had a conversation yesterday; that hadn't been so difficult. Della had explained the pain that had started all of this, and Wint had assured her it was just a common early contraction, not a sign of disaster.

Still, this was the road that led to screaming.

"Lady," said the doctor, "we'll do this at your pace."

Lady Selemei sat in a chair by the head of her bed. "I'm here for you, Della," she said. "I know this is hard for you. Wint is my doctor, and she's been through a lot with me. I trust her. I promise, she will be kind."

"I wish Tagaret were here."

"Of course you do." Lady Selemei's voice took on a note of sadness. "I entirely understand."

"Lady," said Doctor Wint, "I'm happy to wait for your partner's return, but I want to make sure you're certain his presence will help. For your protection, I'm not planning to take his orders." She glanced at Selemei, who nodded firmly. "Do you remember what I explained yesterday? You understand what I'm hoping to do?"

Images flooded in. Kartunnen hands, grabbing her, pulling her backward, holding her down. Needles, instruments. Pain. Della started shaking. She clasped her hands together, tightly.

No.

No, that wasn't Wint. Selemei was here to protect her. Wint had told her what she wanted to do. Remember. Say it aloud, grasp it.

"To—" She squeezed until her knuckles turned white. "To make sure my womb is not weak. To make sure it's capable of sustaining."

"That's right, Lady," said Wint gently. "With your permission, I will observe its opening with my eyes."

"Also, to examine the, the—it."

"The germinal, Lady. May Elinda bless it."

What was it? A growth, or a child? Was she a failure to the Race, again? Or a victory against the decline? She shook her head. Then someone knocked on the door. She yelped and covered her mouth with both hands.

"Who's there?" Lady Selemei asked.

"May I come in?" A sweet, welcome voice: Tagaret.

It seemed like he understood, now. He'd apologized, at least, and promised to do better. Yes, he had panicked when the doctor came, but so had she. Her breath felt shallow, and the way her bottom clenched reminded her of her lack of underwear. Tagaret didn't know about that. She nodded.

"Come in," said Lady Selemei.

The door cracked open. Tagaret looked nervous. He wasn't alone; shadows blocked light behind him. "Mother wanted to be here for you, Della, if you think that's all right."

She glanced at Wint. The doctor's face was solemn, cautioning.

But Tamelera was the one who had made Tagaret understand. "I think that's all right. Thank you for caring, Mother."

Tagaret came to the near side of the double bed and sat down on it. Tamelera didn't stay with him. She walked closer, behind Lady Selemei's chair, and gave the Lady's shoulder a quick pat.

Doctor Wint crossed her ankles and leaned forward. She didn't look at the newcomers, but square at Della as if to say, *you and I are the ones who matter here.* "Lady, may I have your permission to use an instrument to take images?"

Della pressed a hand against her belly without thinking. "What kind of images?"

"Do you mean photographs?" Lady Tamelera asked. "I've had photographs taken before."

"Photographs are permanent images, Lady," the doctor explained. "These are temporary ones. The instrument allows me to see the germinal and assess its health."

A twisted, quivering mass covered in blood.

"Holy Mother of Souls," Della whispered. Was it a child, or not? "Yes, you may."

"I ask your permission to begin."

Della's heart beat against her throat. She tried to gulp it down.

"Lady," the doctor said, "as I told you yesterday, I will always tell you what I'm going to do before I do it. You may ask to stop at any time."

Part of her mind was already screaming, *Stop, stop . . .*

But if I stop now, I learn nothing. I only wrestle with this fear until the blood starts.

She took a shuddering breath. "You may begin, Doctor."

"Thank you, Lady. I would like to do the visual examination first. It will proceed smoothly if you lie down on your back with your legs bent. I will go into the bathroom and wash my hands while you do this. Please tell me when you are ready."

Della's body twitched in fear, but it was all right—see, the doctor was leaving, pushing the bathroom door mostly closed. Yesterday, she'd told Wint about her terror: the hands, always the hands, grabbing, pushing her down. Now the doctor was nowhere near, and she would lie down by herself. She eased down sideways until her shoulder landed and her ankles came up to the bed, and then rolled slowly to her back. Her belly shifted disconcertingly, and the interloper jabbed her. She hissed, but resettled.

She glanced toward Tagaret.

"I love you," Tagaret said. He was wringing his hands.

The bathroom door opened; the doctor had apparently opened it with her foot while keeping her gloved hands clasped together. "May I approach, Lady?"

Della swallowed. "Yes."

Doctor Wint moved carefully to the foot of the bed, to her rolling stand of instruments. There were small sounds. Della winced with each one.

If she touches me I'm going to scream.

She wrestled with the urge that climbed up her throat.

"Please take a breath, Lady," said Doctor Wint.

She gasped.

"Excellent, thank you, and one more, please."

Another breath gave her the ability to speak. "Tagaret?"

Tagaret startled out of his tight posture. "Yes, love?"

"Can you come here?"

He only had to stand and take a step. She grasped his hand in both of hers, and pressed the back of it against her face.

"Squeeze as hard as you like," he whispered.

She nodded, and remembered to breathe. "What comes next?"

"Lady, I'm holding an instrument that will allow me to inspect the opening of your womb," the doctor said. Over her own fabric-draped knees, Della couldn't see it, but its glow lit Wint's face. "With your consent, I will introduce it. I understand this may be difficult, and if you wish me to stop, say, 'stop.'"

Della held tight onto Tagaret's fingers; they kept her from falling into the fear. "I consent."

"I'm moving your nightgown," said the doctor. "In a moment you will feel the instrument touch you. It's no wider than my little finger."

A whine escaped her lips; she clutched Tagaret's fingers. The touch came, warm, wet-feeling and entirely impersonal. It pressed at her, invaded.

"Stop!"

"I've stopped, Lady. Please take a deep breath for me."

She took a breath. Tears pushed against her tight-shut eyes, and one ran away down her cheek. What if her womb was weak? What if there was no hope? What would they do then?

"When you're ready, I will need to push a little bit farther, and then you will feel a slow expansion. I will wait for your word."

"Tagaret . . ."

"I love you," said Tagaret. "I will stand with you against the whole world."

She managed a breath, too shallow; another. "All right, Doctor."

The feeling of the instrument moving sent a shudder up her back, and then came the expansion—weird, oh, gods it felt so weird . . . "Stop!"

"Well done, Lady," the doctor said. "We're all done with that part. I can see what I need to."

Two seconds of concentrated doubt filled the silence.

Della pressed her forehead into Tagaret's hand. "Heile, have mercy . . ."

"It looks normal, Lady," the doctor said. "I see no sign of thinning or weakness. I will collapse my instrument and remove it now."

"Yes." She clung to Tagaret's hands. More tears escaped her eyes as her insides slid back together. By luck or mercy, the interloper seemed to have had no reaction to the invasion at all, though she could hear both Tamelera and Lady Selemei murmuring Heile's name.

Remember to breathe. Yes—breathe.

At last she was able to release her awful grip on Tagaret's fingers. He slipped his hand free and gave her the other one. She used it to sit up. That restored some sense of control. Seconds passed, placing merciful distance between her and the invasion. But a new question had lodged in her mind.

"Doctor, if I don't have a womb weakness, then what's wrong with me?"

"That's not a question I can answer clinically, Lady," Doctor Wint said. She frowned, removed her gloves with a snap-snap, and bent out of view for a few moments. Clicks and mysterious noises came from the rolling stand. Then she came up again. "Lady, may I ask you to please cover your legs and expose your belly while I set this up?"

Della nodded. Tagaret moved closer to her knees and helped her to arrange a sheet covering while Doctor Wint moved an instrument from below to the top shelf of her stand. It was strange, with a screen in its upper half.

"Della," said Lady Selemei from her chair, "I don't think it's fair for you to ask what's wrong with you. We don't know that anything is wrong with you at all. The basic tests your Yoral and others have given you have always been normal."

Della shook her head, tucking the sheet around her legs and trying to pull her nightgown up so it wouldn't fall over her belly. "But there must be something. I never feel right. There's always something wrong."

"I never felt right when I was pregnant," Tamelera said softly. "And for you, it's been so many, many times . . ."

Selemei was angrier. "Della, I've heard an awful lot of people tell you there's something wrong with you. They never once think of *you*; they think only of whether or not you can fulfill your duty to the Race. When you hear that enough times, it's easy to start believing it."

So many, many times. "But I think there must be, though," she said. "With the decline . . ."

"Lady," said Doctor Wint. "Decline or not, every person is different. And every pregnancy is different, because every germinal is different. I'll need permission to touch you, so I can apply this cream to your skin, and then this instrument." She held up a small blunt thing the size of a bar of soap.

This instrument was nothing. What terrified her was the question it would answer. Was this a child, or not?

"Tagaret," she said. "I don't know how to do this."

He took her hand again. "Think of something else. Think of Selimna."

Selimna. The cold air, the cliffsides, the Ride. That was better.

"Doctor," she said, "you have permission to touch me."

The cream was warmer than she expected, and the soap-device tickled. The interloper appeared to notice it, though, and started jabbing her. As if in response, her womb hardened into a stone.

Della gasped. "It's happening again—"

The doctor paused the movement of her device. "Please breathe, Lady. We'll wait for it to pass."

Breathe. Think about Director Aimali, and Venorai Castremei, and Melumalai Forder. All those people who deserve better. And Vant. He deserves better, too.

At last, the hardness released.

"May I resume, Lady?"

"Yes."

The doctor scrubbed the soap-device repetitively over the same area. Della tried to shift her position to get the interloper to settle down. It wouldn't. The doctor kept her eyes and one hand on the machine, never saying a word. Then, a wrinkle of puzzlement formed between her brows.

Name of Elinda—it was going to be bad news. Dread swept over her and nausea came with it; she panted, trying not to panic. What did it mean if her womb was perfect this time, if it was only perfectly able to hold in some kind of horror?

"Stop," she said.

Doctor Wint's hand stopped moving the soap-device, and she looked at her. "Lady?"

"I can't do this. I can't do this." She clenched her fists and hit them against her forehead over and over. The banging was a barrier against seeing and feeling, but it wasn't enough. "It's going to kill me."

"Della," said Tagaret. "Della, listen." His hand touched her shoulder. "You'll live. I know you will. You traveled, and you survived. You went to the Venorai tributary, and you survived. You climbed out the window, and you survived. You saved Lady Falya and Arissen Melín from assassins, and you survived. You're my Maiden Eyn, and you always come back."

She nodded, the heels of her hands clutched against her tear-wet face.

"We'll get out of here," Tagaret said. "We'll go back to Selimna, just you and me. We'll drink tea at Bread in Hand."

The memory of perfect bread helped her hear him. They *would* go back. Think of what they could do, now that she'd finally managed to see the entirety of the problem they were trying to solve!

But that was what would happen if she failed.

What would happen if she *succeeded?* Children didn't travel. She'd have to stay in Pelismara. She'd have to relinquish everything they'd worked for.

This *was* a game. Just another game with no way to win. And that meant she had to find another way—a way to refuse to play.

Della opened her hands, and let them fall to the covers beside her.

"I won't give up," she said. "We will go back to Selimna, whether I bear a child or not. What I can do for Varin is more important than what the Society and the Race think of me."

"Lady," the doctor said. "It's not bad news."

"What?" She looked around. The doctor was no longer touching her, and the screen showed nothing.

"Lady," Doctor Wint said. "I was confused, because I was led to believe you'd been pregnant for twenty weeks, but you're further along than that. I believe you've passed the germinal stage."

"I—I don't know what you mean."

"May I look again, please? You may look with me, or not, as you wish."

Della gulped and nodded. When the doctor resumed scrubbing her with the soap-device, she looked. What the screen showed was nothing like a portrait; it was a changing fog of tiny green dots that suggested form gradually, a little at a time.

"Lady, the first three fifths of a pregnancy are the germinal stage,"

Doctor Wint explained. "This one has reached early essential stage." She stared at the screen while its dots fogged and changed. "The anchor is normal. The brain, heart, and spine are normal. Limbs are in good order."

Normal—good order—there could be no words more unexpected or out of place. Della shook her head. "How is that possible?"

Doctor Wint pulled away, handed Della a towel, and began wiping her device with another. "Often when a pregnancy fails, it's because of poor genetic health in the germinal. But on inspection, I suspect this essential will be born. You may yet labor early, but even if you began today, medical facilities might be able to sustain the essential into childhood. Mind you, I'd far prefer to see this one after four fifths, because one's likelihood of confirmation would go way up."

Confirmation. Seriously? Della wiped the film of cream from her belly with the towel. That was the word her own mother had always worried about when they'd discussed the future—whether her child would be able to join in the public life of the Pelismara Society. But, as Mai was her witness, it didn't matter. She would love to have a private child. They required care, but like her own sister, would be safe from the Society's predatory expectations.

That was a question for later. Today, by some miracle, Elinda had looked on her kindly for the first time. "Thank you, Doctor."

"Wint," said Lady Selemei, "do you have a recommendation for Della's level of daily activity?"

The doctor shrugged, still looking at Della. "Lady, if you have sustained or repetitive contractions, lie down until they subside. But so long as you're not having pain or bleeding, you can do anything you like."

Anything I like. "I'm going to get up and take a shower, to start with." Della slid off the hospital bed. "I don't think we should be needing this extra bed."

"Della, I'm sorry," said Tagaret. "We should have done these tests long ago, whenever you were pregnant."

She embraced him, listening to his heartbeat. "The tests didn't make this child whole," she said. "That was Sirin's hand, and Elinda's. The decline hasn't stopped. You heard the doctor—every pregnancy is different."

Tagaret pulled back from her and stroked her hair away from her face. "I know, but this isn't about the child. This is about *you.* If we'd been doing this all along, we would have known what treatment you needed. When I think of everything you've been through in the name of the Race, just because I was telling doctors what to do, instead of listening—" His brown eyes glistened with tears, and he whispered close to her ear. "It shows me that our project is more important than ever. So you can never be hurt by my ignorance again."

CHAPTER FORTY

Under Attack

What kind of nobleman sits by a poisoned bodyguard's bed?

Not that thought again—not right as she was going to work . . .

But it was kind of inevitable. Just going to work at all, these days, was winding her extra tight.

For lots of reasons.

Melín nodded to her Cohort mates at the gate of the Residence grounds, and passed through. She'd much prefer to skip the Cohort offices, but it was the only place she could be briefed with special instructions, if the Eminence had left her any.

Trudging along the gravel pathway, she thought of Pyaras again, and grunted. Both Drefne and Aripo had called her on being irritable, but she was too angry to explain.

She'd been prepared for Pyaras to lie. She hadn't been prepared for him to tell the truth. And he had, gnash him. His face, when he'd tried to tell her—well, she knew what panic looked like.

What kind of nobleman sits by a poisoned bodyguard's bed?

And if she believed that much, it pushed her toward believing other things he'd said. Things she wasn't comfortable knowing, if they were true.

For one night, I knew how to celebrate being alive—and now I don't know what to do.

That wasn't healthy. That wasn't the kind of person she should want to have a relationship with. She wanted the playful man, the considerate lover, the man who could think of picking a weapon holster or finding doctors at exactly the critical moment. She wanted him hard enough that it was difficult being in the same room.

Why did he have to be Grobal?

Why did he have to be the blasted Executor, of all things?

Quick crunching footsteps brought her attention back to the path. It was Fifth Sahris, running toward her. Melín sped up for a few steps; Sahris reached her, panting, and grabbed her arm.

"Get out."

She blinked. "Where to?"

"We have orders to grab you and hold you. The others'll be here any second. Go."

Go? She didn't have a lot of options; the grounds gate was quite a distance behind her by now, and if she approached it with pursuit, the guards there would seize her. Same with the Residence doors. She turned away from the Arissen section and sprinted directly toward the fence at the edge of the grounds.

Orders to grab and hold—those had to have come straight from Nekantor.

Varin's teeth, why? So he could punish her personally? For what?

There were shouts behind her: Sahris claiming to have bumped into her accidentally and failed to take advantage, and Crenn and the others barking fury at her.

Thank you, Sahris . . .

The gardens on this side of the Residence were broad, flat, and essentially without cover. Right by the fence, the gravel paths ended, giving her stone to run on. Thank Plis, that gave her a speed advantage. One that, given their longer strides, she sorely needed. She turned right and accelerated along the fence toward the Ring.

More barks behind her. They hadn't lost too much time over Sahris, and that meant they'd be on her faster than she wanted.

Could she reach the Ring in time to hide?

Where could she hide that they wouldn't find her?

By the time she reached the curving wall of the Ring, they were way too close. She weaved in through the entrance. The low circular wall was no cover at all, and unless she wanted to lock herself in a locker, there was no place to hide here. She hopped the wall and backed across the center of the sand, watching the exits.

"We've got her now! Second, you go that way. Fourth and Fifth, that way."

Covering the exits so she couldn't escape. It wouldn't have been any better if she'd kept going, though. They'd have caught up eventually.

Her heel hit the low wall. Here behind her was the chair where the Eminence had sat—and it had a roof. Could she get up there?

Too far to jump from the top of the low wall. The Eminence's chair wasn't much better, but the support poles looked good. She leapt onto the nearest one, clamping it between her legs and pulling herself higher, higher. She caught the edge of the roof with her left hand.

"You little tunnel-hound!"

Gods, was that—?

Going for a grip with her right hand, she missed it; her legs slipped off the pole, and she clung desperately with her left. Her body twisted awkwardly, and she saw the owner of the voice running toward her.

First Karyas—it *was.*

I will not be hauled off a roof by First Karyas!

Melín pulled herself up, hard, and caught the right-hand grip, backward. She swung, and with her good leg, caught Karyas with a kick in the helmet that sent her reeling back into the others coming up behind.

Quick, quick, now . . .

She swung back, kicked up, and tucked, hauling hard with her arms for the inversion and pull over. Her legs smacked down onto the roof. She shimmied backward, curled to a crouch, and pulled her knife.

"Anyone tries to climb up here's gonna lose fingers!" Merciful Heile, why was it always fingers?

First Crenn growled and made a leap for the edge of the roof, but she struck his knuckles with her knife-hilt, and he fell back again.

She pulled her bolt weapon with her other hand.

"Try me, carrion-face." Maybe she could light his hair on fire.

"Wait!" Karyas barked. "That's good enough."

"Sir," Second Fetti protested.

"I said, it's good enough." Karyas gestured them to spread out. Her hands had been seriously damaged. They were scarred, weakened by the disruption burns. She wouldn't be able to climb this roof—but it was a good bet she could still shoot. "Cover the edges of the roof so she can't get down."

"Why are you doing this?" Melín demanded.

Karyas pulled a smirk. "I hope you're ready to sit up there a while."

"Go die in a hole." Just because they said they wanted her to sit didn't mean they wouldn't change their minds and start shooting, so she kept low. Then she wondered: "Am I fired?"

"Better hope that's all you are."

Crown of Mai, I'm fired! Finally! It was so ridiculous and perfect she started to laugh, and couldn't stop.

"Shut up!" Karyas snapped.

She kept laughing.

"Shut up or I'll forget Nekantor wants you alive."

Melín gulped and stopped laughing. "He does?" she asked. "What does he want from me?"

"Oh, he doesn't want anything from *you*."

Oh, Sirin and Eyn . . . If this wasn't about her, then she wasn't about to be punished—she was being held hostage. And she could only think of one reason why Nekantor would do that.

What did he want from Pyaras?

CHAPTER FORTY-ONE

Missing

Pyaras walked into Father's room, not because he wanted to, but because Father would expect it. That was what you did during Selection; everyone had to stay informed.

"Father," he said. "How are you feeling?"

"What is it, my Pira? What's the news?"

"No news," Pyaras sighed.

"I can't believe it."

"Yeah, it's weird, I know. Everyone is worried about it. I'm heading out to Tagaret's. The Round of Eight is this afternoon; I'm sorry you can't come to the announcement of the last four."

Father gave a slight smile. "I wouldn't have gone, even if I were well enough. I hate big events. Are you sure you're all right?"

"Fine," he said. Having a bad day wasn't the same thing as being upset. He'd missed jogging this morning: when he'd reached the pole, eight minutes late, there'd been no Evvi, and no Veriga. It was all his own fault for oversleeping, but he still hated to think of Veriga waiting for him and being disappointed, again.

"I'm proud of you," Father said.

"Oh? Uh, thank you."

"You did the right thing, stepping back and letting your cousin compete. Adon's still safe, is he?"

No, not at all, in any way. "Yes, he's safe."

"I'm glad. I'm sure he'll do well in the question session today."

Pyaras couldn't stand it anymore. "So I'll just go," he said. "I don't want to miss seeing Adon before he leaves."

"Give them my best," Father said. "I love you, Pira."

"I love you, too."

"Don't be too jealous, now; you'll be all right."

"Sure."

Jarel met him in the vestibule, gave him his gloves to put on, and accompanied him downstairs. His time with his cousins wouldn't be particularly personal today; Selection events meant lots of people gathering, and lots of chaotic preparation. Imbati Serjer greeted him at the front door, and allowed him into the sitting room where Lady Selemei and Speaker Fedron were already talking with Tagaret and Della.

"Good afternoon, everyone," Pyaras said.

"Pyaras!" Tagaret came and thumped him on the back. "Come to wish Adon luck?"

"All the luck in the world," he agreed. Preferably luck that would get him eliminated as soon as possible. Though an Heir from another Family would cause a whole cluster of different problems.

"Pyaras, I'm glad to see you," said Lady Selemei. "I'm glad Adon can count on you supporting him."

"Where *is* Adon?" he asked.

"He's in the back with his Dexelin, getting dressed," said Della. She was dressed up in a new gown today. It made her look even more pregnant than she had yesterday, but she seemed a great deal better. "We're still waiting on Arissen Melín."

"You're *waiting* on her?" Anxiety struck him in the chest. "What do you mean? She's not here yet?"

"No."

Pyaras shook his head. "That's not like her."

"Well," said Speaker Fedron, "it's likely she's been fired. For a Selection bodyguard, she's terribly presumptuous."

"That doesn't make any sense, though." Not after what she'd said yesterday. Nekantor was counting on her to get Adon through this, wasn't he? Nek had hated having to replace Veriga in the last Selection; he wouldn't want to have to replace Melín.

That was when Adon emerged from the back of the house, with his Dexelin behind him. The Selection stress was obviously getting to him; he seemed distant and distracted, barely making eye contact with anyone. He was, however, impeccably well dressed in a suit of peridot velvet with embroidered hems and sparkling buttons.

Pyaras walked over to him and squeezed his shoulder. "Hey, Adon."

Adon jumped a little, and looked up. "Oh hey."

"Hang in there, today, all right? Maybe you'll get voted out this round so we can all relax."

"Pyaras," said Speaker Fedron, chidingly.

Adon nodded as though he hadn't really heard. "Where's Melín?" he asked. "Isn't she supposed to be here?"

The cold feeling in his chest grew worse. "You know what? I'll go look for her," he said. "How much time is there before you need to leave?"

The doorbell rang. Serjer admitted Arbiter Lorman, who was all in a fluster, waving his hands in shooing motions. "So, so, what are you doing? Don't wait around here! Let's go, let's go. Adon, so, you're first up in the question session. We can't have you be late."

"We're having a problem of a missing Arissen," said Selemei. She turned to her servant. "Ustin, would you and Fedron's Chenna feel comfortable teaming with Adon's Dexelin and Lorman's Oidi as far as the cabinet room?"

The broad-shouldered Imbati woman bowed. "Of course, Mistress."

That seemed agreeable to everyone, and within moments, Selemei, Fedron, and Lorman had surrounded Adon and proceeded out the door, with the four Imbati on the alert around them.

As soon as the door shut, Tagaret gave a deep sigh. "Holy Mai, please let him be eliminated from Selection today."

"Oh, dear," said Della, shaking her head. "Oh, dear."

"Pyaras," said Tagaret, "the announcement of the last four candidates is planned for the Hall of the Eminence today; will you come in with us?"

"Oh, absolutely." He nodded. "I can't stay with you and wait, though. I'm worried something's happened to Melín. I'm going to see if I can find her. I'll be right back."

"Eyn go with you," said Della.

Pyaras whooshed out a breath. "Yeah, thanks."

Outside in the hallway, Adon's party was still within sight, moving at Lady Selemei's slow pace near the junction where the suites wing met the central section. Pyaras glanced back to make sure his Jarel was with him, then ducked down the hall in the opposite direction until he reached the side exit.

He walked out between guards of the Eminence's Cohort into the gardens. No one was in sight. It would be hard to miss anyone crossing the gardens, unless they hid behind one of the garden shrubs. But Melín would never hide behind a shrub.

"Jarel," he said. "Where could she be?"

"Perhaps at the Arissen section, sir?"

It was the only reasonable guess. He was tempted to jump the border and cut across the plantings, but taking the path would be just as fast if he jogged. He crunched along, Jarel more lightly echoing his steps, until he reached the pole where he'd missed Veriga this morning. A soft warble stopped him in his tracks.

It couldn't be.

He called anyway. "Evvi?"

From between two nearby shrubs appeared a broad black snout, and then the tunnel-hound's eyeless head. She lolloped toward him.

Oh, Heile have mercy.

Stomach churning, Pyaras crouched down to greet her. "Evvi pup . . . come here, pup."

Evvi didn't hesitate; she dived into his hands. He scrubbed her velvety head automatically.

But this was bad. She hadn't been tied to the pole. She wasn't even wearing her lead. She would have been, if Veriga were here.

Were Melín and Veriga both missing?

Panic tried to strangle him. But rather than holding his head, he focused on stroking Evvi. *Think, Pyaras, think.* Nekantor must be responsible. It had to have something to do with . . . the murder investigation, maybe? Or the Round of Eight today?

Something was attached to Evvi's collar—a small cloth bag. With his fingers in a panicked rush, he had difficulty untying it. He patted his knee, so Evvi would place her head there and hold still. At last, it came free.

Inside the bag was a small, oddly shaped object that had a polymer case, and some kind of metal plug.

"Jarel?" he whispered hoarsely. "What is this?"

"It's an ordinator storage device," the Imbati replied. "They're in common use in the bureaucratic offices. I believe Household Director Samirya also uses them."

"What does it store?"

"Sir, I couldn't tell you. You have to plug it into an ordinator that can read the information."

He'd bet anything this was information about the murder investigation. If Veriga had come under threat, it would have made perfect sense to give the information to Evvi, because no Grobal would ever stoop to approach a tunnel-hound. Except him. It was possible Veriga had sent Evvi here with it on purpose, and meant for him to find it.

"There are ordinators in the Division offices," Pyaras said. "Come on."

CHAPTER FORTY-TWO

The Cabinet

Am I safe?

Adon walked slowly, staying behind the diaphanous hem of Lady Selemei's gown. Step, step, step, step.

It was impossible to know what *safe* was anymore.

He had four Imbati bodyguards. And Lady Selemei, and Arbiter Lorman, and Speaker Fedron. There were no shinca in the spiral stairway to the second floor, or in the hallway to the cabinet meeting room. There was no Melín.

There were no sounds of shooting, but that was only Sirin's luck.

He should have stayed home. Just said no to Arbiter Lorman and Nekantor and everyone else, and stayed in the drawing room with Tagaret and Della, and Mother, and Aloran. Imagine the size of the breath he could take, then, rather than standing and answering questions in front of the cabinet, with Nekantor watching. Imagine what it would be like to look at them, and smile, and say all the assassins were now someone else's problem.

There were cabinet members standing in the hall when they arrived—all of them effectively strangers, though a few faces were familiar. All were dressed in the sober tones of amber, green, or jasper favored by older men. Speaker Fedron moved away to greet them. Adon stuck behind Lady Selemei, who walked with her cane straight to the cabinet room door. Her Ustin opened it for them, and stayed outside while they went in.

The cabinet meeting room was quite large, windowless, with a big table and cushioned brass chairs nearly as tall as he was. Heavy portraits of Eminences hung on the walls. The men in them wore collar fashions from different eras dating back over two hundred years. They all looked as if someone had sat them down in the throne and lectured them about the Grobal Trust and the responsibilities of their exalted station. Their expressions varied: some sour, some proud, some gloating, some scowling—but none of them were happy.

"Lady Selemei," Adon said. "Can I talk to you about something?"

"Arbiter?" Lady Selemei exclaimed suddenly. "Why are you here? Is everything all right?"

Adon leaned to one side of a chair that had been blocking his view and discovered Innis of the Fifth Family sitting in one of the chairs.

"Good afternoon, Lady Selemei," said Innis, in his nasal voice. "I occupy this seat for the Fifth Family."

Lady Selemei turned to Adon. "Please look out the door and call everyone in, as quickly as you can. It's urgent."

"All right." Adon went back to the bronze door. Immediately outside it was a manservant he didn't recognize. "Imbati, please call the cabinet members in, right away."

"Yes, sir."

In seconds, everyone from the hallway began hurrying in. Adon stepped to one side of the door, and squeezed his shoulders between two heavy wooden portrait frames so he could press himself to the stone. This didn't seem to be about the Heir Selection. The Arbiter of a Family Council shouldn't be sitting in a cabinet chair.

Speaker Fedron strode quickly past Adon to the head of the table. "Innis, what brings you?" he asked.

"I'm sorry to inform you that this morning, in his bed, my cousin Kaspri has joined the stars."

Adon caught his breath. Whatever murmurs of talk had remained among the other cabinet members fell instantly into silence.

"Elinda keep him," said Lady Selemei.

"I therefore occupy this seat for the Fifth Family," said Innis.

"I'm very sorry for your loss, Innis," said Speaker Fedron. "I'm troubled by several irregularities we're coping with this afternoon, one of which is that the Eminence Nekantor has not hired another manservant who can call the meeting to order. I believe for your sake we shouldn't wait to convene."

Adon stood straighter. He knew how to fix this. The door to the room was still open, so he went and ducked his head out. "Dexelin? Can you come and call us to order?"

"If they'll permit me, sir," said Dexelin.

"I'll ask," Adon said. "Speaker Fedron? Can Dexelin do it?"

For a second, Speaker Fedron looked baffled by the question, but then he nodded. "Members, I'll invite Adon's Dexelin to convene the meeting, since he has previous experience. If you agree to this, put your right hand on the table in front of you."

The vote was unanimous, and very quick—so quick it reminded Adon of the lack of news over the last few days. A strange unity among the Families. It could only have grown out of their understanding that Nekantor was behind all of this. Nekantor, who wasn't here yet. Maybe they wanted to do something important before he arrived?

Did that mean *he* wasn't supposed to be here yet? He returned to his position between the portrait frames and tried to disappear into the wall.

Dexelin spoke solemnly. "I call to order this meeting of the Pelismar Cabinet, and serve as a reminder of the Grobal Trust: giving to each according to need, the hand of the Grobal shall guide the eight cities of Varin."

"So noted," said Speaker Fedron. He leaned forward and flicked a switch below the level of the table. Screens embedded in the table at each seat flickered to life. "We'll begin with the question of the seat formerly occupied by Kaspri of the Fifth Family."

"Speaker, sir," said Dexelin, "do you also wish me to announce the vote totals?"

"No, thank you," said Fedron. "Members, please enter your votes into the ordinator and place your right hand on the table if you wish to certify the seat empty." When no hands hit the table, Fedron smiled tightly. "The seat remains occupied by the Fifth Family. Welcome to the cabinet, Innis."

"Thank you," said Innis. "I'm sorry to bring bad news as my first contribution to this august assembly. My cousin Kaspri did die in his bed this morning, but not naturally. A Paper Shadow broke his bedroom window and shot him dead. I think we can all see what's going on."

The entire room fell breathless and silent.

Nekantor murdered a cabinet member. The truth washed over Adon with a wave of nausea, and he pressed both hands over his mouth. The moment he felt able to speak, he said, "I can't do this. I'm going home."

Before he could reach the door, it opened toward him. Nekantor was on the other side, with two guards of the Eminence's Cohort behind him.

"Right on time, Adon. Well done," said Nekantor.

"I'm leaving," said Adon.

"You're not," Nekantor said. "Move; I'm coming in." He walked forward, forcing Adon backward into the room.

"Nekantor!" exclaimed Speaker Fedron. "Do you have no shame?"

None. None at all. Adon shook his head. His whole body tensed with dread.

"I can't imagine what you mean," Nekantor said. He walked to his chair at the front of the room, and sat down. "I believe it's time for us to begin the Round of Eight questioning."

"You have some nerve, Nekantor," said Innis.

"Arbiter Innis?" Nekantor frowned. "Why are you here?"

"I've joined the cabinet."

"Well, then, that means we can start." Nekantor lashed a look at Fedron. "Start."

"Your Eminence," said Fedron, "you know how this process is supposed to work."

"I do," Nekantor said. "Adon of the First Family will be questioned first. He's here, and he's ready."

"I'm not," Adon said sharply. "I won't be questioned."

"Process and rules," Nekantor countered. "We're moving forward."

Innis gave a dramatic sigh. "So I guess that's it. You're planning to pretend that nothing happened, and that the Paper Shadows didn't assassinate my cousin Kaspri this morning."

"Process and rules," Nekantor insisted. "Respect for our noble ancestors and for the Great Grobal Fyn who established the Grobal Trust. Have we all agreed to those rules? We have, haven't we?" He looked around at the cabinet members. Their fear made the air feel heavy. "Every family uses the Paper Shadows in one way or another. I'm not that special, am I, Innis? You used them first."

Innis said nothing.

Adon breathed shallowly. This was bad. How long was a single candidate's question session supposed to last? Would people outside this room realize what was going on? He glanced at Dexelin, but when Dexelin opened the door, Nekantor's orange-uniformed guards walked into the room. One of them stayed by the main door, and the other crossed to the Maze door, blocking it.

"Nekantor," Adon whispered.

His brother was looking at him, with that gaze that felt like a clamp.

Adon straightened and tugged at the bottom edge of his coat.

"Don't do this, Nekantor. I'm not worth it. I can't be the kind of Heir you want."

"Of course you can. You're your father's son; you can learn how, and I'll help you."

"But I don't want you to help me!"

The main door to the room opened. Both of Nekantor's Cohort guards drew weapons; every member of the cabinet shrank back in their seats. Who was coming? Would the guards shoot anyone who walked through that door?

A woman in an orange uniform entered and saluted Nekantor. "Your Eminence," she said.

"You're out of order!" Nekantor snapped. He waved his hands angrily at the cabinet members. "This was supposed to be resolved. Process and rules!"

"I'm sorry, your Eminence," said the Cohort woman. "I'm here to inform you that the two items you requested are under control, and we've located your cousin."

"The pattern." Nekantor gritted his teeth. "I can still control the pattern." He raked his gaze over the terrified cabinet members. "I'll be back in a few minutes. Guards, keep them here." He left his chair and walked along the wall toward Adon and the exit.

Adon stepped into his path. "Nekantor, I don't know what you're planning, but don't do this. We should just follow the rules—and if that means I lose, I don't care."

Nekantor looked down at him. "I see."

"What?"

"You've reminded me why I have to do this. I'll be back in a few minutes." He gestured across the room. "Nobody leaves."

CHAPTER FORTY-THREE

The Arissen

Pyaras managed not to burst into the Division offices as if fleeing rockfall. He was carrying Evvi, though, which surprised quite a number of the officers at the nearby desks. Once they'd recognized him and Jarel, most of them just nodded respectfully and went back to their work. Pyaras approached the young man at the closest desk, a pale Cohort Third with a sprinkling of sunmarks over his nose.

"Third, I'd like to request your help with something." He set Evvi down, told her to stay, and fished the device from his pocket. "I found this, and I'm wondering if someone here lost it. Can we use your ordinator to look?"

"Certainly, Executor, sir," the Third said. And added, a bit incredulously, "Is this your hound?" He bent for a second and offered Evvi his fingers. She seemed to have that effect on everyone.

"She belongs to an Arissen friend of mine," Pyaras said. "Here."

The Third took the device, but had scarcely had a chance to plug it in when muffled shouts echoed into the offices from the door to the foyer. "Pyaras! I know you're in there. Come out!"

Mercy, that was Nekantor. What was he doing here? Wasn't he supposed to be at the Round of Eight?

He wouldn't be looking for the storage device, though; he wouldn't know about Evvi, or he'd have captured her before.

What could this be about?

Pyaras gave the young officer a deliberate smile. "Third, I'm going to need to talk to the Eminence in the foyer for a few minutes. Please take my Jarel's guidance on this until I come back."

"Yes, sir."

"I have reason to believe this may be sensitive information, so please allow her to study it first."

"Understood, sir."

Pyaras drew himself up, though it felt like he'd swallowed a stone. Most important: he mustn't give Nek any reason to suspect what was going on behind this door.

He walked out into the foyer with his head held high. There was Nekantor, with a Cohort guard behind him.

"Your Eminence," Pyaras said. "Are you here to speak to the Executor?"

Nekantor didn't look good. He was scowling, and his gaze bounced around the foyer, from the woven mat on the floor, to the metal benches, to the door to the Executor's playroom. He was straightening his clothes as if he'd had to hurry here and didn't like it. He lashed a glance at Pyaras.

"Yes," he said. "Yes, I am. Here to speak to the Executor."

"You found him."

Nekantor glanced back the way he'd come in, as though he'd forgotten something, and his fingers flickered over his buttons. "Do you have any idea why I gave you this job?"

"That's easy. I'm the only one in the Family who knows anything about how to deal with Ar—"

"To stop you being an embarrassment!" Nekantor snapped.

Gnash Nekantor. "Great. I hope that worked out for you."

Nekantor's eyes flashed, and he flung up both hands. "Of course it didn't work. You're worse than I thought. You're not just stubborn. You're utterly useless!"

Pyaras gritted his teeth. He couldn't help thinking about what Jarel might be discovering, behind the office door; but for now, apparently, he had to stand here and let his cousin insult him.

"Fantastic."

"You think you're funny?" Nekantor demanded. "Well, I've had enough. That ends now. Starting today, you're going to show me some respect."

"Make me."

His cousin's lips stretched into a snarling smile. "Oh, I plan to. Don't tell me you're too stupid to notice some people aren't where they should be."

Veriga. Melín. His skin flashed hot, then cold. Mercy of Heile, this wasn't about the investigation, or about the Selection, it was about *him?*

"You're not going to be refusing my orders again," Nekantor said. "From now on, you'll do exactly as I say."

He tried not to give away his horror. "Or else?"

"Or else your friends will have a more painfully difficult day than they are already."

What was Nekantor doing to Melín and Veriga? He wasn't the type to engage in physical tortures . . . but members of the Eminence's Cohort might be. "Uh," he said. "Let me just—"

"No."

Pyaras snapped his mouth shut.

"I don't recommend you try to rescue them," said Nekantor. "They're in two separate locations. If you want to try, you're going to have to choose."

Choose, between Veriga and Melín? No blasted way. But to do as Nekantor said?

"All right, I'll do as you say," Pyaras said. "Let them go."

"You're a bad liar."

His face flushed hot.

Nekantor poked a finger at him. "Prove to me that you're not lying. Send a hundred soldiers into the northern neighborhoods, right now."

"What? Why?"

Nekantor crossed his arms and narrowed his eyes. "I'm the Eminence. I don't need to explain myself to an Executor."

It was true; he didn't. The answer was obvious enough. A guard of the Eminence's Cohort had killed Herin, and Nekantor had publicly purged any guards deemed 'suspicious.' As a result, the Eminence's Cohort, fully controlled by Nekantor, now guarded every gate and door on the Residence grounds—but after the purge, there were too few guards to control the northern neighborhoods. If he allowed Nekantor to control *him*, then Nekantor could control the Division—and that meant he could control every Grobal in Pelismara.

He couldn't allow that to happen.

Holy Sirin, help me to be a better liar.

"All right," Pyaras said. "I'm going to relay the new orders to Commander Tret; be right back."

He turned his back on Nekantor, trying not to think about the Cohort guard's weapon, or about what Nekantor might have done to

Veriga, or what he might have done to Melín. He returned through the door into the offices and pulled the door shut behind him.

For a second, he could only stand there, breathing.

The young Cohort Third turned to look at him. So did his Jarel.

"Sir," said Jarel. "It's exactly what we thought."

"Hide it, Jarel," Pyaras said. "Tell no one where you've hidden it."

"Yes, sir." She bowed to the floor. "My heart is as deep as the heavens. No word uttered in confidence will escape it."

"Thank you," he said. "Thank you for your service, Jarel. You've always been better than I deserved."

She must have seen his desperation in his face, because her eyes widened. "Sir . . ."

Pyaras walked between the desks toward the glass-enclosed offices at the back of the room, and knocked on Commander Tret's door.

The Commander looked up from his desk and smiled, beckoning him in. "Executor, I thought I told you not to come back until the Selection was over."

"I think it *is* over, Commander."

Tret's smile vanished. "What's happened?"

"The Eminence is in the foyer. He is attempting to coerce me into ordering the Division to take control of the northern Grobal neighborhoods."

Tret looked horrified. "Executor—"

"I hereby request asylum in the Arissen," Pyaras said. "Commander Tret, sir, I hope you will be willing to serve as my sponsor. If I can no longer serve as Executor, it doesn't matter what he tries to do; I will no longer be able to enforce his orders."

The Commander understood instantly. He stood and strode past Pyaras to the office door. "Hand! I need you to print some paperwork, as fast as you can. And someone get me the quartermaster; or if she's not available, get me someone about the Executor's size."

It was shockingly quick. The Captain's Hand produced the papers—not more than four pages—and he and Commander Tret filled them out. Pyaras kept thinking of Nekantor, waiting in the foyer for his satisfaction . . . but then, he reached the last line and had to sign his name. The supreme effort of that act pushed everything else out of his mind.

Sign your name. Do it.

Arissen Pyaras.

The quartermaster was too slow, but one of the Seconds stripped to underwear right in front of everyone, and gave him a uniform. He apologized to the man, shucked out of his suit, and put the new clothes on. Bright rust-red.

"Are you ready?" the Commander asked.

He swallowed. "I think so. Sir, please come with me."

"You're not going out there by yourself. You, you, you, and you, and let's get at least two more—" Tret waved over several officers, until he was entirely surrounded. "All right, let's go."

His heart pounded so hard he felt dizzy. Commander Tret led the way, opened the door. Nekantor was still standing there, impatient, frustrated, furious.

"Varin gnash you, what took you so long? You—" Then he seemed to see what he was looking at, and recoiled. "Pyaras?!"

Commander Tret glanced at Pyaras, encouragingly.

Pyaras took a deep breath. "I'm sorry I can't help you, your Eminence, sir. I'm no longer the Executor of the Pelismara Division."

Nekantor shouted, "No!"

"I'm an Arissen."

CHAPTER FORTY-FOUR

Control

There were two Arissen on the main door, and another on the Maze door, all three of them holding weapons. Pointing them at the members of the cabinet, who sat in their chairs, terrified and silent. At his Dexelin. And at him.

Adon tried to keep breathing. This shouldn't have been possible. It shouldn't be—it *wasn't* possible—like the distortion in the air when he'd been barraged with weapons fire beside the shinca, except now the distortion was in reality itself. This was supposed to be the Round of Eight. Other candidates were supposed to come. There was supposed to be voting. This was supposed to be a competition.

He was supposed to be allowed to lose.

"Lady Selemei," Adon whispered. The sound of his own voice frightened him, but the three guards didn't seem to react. "What are we going to do?"

"We know what he wants," Lady Selemei said quietly. "The only question is whether we have any choice about giving it to him. Caredes, Boros, Amyel . . . what do you think?"

Caredes of the Eighth Family shook his head. Boros of the Second Family, who'd had such a booming voice at the Accession Ball, was silent. Amyel, who had a kind face, only said, "I don't know."

A soft grunt came from the youngest of the men at the table. He hissed, "He started all this by killing my cousin Herin at dinner. We can't just—"

One of the guards trained a weapon on him, and he stopped talking.

Adon pressed his back into the stone. If only he could move through it like a wysp—just disappear . . .

"Innis," said Selemei. "Fedron and I don't condone this. You suspected the truth before anyone else. What do you think we should do?"

Innis of the Fifth Family rubbed his hand across his receding forehead. "Honestly? Stay alive," he said. "That's what we have to do now. Two months ago, when I tried—*that* was the time to stop him."

The young cabinet member spoke again, indignantly. "But that means this isn't an Heir Selection."

"It's not," Innis agreed. "And we shouldn't pretend it is. We shouldn't go through the motions of final rounds as if this were being conducted fairly."

Heile's mercy. Adon could tell what that meant, and it made him sick. "Don't," Adon said. "Don't choose me. Please."

Innis looked at him. "You've shown us you're brave, young Adon. I'm sorry, but that's what you'll need to be."

"Members," said Speaker Fedron. His voice sounded old and tired. "I think Innis is right. There's only one way to end this process here and now, and make sure nobody else dies. Cast your votes."

Adon looked across the group as their hands moved to the screens set in the table. He looked for Dexelin. Dexelin's face was as expressionless as stone.

No one called the vote, but they didn't have to.

They sat in silence for a long time. At last the door to the hallway opened.

Nekantor was back. Sirin had not intervened, to strike him with a stalactite at the last minute. Mother Elinda had not stolen his soul from his body. Mai the Right was silent, and Heile had offered no mercy.

Nekantor didn't seem well, though. He was panting, and his face twitched. He held one hand in a fist, while with the other he frantically twisted the ring on his little finger.

"C-control the pattern," he said. "The cabinet must vote."

"They already did," said Adon.

Nekantor lunged forward between the two nearest cabinet members, who cowered away from him. He looked into their screens.

"The cabinet has voted unanimously," said Speaker Fedron, in that old, tired voice. "Adon will be the Heir."

"Good," Nekantor said. "Good. Adon wins, at the end of the game."

And what would happen next? Would he let them go? Or if anyone asked to leave, would the guards just start shooting?

Process and rules.

"Dexelin," Adon whispered. "Adjourn the meeting."

Dexelin straightened, holding one hand behind his back, and spoke clearly. "This meeting is hereby adjourned."

For an instant, there was only silence, no one daring to move. Then Nekantor wheeled on Adon, and grabbed him by the arm.

"Ouch!" he yelped. "Nekantor!"

"Guards, with me," Nekantor ordered, and dragged him out into the hall. The guards followed—one, two . . . three. Oh, thank Heile. Adon ran to keep up, while his brother's thumb and fingers dug into his arm. Dexelin—where was Dexelin?

"Dexelin," he called.

"Sir." Behind them, but not far behind.

"Make my brother let go of my arm."

Luckily, Nekantor released him with a snort before Dexelin could do anything that might put him in danger. "Fine," he said. "We're going to your suite, now. Keep up."

His suite? The Heir's suite was at the end of the hall, on the other side of the rotunda where the light poured in from above. Adon followed Nekantor there, rubbing the bruises on his arm.

The door to the Heir's suite was huge. The statues that held it up were larger than men. He didn't belong here. Nekantor pressed his hand to the lock pad, and the huge door opened—proof, if he needed any, that none of this was right.

The Heir's suite had its own vestibule. On the other side of the curtain, it had an enormous sitting room as large as both the sitting room and drawing room at home, put together. There were curtained bay windows on the far side.

He should have been at home with Tagaret, and Della, and Mother, and Aloran. He drew a shuddering breath.

"You can go, now, Nekantor. You got what you wanted."

"Not entirely," said Nekantor, who had come in behind him. "Business. Complete the pattern."

Adon shook his head, turning around. "What does that mean?"

"You're the Heir, that's what it means!" Nekantor snapped. "You have the power of appointment, and I expect you to use it to the First Family's advantage. The first thing we need is a new Executor to the Pelismara Division."

Was Nekantor saying what he thought he was saying? "What? Did something happen to Pyaras?"

Nekantor whirled around, grabbed the vestibule curtain, and tore it down. He snarled between clenched teeth. "Dexelin, get some paper."

too far away, still out in the adjunct local station, so she'd have to go directly to the Commander.

She ran up, pulled open the heavy main door, crossed the foyer and entered the offices—and stopped.

The whole place was abuzz. Officers who should have known their assignments clustered here and there talking. A great many of the desks and ordinators sat abandoned. Whatever had happened had affected everyone.

Except maybe the man sitting on the bench outside the Commander's office. He held a tunnel-hound on his knees, and they were rubbing faces. Sirin and Eyn, he looked shockingly like . . .

"Seni, can I help you?" a man's voice demanded coldly.

Melín snapped around to look at a pale Cohort Third who had approached her. Mai help her, she was wearing orange! Without thinking she tore off her helmet, and dropped it onto the floor.

"Captain's Hand Melín, Division cohort on adjuncts under Captain Keyt, reporting," she said. "I've been under cover in the Eminence's Cohort. I need to see Commander Tret, right away."

The pale Third's cold defensiveness dropped all at once, suddenly betraying the same fluster as everyone else in the office. "Sorry for the confusion, Hand. I thought the Eminence had sent you, and after what happened, we're under orders to turn away any of his messengers."

"After *what* happened?"

"The Eminence tried to coerce the Executor into an illegal order, sir. To move the adjunct cohorts against the Grobal in the zone north of the Residence."

So *that* was why she'd spent an hour on a roof. She could easily imagine Nekantor would kill for that. But Fifth Sahris had said the target escaped . . .

"Please tell me he failed."

"Yes, sir. The Exe—" He glanced nervously over his shoulder. "The, that is, we have no more Executor. He Fell rather than give the order."

He Fell.

The man on the bench. The only one here who wasn't flustered, who seemed to have nothing to do. And who looked shockingly like—

"Excuse me, Third," she said.

"Hand."

Melín walked between the desks toward the man sitting outside the Commander's office. Gods above, just look at him! Close up, you could see that his rust-red jacket had come out of storage so recently it still had creases. He sat there, in uniform, lavishing love on a tunnel-hound as though it were the most natural thing in the world. But maybe it was, for someone who'd just given up everything.

"Pyaras?"

Pyaras looked up. "Oh, Sirin and Eyn, you're all right! I thought—" His eyes shone with tears. "I thought he was going to—"

"He didn't, though," she said. "I got fired."

"Oh, thank Heile. Now my family can't—" He choked off, and hugged the tunnel-hound against his chest.

Melín sat down on the bench beside him. She squeezed his arm, just above his elbow. "Well, they can't hurt you, either."

He shook his head. "Now I don't know what to do."

"Celebrate being alive. Come here." She pulled his head down, and kissed him on the mouth. "To life, Pyaras."

"To life, Melín," he whispered.

The taste of him on her lips reminded her of everything she wanted. But he had a lot of things to figure out, first. Where to live, and how. She could help him with that, introduce him to people so he wouldn't be alone. For one thing, he'd definitely need a therapist.

"Whose hound is that?" she asked.

"Veriga's." His voice shook. "If you're safe, maybe he is, too. I don't know. Nekantor threatened both of you."

Gnash it—of course he had. And that had implications she really didn't like. "Hang on," she said. "I'll be right back." She stood up and knocked on the Commander's door.

"Come in."

Commander Tret looked suspicious of an officer in an orange uniform, until she gave him her name and rank. Then he nodded. "Captain Keyt has told me about you and your mission, Hand."

"Thank you, sir. I believe we have a problem, sir."

"Several," he agreed. "Explain."

"You're already aware, sir, that the Eminence has controlled his own Cohort and trained them into illegal actions. We also know that today, he attempted to control the Division. Pyaras has just told me that the Eminence took his police friend, Veriga, hostage. I believe he is attempting to control the Arissen entirely."

"The police." Commander Tret stood up, and walked out into the main room. "Attention!" he shouted. Every person in the room snapped around at once. "This is Hand Melín, and she's Division. She's just informed me the police are also in danger. I need two eights to assure the safety of the Chief of Police, and of an officer named Veriga. Go now. There may be Eminence's Cohort threatening the station, so be careful. Radio the adjunct teams if you need reinforcements."

Melín faced him as he came back through the door.

"Commander, the Paper Shadows may also be under threat."

Tret scowled at that.

"Sir," she said. "I acknowledge that their actions are extrajudicial, but that only means they would be terrible tools in the hands of the Eminence."

"Where?"

She reached into her pocket for Tremi's card, but it wasn't there; the only card in her pocket was her credential as Selection bodyguard. "Seven forty-two Drepli Circumference, in the northern neighborhoods."

Tret gave a curt nod. "Go."

"Melín." Pyaras called after her as she left Tret's office. "What should I do?"

She turned back to him. "For now, stay here, where you'll be safe. Once we've assured Veriga's safety, you can probably stay with him temporarily. I'll help you in any way I can. But right now, I think Nekantor is moving on someone else, and I have to get there before it's too late."

Pyaras held the tunnel-hound tightly. "Eyn go with you."

Reaching the end of the Imbati Household neighborhoods, Melín scanned up and down Drepli Circumference. No sign of an orange uniform anywhere. Maybe Nekantor didn't know where this office was.

She couldn't count on that, though. His people still might be here, hidden, out of uniform and out of sight.

She turned left into the crowd of Lowers on the sidewalk. People moved quickly out of her way, but this mercantile area was very popular. It was impossible to run the way she wanted. Two more shopfronts until the stairway, which would be right about where that Imbati was standing.

That Imbati was someone she knew.

"Imbati Yoral?" Coming level with him, she discovered Lady Della sitting just behind, a cascade of gorgeous copper hair and fine silk on Treminindi's concrete stairs. What in Varin's name? "Lady Della? You haven't seen anyone go up these stairs, have you?"

"No one," the Lady said. "But we just got here."

"How did you know to find this place?"

Lady Della's cheeks flushed red. "You dropped a card in my room. I came here to—well. When I left the house, I knew what I wanted to do. I mean, what else can be done, to stop this? But now that I'm here, I don't think I can do it."

Name of Plis. Assassinating Nekantor *was* the only logical solution left at this point. It was just that Lady Della was the last person she'd have expected to think of it. She wasn't bloodthirsty.

"I've been trying to find this place," the Lady said. "But I never wanted to use the Paper Shadows. I wanted to see them brought to justice for their crimes. If I use them now, how can there ever be justice?"

"Not only that, Lady," Melín said. "A thirteen-year-old would be Eminence, and we would need an Heir. Again."

"Oh, sweet Heile." Her green eyes lit. "Maybe Pyaras—"

"Pyaras Fell."

Lady Della's face changed utterly. "He *what?*"

"It's true, Lady. He's Arissen, now."

A sudden sound electrified Melín's backbone: *hsssssscrack!*

Superheated glass—weapons fire. She looked up at the second floor window.

They were already here!

She grabbed the stair rail and vaulted over Lady Della's shoulder; the Lady dodged aside with a shriek. Melín took the remaining stairs three at a time despite the strain on her ankle, drawing her weapon and her knife. At the top, she backed to the rail, then charged in through the door.

The door slammed into someone just as Tremi popped up from behind her desk and loosed a shot.

Zzap! The man she'd hit with the door screamed and fell.

Just past him was Crenn, turning toward her—Melín shot him in the weapon hand, and he howled. Then Tremi popped up again—

Zzap! Crenn's head exploded.

Zzap! A shot came from close behind the door. Tremi gave a grunt and fell back behind the desk.

Melín looked around the door and found Karyas still holding her weapon aimed toward the spot where Tremi had fallen. Melín slashed her across the wrist with her knife, stepped up onto the body of the man she'd hit with the door—Fetti—and slammed an elbow across her chin.

Karyas toppled.

Melín found herself the only one left standing. Panting, she climbed over Fetti's body and wrestled Karyas' limp form until she could tie her arms behind her, and bind her legs. The knife slash had cut through burn scars, and was bleeding pretty badly, so she wrapped her handkerchief around it and tied it tightly.

The whole room smelled of blood and smoke. The bodies on this side of the desk belonged to the four people Karyas had pulled away from the Ring. None were in uniform. Melín picked her way among the dead, over to the desk. What had happened to Tremi?

Heile's mercy—there were three more people here. One body belonged to Third Solnis, another to a mate she didn't recognize. The third was Tremi, who was panting and shuddering. She'd been shot through the arm near the shoulder, and the bone was visible. Blood slicked all down her side.

"Tremi," Melín cried. "Blast it—" She searched the pockets of the nearest uniformed body for more binding twine. Then she returned and wound it high around Tremi's arm, tying it as tight as she could. She couldn't get as high above the wound as she wanted. The veteran had lost a lot of blood.

She turned toward the door and shouted, "Yoral! Lady Della, help!"

Tremi's voice came from behind her. "Wait."

"I'm getting you help."

"Don't," Tremi spat weakly, "fix me up and stick me in some prison . . ."

Melín shook her head. "You'd rather die?"

"They came for the Shadows," Tremi said. "Karyas came. To take them from me."

"Well, she won't have them now."

"Right drawer keypad. Four two eight nine. Panel."

What did that mean? Footsteps sounded on the steps outside. Imbati Yoral took one look into the room, spun away, and vanished back down the stairs. Lady Della stopped in the door, staring in horror. She fumbled a silk handkerchief from her sleeve and held it over her nose and mouth.

"You take them," said Tremi. "For me. You . . . master assassin."

That thought was as revolting as the dead bodies that surrounded them. "Tremi—"

"Don't do it," said Lady Della.

"Protect them," said Tremi. "Don't let the Eminence . . ." She panted a few breaths. "Or p-police . . ."

"Of course I will," Melín said. "Don't you worry."

"No," said Lady Della. "No."

Treminindi gave a moan, and didn't speak again. If medics didn't get here fast, she wouldn't live to see the inside of a prison cell. Melín took off her jacket and laid it over the veteran, hoping it might help even a little. Then she stood up.

"Melín," said Lady Della softly. "Don't take over the Paper Shadows. Please, tell me you won't do it."

"Gods, no!" Melín snorted. "If I did, Nekantor wouldn't rest until he made me his personal tool. He's tried to take over all of the Arissen, today, Lady. He'll be trying to control your brother, too. You should go help him."

The Lady nodded and vanished, probably all too relieved to leave the scene of death behind. She'd have to find Imbati Yoral, who was probably summoning firefighters and police.

Four two eight nine. Melín opened the desk's right-hand drawer, and discovered a basic keypad and a glass panel unit. Only the Grobal still used that kind of classical technology, on their doors. She entered the numbers, and the panel flashed, so she pressed her hand to it.

What was supposed to happen now?

She pressed the glass again. This time, a lock clicked—she could feel its vibration in the surface under her hand.

She opened the drawer below. It contained a single file.

She pulled it out, opened it. Inside were five sheets of paper, made from the blasted plant she'd so often been asked to defend. They listed names, addresses, skills.

Right.

The top of the metal desk was a plausible spot to have been hit by a stray bolt from the earlier fight. She opened the file in its center, and shot it. It ignited, flames licking up, sending smoke toward the ceiling. Within a minute, nothing was left but ash.

Let Nekantor and his cohorts search as they liked. There would be no new master assassin—the Paper Shadows had just gone up in smoke.

Voices came from outside.

Melín walked out onto the landing and found Yoral had done his job well. Two firefighter medics ran up the stairs past her into the room, and the police came behind them. The first officer up the stairs was Veriga.

"Crown of Mai, Veriga," Melín said. "How are you first on the scene for everything?"

The police officer didn't exactly smile. "I put myself there," he said. "Your Commander's team helped me and my station-mates out of a dangerous situation. A messenger told us you were involved, and where you were going, so I made sure to come. I'm glad you're out of danger."

"You, too. There's serious carrion up here, be warned, but Eminence's Cohort First Karyas is alive, and I'm giving her to you."

"Good." Veriga nodded. "I'll need your full report. But first—what happened to Executor Pyaras?"

Melín chewed her lip. "Yeah, I'm going to need your help with that."

Veriga tensed. "Tell me he's alive."

"He's alive, yes, he's alive—sorry, it's just that—he Fell. So it looks like he's on us, now. He's in the Division offices, and he has your hound."

The police officer visibly relaxed. "That's probably a blessing." He looked her in the eye. "He can do it, you know. He learns, but he needs time."

"Sirin and Eyn, I hope you're right. For now—"

"He should stay with me."

"I was hoping you'd say that." She took a deep breath. "I'll help any way I can."

"I do need your help, actually."

"In there?" she asked. "I'm ready when you are."

Veriga shook his head. "Just a second. You were a Wysp Specialist, weren't you."

Were. She winced. "I was. I'm Captain's Hand now. And you?"

"I'm a Hand, also," said Veriga. "The fact is, the targetball disaster convinced me that the Pelismar Police need to know a lot more about wysps and shinca. I spoke about it with the Chief of Police, and we'll be reaching out to Commander Tret. I hope you'll consider helping us create a training program to enhance our protocols for weapons instruction and crowd management."

"That's the right kind of idea, right now," Melín agreed. It wouldn't just make the city safer. It would bring the Division and Police together in a time when they needed each other more than ever. "I'll be happy to work for the good of all Arissen."

CHAPTER FORTY-SIX

Gathering

Della gathered her skirts in her hands as she walked, trying to gather her thoughts with them. Yes, everything had come apart, but this wasn't the first time her world had fallen in pieces. The difference now was that, for the first time in thirteen years, she hadn't fallen apart with it—and that sent her mind orbiting back to a single overwhelming demand:

Do something.

In the suite vestibule, Serjer did not appear. Cautiously, with one finger, she pulled the left-hand curtain back and found the service door cracked open; Serjer sat behind it, motionless on a stool with his face in his hands. She dropped the curtain and turned to her Yoral.

"Yoral, can you talk to him? Make sure he's all right, and that he has help to call the Household and the ashers if he needs it?"

Yoral inclined his head. "Of course, Mistress."

When she entered the sitting room, Tagaret came and flung his arms around her. "Oh," he said. "Oh, Della, you're back."

"Tagaret, you have to know what's happened."

He leaned away from her. "More deaths?"

The image of the room full of Arissen bodies washed over her, and she panted until she could shove it away. "Nekantor tried to control the Arissen. All of them."

"Mercy of Heile—*tried?*"

"The Cohort first. The Division second, and then the Police. Pyaras is the only reason he failed."

Tagaret stared at her, speechless, his face white.

"Pyaras Fell."

For a second, Tagaret's knees wobbled; she held him up. "No," Tagaret said. "I can't lose him. He's not dead; I refuse to pretend he is. He's my *cousin* . . ."

"Maybe we can see him in secret," Della said. "We'll manage something."

"Look at us," Tagaret said, mournfully. "What happened? We were going to change Varin . . ."

"We *all* wanted to change Varin," she agreed. "Nekantor did, too; and his plan worked, because he had so few people he cared enough to protect. Think where we might be if he didn't love order so much."

"Chaos." Tagaret leaned his head against hers. "Violence."

"We're so close to that abyss, still," she whispered. "Right now, Adon is the only bridge that can get us across. And that means, even if we can't do it the way we used to, we still have to protect him."

"But he's Heir," Tagaret said. "Everyone will be watching. How do we make sure he won't be found out?" He gave a heavy sigh. "There's only one answer. I didn't want him to be right . . ."

"Come into the drawing room. We need to talk to Mother."

She knocked on Tamelera's door, but got no answer. Tamelera might be too upset to respond . . . she tested the handle, and, finding it unlocked, cautiously cracked the door open.

Tamelera sat at the foot of her bed, holding Aloran, who had his face buried in her neck. "Aloran," she said, softly. "Love, look at me."

He leaned back from her. His face was wet with tears. "My Lady . . ."

She gently brushed the tears from his cheeks with her fingers. "We knew, didn't we? At the Academy, or here, it was always going to happen. One way, or the other. We just didn't know when. Just remember, I will give up everything before I lose you."

Aloran leaned to kiss her . . .

Della realized what she was doing, and shoved the view closed, blushing furiously. She knocked again, harder. "Mother? Mother, can you come out, please?"

A second later, Tamelera opened the door herself.

"Please don't Fall," Della blurted. "We just lost Pyaras to the Arissen—please, please don't. Adon still needs you. We'll find another way."

Tamelera stared, icy eyes wide, for an instant, as if about to fly into a rage. But then she exhaled. "Really? Pyaras?"

"Really. Can you and Aloran come out? I'm going to get Adon. We have to plan."

She tiptoed to Adon's door. This was going to be the hard one.

What would she do if he'd locked himself in? She couldn't possibly ask Aloran to intervene with him right now. She knocked.

"Who is it?"

Easier than expected. "It's Della. Can you come out to the drawing room?"

"No. It's not safe."

"It's not?"

"No. Nekantor might come in."

"What if we come in where you are? It's just me, and Tagaret, and Mother."

The lock clicked, and the door swung slightly open.

They all gathered on the floor, on Adon's carpet, amid the layers of colorful silk. Della sat down heavily across from Adon, while Tagaret and Mother sat to either side of them. Adon would hardly look at anyone.

"We'll keep this room for you," Della promised. "So you can always come here and get away from Nekantor. And be safe."

"You shouldn't," said Adon. "You should leave."

"Adon," said Tagaret, "here's something you need to understand about Nekantor. He's always harmed us, but we've always survived it. He won't kill us, or damage us too severely, because we're still his kuarjos pieces. And without all the pieces—"

"You can't play the game." Adon looked up for the first time.

"I'm going to stay," Tagaret said.

"So will I," said Della. "We won't leave you."

"Then help me," Adon said. "Nekantor is expecting me to appoint an Executor to the Pelismara Division. He wanted me to appoint Corrim, but I can't stand to do that to him. Or to Lady Selemei."

"You'll want someone whose Family hates him, and is powerful enough to resist him," said Tagaret. "Fifth, I'd say, or Third. My Kuarmei can write up the order."

"Unger of the Fifth Family," said Adon.

"Perfect," Della said. "That means you also get to appoint an Alixi of Selimna. But don't appoint Tagaret. Not now; we need to stay here with you in Pelismara at least until our child is born." Had she really just said that? She shivered.

"Someone we trust, though," said Tagaret. "Who won't do violence against the Selimnai, and who might consider accommodating us later."

Adon nodded. "A friend of yours."

"Gowan," said Tagaret. He got up and rang the service call button. Kuarmei came quickly and wrote up the papers on Adon's desk. Adon stood to sign them, but hesitated.

"What if he's angry?" His voice shook. "What will he do?"

"Nekantor loves order," said Tagaret. "He'll cling to it until he can't anymore, before he causes chaos. We have to count on that."

Adon looked at him for several seconds, and pressed one hand against a pocket of his coat. Then he nodded. "All right." He signed the papers and handed them to Kuarmei, who bowed and left through the door into the Maze.

"I'm going to have to leave Pelismara," said Tamelera.

Adon's body jerked as if she'd hit him, but when he spoke, he spoke in a calm and distant voice. "Of course you will. That's why you weren't at the Selection events, wasn't it. You were afraid of what he would do."

Tamelera looked down at her hands. "Yes. Adon, I love you. I'll write to you." Tears came into her voice. "I'm so sorry." She stood up, straightened her skirts, and left the room.

"Mother, wait," Della called. Standing up was awkward. She just managed to catch Tamelera still in the drawing room, with one hand on her open bedroom door. "Mother, let's think about this. You can go; and you should. But you don't have to run."

Tamelera's brows pinched. "What do you mean?"

"Yes." Tagaret had come up behind her. "What *do* you mean?"

Della turned so she could look between them. "We want to go back to Selimna, right? But it's not Selimna we want. It's a new Varin—the Varin our child would want to grow up in. We found a way to make a difference in Selimna without you as Alixi, Tagaret. We can find a way to make a difference without being there. Mother, you know Household Director Aimali already."

Tamelera nodded slowly. "I do."

"And you know you already changed the Circle to the Lady's Walk. You also know Melumalai Forder, now, which means you can speak to Dorlis and Nenda. We can send you with letters that will allow you to speak with Venorai Castremei. And Tagaret and I can stay here and work with Pyaras and Veriga and Melín, and even Vant, and send you ideas. You can begin this work, to make Selimna the place where you and Aloran deserve to live together."

"I wish to do this, my Lady." Aloran emerged from the open bedroom door and resumed his place at Tamelera's shoulder.

"If you wish it, then of course we'll do it," said Tamelera. She looked at Della solemnly. "We'll go to Selimna, and do what you can't."

"And we'll do what *you* can't," Della said. "Adon needs love. He needs a reason to believe he will have a future, to give him strength."

"The most important thing is, we won't give up," said Tagaret.

"We won't give up," Della promised. "We'll save one life."

To Master Adon,

I know it's selfish of me to leave you like this. It's not your fault. I've made my choice: I choose death for myself before he uses me to control you. At least I won't die still carrying his name. You gave me that.

He's not strong. Never forget it. He is searching, always searching for calm. Once he finds something that will give it to him, he will be completely dependent on it and will never consent to give it up.

It doesn't mean he's not dangerous, though. He perverts people. Careful he doesn't do it to you.

I would have served you faithfully. May Mai forgive me for my transgressions.

Sincerely,

Adon's Dexelin of the Household of the First Family

Liadis—Della's little sister
Lorman of the First Family—Arbiter of the First Family Council
Menni of the Second Family—a friend of Tagaret's
Nayal of the Second Family—a school friend of Adon's
Nekantor of the First Family—Heir to the Throne of Varin, brother of Tagaret and Adon
Odil of the Eleventh Family—a friend of Corrim
Orindi—leader of Down-Bend, Selimna
Pelli of the First Family—youngest daughter of Lady Selemei
Plist of the Third Family—Arbiter of the Third Family Council
Preines of the Sixth Family—an Heir candidate
Pyaras of the First Family—cousin of Tagaret, Nekantor, and Adon
Reyn of the Ninth Family—Tagaret's best friend
Rorni of the Tenth Family—an Heir candidate
Satenya of the Seventh Family— the newly appointed Alixi of Peak
Selemei of the First Family—cabinet member, distant cousin of Tagaret, Nekantor, and Adon
Tagaret of the First Family—partner of Della, brother of Nekantor and Adon
Tamelera of the First Family—mother of Tagaret, Nekantor, and Adon
Tass of the Tenth Family—a cabinet member
Unger of the Fifth Family—a distant cousin of Innis
Venmer of the Eighth Family—a schoolmate of Adon's
Vix—leader of the Venorai Tributary, Selimna
Vull of the First Family—a retired Administrator, father of Pyaras
Wenmor of the Ninth Family— the new appointee to Director of the Pelismar Secure Facility
Xeref of the First Family—a cousin of Adon's

Arissen

Abru—Commander of the Eminence's Cohort
Aripo—a Division Therapist, lover of Melín
Berios—a Division Second
Budrien—a hero

Cast of Characters
(alphabetical by caste)

Grobal

Adon of the First Family—a young man, brother of Tagaret and Nekantor
Amyel of the Ninth Family—a cabinet member
Boros of the Second Family—Cabinet Secretary
Cahemsin of the First Family—a cousin of Adon's
Caredes of the Eighth Family—a cabinet member
Chaile—leader of Up-Bend, Selimna
Churon—a Schoolmaster at the Grobal School
Corrim of the First Family—son of Lady Selemei
Della of the First Family—partner of Tagaret
Fedron of the First Family—Speaker of the Cabinet, a distant cousin of Selemei and Tagaret
Falya of the Third Family—partner of the Eminence Herin
Fyn—the founder of Modern Varin
Ganni—a schoolmate and cousin of Adon's
Garr of the First Family—deceased father of Tagaret and Nekantor
Gosek of the Eleventh Family—an Heir candidate
Gowan of the Ninth Family—a friend of Tagaret's
Herin of the Third Family—the Eminence of Varin
Igan of the Ninth Family—a school friend of Adon's
Indal of the Fifth Family—deceased former Eminence of Varin
Indelis of the First Family—deceased mother of Pyaras and partner of Vull
Innis of the Fifth Family—Arbiter of the Fifth Family Council
Jorem—an older cousin of Adon's
Kaspri of the Fifth Family—a cabinet member
Kudzina—leader of Bend, Selimna

Sirin the Luck-Bringer—God of luck, youth, and love; one of the Lovers who together symbolize love and faithfulness. A planet. Symbolized by garnet and the color dark red.

Eyn the Wanderer—Goddess of exploration, independence, and beauty; one of the Lovers who together symbolize love and faithfulness. A comet. Symbolized by diamond and the color white.

Deities of the Celestial Family

Father Varin—Source of all life; punishes the wicked after death by gnashing them in his fiery teeth. The sun. Symbolized by gold.

Mother Elinda—Goddess of childbirth and death; brings souls to children, sets the souls of the virtuous dead in the heavens as stars. The moon. Symbolized by silver and the mourning color, pale yellow.

Mai the Right—Deity of justice; takes male, female, and nonbinary embodiments, can see all sides of a problem, chooses humans who share one's nature. A planet. Symbolized by bronze, often worn as a medallion by the chosen.

Plis the Warrior—God of strife and war. A planet. Symbolized by iron.

The Silent Sister—Goddess of earth and agriculture. A planet. Symbolized by any sedimentary stone.

Bes the Ally—God of charity and negotiation; one of the Twins who together symbolize unity, peace, and love. A planet. Symbolized by lapis.

Trigis the Resolute—God of steadfastness and rescue; one of the Twins who together symbolize unity, peace, and love. A planet. Symbolized by malachite.

Heile the Merciful—Goddess of mercy, music, art, and medicine. A planet. Symbolized by peridot, the color light green, and a green lamp.

The silk paper was entitled, *Honoring the Heroes*. She read down the names solemnly until she saw the last two.

Arissen Pyaras
Grobal Della of the First Family

She started to cry.

Thank Heile for mercy. She followed him.

"Ohhh," Adon sighed. "Look at it."

It really was breathtaking. The inside of the Eminence's Library had been designed to look like a clearing up on the surface. It had a lush, thick carpet in a color that was not Grobal, but grass-green. At the head of the room, a shinca trunk had been built into the wall, filling the space with clear silver light. The ceiling was designed to imitate it, with white marble branches that split, and split again, and orange-lit globes hanging everywhere. "It's beautiful," she whispered.

Adon, clearly in awe, wandered forward into the space.

Tagaret joined her at her shoulder, then; she squeezed his arm, and he smiled. It couldn't have been more perfect. Tall, mostly empty bookshelves extended into the room from the sides, creating little alcoves of privacy. The ones on the right-hand wall had windows between them. Stuffed chairs sat here and there, not aligned with anything, scattered without a pattern. It truly felt like freedom within walls.

"Tagaret," Della whispered. "This is so lovely, I think Adon might even forgive you."

Adon didn't stop until he reached the other side of the room. He laid one hand on the back of a chair beside the shinca, and the other directly on the tree itself, and stood there for several seconds. Then he turned around and looked at them—really looked at them both, for the first time in weeks. Hope kindled in her heart.

"I could be safe here," Adon said.

"Yes," said Tagaret. "This place can be just for you."

Della sighed. "Oh, Adon, I'm so glad. I love you so much."

Adon looked about the room again, taking everything in. "Oh," he said, suddenly. "So that's where those went. I had the list redone, Della, look."

"List? What do you mean?" She walked forward until she passed the last bookshelf, and found two long scrolls of paper hanging on the library wall: one black with writing in gold, the other, black ink on paper the striking golden color of pure tillik-silk.

The black paper was entitled, *Honoring the Dead.* A paragraph described the terrible events surrounding Eminence Herin's death, and there was a list of names below; she scanned them with a thick feeling in her throat.

Chezzy—a waiter at the Blades bar
Crenn—a First in the Eminence's Cohort
Demni—hearing Arbitrator
Drefne—a Division soldier, lover of Melín
Drenas—the Eminence Herin's bodyguard
Durkinar—bartender at the Blades bar
Elovin—a demoted Wysp Specialist of the Pelismara Division
Fetti—a Second in the Eminence's Cohort
Figo—a Division soldier
Gul—a First in the Eminence's Cohort
Helis—an Eighth in the Eminence's Cohort
Jos—a Division soldier
Karyas—a First in the Eminence's Cohort, Nekantor's favorite
Keyt—a Captain in the Pelismara Division
Luun—a Division Fourth and targetball fan
Melín—a First, and Wysp Specialist in the Pelismara Division
Ostem—a Division soldier
Sahris—a Fifth in the Eminence's Cohort
Solnis—a Third
Treminindi—a Division veteran and former Wysp Specialist, master assassin of the Paper Shadows
Tret—Commander of the Pelismara Division
Veriga—a police officer, friend of Pyaras
Xunir—a guard of the Eminence's Cohort

Imbati

Aimali—Household Director of the Selimna Residence of the Grobal
Tamelera's Aloran—manservant of Lady Tamelera of the First Family
Herin's Argun—manservant to the Eminence
Innis' Brithe—manservant of Grobal Innis of the Fifth Family
Fedron's Chenna—manservant of Speaker Fedron of the First Family
Nekantor's Dexelin—manservant of Nekantor of the First Family
Unger's Fyani—manservant of Alixi Unger of the Fifth Family
Pyaras' Jarel—manservant of Pyaras of the First Family